P9-EES-805
RANDOM HOUSE
LARGE PRINT

Also by Isabel Allende
Available from Random House Large Print

A Long Petal of the Sea

The Soul of a Woman

VIOLETA

VIOLETA

a novel

Isabel Allende

TRANSLATED FROM THE SPANISH
BY FRANCES RIDDLE

RANDOM HOUSE
LARGE PRINT

Published in the United States of America by Random House Large Print in association with Ballantine Books, an imprint of Random House, a division of Penguin Random House LLC, New York.

Published in Spanish by Plaza & Janes, a member of Penguin Random House Grupo Editorial, Barcelona, Spain.

Cover design: Elena Giavaldi
Cover illustration: Amanda Arlotta

The Library of Congress has established a Cataloging-in-Publication record for this title.

ISBN: 978-0-593-55871-3

www.penguinrandomhouse.com/large-print-format-books

FIRST LARGE PRINT EDITION

Printed in the United States of America

1st Printing

This Large Print edition published in accord with the standards of the N.A.V.H.

TO

Nicolás Frías and Lori Barra, pillars of my life

Felipe Berríos del Solar, beloved friend

Tell me, what is it you plan to do
with your one wild and precious life?

—MARY OLIVER

VIOLETA

Dear Camilo,

My intention with these pages is to leave you a testimony of my life. I imagine someday, when you are old and less busy, you might want to stop and remember me. You have a terrible memory since you're always so distracted, and that defect gets worse with age. I think you'll see that my life story is worthy of a novel, because of my sins more than my virtues. You have received many of my letters, where I've detailed much of my existence (minus the sins), but you must make good on your promise to burn them when I die, because they are overly sentimental and often cruel. This recounting of my life is meant to replace that excessive correspondence.

I love you more than anyone in this world.

VIOLETA

Santa Clara, September 2020

PART ONE

EXILE

(1920–1940)

1

...

I CAME INTO THE WORLD ONE STORMY FRIDAY in 1920, the year of the scourge. The evening of my birth the electricity went out, something that often happened during storms, so they lit candles and kerosene lamps, which were always kept on hand for these types of emergencies. María Gracia, my mother, began to feel the contractions—a sensation she knew well since she'd already birthed five sons—and she surrendered to the pain, resigned to bringing another male into the world with the help of her sisters, who had assisted her through the difficult process several times. The family doctor had been working tirelessly for weeks in one of the field hospitals and she felt it imprudent to call him for something as prosaic as childbirth. On previous occasions they had used a midwife, always the same one, but the woman had been among the first to fall victim to the flu and they didn't know of anyone else.

To my mother it seemed she'd spent the entirety of her adult life either pregnant, recovering from childbirth, or convalescing after a miscarriage. Her oldest son, José Antonio, had turned seventeen, she was sure of that, because he had been born the same year as one of our worst earthquakes, which knocked half the country to the ground and left thousands of deaths in its wake. But she could never precisely recall the ages of her other sons nor how many pregnancies she'd failed to carry to term. Each miscarriage had left her incapacitated for months and after each birth she'd felt exhausted and melancholic for a long while. Before getting married she had been the most beautiful debutante in the capital—slender, with an unforgettable face, green eyes, and translucent skin—but the extremes of motherhood had distorted her body and drained her spirit.

She loved her sons, in theory, but in practice she preferred to keep them at a comfortable distance. The exuberant band of boys was as disruptive as a battle in her peaceful feminine realm. She'd once admitted during confession that she felt doomed to bear only sons, like a curse from the Devil. In penitence she was ordered to recite a rosary every day for two years straight and to make a sizable donation to the church renovation fund. Her husband forbade her from returning to confession.

Under my aunt Pilar's direction, Torito, the boy we employed for a wide range of chores, climbed a ladder to hang a labor sling from two steel hooks that he himself had installed in the ceiling. My mother, kneeling in her nightdress, each hand pulling at a strap, pushed for what felt like an eternity, cursing like a pirate, using words she'd never utter under normal circumstances. My aunt Pía, crouched between her legs, waited to receive the newborn baby before he could fall to the floor. She had already prepared the infusions of nettle, artemisia, and rue for after the birth. The clamor of the storm, which beat against the shutters and ripped tiles from the roof, drowned out the low moans and then the long final scream as I began to emerge, first a head, followed by a body covered in mucus and blood, slipping through my aunt's fingers and crashing down onto the wood floor.

"You're so clumsy, Pía!" Pilar shouted, holding me up by one foot. "It's a girl!" she added, surprised.

"It can't be, check him good," my mother mumbled, exhausted.

"I'm telling you, sister, she doesn't have a willy," Pilar responded.

THAT NIGHT, MY FATHER returned home late, after dinner and several hands of cards at the club, and went directly to his room to change his clothes and rub himself down with alcohol as a precautionary measure before greeting his family. He ordered a glass of cognac from the housekeeper on shift, who didn't think to give him the news because she wasn't accustomed to speaking to the boss, and then he went to say hello to his wife. The rusty smell of blood warned him of what had occurred before he'd even crossed the threshold. He found his wife in bed, flushed, her hair damp with sweat, wearing a clean nightdress, resting. They'd already removed the straps from the ceiling and the buckets of soiled rags.

"Why didn't anyone tell me!" he exclaimed after kissing his wife on the forehead.

"How could we have? The driver was with you and none of us were going out on foot in that storm, assuming your henchmen would even let us," Pilar responded coldly.

"It's a girl, Arsenio. You finally have a daughter," Pía interrupted, showing him the bundle she held in her arms.

"Thank God!" my father muttered, but his smile faded as he saw the creature peeking out from the folds of the blanket. "She has a lump on her forehead!"

"Don't worry. Some babies are born that way. It goes down after a few days. It's a sign of intelligence," Pilar improvised.

"What are you going to name her?" Pía asked.

"Violeta," my mother said firmly, without giving her husband a chance to chime in.

It was the name of our illustrious great-grandmother who had embroidered the shield of the first flag after independence, in the 1800s.

THE PANDEMIC HAD NOT taken my family by surprise. As soon as word spread about the dying people in the streets near the port and the alarming number of blue corpses in the morgue, my father, Arsenio Del Valle, calculated that the plague would not take more than a few days to reach the capital, but he did not lose his calm. He had prepared for this eventuality with the efficiency he applied to his business. He was the only one of his brothers on track to recover the prestige and wealth that my grandfather had inherited but lost over the years because he'd had too many children and because he was an honest man. Of my grandfather's fifteen children, eleven survived, a considerable number that proved the heartiness of the Del Valle bloodline, as my father liked to brag. But such a large family took a lot of effort and money to maintain, and the fortune had dwindled.

Before the national press ever called the illness by its name, my father already knew that it was the Spanish flu. He kept up to date on the news of the world through foreign newspapers, which arrived with considerable delay to the Union Club but provided better information than the local papers, and via a radio he had built himself, by following the instructions in a manual, to keep in touch with other enthusiasts. And so, punctuated by the static and shrieks of the shortwave, he learned of the havoc wreaked by the pandemic in other places. He had followed the advance of the virus from the beginning, and he knew how it had blown through Europe and the United States like a deadly breeze. He deduced that if civilized countries had experienced such tragic consequences we should expect worse in ours, where resources were more limited.

The Spanish influenza, "the flu" for short, reached us after almost two years' delay. According to the scientific community, we'd be spared infection entirely due to our geographic isolation, the natural barrier afforded by the mountains to one side and the ocean to the other, as well as our remoteness. Popular opinion, however, attributed our salvation to Father Juan Quiroga, in whose honor precautionary processions were held. Quiroga is the only saint worth worshipping, because no one can outdo him when it comes to domestic miracles, even if the Vatican has failed to canonize him. Nevertheless, in 1920 the virus arrived in all its majestic glory with more force than anyone could have imagined, toppling the notions of scientists and theologians alike.

The onset of illness brought first a terrible chill from beyond the grave, which nothing could quell, followed by fevered shivering, a pounding headache, a blazing fire behind the eyes and in the throat, and deliriums, with terrifying hallucinations of death lurking steps away. The person's skin turned a purplish-blue color that soon darkened until the feet and hands were black; a cough impeded breathing as a bloody foam flooded the lungs, the victim moaned and writhed in agony, and the end arrived by asphyxiation. The most fortunate ones were dead in just a few hours.

My father suspected, on good grounds, that the flu had reaped a greater death toll among the soldiers in Europe, huddled in the trenches with no way to mitigate the spread, than the bullets and mustard gas had. It ravaged the United States and Mexico with equal ferocity and then turned toward South America. The newspapers said that in other countries the bodies were piled up like cordwood along the streets because there was not enough time or cemetery space to bury them all, that a third of humanity was infected, and that there were more than fifty million victims. The reports were as contradictory as the terrifying rumors that circulated. It had been eighteen months since the armistice had been signed, putting an end to the four horrific years of the Great War in Europe. But the full scope of the pandemic, which military censorship had covered up, was only just starting to be understood. No nation had wanted to report the true number of deaths. Only Spain, who had remained neutral in the conflict, shared news of the illness, which is why it ended up being called the Spanish influenza.

Before, the people of our country had always died

from the usual causes, which is to say, crushing poverty, vices, violence, accidents, contaminated water, typhus, or the normal wear and tear of years. It was a natural process that culminated in a dignified burial. But with the arrival of the flu, which pounced on us like a voracious tiger, we were forced to dispense with consolation for the dying and the regular rituals of mourning.

THE FIRST CASES WERE detected in the houses of ill repute near the port in late autumn, but no one except my father paid them much mind, since the victims were mostly women of dubious virtue, criminals, and smugglers. They said it was a venereal disease brought over from Indonesia by sailors passing through. Very quickly, however, it was impossible to ignore the widespread catastrophe or continue blaming promiscuity and happy living, because the illness did not discriminate between sinners and saints. The virus triumphed over Father Quiroga and moved freely through the population, viciously assailing children, the elderly, rich and poor alike. When an entire company of zarzuela singers and several members of Congress fell ill, the tabloids announced the Apocalypse and the government decided to close the borders and restrict the ports. But it was already too late.

Masses presided over by three priests with little bags of camphor tied around the neck did nothing to ward off infection. Winter was just around the corner and the first rains made the situation worse. Field hospitals sprang up on soccer pitches, makeshift morgues appeared in the meat lockers of the local slaughterhouse, and mass graves were dug for the bodies of the poor to be dumped and covered in lime. Since it was already understood that the illness entered the body through the breath and not from a mosquito bite or stomach worms, as had been widely believed, the use of face coverings was ordered. But since there weren't even sufficient masks for health workers, who fought on the front lines, there certainly weren't enough to go around for the general population.

The president of the nation, son of an Italian immigrant, with progressive ideas, had been elected a few months prior thanks to the vote of the emerging middle class and the workers' unions. My father, like all his Del Valle relatives, friends, and acquaintances, distrusted the man because of the reforms he'd vowed to implement—highly inconvenient for the conservatives—and because he was an upstart without an old Spanish-Basque surname, but my father did approve of how he'd tackled the public health crisis. The first measure was a stay-at-home order to curb the spread, but since no one heeded it, the president decreed a state of emergency, a nightly curfew, and a ban on free circulation of the civil population without due cause, under penalty of fine, arrest, and, in many cases, beatings.

Schools were closed, as well as shops, parks, and other places where people typically congregated, but some public offices and banks remained open. The trucks and cargo trains continued to deliver supplies, and liquor stores had license to operate, since it was believed that alcohol with a large dose of aspirin would kill the virus. No one counted the number of people poisoned by that combination of alcohol and aspirin, as pointed out by my aunt Pía, who did not drink and didn't believe in pharmaceutical remedies either. The police were overwhelmed and unable to impose order and prevent crime, just as my father had feared, and soldiers were called in to patrol the streets, despite their well-earned reputation for brutality. This rang an alarm bell for the opposition parties, intellectuals, and artists, who had not forgotten the massacre of defenseless workers, including women and children, carried out by the military a few years prior, as well as other instances in which they'd brandished their bayonets against civilians, treating our people like foreign enemies.

The shrine of Juan Quiroga was thronged with devotees seeking to cure themselves of the influenza, and in many cases they saw improvement. The skeptics, who can always be counted on to give their two cents, said that any person who could climb the thirty-two steps of the San Cerro Pedro Chapel was already on the mend. This did not discourage the faithful. Despite the fact that public gatherings were prohibited, a crowd led by two bishops marched to the shrine but were quickly scattered by soldiers doling out bullets and beatings. In under fifteen minutes they left two bodies dead in the street and sixty-three wounded, one of whom perished later that night. The bishops' formal protest was ignored by the president, who refused to receive the prelates in his office and instead answered in writing through his secretary that "anyone, even the Pope, who disobeys a public ordinance will feel the firm hand of the law." No more pilgrimages were attempted after that.

There wasn't a single infected person in our family because, before the government had even issued measures to curb spread, my father had already made preparations, taking his cue from methods of combatting the pandemic in other countries. He got on the radio and contacted the foreman of his sawmill, a highly trustworthy Croatian immigrant, and had two of their best loggers sent up from the south. He armed the men with ancient rifles, planted one at each entrance to our property, and assigned them the task of ensuring that no one entered or exited the premises except himself and my oldest brother. It was a ridiculous order, because they couldn't realistically shoot members of the family, but the presence of these men was mostly meant to dissuade looters. The loggers, transformed overnight into armed guards, never entered the house; they slept on pallets in the garage, ate food that the cook served them through the window, and drank the mule-killer aguardiente that my father provided in limitless supply, along with handfuls of aspirin, to keep the illness at bay.

For his own protection, my father bought a contraband Webley revolver, of proven efficacy in war, and began target practice in the service yard, terrorizing the hens. In reality he wasn't as scared of the virus as of the desperation it would sow among the masses. In normal times there were already too many poor, beggars, and thieves in the city. If what had happened in other places was any indication of what we could expect, unemployment would rise, food would become scarce, panic would set in, and even honest people, who up to that point had merely protested outside Congress demanding jobs or justice, might turn to crime. It had happened before, when laid-off miners from the north, furious and starving, had invaded the city and spread typhus.

My father bought enough supplies to last the winter: bags of potatoes, flour, sugar, oil, rice and beans, nuts, strings of garlic, dried meats, and crates of fruits and vegetables for preserves. He sent four of his sons, the youngest of whom had just turned twelve, down south before the San Ignacio school suspended classes by government decree. Only José Antonio stayed on in the capital, because he was going to start university as soon as the world went back to normal. All travel had been suspended, but my brothers managed to take one of the last passenger trains to San Bartolomé, where Marko Kusanovic, the Croatian foreman, met them at the station armed with instructions to put them to work alongside the rugged local loggers. No coddling. This would keep them busy and healthy and keep things quieter at home.

My mother, her two sisters, and the maids were ordered to remain indoors and not leave for any reason. My mother, who'd had weak lungs ever since a bout of tuberculosis in childhood, was of a delicate constitution and could not risk exposing herself to the flu.

THE PANDEMIC DID NOT greatly alter the closed universe of our home. The front door, of carved mahogany, opened onto a wide, dark vestibule that led to two sitting rooms, the library, the formal dining room, the billiards room, and another room that was always locked. We called that room the office because it contained half a dozen metal cabinets filled with documents that no one had looked at since time immemorial. The second wing of the house was separated from the first by a courtyard paved in blue Portuguese tile with a Moorish fountain that had a broken water pump, and a profusion of potted camellias; these flowers gave their name to the property: Camellia House. Along three sides of the courtyard ran a long corridor we called the conservatory, lined with beveled-glass windows, that connected the rooms for daily use: casual dining room, game parlor, sewing room, bedrooms, and bathrooms. The conservatory was cool in summer, and was kept more or less warm in winter with coal braziers. The back part of the house was the realm of the servants and the animals: consisting of the kitchen, laundry sinks, cellars, garage, and a line of pathetic cubicles where the domestic employees slept. My mother had entered that back courtyard on very few occasions.

The property had once belonged to my paternal grandparents, and when they died it was the only significant thing their children inherited. Its value, divided in eleven parts, represented a very small amount for each child. My father, the only one with any vision, offered to buy out his siblings in small installments. At first they thought he was doing them a favor, since that old mansion had endless structural issues, as he explained to them. No one in their right mind would live there, but he needed the space for his sons and the other children, who would come later, as well as his mother-in-law, already advanced in age, and his wife's two spinster sisters, who relied on his charity. Later, when he began to make late payments, proffering only a fraction of the promised amount, and then finally stopped paying altogether, the relationship with his siblings began to deteriorate. He truly never intended to swindle them. He was presented with investment opportunities that he had to seize, promising himself he would pay them back, with interest, but the years passed with one deferment after another, until he eventually forgot about the debt.

The house was truly a neglected ruin, but the lot took up half a block and had entrances from two streets. I wish I had a picture to show you, Camilo, because that's where my life began and my first memories were made. The old house had lost its former luster from before the financial setbacks, when my grandfather still reigned over a clan of children and an army of servants who kept the house in impeccable condition. The gardeners cared for a paradise of flowers and fruit trees with a glass greenhouse that held orchids from other climes. There were four marble statues of mythological Greek figures, popular at the time among the families of noble lineage and sculpted by the same local artisans who carved their elaborate family crypts in the cemetery. The old gardeners no longer existed, and the new ones were a bunch of lazy bums, according to my father. "If we keep going at this rate, the weeds are going to overrun the house," he would say, but he did nothing to rectify the problem. He considered nature something nice to admire from a distance, but it did not merit his attention, which was better reserved for more profitable activities. He was unconcerned by the progressive deterioration of the house because he planned to stay there only as long as necessary: The structure itself was worth nothing, but the lot was magnificent. He planned to sell it as soon as it had appreciated enough in value. His motto was a cliché: Buy low, sell high.

The upper class had begun moving to more-residential neighborhoods, far from the public offices, markets, and dusty plazas covered in pigeon poop. The trend was to demolish the old mansions like ours and construct office buildings or apartments for the middle class. The capital was and still is one of the most segregated cities in the world, and as the lower classes began to encroach onto those streets, which had been the city's main thoroughfares since colonial times, my father would have to either move his family or risk being looked down upon by his friends and acquaintances. At my mother's insistence, he modernized the house, adding electricity and installing toilets, as the home otherwise silently deteriorated all around us.

2

MY MATERNAL GRANDMOTHER SAT ALL day in the conservatory, in a high-backed armchair, so lost to her memories that she hadn't uttered a single word in six years. My aunts Pía and Pilar, several years older than my mother, also lived with us. The first was a sweet lady, knowledgeable in the healing properties of plants, gifted with a talent for curing through the laying on of hands. At twenty-three she had been engaged to marry a second cousin, whom she'd been in love with since age fifteen, but she never got to wear her wedding dress because her fiancé died suddenly two months before the wedding. The family refused an autopsy and the cause of death was attributed to a congenital heart defect. Pía considered herself a widow who'd lost her only love, dressed religiously in mourning clothes from then on, and never accepted any other candidates for marriage.

Aunt Pilar was pretty, like all the women in her family, but she did her best to hide her looks and she mocked the virtues and adornments of femininity. A few brave men had tried to court her in her youth, but she'd managed to frighten them away. She lamented not having been born a half century later, when she could have fulfilled her dream of being the first woman to climb Mt. Everest. The day the Sherpa Tenzing Norgay and the Englishman Edmund Hillary achieved the feat in 1953, Pilar cried in frustration. She was tall, strong, and agile, with the authoritarian temperament of a colonel; she managed the household and saw to repairs, which were endless. She had a talent for mechanics, invented her own domestic appliances, and came up with ingenious ways to solve problems, which is why everyone said that God had made a mistake when he chose her gender. No one was surprised to see her straddled atop the house, directing the replacement of roof tiles after a quake, or helping to slaughter hens and turkeys for the Christmas celebration without a hint of disgust.

The quarantine imposed by the influenza didn't change much for our family. In normal times, the maids, cook, and washing woman were off only three afternoons per month; the driver and the gardeners had more freedom, because the men were not considered part of the staff. The exception was

Apolonio Toro, a gigantic adolescent who had come knocking at the Del Valles' a few years prior asking for something to eat, and had stayed. They supposed he was an orphan, but no one had bothered to verify this. Torito rarely went out, because he was afraid he would be bullied, as had happened on many occasions; his almost beastly appearance combined with his childlike innocence elicited cruelty from others. He was tasked with hauling firewood and coal, sanding and waxing the parquet floors, and other hard physical chores that did not require critical thinking.

MY MOTHER WAS NOT particularly social, and went out as little as possible. She accompanied her husband to Del Valle family gatherings, so many that you could fill up the entire calendar with all the anniversaries, baptisms, weddings, and funerals, but she did so grudgingly, because the noise gave her headaches. She would use her ill health or another pregnancy as an excuse to stay in bed or escape to a tuberculosis sanatorium in the mountains, where her bronchitis would clear up and she'd have a chance to rest. If the weather was nice, she liked to go for rides in the flamboyant automobile that her husband had purchased as soon as they'd come into fashion, a Ford Model T, which reached the suicidal speed of thirty miles an hour.

"One day I'm going to take you flying in my very

own airplane," my father promised her, although it was the last thing she would have chosen as a mode of transport.

Aeronautics, which was considered a vagary of adventurers and playboys, fascinated my father. He believed that in the future those mosquitos made of wood and cloth would be readily accessible to anyone who could afford them, like automobiles, and he would be among the first to invest in them. He had thought it all out. He would buy planes secondhand in the United States, have them disassembled and brought into the country as parts, to avoid tariffs, and then after careful reassembly he would sell them for a fortune. By a strange twist of fate, I would end up fulfilling a form of his dream many years later.

The driver took my mother shopping at the Turkish market or to meet one of her sisters-in-law at the Versailles tearoom, where they would fill her in on the family gossip, but almost none of that had been possible in recent months, first due to the weight of her belly and later because of the quarantine orders. The winter days were short and they passed quickly over games of cards with my aunts Pía and Pilar, or sewing, knitting, and praying the rosary in penance with Torito and the servants. She had the rooms of her absent sons closed up, as well as the two sitting rooms and the formal dining room. Only her husband and her oldest son used the library, where Torito kept the fire lit so that the damp wouldn't creep into the books. In the rest of the rooms and in the conservatory they set up coal braziers topped with pots of boiling water containing eucalyptus leaves to cleanse the lungs and dispel the ghost of influenza.

My father and my brother José Antonio did not adhere to the quarantine or respect the curfew, my father because he was one of the business tycoons considered indispensable to the proper functioning of the economy and my brother because he went everywhere our father went. They had a permit to circulate, something granted to certain industrialists, businessmen, politicians, and healthcare workers. Father and son went to the office, met with colleagues and clients, and dined at the Union Club, which remained open; closing it would've been like shuttering the cathedral itself, although the quality of service declined as the waiters began dying off. On the streets they safeguarded themselves using felt masks sewn by my aunts, and they rubbed themselves down with alcohol before getting into bed. They knew that no one was immune to the flu, but they hoped that with these measures, along with the cleansing eucalyptus, they could keep the virus from entering our home.

Back when I was born, ladies like María Gracia shut themselves away to hide their pregnant bellies from the eyes of the world, and they did not nurse their infants, which was considered vulgar. It was common to hire a wet nurse, some poor woman who had to rip the breast from her own child's mouth and rent it to another more fortunate babe, but my father would not allow any stranger into our home. They might bring in the influenza and infect us all. They solved the problem of my nourishment with the milk of a goat that they brought to live in the back courtyard.

From my birth until five years old, I was left in the exclusive care of my aunts Pía and Pilar, who spoiled me to the point of almost completely ruining my character. My father contributed as well, because I was the only girl in a pack of sons. At the age when other kids learned to read, I was still unable to use silverware, having always been spoon-fed, and I slept curled up inside a bassinet beside my mother's bed.

One day my father dared to scold me for shattering my doll's porcelain head against the wall.

"Spoiled brat! I'm going to give you a good spanking!"

Never before had he raised his voice to me. I threw myself facedown onto the floor, panting like I was possessed, one of my usual tricks, and for the first time he lost his infinite patience, picked me up by the arms, and shook me so hard that, if my aunts hadn't stepped in, he might've broken my neck. The shock put an instant end to my tantrum.

"What this child needs is an English governess," my father decreed, furious.

And that's how Miss Taylor came into the family. My father found her through the commercial agent that managed some of his business interests in London, who simply put an ad in the **Times**. The two men communicated via telegram and letters that took several weeks to arrive at their destination and several more to return with a response. Despite the obstacles imposed by the distance and the language, since the agent didn't speak Spanish and my father's English vocabulary was limited to exchange rates and exportation documentation, they managed to hire the ideal person to fill the role, a woman of proven experience and respectability.

FOUR MONTHS LATER, MY parents and my brother José Antonio took me, dressed in my Sunday best with a blue velvet coat, straw hat, and patent-leather boots, to meet the Englishwoman at the port. We had to wait for all the passengers to disembark down the gangplank, greet whoever had showed up to welcome them, photograph themselves in huge groups, and sort out their complicated luggage, before the dock finally cleared and we made out a lone figure with a lost look on her face. That's when my parents saw that the governess was nothing at all like they had pictured based on a correspondence plagued with linguistic misunderstandings. In reality, the only personal detail my father had asked in one of his telegrams before hiring her was if she happened to like dogs. She had responded that she preferred them to humans.

Due to one of my family's many deep-rooted prejudices, they had expected a matronly, old-fashioned woman with a sharp nose and bad teeth, like some of the ladies from the British community they were vaguely acquainted with or had seen in the society section of the paper. Miss Josephine Taylor was a young twentysomething woman, short in stature and slightly curvy, without being fat, and she wore a loose mustard-colored dress with a drop waist, a felt hat shaped like a chamber pot, and slingback heels that buckled around the ankle. Her round, light-blue eyes were painted with black kohl, which set off her startled expression. She had strawlike blond hair, and that skin as transparent as rice paper that girls from cold countries sometimes have, which over time becomes spotted and mercilessly wrinkled. José Antonio was able to communicate with her using the basic English he had acquired through an intensive course but had never gotten a chance to put into practice.

My mother was enchanted with Miss Taylor from her first glimpse of the woman, fresh as an apple, but her husband considered himself swindled, because his sole objective for bringing her from so far away was to impose discipline and good manners and to lay the foundation of an acceptable education. He had decreed that I would be homeschooled to protect me from harmful ideas, vulgar customs, and the illnesses that decimated the young population at that time. The pandemic had taken some victims among our more distant relatives but everyone within our immediate family had gone unscathed. Nevertheless, there was a fear that it could return with renewed fury and sow death among children, who had not been immunized by the first wave of the virus like the surviving adults had. Five years on, the country had not yet fully recovered from the tragedy caused by the flu; the impact on public health and the economy was so devastating that, while in other parts of the world the Roaring Twenties were in full swing, in our country people still lived guardedly. My father feared for my health, never suspecting that my fainting fits, convulsions, and explosive vomiting were the result of my extraordinary talent for theatrics. He took it for granted that the trendy flapper he met at the port couldn't possibly be up to the task of taming his daughter's wild temperament. But that foreign woman would surprise him in more ways than one, down to the fact that she wasn't actually English.

BEFORE HER ARRIVAL, NO one was clear on the precise position that Miss Taylor would occupy in the domestic order. She didn't fit into the same category as the maids, but she definitely wasn't a member of the family. My father said that we should treat her with courtesy and distance, that she should eat her meals with me in the conservatory or in the pantry but not in the dining room. He assigned her to the bedroom that had been previously occupied by my grandmother, who had died sitting on her chamber pot a few months earlier. Torito moved the old lady's worn, heavy furniture down into the basement, and it was replaced with other less gloomy pieces, to keep the governess from getting depressed since, according to Aunt Pilar, she'd have enough to worry about between me and adapting to a barbaric land at the end of the world. Pilar chose an understated striped wallpaper and faded pink curtains, which she thought appropriate for an old maid, but as soon as she laid eyes on Miss Taylor, she understood that she had been mistaken.

Within a week, the governess had integrated into the family much more intimately than her employer had expected, and the issue of her place in the social hierarchy, so important in this classist country, melted away. Miss Taylor was friendly and discreet, but not at all shy, and she gained the respect of everyone, including my brothers, who were now grown but still behaved like cannibals. Even the two mastiffs my father had acquired in the time of the pandemic to protect us from possible assailants, and which had now turned into spoiled lapdogs, obeyed her. Miss Taylor only had to point at the floor and give them an order in her language, without raising her voice, and they would jump from the sofas with their ears folded. The new governess quickly established routines and started the process of teaching me basic manners, after getting my parents' approval on a plan of studies that included outdoor physical education, music lessons, science, and art.

My father asked Miss Taylor how she had acquired so much knowledge at such a young age and she responded that that was what reference books were for. Above everything else, she touted the benefits of saying "please" and "thank you." If I refused, and threw myself to the floor howling, she would stop my mother and her sisters with a mere gesture before they could rush over to console me. She let me kick and scream until I got tired, as she continued reading, knitting, or arranging flowers from the garden, unfazed. She was also wholly unmoved by my feigned epilepsy.

"Unless she's bleeding, we're not going to interfere," she declared, and they obeyed, intimidated by the woman and never daring to question her didactic methods.

They supposed that, since she came from London, she must be well qualified.

Miss Taylor deemed me too big to sleep curled up in a bassinet beside my mother, and asked for another bed to be placed in her own room. For the first two nights she pushed a dresser against the door so that I couldn't escape, but I quickly resigned myself to my fate. She immediately taught me to dress and feed myself, through the method of leaving me half-naked until I learned to put on at least some of my clothes and sitting me in front of my plate, spoon in hand, waiting with the patience of a Trappist monk until I finally succumbed to hunger. The results were so dramatic that in a short while the monster that had grated on the nerves of the entire household had become a normal little girl who followed the governess everywhere she went, fascinated by the smell of her bergamot perfume and her chubby hands that fluttered in the air like pigeons. Just as my father had always maintained, I'd spent five years yearning for structure, and I finally received it. My mother and aunts took this as a criticism, but they had to admit that there had been a fundamental shift. The air had sweetened.

MISS TAYLOR POUNDED AT the piano with more enthusiasm than talent, and sang ballads with an anemic but well-tuned voice; her good ear allowed her to quickly acquire a watered-down but intelligible Spanish that even included some curse words she'd picked up from my brothers, which she sprinkled into her sentences without understanding their meaning. The insults didn't sound as offensive with her accent, and since no one ever corrected her, she continued to use them. She couldn't stomach rich food but she kept her British stiff upper lip when it came to the local cuisine, just as she did during the winter rainstorms, the summer's dry, dusty heat, and the earthquakes that made the light fixtures dance and rearranged the chairs while everyone went about their business. What she couldn't stand, however, was the slaughter of animals in the service yard, which she classified as a cruel and primitive custom. She thought it savage to eat a stew made with a bunny or hen that we'd known personally. When Torito slit the throat of a goat he'd been fattening up for three months for his boss's birthday, Miss Taylor fell sick in bed with a fever. From then on Aunt Pilar decided to start buying meat from a butcher, even though she didn't see any difference between killing the poor animal in the market or at home. I should clarify that it wasn't the same goat that served as my wet nurse in infancy; that one died of old age several years later.

The two green metal trunks that comprised Miss Taylor's luggage contained textbooks and art history tomes, all in English; a microscope; a wooden box with everything needed for chemistry experiments; and twenty-one volumes of the most recent edition of **Encyclopædia Britannica**, published in 1911. She maintained that anything that didn't appear in the encyclopedia didn't exist. Her wardrobe contained two nice outfits, with their respective hats, one of which was the mustard-colored dress in which she'd stepped off the boat, and a coat with a fur collar made from some unidentifiable mammal; the rest was all skirts and plain blouses, which were covered in an apron all day. She took off and put on her clothes with the skill of a contortionist, in such a way that I never once saw her in her slip, much less naked, even though we shared a room.

My mother made sure that I prayed in Spanish before I got into bed, because the English prayers could be blasphemous and who knew if they'd even be understood up in heaven. Miss Taylor belonged to the Church of England, and that made her exempt from coming to Catholic mass with the family and from praying the rosary with us. We never saw her read the Bible she kept on her nightstand, or heard her speak with any religious zeal. Twice a year she went to the Anglican service held in the home of a member of the British community, where she sang hymns and talked to the other foreigners she often met with to have tea and exchange books and magazines.

With her arrival my existence was notably improved. The first years of my life had been a tug of war; I was constantly trying to impose my will and, since I always got my way, I didn't feel safe or protected. My father had always said I was stronger than the adults around me and so I didn't have anyone to lean on. The governess could not completely tame my rebelliousness, but she taught me the basic societal norms of acceptable behavior and managed to break me of my obsession with bodily functions and illness, which were popular topics of conversation in our country. Men talk about politics and business; women talk about their ailments and their servants. Every morning when my mother woke up, she took inventory of her aches and pains, writing them down in a notebook where she also kept a list of past and present medications, and she often entertained herself by flipping through those pages with more nostalgia than she felt for our family photo albums. I was on the same path as my mother; from so much pretending to be sick I had become an expert in a variety of afflictions, but thanks to Miss Taylor, who paid them no mind, they all cleared up on their own.

At first I did my schoolwork and piano exercises just to please her, but later out of a simple joy for learning. As soon as I could write legibly, Miss Taylor had me start keeping a diary in a beautiful leather notebook with a tiny lock, a custom I've maintained almost all my life. As soon as I could read fluently, I commandeered the **Encyclopædia Britannica**. Miss Taylor made up a game in which we memorized the definition of uncommon words and tested each other. Soon José Antonio, who was about to turn twenty-three without the vaguest intention of leaving the comfort of the family home, also joined in the game.

MY BROTHER JOSÉ ANTONIO had studied law, not out of interest, but because at that time there were very few acceptable professions for men of our class. Law had seemed better than the other two options: medicine or engineering. José Antonio worked with my father, assisting him in his business dealings. Arsenio Del Valle introduced him as his favorite son, his right-hand man, and my brother repaid our father's favor by remaining constantly at his beck and call, even if he wasn't always in agreement with the man's decisions, which he often found reckless. More than once my brother warned him that he was taking on too much debt but, according to my father, big business was done on credit and no entrepreneur with any commercial vision invested his own money if he could use someone else's. José Antonio, who had seen the creative bookkeeping for those businesses, thought that there must be a limit, that you could only pull a cord so tight before it would break, but my father assured him that he had everything under control.

"One day you're going to run this empire that I'm building, but if you don't wise up and learn to take risks, you won't be able to handle it. And, by the way, I've noticed you seem distracted, son. You spend too much time with the women of the house; they're going to make you foolish and weak," he told him.

The encyclopedia was one of the interests that José Antonio shared with Miss Taylor and me. My brother was the only one in the family who treated the governess like a friend and called her by her first name; for everyone else she would always be Miss Taylor. On lazy afternoons, my brother would chat with her about the history of our country; the forests in the south, where one day he'd take her to see the family's sawmill; the political news, which he was greatly concerned with ever since a colonel had presented himself as the only candidate for the presidential elections, obtaining one hundred percent of the votes, logically, and running the government like a military regiment. He had to admit that the man's popularity was justified when it came to the public works and institutional reforms he'd undertaken, but José Antonio talked to Miss Taylor about the danger to democracy posed by an authoritarian military leader of the kind that had plagued Latin America since the wars for independence.

"Democracy is vulgar. You'd be better off with an absolute monarchy," she joked, but in reality she was proud to have an Irish grandfather who had been executed in 1846 for defending the rights of workers and demanding universal suffrage for all men, even if they weren't landowners, as the king had decreed.

Josephine had told José Antonio, thinking I wasn't listening, that her grandfather had been accused of affiliation with the Chartist movement and of treason to the Crown, for which he'd been hung and quartered.

"A few years earlier and they'd have slit him open, pulled out his guts and castrated him, then strung him up, still alive, and cut him into pieces, before a crowd of thousands of cheering spectators," she explained dryly.

"And you call us primitive for killing chickens!" José Antonio exclaimed, horrified.

These grisly tales filled my nightmares. She also told my brother about the English suffragettes, who fought for the women's vote, risking prison and public humiliation, going on hunger strikes, which authorities put an end to by force-feeding them through a tube down their throats, in their rectums, or in their vaginas.

"They endured terrible tortures like true heroines. They've managed to secure a partial right to vote but continue fighting to obtain the same rights as men."

José Antonio was convinced that this would never happen in our country, but he had never stepped outside of his conservative bubble. He had no idea of the strength brewing in that very moment among the middle class.

Miss Taylor carefully avoided such topics around the rest of the family; she didn't want them to send her packing back to England.

3

"SHE HAS A DELICATE GUT," MY AUNT PÍA declared when Miss Taylor was stricken with diarrhea the day after her arrival.

It was a common affliction for foreigners, who got sick from their first sip of water, but since they almost all survived no one worried much about it. The governess, however, never really adapted to our bacteria, and spent two years struggling with a distressed digestive system, medicated by Aunt Pía with infusions of fennel and chamomile and powders that the family doctor doled out to her. I think it was all too rich for her, the desserts of dulce de leche, the pork chops with hot sauce, the corn cakes, the cups of hot chocolate with cream at five o'clock every afternoon, among other foods that it would've been bad manners for her to refuse. She stoically endured stomach cramps, vomiting, and diarrhea without ever saying a word.

Miss Taylor grew silently weaker until the family stepped in, alarmed by her weight loss and her ashy coloring. After examining her, the doctor prescribed a diet of rice and chicken broth and a half glass of port with drops of opium tincture twice a day. In private, he told my parents that the patient had a tumor the size of an orange in her stomach. There were local surgeons as good as the top doctors in Europe, he said, but he thought it was too late for an operation and that the most humane thing would be to send her back to her family. She had only a few months left to live.

José Antonio was assigned the difficult task of telling her, divulging only part of the truth, but she immediately guessed the rest.

"How inconvenient," said Miss Taylor, without losing her composure.

José Antonio informed her that our father would make the necessary arrangements for her to travel to London first-class.

"You want to get rid of me?"

"My God! No one wants to get rid of you, Josephine! We only want you to be with your family, dear, taken care of . . . I will explain the situation to them."

"I'm afraid you lot are the closest thing I have to a family," she replied, and then she proceeded to tell him what no one had ever bothered to ask.

. . .

IT WAS TRUE THAT Josephine Taylor had descended from an Irish grandfather who had been executed for angering the British Crown, but when she'd told my brother the story, she had omitted the fact that the justice warrior's son, her father, was an abusive alcoholic. Her mother, abandoned to poverty with several children, had died young. The smaller children were scattered among distant family members; the oldest, at age eleven, was sent to work in the coal mines; and she, at nine years old, went to live in an orphanage run by nuns, where she earned her keep doing washing, the institution's main source of income, and waited for some kind soul to adopt her. She detailed the Herculean task of soaping, thrashing, and brushing all those clothes, the immense pots of boiling water, then the endless rinsing, starching, and ironing.

At twelve years old, when she had not yet been adopted, she was placed as an indentured servant in the house of a British military officer, who, when she became a teenager, granted himself the right to systematically rape her. The first time it happened he'd burst into the small cell beside the kitchen where she slept, covered her mouth, and climbed onto her without any warning. From then on a routine was established, always the same, which Josephine grew to know and fear. The officer would wait until his wife was out, a frequent occurrence since she was always busy with charity work and social calls, and, with a gesture, he would let the girl know what was to come. Josephine obeyed, terrified, without ever imagining it possible to refuse or escape. The man would take her into the coach house, where he beat her with a riding crop, careful not to leave visible marks, and submitted her to perverse practices, which she survived by surrendering her body to the nightmare and closing her mind to the possibility of mercy. "This will eventually be over, this will end soon," she silently chanted.

Finally, after several months, the wife began to notice that her servant behaved like a beaten dog, scurrying into the shadows and trembling when her husband arrived home. In the years they'd been married she'd noticed many signs of perversion in him, but had preferred to ignore them with the theory that what is not named does not exist. As long as they kept up appearances, there was no need to scratch below the surface. Everyone had secrets, the woman told herself. But she realized that the other servants whispered behind her back, and a neighbor asked if her husband had taken to whipping the horses, because they heard blows and whimpers coming from the coach house. That's when she understood that she had to get to the bottom of what was happening under her roof before other people found out. She managed to catch her husband, whip in hand, and Josephine, half-naked, bound, and gagged.

The woman didn't put Josephine out on the street, as often occurred in such cases, but sent her to London to serve as companion to her mother, making her vow not to utter a word about her husband's conduct. Scandal had to be avoided at all costs.

HER NEW BOSS TURNED out to be a still-vigorous widow who had traveled the world extensively and aimed to continue doing so, for which she required a companion. She was haughty and tyrannical, but she had a knack for teaching and set out to convert Josephine into a polite young lady, since she did not wish to keep company with an Irish orphan who had the manners of a washerwoman. The widow's first task was to eradicate the girl's accent, which was torture to the ears, and to teach her how to speak like an upper-class lady of London; the next step was converting her to the Church of England.

"All papists are ignorant and superstitious; that's why they're poor and they reproduce like rabbits," the lady declared.

She achieved her objective without any difficulty because Josephine saw little difference between one religion and the other; and in any event she preferred to keep her distance from God, who had treated her so badly since the day she was born. She learned to conduct herself with impeccable manners in public, and to maintain strict control over her emotions and posture. The lady granted her access to her library and guided her reading, instilling in her a weakness for the **Encyclopædia Britannica**, and took her to places she'd never dreamed of seeing, from New York to Cairo. The woman eventually had a stroke and died soon after, leaving a small amount of money to Josephine, which she was able to live on for many months. When she saw an ad in the newspaper offering employment as a governess in South America, she applied.

"I got lucky, because I found your family, José Antonio, and you have treated me very well. To put it bluntly, I have nowhere to go. I'd like to die here, if you don't mind."

"You're not going to die, Josephine," José Antonio muttered, his eyes teary, because in that moment he realized how important she'd become to him.

WHEN MY FATHER FOUND out that the governess was going to wither away and die under his roof, his first instinct was to force her onto the next transatlantic ship leaving the port, to save me the trauma of seeing a woman I loved so dearly suffer. But, for the first time, José Antonio stood up to him.

"If you kick her out, I'll never forgive you, Dad," he vowed, and then he persuaded our father of his Christian duty to try and save her by any means he had at his disposal, despite the doctor's grim prognosis. "Violeta will be devastated if Miss Taylor dies, but she will understand. She's old enough now.

What she would never be able to accept is if her governess suddenly disappears. I'll take responsibility for Miss Taylor, Dad; you don't have to concern yourself," he said.

He kept his word.

A team headed by the most celebrated surgeon of his generation operated on Miss Taylor at the Military Hospital, the best in the country at that time, which she accessed thanks to the British consul, with whom my father had a relationship through his export business. Unlike the public hospitals, as poor as their patients were, and the scarce private clinics, where patients paid dearly for mediocre attention, the Military Hospital could compete with the most prestigious clinics in the United States and Europe. It was reserved exclusively for members of the armed forces and diplomats, but exceptions were made for patients with the right connections. The building, modern and well equipped, had large gardens where the convalescent could stroll. And the hospital staff, headed by a colonel, ensured impeccable hygiene and first-rate medical attention.

My mother and my brother accompanied Miss Taylor on her first consultation. A nurse in a uniform so stiffly starched it crunched with each step led them to meet the surgeon, a man of about seventy, bald, with a somber face and the arrogant manners of someone used to exercising authority. After examining her for a long while behind a partition that divided the room, he explained to José

Antonio, completely ignoring the presence of the two women, that the tumor was most likely cancerous. They could try to reduce it with radiation, but removing it surgically was too great a risk.

"If I were your daughter, doctor, would you attempt it?" Miss Taylor asked, as calm as ever.

After a pause, which felt endless, the doctor nodded.

"Then tell me when you can operate," she said firmly.

SHE WAS ADMITTED TWO days later. Faithful to her motto that honesty was always the best policy, before leaving for the hospital she told me that she had an orange in her stomach and they had to take it out, but it wasn't going to be easy. I begged her to let me go and hold her hand through the operation. I was seven years old and just as clingy as I'd been as a small child. For the first time since we'd met her, Miss Taylor cried. After she'd said goodbye to each of the servants, she hugged Torito and my aunts, whom she instructed to distribute her belongings, if necessary, among whoever might want something to remember her by, and she gave my mother a packet of sterling pounds tied up with a ribbon.

"For your poor, ma'am."

She had saved up all her earnings so that she might one day return to Ireland and seek out her displaced siblings, one by one.

She gifted me with her greatest treasure, the **Encyclopædia Britannica,** and assured me that she would do her best to return, but that she couldn't promise it. I knew something terrible could happen in the hospital; I was familiar with the unwavering power of death, since I'd seen my grandmother in her coffin, her face like a wax mask resting against the folds of white satin, as well as the dogs and cats that died of old age or accidents, and birds of all kinds, goats, sheep, and pigs that Torito slaughtered for the soup pot.

The last person Josephine Taylor saw before they wheeled her into the operating room was José Antonio, who stayed with her until the last minute. They had given her a powerful sedative and her friend's image seemed shrouded in mist. She didn't comprehend his encouraging words or his confession of love, but she felt a kiss on her lips and smiled.

THE OPERATION LASTED SEVEN long hours, which José Antonio spent in the hospital waiting room drinking coffee from a thermos and pacing back and forth, recalling the card games, teatime in the garden, their excursions outside the city, the encyclopedia guessing game, the afternoons of piano ballads, and byzantine discussions of drawn-and-quartered grandfathers. He determined that those had been the happiest hours he'd spent in the entirety of his regulated existence, in which his path had been laid out since birth. He was convinced that Josephine was the only woman with whom he could escape from under his father's tutelage and the web of complicity that trapped him. He had never made his own decisions, but simply did what was expected of him without a peep. He was the model son, and he was sick of it. Josephine challenged him, shook up his beliefs, and made him see his family and their social environment in a harsher light. Just as she'd made him dance the Charleston and taught him about the suffragettes, she pushed him to imagine a future different from the one that had been assigned to him, a future filled with risk and adventure.

At twenty-six, my brother already had a reserved and prudent nature, something he detested. "I'm old ahead of my time," he would mutter in disgust as he shaved in front of the mirror. He had been our father's second-in-command for years, but he was uninterested in the suspect business dealings and struggled to keep afloat in a social environment full of people with whom he shared no interests or ideals.

Pacing that hospital waiting room, he imagined starting a new life somewhere else with Josephine; they could go to Ireland and set up a modest home in the town where she'd been born. She could give classes and he would work as a laborer. The fact that Josephine was five years his senior and had never showed the slightest romantic inclination toward him were minor details compared to the sharp focus of his determination. He imagined the avalanche of gossip when he announced their wedding, our family surely seeing it as a disgrace since they expected him to wed an upper-class Catholic girl from a well-known family, such as cousin Florencia. But none of that would matter to him and his bride as they sailed off to Europe. How do I know all this, Camilo? In part because I wheedled it out of my brother over the years, and in part because I can imagine it since I knew him so well.

THE ORANGE IN MISS Taylor's stomach turned out to be benign, thanks to the celestial intervention of Father Quiroga, according to my aunts. The surgeon explained that the tumor had damaged her ovaries and they'd had to be removed. The patient would never be able to bear children, but since she was no longer young and still unmarried, that detail was of little importance. The operation had been a success, he assured us, but as was normal in these types of cases she had suffered massive blood loss, and was very weak. With rest and proper care, she'd slowly recover. My aunts Pía and Pilar took on the task of nursing her back to health, and I kept her constant company, as loyal as the two mastiffs, who never left her side.

Miss Taylor had become a shadow of the glowing young woman who had arrived dressed as a flapper years before. Ravaged by months of enduring pain without complaint and the brutal operation, nothing remained of her curves except the dimples in her hands, and her skin had acquired a disquieting yellow tone. When she finally stood, after almost a month subsisting on chicken soup and healing herbs, boiled seasonal fruits with bee pollen, opium drops, and a disgusting drink of beets and brewer's yeast for her anemia, we saw that her clothes hung from her frame and half of her hair had fallen out. José Antonio thought she'd never been lovelier. He lurked around the sick woman's room like a lost soul, waiting for our aunts to leave so that he could sit by her bedside and read poems to her in Spanish, which she only halfway understood through the haze of opium, eyelids heavy. I suggested that my brother read the encyclopedia to her instead, but he was lost in a dreamy fog of love.

Her convalescence went on for several more months and during that time Miss Taylor continued my education from an armchair in the conservatory. The life of the house was concentrated there. My mother brought her sewing machine out; Torito used the space to repair rickety pieces of furniture; Aunt Pilar built a complicated contraption she'd invented to dry bottles; and Aunt Pía prepared tinctures, powders, capsules, and wafers from her vast repertoire of natural remedies. She had gotten ahold of some fruits of the mocatú palm, sent from the Amazon basin of Bolivia, which she crushed to extract an oil said to cure baldness. She shaved off poor Miss Taylor's last four strands of hair and massaged her scalp twice a day with the miracle oil. Seven weeks later, she had sprouted a soft fuzz, and a short while after that she had begun to grow a lush dark mane. Aunt Pilar said, scornfully, that the governess had grown the coarse hair of the Altiplano Indians, thanks to those fruits, but she had to admit that it suited the woman better than her former strawlike strands.

The days passed slowly and peacefully. Only José Antonio was impatient, waiting for the moment he could take Miss Taylor to the Versailles tearoom and declare his intentions. He never doubted that she would accept; his only reservations concerned their economic situation, because the idea of earning a living as a laborer in Ireland seemed increasingly less attractive, and his future wife would need the safety and support of a family. He'd worked alongside our father from age seventeen but he'd never received any salary, only sporadic compensation more like generous tips, and nothing that permitted him to build savings.

Our father assured him that he'd receive a more than adequate portion of the earnings from the family business, but in practice the profits were instead reinvested in other enterprises. Arsenio Del Valle took out loans to finance one venture, which he would sell as soon as he could to fund another, repeating this cycle over and over, confident that the money would multiply in the invisible universe of banks, stocks, and bonds. José Antonio had warned his father against this approach, which he likened to a lab rat running tirelessly on a wheel, going nowhere. "At this rate you'll never get out of debt," he said, but our father maintained that no one got rich from a steady job or by investing prudently; according to him, the future belonged to the bold.

4

.....

THANKS TO HER LONG CONVALESCENCE AND Aunt Pía's therapeutic concoctions, Josephine Taylor had been restored to health and she was eager to get out of the house; she had spent too long inside the glass conservatory. She was very thin, but her coloring had improved, and her new short hair gave her the look of a half-plucked bird. For her very first outing she accompanied my mother, my aunts, and me to one of the Del Valle nieces' bridal shower. The simple, inconspicuous card, inviting the women of the family to join them for a light afternoon snack, downplayed the extravagance of the event, as was proper in a country where ostentation was once considered terribly tacky. It hasn't been that way for some time now, Camilo. These days everyone pretends to have more than they do and to be more than they are. The "light snack" turned out to be a scandalous spread of decadent pastries, silver pitchers of hot chocolate, ice cream, and sweet liqueurs served in Bohemian crystal glasses. All this was accompanied by a women's string orchestra for entertainment along with a magician vomiting silk scarves and pulling bewildered pigeons from the ladies' necklines.

I'd estimate there were about fifty women in those rooms, counting all of our female relatives and friends of the bride. Miss Taylor felt like a chicken in the wrong coop, underdressed, unconnected, and foreign. When a three-tiered cake was wheeled in to a chorus of exclamations and applause, she took the opportunity to escape to the garden. There she encountered another guest who'd fled outdoors just as she had.

Teresa Rivas was one of the few women who dared to sport the wide-legged pants and men's vests that had been recently introduced by a French designer, paired with a starched white shirt and tie. She was smoking a pipe with a bone mouthpiece and bowl carved in the shape of a wolf's head. In the dim afternoon light, Josephine first mistook her for a man, which was exactly the effect the woman had been aiming for.

They sat and talked on a bench nestled between the trimmed hedges and patches of flowers, enveloped in the scent of spikenards and tobacco. Teresa learned that Josephine had been in the country for several years and that her only acquaintances were the family she worked for and the members of the British community, whom she saw at the Anglican service. Miss Taylor talked about her home country with its working class and several layers of middle class, and about life in the provinces, about miners, farmworkers, and fishermen.

When Josephine finally heard me calling to her in the garden, she realized that the party had been over for some time and it was getting dark. The women hurriedly said their goodbyes. I overheard Teresa tell Miss Taylor where to find her, handing over a card with her name and work address on it.

"I am going to get you out of your cave, Jo, and show you some of the world," she said.

Josephine liked the nickname that this strange woman had given her, and she agreed to accept the offer; perhaps this would be her first friend in this foreign land where she'd begun to put down roots.

BACK AT HOME, I voiced what everyone was thinking: The time had come for us to adopt the modern fashions, with calf-length skirts, patterned fabric, and low-cut sleeveless blouses. The aunts always wore black dresses down to their ankles, like nuns, and my mother wouldn't have thought it necessary to modernize her wardrobe either, since she now managed to avoid social life almost entirely; her husband had tired of begging her to go places with him. Miss Taylor had attended the Del Valle bridal shower in the old mustard dress, after taking it in by several inches. My mother sent the driver to pick up some of the women's magazines that came over from Buenos Aires so we could gather ideas. The only thing Miss Taylor was interested in was Teresa Rivas's style. She bought several yards of gabardine and tweed, despite the fact that the climate wasn't suited to those thick fabrics, and with the help of some patterns she began sewing discreetly.

"I look like a street urchin," she murmured when she saw herself in the mirror wearing the completed outfit.

She was right. With her five-foot, hundred-pound frame, and her short, untidy hair, the pants, vest, and blazer made her look like a little boy wearing a men's three-piece suit. I was the first person who saw her in the new clothing, in the privacy of our bedroom.

"My parents aren't going to like those clothes at all," I said.

THAT SUNDAY, MISS TAYLOR took me on an outing to the Plaza de Armas, where Teresa Rivas was waiting for us. She hooked her arm through Miss Taylor's without making any comment on her clothes, and we strolled toward the ice-cream shop run by a Galician family. The two women were absorbed in conversation, and I perked my ears up to catch some of what they were saying.

"Shameless dykes!" a gentleman with a hat and cane commented loudly as he passed.

"And proud of it, sir!" Teresa answered with an insolent cackle while Miss Taylor blushed in embarrassment.

After the ice cream, Teresa drove us to her house, which was quite different from what we had imagined.

Miss Taylor had been of the notion that Teresa, because of her rebellious attitude and her natural elegance, was a member of the upper class; thinking perhaps she was one of those heiresses who could buck convention because she had money and a good name behind her. Miss Taylor was still unable to tell the difference among our social classes, partly because she'd had contact only with my family and the servants in the house.

That fairy tale that all humans are equal before the law and in the eyes of God is a lie, Camilo. I hope you don't buy into it. Neither the law nor God treats everyone the same. That is especially obvious in this country. A mere glance, based on any slight inflection, the way a fork is held at the table, or the ease in dealing with a person of inferior standing, is enough to instantly identify where a person falls in the intricate social hierarchy. This is a skill that few foreigners ever master. Excuse me if I harp on this topic, Camilo. I know you can't stand the whole class system, so exclusionary and cruel, but I have to mention it to help you understand Josephine Taylor.

Teresa lived in the attic apartment of a big old house on a poor-looking block of a dusty street. The first floor was occupied by a shoe repair shop, and on the second floor seamstresses sewed nurses' uniforms and white lab coats for doctors. The attic was reached by a dark hallway and stairwell, the wooden steps worn from use and carved up by the patient work of termites.

We found ourselves in a wide room with a low ceiling and two grimy windows that barely let in any light, a divan used as a bed, furniture that looked to have been salvaged from the dump, and a stately wardrobe with mirrored doors, the lone vestige of a past splendor. A hurricane-like disorder reigned, with clothes strewn about and piles of newspapers and magazines tied with string; I deduced that no one had cleaned the place in months.

"What is your connection to the Del Valles?" Miss Taylor asked Teresa.

"None. I went to the party with my brother, Roberto, the magician. Remember him?"

"Your brother is fantastic!" exclaimed Miss Taylor.

"Magic is only a hobby; no one can earn a living swallowing swords and making bunnies disappear."

TERESA LIT A BURNER to boil water and served us tea in chipped cups, mine with sugar and Josephine's with a shot of cheap aguardiente. They smoked dark, bitter cigarettes, which according to Teresa cleansed the lungs. She told us that her parents were both teachers in a southern province, which she and her brother had left as soon as they could—him to study at the university and she in search of adventure. She told us she'd never felt comfortable in her parents' environment, defining herself as bohemian. Her father had contracted the Spanish influenza years before and survived, but he'd had trouble with his lungs ever since.

"My parents recently retired. Teachers are paid next to nothing here, Jo. The new pension system was implemented too late for them to benefit, and they didn't have any savings, so they moved out into the country, where they don't need much to live, and now teach classes for free. I'd like to help them, but I'm a lost cause—I barely make enough to eat. Roberto, on the other hand, will have a good career and he's a responsible and generous son; he'll have to support my parents."

Teresa explained to Miss Taylor that her brother had entered military service at a young age, which had delayed his studies, but that in a few years he would graduate as an agricultural specialist. He studied during the day and worked as a waiter at night and a magician whenever he had a chance. Teresa had a job as an operator with the National Telephone Company.

"Of course, I can't turn up there dressed like a man," she added, laughing.

She showed us a few photos of her parents, taken

in the town square, and one of her brother as a new recruit in uniform, a clean-shaven boy who looked nothing like the entertaining mustached magician we'd seen at the party.

Many years later, in her old age, Josephine Taylor would tell me how that afternoon she and Teresa had cemented a friendship that would transform her life. Her only sexual experience had been the rapes and beatings from that British officer in her adolescence, which had left scars on her body and mind, as well as a profound rejection of all physical intimacy. The notion of sexual pleasure was inconceivable to her, and maybe for this reason she didn't know how to interpret José Antonio's attentions. With Teresa she discovered love and was able to cultivate sensuality, something she didn't even know existed. At thirty-one years old, she still maintained a rare innocence.

Teresa bragged about her willingness to try anything new, never minding morals or rules imposed by others. She mocked religion and the law alike. She explained to Josephine that she'd had affairs with both men and women, and considered monogamy to be an absurd constraint.

"I believe in free love. Don't try to tie me down," she warned Miss Taylor a few weeks later, as they lay naked on the divan caressing each other.

Miss Taylor accepted this condition with a lump in her throat. She never imagined that over their long and intimate relationship, she'd never have cause for jealousy, because Teresa would be the most faithful and devoted of lovers.

IN SEPTEMBER 1929, THE United States stock market suffered an alarming drop, and in early October it plunged further. My father calculated that, if the strongest economy in the world were to topple, all the other countries would feel a cataclysmic impact, and ours would be no exception. He knew it was a matter of time, maybe only a few days, before his financial empire fell and he'd be ruined, like so many men of great wealth in America. What would happen with his businesses, with the sale of the house, which was almost finalized, and the construction project he'd sunk so much money into? He'd mortgaged his assets to invest in the stock market, taken money from loan sharks, and involved himself in illegal schemes that forced him to keep one official register and one secret one, which he shared only with José Antonio.

Arsenio Del Valle felt panic rise like flames inside him and a glacial cold on his skin, so anxious that he couldn't sit still as his mind clouded with worry; he panted and sweated. He tallied the number of people who depended on him, not only his family, but also his servants and the employees in his office, the workers at the sawmill and in his vineyards to the north, where he'd begun to fulfill his dream of distilling refined brandy to compete with Peruvian pisco. They'd all be forced out into the streets. None of his sons except José Antonio helped him run his businesses; the other four took full advantage of the prosperity that he provided without ever asking how hard it had been won. He was desperate, consumed with stress over how he'd support his wife, his sisters-in-law, and me, how to save himself from bankruptcy and the humiliation of failure, how he'd face society, his creditors, my mother.

He wasn't the only one in this position. Among the members of the Union Club paralyzing fear spread from one man to the next. In the sitting rooms decorated in the green and maroon English style, with scenes of foxhunting that had never taken place in our country and authentic Chippendale furniture, the upper-class gentlemen—who had always had economic clout, although not always political power—accustomed to the security of their privilege, followed the news in disbelief. Up to then calamities of all kinds, so frequent in this land of earthquakes, floods, droughts, poverty, and eternal discontent, had rarely touched them.

The waiters ran around serving liquor and passing trays of raw oysters, crab legs, pickled quail, and fried empanadas, the anxiety so great that no one even sat at the tables. An optimistic voice rose up to declare that, as long as the price of certain minerals remained stable, the country could weather any storm looming on the horizon. This delusion was immediately quashed. The numbers showed an unavoidable reality.

JUST AS MY FATHER had expected, with a knot in his stomach, the last Tuesday in October the entire world found out that the international stock market had collapsed. He locked himself in the library with José Antonio to take a hard look at their situation, conscious that his own denial had kept him from taking steps to avoid disaster. He questioned everything, especially his own judgment. He had failed at the very thing his social position had been founded upon: his natural ability to make money, his clairvoyant vision for opportunities that no one else could see, his bloodhound nose for problems and their solutions, the salesman's charisma he could use to bamboozle people with such skill that they thought he was doing them a favor, and his enviable panache for getting out of tight situations. None of this had prepared him to face the chasm that now opened up at his feet, and the fact that so many others were staring into the same void was no consolation. He knew that his son, unbiased and reasonable, was the best person to counsel him.

"I'm sorry, Dad, I think we've lost everything," José Antonio said after checking the books for the second time, the doctored ones as well as the real ones.

My brother explained that his stocks no longer had any value, that he owed money to half the world, and that there was a real possibility of his being arrested on grounds of tax evasion. There was no way to pay his debts, but no one else would be able to either; the creditors would have to wait. The bank would take the sawmill, the vineyards, the construction projects, and even our house. What would we live on? We'd have to reduce expenses to a minimum.

"So you're saying, we have to cut back . . ." my father stammered in a thread of a voice.

The possibility had never occurred to him.

THE GLOBAL FINANCIAL DEBACLE paralyzed our country. We didn't know it yet, but we'd be the nation most greatly affected by the crisis, because the exportation system that sustained us would collapse. The wealthy families, who despite having lost so much were able to leave the city, fled to their rural estates, where at least they'd have livestock and gardens to provide food, but the majority of the population felt the crushing blow of poverty.

As more companies declared bankruptcy, the number of unemployed increased; in a very short time soup kitchens and community food banks opened where thousands of hungry people lined up for a plate of watery broth. Crowds of men wandered in search of work, and women and children begged in the streets. No one stopped to give alms to the homeless lying on the sidewalks. There were frequent outbursts of violence among the desperate population. The crime rate increased so greatly in the cities that no one felt safe.

The government was in the hands of the iron-fisted general who had sent the previous president into exile. They said that he drowned his political enemies in the port and that anyone who dove down to take a look could see the skeletons laid bare by the fish, blocks of cement tied to their ankles. Despite his repressive measures, the general was losing power by the minute, plagued by massive protests that the new branch of the police, trained with Prussian military tactics, quelled with gunfire. The capital looked like a city at war. Students went on strike, as did teachers, doctors, engineers, lawyers, and other unions, all united by a single demand for the general to step down. The general, barricaded inside his office, couldn't believe that his luck had been turned on its head overnight, and he ordered the police to continue carrying out their duty.

THE SECOND DAY OF the protests, José Antonio and my other brothers went out to participate in the demonstrations, not so much out of political conviction as to vent their frustration and keep from being left out, since their friends and acquaintances were all protesting. White-collar workers wearing hats and ties, shirtless laborers, and beggars in rags all mingled on the streets. There had never been such a crowd marching shoulder to shoulder, so different from the parades of poor families during the worst times of unemployment, which the upper class merely watched from their balconies. José Antonio, accustomed to controlled emotions and an orderly existence, found it to be a liberating experience; for a few hours he had the sense of belonging to a community. He hardly recognized himself in this manic state, shouting to provoke the dense line of police officers who responded with whips of their batons and shots fired into the air.

That's what he was doing when he saw, on a street corner, Josephine Taylor, as excited as the rest of the crowd, and me, gripping her hand, terrified. His euphoria chilled instantly. In his pocket he carried a little box with a ring of garnets and diamonds, the same ring Miss Taylor had delicately rejected when he'd asked her on bended knee to marry him.

"I'll never get married, José Antonio, but I'll always love you as my best friend," she told him, and had continued treating him with the same familiarity as before, as if he'd never made any declaration of love.

But the close and caring relationship they'd had for so long gave José Antonio hope that in time she'd change her mind. The ring would remain in his possession for thirty years.

There were few females among the protestors,

and in her pants, suit jacket, and Bolshevik hat, Miss Taylor blended in with the men. She was with another woman, also dressed in men's clothes, who was unknown to José Antonio. He had never seen Miss Taylor dressed this way; in her role as governess she was the model of traditional femininity. He took her by the arm and grabbed me by the collar of my coat, practically dragging us to the door of a building, away from the police.

"You could get trampled or shot! What are you doing here, Josephine? And with Violeta!" he said, baffled as to why this Irish woman should be concerned with local politics.

"The same as you: protesting." She laughed, her voice hoarse from shouting.

José Antonio didn't get the chance to ask her why she was disguised as a man because Miss Taylor's companion interrupted him, introducing herself as "Teresa Rivas, feminist, at your service." He was not familiar with the term and thought that the woman had perhaps said "communist" or "anarchist," but there was no time to ask for clarifications, because a sudden shout of triumph rose up and the crowd began to jump, throw their hats in the air, and climb onto the roofs of cars, waving flags and cheering in unison, "He's fallen! He's fallen!"

And it was true. When the general finally understood that he had completely lost control of the country and that his orders were no longer obeyed by the military or the police force that he himself had created, he escaped from the presidential palace and fled the country with his family by train, the same train on which the recently exiled president would soon return. That night, Miss Taylor said once again that we'd be better off with a monarchy, and my father was in total agreement. The celebrations in the streets went on for hours, but that brief political victory did nothing to mitigate the poverty and destitution in which the country was already mired.

5

.....

MY FATHER HELD OFF THE BANKS AND creditors for a full year, as his last resources were diminished. He managed to delay the impending shipwreck through a pyramid scheme that had already been outlawed in other countries but was still unknown in ours. He knew it was a short-term solution, and when it folded, he hit rock bottom. He understood by then that he had no one left to turn to; he had made too many enemies over a career singularly focused on earning more and more money. He'd swindled several acquaintances with the pyramid scheme; others had been his partners in failed ventures in which they'd lost everything while he'd walked away unscathed. He certainly couldn't expect help from his siblings, who at the start of the crisis had turned to him seeking loans. He'd explained that he was bankrupt, but they didn't believe him and went away angry; they hadn't forgotten how he'd made off with the family inheritance. He stopped going to the Union Club because he couldn't afford membership and was too proud to let them temporarily waive the fees, as had been done with other members in similar situations. He'd climbed too high and wagered too much. His fall was spectacular.

José Antonio was the only person who knew the whole truth; my other brothers, stripped of their monthly allowance, took refuge with cousins and friends, trying to steer clear of their father's disgrace. The women of the family had to reduce their expenses and say goodbye to almost all of the servants, but they didn't realize how serious things truly were. Like so many other matters, it didn't concern them; it was a problem for the men to solve.

My father's enthusiasm, which had been the main driving force in his life, vanished. He bore the pain of each day with the help of gin and combatted his nighttime insomnia with his wife's miracle drops. He awoke in the morning with a foggy mind and weak knees, sniffed white powders, dressed himself with difficulty, and, to avoid my mother's questions, scurried to the office, where there was nothing to do except wait for the hours to pass and the situation to worsen. The alcohol, cocaine, and opium enabled him to function but gave him acid reflux and suppressed his appetite. He became thin, with dark circles under his eyes, his skin sallow and his shoulders hunched. He'd aged a century within a few months, but I was the only one who seemed to notice his weakened state. I followed him around the house, silent as a cat, and, breaking the rule against entering the library, I sat at his feet as he lay on the leather sofa and stared blankly at the wall.

"Are you sick, Dad? Why are you sad?" I asked over and over, without expecting a response.

My father was a ghost.

TWO DAYS AFTER THE fall of the government, Arsenio Del Valle learned that we were being evicted from Camellia House, where he and all his children had been born. He had one week to vacate the premises. The final nail in his coffin was the arrest warrant for fraud and tax evasion that his son José Antonio had long feared would come.

In that big old house of so many rooms filled with rumbling pipes, creaky floors, rats scurrying between the walls, and the inhabitants clomping around, no one heard the gunshot. I found him the next morning, when I went into the library to take him his cup of coffee, as I often did since they'd fired the maids. The heavy velvet curtains were closed and the only light came from a Tiffany desk lamp with a stained-glass shade. It was a big room with high ceilings, the walls lined with bookshelves and reproductions of classic oil paintings that a Uruguayan artist copied so accurately they could fool an expert buyer, something my father had proven on a few occasions. All that remained was an enormous Judith with the severed head of Holofernes resting on a platter. The Persian rugs had disappeared, along with the bearskin, two baroque chairs, huge Chinese porcelain vases, and the majority of the various collections. This room, which had previously been the most luxurious in the house, was now a naked space.

Blinded by the morning light of the conservatory, I paused for a few seconds to adjust to the darkness, and then I saw my father slumped in the chair behind his desk. I thought he was sleeping, but the stillness of the air and the faint smell of gunpowder alerted me that something was amiss.

My father shot himself through the temple with the English revolver he'd bought during the pandemic. The bullet lodged cleanly in his brain, the entry point a black hole the size of a coin, a thin trail of blood trickling from the wound down to the paisley design on his Indian smoking jacket and from there to the carpet, which absorbed the stain. I remained frozen at his side for an eternity, observing him, the coffee mug trembling in my hands, whispering to him, "Dad, Dad." I can still remember with perfect clarity the feeling of emptiness and terrible calm that came over me and would last until long after the funeral. Finally, I set the mug on the desk and went quietly to look for Miss Taylor.

This scene is etched in my memory with the

precision of a photograph and has reappeared in my dreams many times. Around age fifty I spent several months in therapy with a psychiatrist who made me analyze the event ad nauseam, but I have never been able to muster the emotion that should correspond to seeing your father dead from a bullet wound. I don't feel horror or sadness, nothing. I can describe what I saw, the emptiness and calm I felt, but nothing more.

THE ENTIRE HOUSE AWAKENED to the tragedy forty minutes later, after Miss Taylor and José Antonio had cleaned up the blood and hidden my father's wound under the nightcap he always wore in winter. It was a commendable effort, which allowed us to pretend that his heart had burst from stress. No one, within the family nor outside, believed it, but it would've been impolite to contradict the official story, which the doctor corroborated so that we could lay him to rest in the Catholic cemetery instead of in the town graveyard, where the poor and the foreigners who belonged to other religions were buried. He wasn't the first and wouldn't be the last ruined wealthy gentleman to take his own life during that dark period.

My mother considered her husband's suicide an act of cowardice: He'd left her helpless in the midst of a disaster he himself had created. The indifference she'd felt toward him those last years, when they hadn't even shared a bedroom, turned to contempt and rage. This betrayal was much more serious than the minor sins of infidelity, which she had known about but ignored; this was a much greater humiliation. She couldn't bring herself to play the part of the grieving widow or dress in mourning, even though she knew that the Del Valles would never forgive her for it. She buried him immediately, without alerting anyone except her sons, because we still had to vacate the house. A brief note about his passing ran in the paper the following day, after it was already too late to attend the funeral. There was no eulogy and no flowered wreaths; very few people offered their condolences. They did not allow me to go to the cemetery, because after discovering my father's body in the library I began to run a fever and they say I didn't speak for several days. Miss Taylor stayed home with me. My father, Arsenio Del Valle, the powerful man who was respected and feared by so many, left the world like a pauper.

My family mentioned him as little as possible, to the degree that I didn't even suspect economic ruin and fraud had led him to commit suicide until fifty-seven years later. That was when you, Camilo, as a teenager, set out to dig through the past and unearth our family secrets.

For a time, the silence surrounding my father's death made me doubt whether I'd actually seen that hole in his temple; everyone repeated the story about the heart attack so often that I almost began to believe it. I quickly realized that it was a taboo topic, and I processed my repressed grief through recurring nightmares, quietly, exercising the self-control Miss Taylor had taught me.

JOSÉ ANTONIO GATHERED MY other brothers, my mother, and the rest of the women in the family, Miss Taylor included, and, without beating around the bush, detailed the family's financial situation, which was much more dire than they'd ever imagined. They left me out because they thought I was too young to understand, and because I seemed so strongly impacted by the suicide. With great regret, they laid off the last two servants that remained in that desolate house, where even the mastiffs had died and the cats had disappeared. The rest of the servants, the driver, and the gardeners had been let go months prior. Apolonio Toro stayed on, because we were his only family. He'd never received a salary, working only for room, board, clothes, and sporadic tips.

My brothers, who were now adults, distanced themselves from the social scandal, found jobs, and began making their own way. If we'd ever had any kind of familial bond, it was broken the morning we found my father in the library. The numerous Del Valle clan was lost to me at age eleven, which is why you haven't met most of them, Camilo. The only one who never abandoned my mother, my aunts, and me was José Antonio. He accepted his duty as eldest son, confronted the scandal and the debts, and assumed the responsibility of supporting the women of the family.

José Antonio had to come up with a plan, discussing his options with Miss Taylor, because he understood that my mother and aunts, who'd never had to make important decisions before, wouldn't be much help. It was Miss Taylor who came up with the best idea, but her solution was hard for José Antonio to accept. He had lived his life inside a closed circle of people who always protected each other. Miss Taylor had been born poor and could think beyond José Antonio's limitations. She helped him see that we'd been ostracized. Arsenio Del Valle had tarnished the family name, and we, his descendants, would pay the consequences.

With the few jewels and the collection of ivory carvings my father hadn't managed to sell or pawn, José Antonio was able to scrape together enough money to move us out of the city. We had to start over somewhere we could get by on the bare minimum while he looked for a way to make a living. Our father's disgrace was his as well, not only as his son, but because he'd worked alongside the man since adolescence and gave the appearance of being directly involved in those shady business dealings. No one believed that my brother had tried many times to warn our father of the dangers of his behavior, nor that the man never gave him any authority.

José Antonio would not be able to practice as a lawyer until he cleared his name. And, thanks to the Great Depression, which had upended the entire known world, it would not be easy to find work doing anything else either. Miss Taylor's plan was the most practical way forward.

My governess turned out to possess a laudable mettle in the face of misfortune. She firmly believed that her childhood poverty, the orphanage with the nuns in Ireland, and her first boss's cruel perversion had granted her more than her fair share of suffering in this life and nothing the future might hold could possibly be worse. When she saw how lost José Antonio was after burying his father, she thought it would be best for us to get as far away as possible from our familiar environment, at least for a while.

"We don't need anyone's pity or compassion," she said to him, including herself automatically among the Del Valles. She added that they could count on her savings; my mother had returned the bundle of sterling pounds after the operation, and she'd kept it safe in her underwear drawer ever since.

José Antonio asked her for the umpteenth time to marry him, and she repeated once again that she'd never marry, but she didn't offer him the only explanation he would have accepted: She was already wed, in spirit, to Teresa Rivas.

• • •

MISS TAYLOR KNEW JUST the place for us and took care of all the details. The train left us in Nahuel, the end of the line; from there, travel farther south continued in carts, on horseback, and by sea where the land breaks up into islands, canals, and fjords that extend down to the icy blue glaciers. We didn't meet another soul on that desolate train platform half-covered by a corrugated metal roof with a weatherbeaten sign bearing the name of the town. We'd traveled many hours on hard seats, sharing a basket of boiled eggs, cold chicken, bread, and apples. On the last leg of the journey we were the only passengers in the car, the rest having disembarked at previous stops along the way.

We'd packed everything we could fit into our many trunks and suitcases: clothes, pillows, sheets and blankets, hygiene products, and items of sentimental value. In a crate in the cargo hold we placed the sewing machine, a grandfather clock that had belonged to my grandmother, my mother's Queen Anne writing desk, the complete **Encyclopœdia Britannica,** kitchen objects, three lamps, and some small jade figurines my mother considered indispensable to our new life, which we'd managed to make off with before the creditors inventoried the contents of the house and confiscated everything. We also salvaged the piano, moving it to an empty room in the house where Teresa Rivas lived. José Antonio gave it to Miss Taylor since she was the only person who could play it more or less decently. In other boxes my aunts had packed Aunt Pía's apothecary kit, Aunt Pilar's tools, jars of preserves, smoked hams, aged cheeses, bottles of liquor, and other delicacies they couldn't bear to leave behind.

"Enough! We're not moving to a desert island!" José Antonio said, stopping them as they tried to pack a crate of live hens.

"THIS IS WHERE CIVILIZATION ends, Indian territory," the conductor told us, as we waited for Torito and José Antonio to unload our luggage at the Nahuel station.

The comment did not help calm the nerves of my mother and aunts, exhausted from the trip and scared for our future, but it did pique Miss Taylor's interest and my own. Maybe this forgotten corner of the world would turn out to be more interesting than we'd expected.

We were sitting on our suitcases, protected from the drizzle under the station roof, and reviving our bodies with the hot tea we'd been offered by the railway workers—local men, sullen and silent but hospitable—when a mule cart pulled up. It was driven by a man wearing a wide-brimmed hat and a heavy black poncho. He introduced himself as Abel Rivas, shook José Antonio's hand, tipped his hat to the women, and gave me a kiss on each cheek.

He was of medium height and undefined age, with weathered skin, coarse gray hair, round wire-rimmed glasses, and large hands deformed by arthritis. Miss Taylor had arranged for us to come live with her friend Teresa Rivas's parents.

"My daughter, Teresa, told me to meet your train," he said, and added that he would take us to our lodgings. "Then I'll come back for your luggage. I can't put that much weight on the mules. Don't worry, no one will steal anything from you here."

The slow journey by cart bumping along the dirt roads, drenched in rain, felt eternal and allowed us to experience the full force of our self-imposed isolation. José Antonio rode on the driver's seat beside Abel Rivas; Pilar held my mother, who was doubled over with a coughing fit, increasingly frequent and prolonged; Aunt Pía prayed silently, and I, sitting on a plank between Miss Taylor and Torito, scanned the vegetation in hopes of spotting one of the Indians the conductor had warned of, imagining the fierce Apaches in the only movie I'd ever seen, a confusing silent film about the American Wild West.

Nahuel consisted of one short road lined on both sides by ramshackle wooden houses, a small general store that was closed at that hour, and a single brick construction that, according to Abel, served several functions: post office, church whenever a priest passed through, town hall where locals decided on issues that affected the community, and reception room for large celebrations. Mangy dogs, lying beside the houses to keep out of the rain, barked half-heartedly as the mules passed.

The cart left the town behind and continued on for another half mile, turned onto a path lined with trees stripped bare by winter, and finally stopped in front of a house similar to the ones in town, but larger. A woman came out to greet us, sheltered under a large black umbrella. She helped us out of the cart, giving us each a welcoming hug, as if she'd known us forever. It was Lucinda, Abel's wife and Teresa Rivas's mother—tiny, constantly in motion, bossy and effusive in her affection, a woman who did not discriminate between family and strangers, between people and animals. I'd guess she was around sixty years old then, based only on her gray hair and wrinkles, because she was as quick and agile as her husband was slow and taciturn.

And so began the second phase of my life, which our family referred to as Exile, with a capital "E." For me it was a period of discovery. I'd spend the next nine years in that semi-uninhabited province in the south, which is now a tourist destination, a landscape of vast cold forests, snowy volcanoes, emerald lakes, and raging rivers, where anyone with a hook and line can fill a basket with trout, salmon, and turbot in under an hour. The wide skies were an ever-changing spectacle, a symphony of colors, clouds pulled quickly along by the wind, bands of wild geese, and sometimes the outline of a condor or eagle in majestic flight. Night there fell suddenly, like a black blanket embroidered with millions of lights, which I learned to identify by both their classical and indigenous names.

LUCINDA AND ABEL RIVAS were the only teachers for miles around. Teresa had told Miss Taylor how her parents had retired and left the town where they'd taught for decades to move home, where they were more greatly needed. They returned to Abel's family farm, which had been left in the hands of his younger brother Bruno. Santa Clara was a small property, just large enough to support the family and provide a surplus of products, such as honey, cheeses, and cured meats, to trade or sell in the neighboring towns. It wasn't even a shadow of the large estates owned by the German and French immigrants. In addition to the main house, there were a few rustic dwellings, a smokehouse, a covered bathhouse for the metal tub we used weekly, a bread oven, toolshed, pigsty, and stable for the cows, horses, and mules.

Bruno Rivas was much younger than his brother Abel; he was around fifty years old, a salt-of-the-earth, hardworking man with a strong body and heart. He had lost his only child and his wife during her first childbirth, and had no other love. He was somber and quiet but kind, always willing to help, to lend his tools or his mules, to give away any milk or eggs he had to spare.

Facunda, a young Indian woman with an expressive face, broad shoulders, and a body as strong as a stevedore's, had worked in his house for many years. She had a husband somewhere and a couple of kids she seldom saw, who were being raised by their grandmother. She baked amazing bread, tarts, and empanadas, spent her days singing, and adored Señor Bruno, as she called him, whom she scolded and spoiled like she was his mother, although she was young enough to be his daughter.

Lucinda and Abel occupied one of the small cottages located just a few yards from the main house. Bruno liked their company and the help his brother and sister-in-law offered; there was always so much to do, and no matter how early you started out, the day was never long enough. In spring and summer, the seasons that required the most work, Bruno hired a couple of laborers to help because Abel and Lucinda went out to teach classes. They traveled on horseback and mule across a vast area, carrying boxes of notebooks and pencils bought with their own money, since the government had left the children of the most remote locations to fend for themselves. Four years of basic education was obligatory, but it was hard to provide it to the entire country; there weren't enough roads, resources, or teachers to reach those distant parts.

When they arrived at a farmhouse, Abel Rivas would ring a cowbell to call the children out. They'd stay for a few days teaching from sunup to sundown, cultivating friendships with the families, who saw them as angels sent from heaven. People couldn't pay the Rivases for the classes, but they always insisted on giving them some token of appreciation: jerky, rabbit hides, homemade sandals, or textiles. They slept wherever they were offered lodgings, and then continued on to their next destination. Before setting out they gave the students enough work to last several weeks, with the warning that they'd be back to test them so one day they could graduate with an elementary diploma. The Rivases dreamed of having their own school where they could gather all the students and provide them with one hot meal per day, because in some cases it would be the only meal they got, but it was impossible. The students couldn't travel so many miles on foot to school; the school had to go to them.

"My brother Bruno is fixing up the other house for you. It hasn't been lived in for years, but it'll clean up nicely," Abel told us.

We sat around the woodburning stove, the heart and soul of the house, sharing **mate**, the bitter green tea typically drunk in the south, with fresh bread, cream, and quince jam that Facunda served us. Later that afternoon we met Bruno, and the neighbors began arriving to welcome us. They left their dripping ponchos and muddy boots at the door, greeted us timidly, and placed their offerings on the table: jars of preserves, lard, or goat cheese wrapped in cloth. They examined us with curiosity;

who knows what they must have thought of those visitors from the capital, with our white hands and thin coats that were useless against a good rain shower, and our different way of speaking. The only one who seemed human to them was Torito, with his huge hands hardened from work, his large frame hunched to keep from hitting his head on the roof beam, and his eternally kind smile.

When night fell, the neighbors left.

"See you tomorrow. Facunda will bring you fresh bread for breakfast," Lucinda told us, slipping her poncho over her head.

And that's when we realized that Mr. and Mrs. Rivas were going to sleep somewhere else in order to leave their home to us.

"It's just for a few days. Your house will be ready soon. We're repairing the roof and we have to install a woodburning stove," Abel explained.

THE FIRST DAYS PASSED quickly with visits to the nearby farms and Nahuel to introduce ourselves and repay our neighbors' kindnesses. The proper thing to do was take a gift in exchange for the one you'd received; in this country you never show up to someone's house empty-handed. All my aunts' jars were portioned out, although they couldn't hold a candle to the country preserves. José Antonio and Torito joined the men repairing the house we'd been assigned. One week later my mother, my aunts, and

I moved into a home filled with used furniture that Bruno had procured for us.

In those modest clapboard rooms with the wind howling outside, the cherry writing desk and the grandfather clock we'd brought from the city looked out of place, and the Tiffany lamps were useless since there was no electricity. I don't remember what happened to the jade figurines, I think they stayed wrapped in their cloths forever. Just as Bruno had explained, it would've been impossible to survive without the big black stove, which served for cooking, heating the rooms, drying laundry, and gathering around. It remained lit from morning to night, winter and summer alike. My aunts, who before had barely known how to make a cup of tea, learned to use it, but my mother never even tried. She was perpetually languishing on a chair or in bed, exhausted from the cold and an incessant cough.

Torito and I were the only ones who were able to adapt to the circumstances right from the start. The others pretended we were only temporarily camping, because it was hard for them to accept the isolation and sparseness, which no one wanted to call poverty, of our new reality. During those first weeks we felt the damp like a persistent plague. Storms rose up with furious winds lashing at the tin roof. The constant drizzle was infinitely patient. If it wasn't raining, we were shrouded in fog, never fully dry because in the few moments that the sun made its way from behind the clouds it barely warmed us. These conditions caused my mother's bronchitis to worsen.

"My tuberculosis is returning. This climate is going to kill me; I won't make it to spring," she gasped, huddled under blankets and nourished on a diet of soup.

But according to my aunts, the country air improved my character and ironed out my rebelliousness. At Santa Clara I was always busy, the days flew by. I had a thousand chores to do and I loved them all. I was captivated by Uncle Bruno, as I called him from the start, and I am certain that the affection was mutual. To him I was the reincarnation of his daughter who had died at birth, and to me he was a substitute for the father I had lost. In my presence he transformed back into the happy and playful man some still remembered from his youth. "Don't get too attached to that little girl, Señor Bruno; one of these days they'll go back to the city and leave me to take care of you and your broken heart," Facunda warned him.

At his side I learned to fish and trap rabbits, milk cows, saddle a horse, smoke cheeses, meats, fish, and hams in the circular mud hut where a pile of embers perpetually glowed. Facunda took me under her wing because Bruno asked her to. Up to that point she'd never allowed anyone to set foot in the kingdom that was her kitchen, but she ended up teaching me to knead dough, to hunt for the eggs that the hens would lay wherever they pleased, to cook stews in winter. She even shared her recipe for the celebrated apple strudel that German immigrants had introduced to the regional cuisine.

SPRING FINALLY ARRIVED, BRIGHTENING the landscape and the mood of the exiles, as we referred to ourselves when the Rivases were out of earshot. It wouldn't do to offend their hospitality. The ground burst with wildflowers, the trees with fruit and chattering birds; the sun finally permitted us to shrug off our ponchos and slip off our boots, the mud puddles on the roads dried up, and we harvested the first vegetables of the season and honey from the bees.

That's when José Antonio and Josephine Taylor knew it was time for each of them to go, as had been the plan from the start. They'd wanted to get the family set up at the Rivas farm before they went their own ways, as neither of them could make a living in the country.

Miss Taylor decided to return to the capital, where she would be able to find work teaching English.

"You don't need me anymore, Violeta, now that you will be living with two wonderful teachers," she told me.

She refrained from mentioning that we couldn't afford to pay her and in fact she hadn't received a salary since my father went broke. Her true motivation, however, was to be with Teresa. Every minute away from her was a lifetime lost, but we didn't know that at the time.

For his part, José Antonio had to earn enough to support the women of the family, who couldn't depend on the Rivases' charity forever. Although our food and lodgings were free, there were always expenses, be it shoes for me or our mother's medicines. My brother had worked alongside Bruno doing chores on the farm in the winter, helping out wherever he could, but he wasn't made to push a plow or split firewood. He was tempted to follow Josephine to the capital, thinking that maybe with persistence he could win her love, and he'd always planned to return eventually, once the shadow of Arsenio Del Valle had faded.

"You don't have to pay for your father's sins, José Antonio," said Miss Taylor. "If I were you, I'd march straight into the Union Club, order a double whiskey, and look those nosy gossips straight in the face." But she didn't understand the rules of our social class.

José Antonio had to wait; only time could erase scandal.

In the meantime, over those rainy months, my brother had formulated a plan. If it worked out, he could settle in Sacramento, the capital of the province, only two hours away by train.

He began to search for Marko Kusanovic, the foreman of my father's sawmill in the south. My father had offered the mill as collateral for one of his loans, and when he couldn't pay it back the bank had confiscated the mill, firing all the workers and stopping the production of logs while they looked for a buyer; the machinery had sat collecting rust for over a year. Marko had disappeared after the bank closed the sawmill, but from what José Antonio had been able to find out, the majority of the Croatian community had been scattered across the country's southernmost province. Many of the central European immigrants knew each other, married amongst themselves, and welcomed new arrivals with open arms. José Antonio supposed that Marko might have family or friends there.

The radio operator in Nahuel put José Antonio in contact with the Austria-Hungarian Club, where the members of the Croatian community were registered, and nine days later José Antonio was able to speak with Kusanovic. They barely knew each other, but that first conversation, frequently interrupted by the squeals and static of a poor connection, laid the foundation for what would be a long friendship.

"Come to Sacramento, Marko, the future is here," my brother told the Croatian man. And he agreed.

6

......

AFTER MY FAMILY HAD SPENT A FEW YEARS on the farm, as Lucinda and Abel were preparing for another teaching tour of the small towns and homesteads of the region, they declared that it was time for me to put my knowledge to the service of others. They taught me to ride a horse, overcoming my terror of those large beasts with steaming nostrils, and they recruited me as an assistant in their itinerant school. "We'll be back at the end of summer," they announced to my mother.

Torito wanted to join the expedition in order to protect me, so that no Indians tried to capture me, as he said. They explained that if it was the natives he was worried about, everyone around those parts had indigenous blood in them, with the exception of the foreign immigrants. All the pure-blooded Indians had been pushed out through the efficient system of buying their land at ridiculously low prices or getting them drunk and making them sign documents they couldn't read. If that failed, violence would be employed. Since independence, the government had set out to conquer, integrate, force the "barbarians" to submit, and convert them into civilized people, Catholic if possible, through military occupation and repression. The murder of Indians had been going on since the sixteenth century, first by the Spanish colonizers and then by anyone else, with impunity. The native peoples had good reason to hate foreigners in general, and the government in particular, but the Rivases assured Torito that they didn't go around kidnapping little girls.

"Anyway, you have to stay here to help Bruno and look after the women. Violeta will be safe with us."

I SPENT THE SUMMER of my thirteenth year giving classes in the one-horse towns and abandoned outposts of the Rivases' school route. The first days were hard because my rear end hurt and I missed my mother, Miss Taylor, and my aunts, but as soon as I got used to horseback riding I found a taste for adventure. With the Rivases, complaining was futile; they offered me no consolation or sympathy, and that's how they stamped out the final traces of my childhood tantrums and invented illnesses.

The mobile school moved unhurriedly, at the pace of the mule who carried the educational material, blankets for sleeping, and our scant personal items. Our schedule almost always permitted us to arrive at an inhabited place before nightfall, but we sometimes slept in the open air. I invoked Father Juan Quiroga to keep us safe from vermin and beasts of prey, even though the Rivases assured me that the snakes were not poisonous and the only dangerous feline was the puma, who wouldn't come near if there was a campfire.

Abel had bad lungs; he coughed constantly and sometimes had difficulty breathing, like a dying man. But teaching was second nature to him; on nights when we camped under the stars he taught me the names of the constellations, and by day he pointed out local flora and fauna. Lucinda knew endless tales from folklore and mythology, which I never tired of hearing. "Tell me again about the two snakes that created the world," I would say.

A good part of our journey was made on narrow footpaths and there were stretches where the previous winter had erased all traces of a trail, but Mr. and Mrs. Rivas never got lost, charging into forests without hesitation and safely fording rivers. Only once did my horse slip on the rocks and throw me into the water, but Abel was right there, ready to pull me to shore. He gave me my first swimming lesson later that very day.

The students were spread out across a vast territory, which over time I came to know as well as the Rivases, just as I learned to identify every student by name. I saw them grow year after year, as they moved directly into adulthood without passing through awkward adolescence; daily demands left them no time for idle imagination. They were mired in a poverty more dignified than that in the city, but it was a profound destitution nonetheless. The girls became mothers before their bodies had even finished maturing, and the boys worked the land like their fathers and grandfathers, unless they were drafted into military service, which would allow them to escape for a couple of years.

I quickly lost the innocence that my family had so carefully guarded throughout my childhood. Mr. and Mrs. Rivas did not attempt to shield me from the realities of alcoholism, abused women and children, knife fights, rape, and incest. Life here was very different from the bucolic ideal of a rural existence we'd imagined when we first arrived. I realized also that in Nahuel, that town of hospitable neighbors, you only had to scratch the surface to uncover the ugliest of vices, though my mentors insisted that cruelty wasn't inherent to the human condition, merely something born of ignorance and poverty. "It's much easier to be generous with a full belly than an empty one," they said. I've never believed that, though, because I've seen that both kindness and cruelty exist everywhere.

In some settlements we managed to round up a dozen students of various ages, but more often we'd stop at isolated homesteads, where there were only three or four barefoot children to teach. In those situations we'd try to help the adults become literate as well, since quite often they hadn't received any education, but the efforts were generally fruitless; if they had lived up to that point without ever learning the alphabet, it's because they didn't need to know it. Torito gave us the same argument when we tried to convince him of the benefits of reading and writing.

THE NATIVE PEOPLES, POOR and discriminated against by the rest of the population, lived scattered across small landholdings, in huts with only a few farm animals, crops of potatoes, corn, and other vegetables. It seemed to me a miserable existence, until Lucinda and Abel helped me see that it was simply a different way of life; they had their own language, religion, their own economy, they had no need for the material items we placed so much value on. They were the original peoples of this land; all outsiders, with few exceptions, were usurpers, thieves, men without honor. In Nahuel and other towns they were more or less integrated into the broader population—they lived in wooden houses, spoke Spanish, and took whatever work they could get—but the majority of them lived in small rural communities. They always welcomed us, despite their ingrained distrust of outsiders, because they considered teaching to be a noble profession. Mr.

and Mrs. Rivas, however, didn't go to teach, but to learn.

The chief, an old man with a compact, square frame and a face like stone, received us in the community dwelling, a rustic windowless structure made of sticks with straw walls and roof. He wore adornments and ceremonial necklaces, and he was flanked by strong young men with menacing expressions and a band of kids and dogs circling his feet. Lucinda and I stayed outside with the rest of the women until they allowed us to enter, while Abel paid our respects with offerings of tobacco and alcohol.

After a few hours drinking in silence, because they did not share a common language, the chief gave a signal to invite the women in. Then Lucinda, who knew a little of the indigenous language, served as interpreter, aided by one of the young men who had learned Spanish during military service. They talked about horses, harvests, the soldiers stationed nearby, the government that in the past had taken the sons of chiefs as hostages and now wanted the native children to forget their language, their customs, their ancestors, and their pride.

The official visit went on for many hours; there was no hurry since time was measured in rains, harvests, and misfortunes. I fended off boredom without complaint, dizzy from the smoke of the fire smoldering in that unventilated space and intimidated by the men's open examination of me. Finally, when I was about to fall down from fatigue, the visit was over.

LUCINDA TOOK ME TO the hut of the healer, Yaima, where she learned about plants, bark, and medicinal herbs. The woman shared her knowledge with the caveat that the plants would do little good without the corresponding magic. To illustrate this, she recited enchantments and beat rhythmically on a leather drum painted with pictures of the seasons, the cardinal points, the sky, the earth, and the underworld. "But the drum belongs to the people," she clarified, by which she meant her people alone; outsiders were forbidden from touching it because they were not people. Lucinda wrote down the indigenous names for all the plants and sketched images to help identify them. She would share her notes with Aunt Pía, who was expanding her repertoire of herbal remedies but who used the healing energy of her hands in place of a magic drum. During the lessons, I fell asleep on the packed earth floor, curled up beside two or three flea-ridden dogs.

Yaima looked to be no more than fifty, but claimed to remember the Spanish being sent home with their tails between their legs and the republic being born. "There was nothing good before, and after it only got worse," she concluded. If this was true, she would've been 110 years old, Lucinda calculated, but there was nothing to be gained from contradicting her. Lucinda said that each person was free to narrate their life the way they saw fit. Yaima wore the traditional dress of her people, which had at one time been entirely handmade on looms. Over her long, wide dress of flowered cloth, she wore a black shawl held closed with a large pin, a handkerchief over her hair, and silver adornments on her forehead.

When I turned fourteen, the chief asked Abel Rivas for my hand in marriage, for himself or one of his sons. He offered Abel his best horse as payment for the bride. Abel, translated with difficulty by Lucinda, delicately declined the offer with the argument that I had a very bad temperament and also that I was already one of his wives. The chief offered to exchange me for another woman. From then on I stopped accompanying them on that part of the tour, in order to avoid a premature marriage.

MY WORK IN THE nomadic school proved what Miss Taylor had always maintained: Teaching is learning. In my free time I had to prepare my classes under the direction of Lucinda and Abel, deciphering the mysteries of mathematics and memorizing history and national geography. I'd had six years of education with Miss Taylor and could recite the names of every king and queen of the British Empire in chronological order, but I knew very little of my own country.

During one of José Antonio's regular visits, they discussed the possibility of sending me to boarding school three hours away by train: the Royal British College, which had been founded by a pair of English missionaries. The pompous name was too grand for the puny establishment, composed of a single house with room for twelve students and a pair of missionaries as the only teachers, but it had the reputation of being the best school in the province. I practically threw one of my old tantrums. I announced that if they sent me away to school, I'd escape and they'd never see me again.

"I learn more here than at any dumb school," I swore with such conviction that they believed me. Time proved me right.

My life was divided into two seasons, one of rain and the other of sunshine. Winter was long, dark, and damp, with short days and freezing nights, but I was never bored. In addition to milking the cows, cooking with Facunda, tending the hens, pigs, and goats, and washing and ironing, I also had a full social life. Aunts Pía and Pilar had become the heart and soul of Nahuel and the surrounding area. They organized gatherings where everyone played cards, knitted, embroidered, used the sewing machine, listened to music on the hand-crank Victrola, or prayed novenas for sick animals, stricken people, harvests, and fair weather. The unconfessed intention of the novenas was to steal parishioners away from the evangelical pastors, who were gradually gaining ground in the area.

My aunts doled out generous servings of plum or cherry liquor, which they made themselves to lift the spirits, and they were always willing to listen to the complaints and confessions of the other women, who came by in their free time or when they wanted a break from the tedium of everyday life. Aunt Pía's healing hands were known for miles around, although she was discreet to avoid a rivalry with Yaima. The two healers were more sought after than any doctors.

The hours of daylight flew by as I helped Uncle Bruno with the animals or in the pastures when it wasn't raining too hard. In the evenings I would weave on the loom or knit, study, read, help Aunt Pía prepare home remedies, give classes to local kids, or learn Morse code from the radio operator.

MISS TAYLOR AND TERESA Rivas came to stay for a few weeks in the dead of winter, and their joyful presence brightened our bad moods. They were the only two people crazy enough to take vacations to the worst climate in the world, they said. They brought with them news from the capital, magazines and books, school material for Mr. and Mrs. Rivas, yards of cloth for sewing, tools for Aunt Pilar, small items that the neighbors requested, and new records for the Victrola. They taught us the latest dances, to choruses of laughter. Even Uncle Bruno participated in the sing-alongs, enchanted by his niece and the Irish woman. Aunt Pilar had transformed during her time in the country, polishing her knowledge of mechanics, swapping her skirts for pants and boots, and she competed with me for Uncle Bruno's attention; she was in love with him, according to Miss Taylor. They were about the same age and shared a long list of common interests, so it wasn't such a far-fetched notion.

Miss Taylor and Teresa Rivas had the splendid idea that we should celebrate Torito, who'd never had a birthday party and didn't even know what year he'd been born. By the time he came to us and my parents got around to registering him he'd already passed puberty, so his birth certificate showed at least twelve or thirteen years less than his true age. They decided that, since his last name was Toro and he had a stubbornly loyal nature, his zodiac sign must be Taurus, and therefore he must've been born in April or May, but we would celebrate his birthday whenever we were all together.

Uncle Bruno bought a half rack of lamb at the market so that we didn't have to kill the only sheep on the farm, which happened to be Torito's pet, and Facunda made a sponge cake with dulce de leche. Uncle Bruno helped me make a gift for Torito: a little cross that I carved from wood, with his name engraved on one side and mine on the other, tied on a string made from pig leather.

If it had been made of solid gold, Torito couldn't have cherished it more. He hung it around his neck and never took it off. I'm telling you this, Camilo, because that cross would play an important role many years later.

IF THEY LET JOSÉ Antonio know in advance that they planned to visit, he would try to be there when Miss Taylor and Teresa came, always taking the opportunity to once again ask the Irish woman for her hand, out of habit. He worked with Marko Kusanovic within a relatively short distance as the crow flies, but at first, before he'd set up his office in the city, he had to come off the mountain on treacherous paths to catch the train. Uncle Bruno and I would meet him at the station and bring him up to speed on the family, out of earshot of my mother and aunts. We were increasingly concerned for my mother, who waited out the overwhelmingly damp winters in bed, with blankets pulled up to her chin, warm linseed poultices on her chest, and engrossed in a continuous torrent of prayers.

In the third year at Santa Clara, the family decided that she wouldn't last another winter; we had to send her to the sanitorium in the mountains. José Antonio now earned enough to afford it. From then on, Lucinda and Aunt Pía accompanied her first by train and then bus to the sanitorium, where she'd spend four months healing her lungs and her spirit. They would go back to get her in spring, and she'd return to us with enough strength to survive a little longer. Because of those prolonged absences, and because she'd been practically incapable of a normal existence for most of my life, the memories I have of my mother are less vivid than those of other people I grew up with, such as my aunts, Torito, Miss Taylor, and the Rivas family. Her eternal illness is the reason for my good health; in order to avoid following in her footsteps, I've lived my life proudly ignoring any and all ailments. That's how I learned that, in general, things clear up on their own.

Spring and summer left no time for rest on the Rivas farm. For the majority of the warmer months I was on tour with Abel and Lucinda's mobile school, but I also spent time helping out at Santa Clara. We harvested vegetables, beans, and fruit; jarred preserves; made jams, jellies, and cheese from cow, goat, and sheep's milk; and smoked meat and fish. It was also the season in which the farm animals had their babies, a brief and joyful moment when I could bottle-feed and name them, inevitably becoming attached before they were sold off or slaughtered and I had to forget about them.

When the time came to slaughter a pig, Uncle Bruno and Torito made sure to do it inside one of the sheds, but no matter how far away I tried to hide, I could always hear the animal's bloodcurdling squeal. Afterwards, Facunda and Aunt Pilar, up to their elbows in blood, would make sausage, chorizo, ham, and salami, which I'd devour without a hint of guilt. Several times throughout the course of my life I've vowed to become a vegetarian, Camilo, but my willpower always fails me.

THAT'S HOW I SPENT my adolescence, our period of Exile, which I remember as the most diaphanous time of my life. They were calm and abundant years, dedicated to the everyday chores of farm life and a devotion to teaching alongside Mr. and Mrs. Rivas. I read a lot, because Miss Taylor always sent books from the capital, which we would discuss by letter and in person when she came to visit the farm. Lucinda and Abel also shared ideas and readings that expanded my horizons. It was clear to me from a young age that although I respected them, my mother and my aunts were stuck in the past, uninterested in the outside world or anything that might challenge their beliefs.

Our house was small and we lived in very close quarters; I was never alone, but when I turned sixteen I was given a cabin a few yards away from the main house, which Torito, Aunt Pilar, and Uncle Bruno had built in the blink of an eye as a gift for me. I named it the Birdcage, because it looked like an aviary with its hexagonal shape and skylight in the ceiling. There I had my own space with a little privacy and enough peace and quiet to study, read, prepare classes, and dream, away from the incessant chatter of the family. I continued to sleep in my mother and aunts' house, on a mattress I unrolled every night beside the stove and put away every morning; the last thing I wanted was to face the terrors of the darkness alone in the Birdcage.

Uncle Bruno and I celebrated the miracle of life with every chick that hatched from its egg and every tomato that came from the garden to the table; he taught me to observe and listen attentively, to get my bearings in the woods, to swim in freezing lakes and rivers, to start a fire without a match, to enjoy the pleasure of sinking my face into a juicy watermelon, and to accept the inevitable pain of saying goodbye to people and animals, because there is no life without death, as he always said.

Since I didn't have a group of friends my age and my only company was the adults and children around me, I didn't have anyone to compare myself to, and so I didn't experience adolescence as a terrible upheaval; I simply moved from one phase to the next without noticing. I similarly avoided romantic fantasies—so normal at that age—because there were no boys around to inspire them. Apart from that Indian chief who'd tried to trade a horse for me, no one considered me a woman, I was just a girl, Bruno Rivas's adopted niece.

I changed a lot. When I look at the only two

surviving pictures from that period, I see that at age eighteen I was a lovely young woman; denying it would be false modesty. But I didn't know it at the time, because within my family and among the people of the region, looks didn't count for much. No one ever told me I was pretty and the only mirror in the house was barely large enough for me to style my hair. I had dark olive-shaped eyes that contrasted with my pale skin, an untamable mop of dark shiny hair, which I wore in a braid down my back and washed once a week with the soapy foam of local tree bark. My hands, with long fingers and thin wrists, roughened by farmwork and bleach, were more like the hands of a washerwoman, according to Miss Taylor, who had direct knowledge from her experience in the Irish orphanage. I dressed in clothes that had been made for me by my aunts, who thought only of practical utility and never considered fashion: overalls or jumpsuits of rough cloth and clogs made of wood and pig leather for daily use; for going out, a simple percale dress with a lace collar and mother-of-pearl buttons.

UP TO NOW I'VE told you little of Apolonio Toro, unforgettable Torito, who deserves to be paid greater homage since he lived with me for many years of my life and remained with me even after his death. I suppose he'd been born with some genetic anomalies because he looked nothing like anyone we'd ever met. For starters, he was a giant in our country, where people used to be mostly short; not like now, with the younger generations a full head taller than their grandparents. Because he was so large, he moved as slowly as a pachyderm, adding to the appearance of menacing brute that contrasted so sharply with his docile nature. He would've been able to strangle a puma with his bare hands, but if anyone taunted him, as sometimes happened, he didn't even defend himself, as if he were all too aware of his strength and refused to wield it against others. He had a narrow forehead, small, sunken eyes, a prominent jaw, and a mouth that always hung open.

Once, in the market, a group of boys surrounded him, shouting insults of "Retard!" and "Moron!" and throwing rocks at him. Torito bore the abuse without getting agitated or trying to protect himself, even when he received a cut on his forehead and blood began to run down his face. A small circle of curious onlookers had formed by the time Uncle Bruno showed up, attracted by the commotion, and furiously dispersed the boys. "That gorilla attacked us!" "Lock him up!" they shrieked, but they backed off, continuing to jeer as they ran away.

I can still picture him, sitting on a bench, since chairs were always too small for him, a safe distance from the stove, because he tended to overheat, whittling a little animal out of wood for the kids who flocked to the house for Facunda's cookies. The same kids, who were at first terrified of Torito, soon followed him everywhere he went. The women slept in the house, but he preferred the open air and when it rained he put down a blanket to sleep in the shed. We liked to joke that he slept with one eye open, always vigilant. I can't count the number of times I curled up in his arms after waking from a nightmare. Torito would hear me screaming and get there before anyone else to rock me like a baby, cooing, "Sleep, my little girl, go to sleep, the bogeyman is gone and won't come back."

In the country, Torito found his place in the world. I think he understood the language of animals and plants; he could calm a wild horse by talking softly to it, and encourage crops to grow by playing a song on his harmonica. He could predict the weather well before Uncle Bruno saw any of the telltale signs. The clumsy oaf he'd been in the city was transformed out in nature into a delicate being, sensitive to everything happening around him as well as the moods and emotions of others.

Every once in a while, Torito disappeared. We knew that he was going because he would change the soles of his boots, pack his hatchet, knife, fishing pole, trapping material, and provisions from Facunda, who treated him with the same bossiness and gruff affection that she otherwise reserved for Uncle Bruno. He'd wrap everything in a blanket and sling it diagonally across his back, tying it to his chest with rope. He'd say goodbye without many words and then set out on foot. He refused to ride on horseback, saying he was too heavy a load for a horse or mule. He'd wander for weeks at a time and return thin, bearded, browned by the sun, and happy. We'd ask him what he'd been doing, and his answer was always the same: getting acquainted. This expression of his extended to the cold impenetrable rain forest, the volcanoes, cliffs, and stony footpaths of the country's mountainous border, the raging rivers and frothy white waterfalls, the lagoons hidden behind rocky outcroppings. And it also included the locals, who knew the land like the palms of their hands, shepherds and hunters and the indigenous people, who respected him and gave him the nickname Fuchan because of his size. For them, Torito wasn't the village idiot, but the wise giant.

ONE SATURDAY IN LATE autumn, one of the workers on a nearby ranch, who'd seen me at a rodeo, came to the Rivas farm with the excuse of wanting to buy some pigs; I never imagined he was really there for me. I remember that he was unshaven, with an authoritative voice and arrogant posture as he talked down to us from his saddle. The piglets were very small, it wasn't yet time to sell them, and Uncle Bruno told him to come back in a few months, but when the man lingered Bruno invited him inside for a drink. I served them apple chicha and made a gesture to excuse myself, but the man stopped me with the click of his tongue, like he was calling a dog.

"Where are you going, pretty girl?" he said.

Uncle Bruno stood up, more shocked than angry, because we were unaccustomed to such impertinence. He sent me to see my mother while he got rid of the stranger.

That afternoon I had my weekly bath. In the shed, Facunda and Torito lit the fire to heat the water inside the huge tub, which was later emptied into a wooden trough. Torito left and closed the linen curtain that served as a door, then Facunda helped me wash my hair and scrub my body until my skin was red and shiny new. It was a long and sensual ritual, the hot water and the cold evening air, the foam from the tree bark in my hair, the rough sponge on my skin, the clean scent of mint and basil leaves that Facunda sprinkled into the tub. Afterwards I dried off with rags—we didn't have towels—and Facunda detangled my dense hair. I aided in the bathing process with her, Lucinda, and my aunts, but my mother took only sponge baths, to avoid catching cold. The men bathed using buckets of water, or in the river.

It was getting dark when I bid Facunda good night and walked toward our house, wearing my nightdress and a thick vest, to have the cup of broth and bread with cheese that generally made up our dinner. Suddenly I again heard the clicking sound that the strange man had made hours earlier, and before I had time to react he appeared before me.

"Where are you going, pretty girl?" he snarled.

I could smell the drink on him from several steps away. I don't know what idea he had of me; maybe he thought I was one of the servants, someone insignificant who could be taken advantage of. I tried to run, but he cut me off and grabbed me by the neck with one hand, covering my mouth with the other.

"If you scream I'll kill you. I have a knife," he muttered, biting off his words, and he kneed me in the belly, causing me to double over.

He dragged me to my Birdcage, kicked the door open, and I found myself in the pitch-darkness of the cabin. The Birdcage was close to the house, and if I could've screamed someone would've heard me, but my mind was clouded with fear. He threw me down without easing his grip, and I felt my head smash against the floorboards. With his free hand he tried to lift my nightdress and pull down my underwear, as I kicked weakly, flattened under his weight. His calloused hand blocked my mouth and nose; I couldn't breathe, I was suffocating. I scratched at his arm trying to free myself; getting air was much more urgent than defending myself.

I DON'T REMEMBER WHAT happened after that, I might have lost consciousness from lack of oxygen or simply blacked out from the trauma of that violent act. Torito, noticing I was taking too long to come home, had gone out looking for me, and he must've heard something because he came into the Birdcage and managed to grab the man in his huge hands and pull him off before he could rape me. This was explained to me later by my aunts, and they added that Torito had escorted the terrified man out of Santa Clara and given him a swift kick in the rear end, sending him into the middle of the road like a sack of potatoes.

The police showed up two days later to interrogate everyone in the area. Some fishermen had found the dead body of a man named Pascual Freire, who managed the Moreau family farm, among the reeds of the riverbank, about a mile and a half away. It had been easy to identify him because he was well known in the area as a notorious drunk and a troublemaker who'd had more than one run-in with the law. The logical explanation was that Freire had gotten drunk and drowned, but he had lacerations around his neck. The police didn't get any good information as they half-heartedly asked their questions and soon left.

Who accused Torito? I'll never know, just as I'll never know if he was responsible for the man's death. He was arrested that weekend and held in Nahuel, awaiting the order for transfer to Sacramento. We immediately called José Antonio, who took the first train down the next morning. In the meantime, all three members of the Rivas family went to testify that Apolonio Toro was a peaceful person, who had never shown any signs of violence, as many others could attest, including the local children who adored him. They managed to keep him from being moved to Sacramento that day, buying my brother some time.

José Antonio had worked very little as a lawyer, but the humble local police, who could barely read, didn't know that. He showed up at the precinct, which was just a shack with a cage for prisoners, wearing a hat and tie, carrying a black briefcase, empty but impressive, and took the irate tone of an offended king. He made their heads swim with legal jargon, and once they were sufficiently intimidated, he handed them several bills for their trouble. They released the detainee with the warning that they'd keep an eye on him. Torito rode home in Uncle Bruno's truck and had to be helped into the house because he'd been so badly beaten.

No one in my family or on the Rivas farm asked Torito any questions about what, if anything, he'd done to my attacker. Facunda fortified him with the best of her baked goods, while Aunt Pía consulted with her rival, Yaima, to help heal his wounds. Torito's kidneys had been damaged, causing blood in his urine, and so many of his ribs were broken that he could hardly breathe. I didn't leave his side, overcome with guilt, since he'd risked his freedom and possibly even his life to save me. But when I tried to thank him he just repeated the same words he'd said to the police when they'd interrogated him about Pascual Freire: "I didn't know that dead man."

According to José Antonio, that could be interpreted a number of ways.

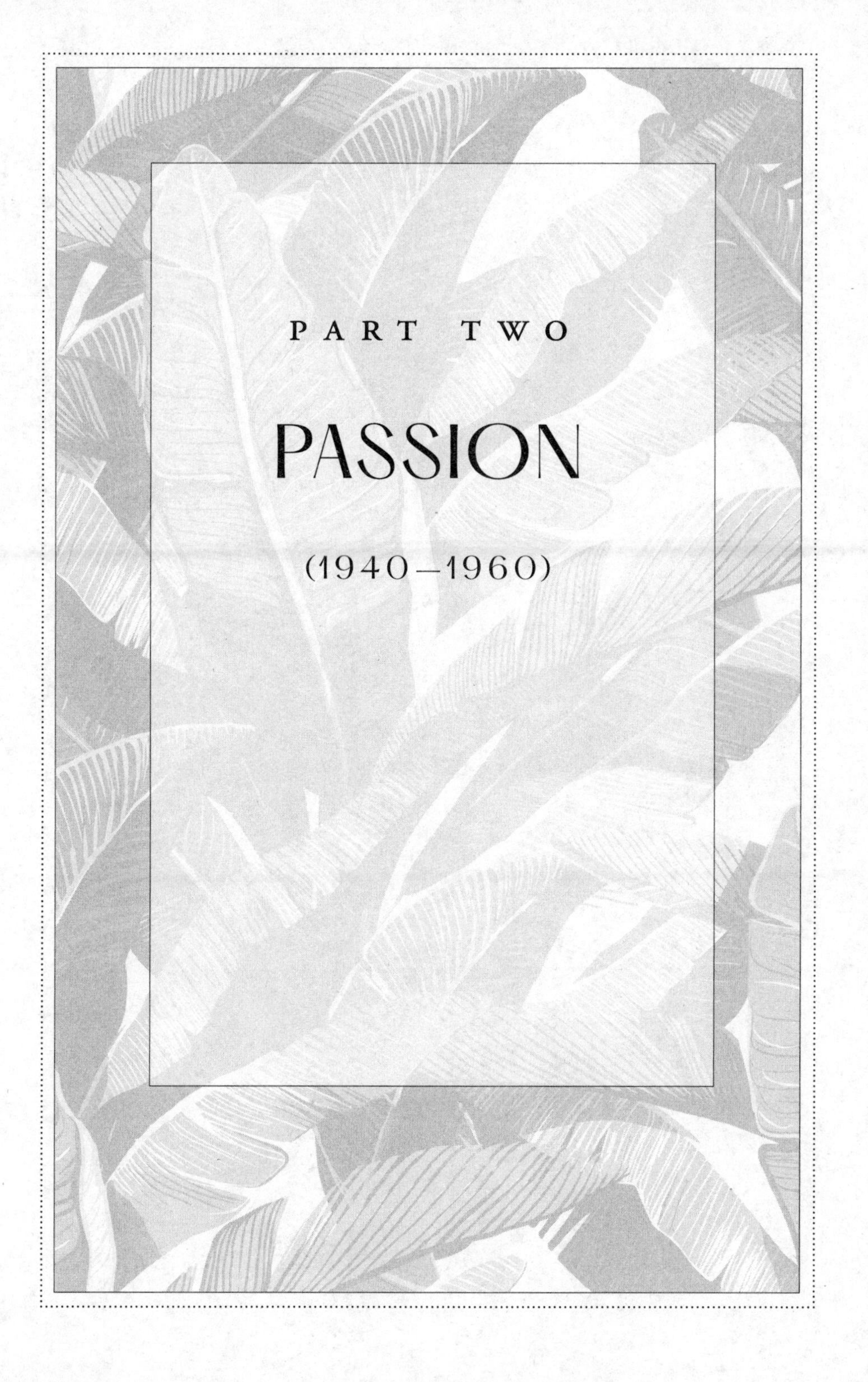

PART TWO

PASSION

(1940–1960)

7

THE FOLLOWING SUMMER, WITH THE GHOST of Pascual Freire still haunting our conversations, I met Fabian Schmidt-Engler. He was the youngest son in a large family of German immigrants who had arrived with nothing, but after a couple of decades of hard work and vision for the future, plus land and loans from the government, had become prosperous citizens. Fabian's father owned the most successful dairy farm in the area, and his mother and sisters ran a charming hotel on the lake a few miles outside of Nahuel, popular with tourists who came from around the world to fish.

At twenty-three, Fabian had already completed his coursework to become a veterinarian and was offering his services to local farmers to gain the practice he needed to receive his degree. He showed up at the Rivas farm on his horse, leather bags hanging from the saddle, thirty pockets in his pants and shirt like some explorer, slicked-back hair, looking for all the world like a lost foreigner—a look he would have for the rest of his life. He'd been born in this country but was so dull and formal, so stubborn and punctual, that he gave the impression of someone recently arrived from far away.

I was on my way out wearing my Sunday clothes, since I was going in Uncle Bruno's truck to the Nahuel station. My brother was arriving that day from Sacramento, where he now shared an office with Marko Kusanovic. Because I was preparing to move to the city in the fall, it was the first summer that I hadn't joined Abel and Lucinda to give classes. When I saw that young man dressed like a geographer, I mistook him for one of the tourists who had turned up a few days prior to watch birds, something new to us. No one could understand the attraction of spending hours staring up at the sky with binoculars waiting to see a turkey vulture and writing about it in a notebook. They were surely only pretending, while secretly scouting out a spot to set up one of those businesses that only the gringos can think up, the neighbors said.

"There aren't any strange birds around here," I said by way of greeting.

"Do you have . . . cows?" the young man stuttered.

"Two, Clotilde and Leonor, but they're not for sale."

"I'm a veterinarian. Fabian Schmidt-Engler . . ." he said, jumping out of his saddle right into a pile of fresh manure.

"No one here is sick."

"Well, they might be," he suggested, his ears turning pink.

"Uncle Bruno and Aunt Pía see to our animals, and if it's really serious we call Yaima."

"Well, if you ever need me, you can find me at the Hotel Bavaria."

"Oh! You're one of **those** Schmidts, from the hotel."

"Yes. There's a telephone there."

"We don't have one here but there's one in Nahuel."

"It's free . . . I mean, I treat animals for free . . ."

"Why?"

"I'm practicing."

"I doubt Uncle Bruno would let you practice on Clotilde or Leonor."

That didn't stop Fabian; he returned the next day at teatime, with a peach kuchen from the hotel. He'd spent all night tormented by the insomnia of sudden love, as I later found out; overcoming his innate caution, he stole the kuchen from his mother's oven and rode forty minutes in hopes of seeing me again. The entirety of the small Del Valle clan received him, along with Uncle Bruno and Torito; they feared that he intended to seduce me. Facunda grudgingly served him tea.

"You don't need to bring food here, young man, we have more than enough," she spat when she saw the kuchen.

FABIAN POSSESSED THE DISCIPLINE and tenacity that had helped his family earn their fortune. He set out to win me over, and would not be dissuaded. Uncle Bruno's open distrust and Facunda's grumbling did not scare him away, and he did not back down in the face of my indifference either. I had no notion of his romantic illusions until much later, treating him like a distant and uninteresting acquaintance. He visited us every day for two solid months that summer, humble as a beggar, stoically withstanding countless cups of tea, praising Facunda's tarts and cakes—he did not make the mistake of showing up with another kuchen—and entertaining my mother and aunts with endless games of cards, as I scurried away to my Birdcage to read in peace. He was so bland and boring that he inspired instant trust.

Once he got comfortable around us, Fabian overcame his irritating stutter, but he was not a talkative guy; unlike all the other men I've known in my life, he preferred not to offer his opinion if he wasn't an expert in the matter. His prudence, which could be interpreted as ignorance, did not keep him from having surprising successes in his profession, which I'll get to later, if I remember. Uncle Bruno, who had gruffly dispensed with other young men, got used to seeing Fabian come and go. When Bruno allowed him to attend the birth of Clotilde's calf, we knew that the young man had been fully accepted.

His presence alleviated the family's tedious cycling through the same old topics of conversation. As was only natural, given that we were so isolated, we always talked about the same things: the fields, the neighbors, food, illnesses, and cures. Only when Miss Taylor and Teresa came to visit did we have lively parties. The news we heard on the radio seemed to come from another planet; it had nothing to do with us. Fabian contributed very little, but he was such a good listener that the family divulged information to him, recounting stories from our past that I'd never heard before. My aunts told him, for example, about the earthquake that occurred the year José Antonio was born, the pandemic that broke out the year of my arrival in the world, and additional catastrophes that aligned with each of my other brothers' births. I don't believe they were signs of our destinies, as my aunts thought, but simply that in this country there are always calamities, and it's not hard to connect them to some life event, be it a birth or a death. I also learned that Grandmother Nívea, my father's mother, had been decapitated in a terrifying automobile accident and her head was lost in a field; there was an aunt who communed with spirits and a family dog that grew and grew until it was the size of a camel.

It turns out that my father's side of the family was much more interesting than I'd ever known; I regretted having lost contact with them. These are your ancestors, Camilo; it would behoove you to learn more about them, especially since certain characteristics tend to be hereditary. Of course, they never mentioned my father, nor our reasons for Exile. The young man was too polite to ever ask.

FABIAN WAS INCAPABLE OF hiding the turmoil of his feelings; it was plain to everyone, except me. Witnessing this, his older sisters looked into the reputation of the Rivases, modest people but well respected in the area, and the Del Valles, aristocrats from the capital, but surely an impoverished branch of the family since there was no other explanation for why we would be living like freeloaders on the Rivas farm. If they'd heard about the scandalous ruin of Arsenio Del Valle, they never mentioned it. I suppose they discussed the situation within their clan and concluded that they had no choice but to get a look at the girl Fabian had chosen. Shortly before I moved to Sacramento, my mother, aunts, and I received an invitation to have lunch at the Hotel Bavaria. Bruno dropped us off in the truck, which had replaced the old mule cart.

We were received by the entire female squadron of the Schmidt-Englers in formation: mother, sisters, and sisters-in-law, plus a horde of children of all ages, just as blond and clean-cut as Fabian—pure Aryans. The hotel was at the time, and still is, a simple Scandinavian-style building made from sequoia, with huge windows. It sits on a hill rising up from the lake with a spectacular view of the snowcapped volcano, which at that time of day shone like a lighthouse in the clear sky. The terraced garden, which descended to the thin strip of beach on the lakeshore, was an orgy of flowers crisscrossed by narrow footpaths for guests to stroll.

They had placed a table on one of the garden terraces, far from the hubbub of the dining room, laid with white linen and fresh-cut roses in glass jars between platters of salad and cold cuts. Afterwards, my aunts said they hadn't enjoyed such refinement since their days at Camellia House, before my father set out on his tragic road to ruin.

I think I made a good impression on those women, with my long braid, modest dress, and appearance of a well-mannered young lady, despite the fact that I was not Aryan and my poverty was impossible to hide. If I married Fabian, I would not be able to offer anything on the economic front and would stick out like a sore thumb among them. They politely kept all this to themselves. It was inevitable that they'd begin to mix with the people of their adopted country sooner or later, but it was a shame it had to happen to their baby brother. In those days, Camilo, the foreign colonizers still lived in closed communities. There were half a dozen lovely, eligible young German girls, of good social standing, who would've been a much better fit for Fabian. Also, he was too young to marry, he had not yet finished his degree or begun earning a living, which he'd have to do since he refused to work for his father.

WHEN HE SAW THAT I hadn't been outright rejected by his family, Fabian decided to act before they changed their minds and I moved to Sacramento. He cornered me the next day while my aunts were distracted, and he announced, quaveringly, that he needed to speak to me in private. I guided him to the Birdcage, my refuge, where no one except me ever set foot. On the door hung a hand-painted sign prohibiting entrance "to persons of both sexes." The afternoon light filled the space, which still smelled like fresh pine. The furnishings consisted of a tabletop on iron legs, bookshelves, a trunk, and a dilapidated divan, which I gestured for him to sit on, as I took the only chair.

"You know . . . what I'm . . . I'm . . . I'm . . . going to say, right?" Fabian stuttered pitifully, wringing one of the three handkerchiefs he always carried in his many pockets.

"No, how would I?"

"Marry me, please," he blurted, practically shouting.

"Get married? I'm not even twenty yet, Fabian. How could I get married!"

"It doesn't have to be . . . right now. We . . . we . . . we can wait . . . I'm going to graduate soon."

My aunts and Uncle Bruno had teased me about the veterinarian's daily visits, which should've been a clue, but nevertheless his marriage proposal took me by surprise. I'd become fond of him, despite the fact that his constant presence annoyed me. If he ever failed to show up at the usual hour, I would start to glance at the grandfather clock, feeling anxious.

The first thing I felt when he proposed was apprehension over how I'd fit in with the German community, where I'd feel like a plucked duck surrounded by swans. Marrying Fabian was a crazy idea, but as I saw him sitting there before me, frightened, treading water in the flood of his first love, I didn't have the heart to reject him outright.

"I'm sorry, but I can't give you an answer right now; I have to think about it. We can wait a while and, in the meantime, get to know each other better. What do you think?"

Fabian heaved a huge sigh, after holding his breath for over a minute, and dried his forehead with his handkerchief, his eyes watering with relief. Fearing he might start to cry on me, I took a few steps toward him and leaned over to kiss him on the cheek, but he pulled me firmly toward him and kissed me full on the mouth. I pulled back, startled by how incongruous this was with his measured and prudent nature, but he didn't let go. He continued kissing me until I finally relaxed in his arms and kissed him back, exploring this newfound intimacy.

It's hard to describe the contradictory emotions that flooded me in that moment, Camilo, because desire fades with time and that kind of lust seems absurd to me now, like some psychotic episode that happened to another person. I suppose I felt a sexual awakening, pleasure, excitement, curiosity, mixed with fear of giving too much of myself and not being able to pull back. But I'm no longer sure of anything related to sex. I've forgotten what it's even like.

I DIDN'T TELL ANYBODY what had happened, but everyone, even Torito, who was usually oblivious, guessed, because the air changed between Fabian and me. We'd find any excuse to disappear to the Birdcage, our anticipation impossible to hide. Our fondling escalated, as was to be expected, but Fabian had fixed notions about what was permitted before marriage and he never wavered, even in the face of his ardent desire and my easy compliance. Despite the danger of getting pregnant and my strict upbringing, I railed against Fabian's sanctimoniousness and would've preferred to get naked and make love to him, as opposed to those exhausting scuffles tangled in clothes. Let me be clear, Camilo, at that time girls of my social class were not supposed to go to bed with their boyfriends, or anyone, before marriage. I'm certain that many of them did, but not even under torture would they have admitted it. Birth control pills hadn't yet been invented.

Before I left, we explored each other in my cabin, in the stable, or hidden in the cornfield, sealing Fabian's determination to tie me down for good, as he would reiterate a thousand times in his letters. It also sparked in me a serene conviction that I would one day marry this man, because the most natural thing for a woman to do was become a wife and mother.

"Fabian is a good guy: decent, hardworking, honest, close with his family, as he should be, and a veterinarian is a respectable profession," said Aunt Pilar.

"That young man is one of those loyal people born to have only one great love," said Aunt Pía, an incurable romantic.

"He's a wet blanket, aunties. He's so predictable that we can already tell exactly what he'll be like in ten, twenty, or fifty years," I added.

"Better a boring husband than an unreliable one."

What did those two old maids know about love and marriage? I liked the sexual play with Fabian, even though it left me both aroused and enraged, but I felt little sentimental attachment to that tall, thin, stiff man with solemn manners and puritan ways. I knew he'd make an excellent husband, but I didn't feel any urgency to marry. I wanted a taste of freedom before settling in to a quiet life by his side, raising children in the immutable safety of his clan. I imagined that future like a peaceful meadow where nothing unexpected could happen—no troubles, chance encounters, or adventures—a clear path straight on until death.

8

.....

Marko Kusanovic had emigrated from Croatia in the late 1800s, at age fourteen, alone and penniless with nothing but a scrap of paper bearing the name of a relative who had gone to South America ten years prior. He'd never seen a map and had no notion of the distance he would have to travel; he wasn't even sure which direction he was going and he didn't speak a word of Spanish. He paid his way by working on a cargo ship whose captain, another Croatian, took pity on the boy and hired him as a cook's assistant. When he arrived he was unable to find his relative, because he'd gotten the country wrong. But he was strong for his age and able to earn a living as a stevedore at the port, as a miner, and doing other odd jobs until he landed the role of foreman at the sawmill owned by Arsenio Del Valle. He had a gift for leadership and he enjoyed the rustic lifestyle of the Andes. He worked at the mill for eleven years until it closed; then he prepared to start over. José Antonio's call was fortuitous.

When my brother entered into partnership with Kusanovic, they sealed the deal with a handshake, which had been good enough for both of them, but for legal reasons they had to register the company with a notary in Sacramento. When they signed the documents, José Antonio changed his last name to Delvalle, a symbolic gesture to cut ties with the past, and a practical gesture to distance himself from our father.

Prefab wooden houses already existed in other parts; José Antonio had read about them in a magazine, but no one had previously thought to build them in our country, where earthquakes sporadically leave everyone scrambling to rebuild. Marko knew a lot about wood and José Antonio knew how to get loans and run the legal and administrative aspects of a business. He'd learned from his father's success, as well as from his ultimate ruin.

"We're going to be known for our honesty," he said to Marko.

The first thing they did was design a basic floor plan to be built from panels, some solid and others with doors or windows cut out. They could make the construction larger by simply multiplying the number of modules, allowing them to build anything from a tiny dwelling to a large hospital. With the blueprints under his arm, José Antonio showed up at the Regional Bank of Sacramento and got the loan he needed to save our father's sawmill. The loan officer granted the request and was so taken with the project that he asked to be brought in as a partner. This gave my brother a foot in the door of the financial world of the province, where no one questioned the Delvalle name, and so he began his company. Rustic Homes still exists, although it is no longer owned by our family.

IN THE EARLY DAYS of the company, José Antonio camped with Marko in the Andean forests, while they breathed new life into the sawmill and organized transportation of the boards to the modest panel factory they'd set up on the outskirts of Sacramento. After that they divided up the work; Marko was in charge of production and José Antonio opened an office to sell their products. The first orders came from local landowners in need of basic homes for their seasonal laborers, and then they started getting orders from families of little means. Such efficiency had never been seen in those parts. A couple of construction workers would go out on site to lay the foundation and install the plumbing, and as soon as the concrete was dry the truck carrying the modules showed up. A house could be built in under two days; on the third day the roof was added and the new homeowners and builders celebrated with a barbecue washed down with plenty of wine, all courtesy of Rustic Homes. It turned out to be good publicity.

By the time I joined them, there was beginning to be a market for young middle-class couples. The first home they built as a model was functional, but it looked like a doghouse. It was so basic that it bordered on pathetic, something Marko, José Antonio, and I all agreed on. They suggested trying to soften it with landscaping, but it would've taken a forest to hide it completely. In a burst of inspiration, I had the idea to put a thatched roof on the house, as I had seen on the huts of the indigenous peoples, which further served to justify the name "Rustic Homes" and hide the ugly corrugated metal roof. It was a success. José Antonio was photographed in the provincial newspaper beside his model home, with the caption noting that in addition to being comfortable and cheap, the houses were adorable with their little straw wigs. Soon there was so much business they had to expand the factory and hire an architect.

When I began to feel suffocated by Santa Clara and was itching to see a bit of the world, I convinced my brother to hire me. The Rivases hoped I would study to become a teacher, since I had a knack for it and plenty of experience, but I didn't like children. The only good thing about kids is that they grow fast.

My mother and my aunts were in agreement that

it would be good for me to spend a year or two in Sacramento; the only people who raised objections were Torito, because he couldn't imagine life without me, and Fabian, for the same reason. The Schmidt-Engler family, on the other hand, almost certainly celebrated that temporary separation, which, with a little luck, they hoped would be for good. They probably thought I would meet a new and more appropriate young man in the city, and in the meantime they could rustle up a more fitting candidate for Fabian among the German community.

THE PREPARATIONS FOR MY trip began early, because I needed a new wardrobe; I couldn't walk around Sacramento in canvas coveralls, wooden clogs, and a poncho. Miss Taylor sent several dress patterns down from the capital, along with material for hats, and the sewing machine ran nonstop for weeks. Even Aunt Pilar, who usually preferred shoeing horses and plowing the fields with Uncle Bruno, joined the collective effort. They improvised a clothes rack from an iron bar, and there my city outfits hung, dresses copied from Miss Taylor's magazines, jackets, a coat with a rabbit fur collar and cuffs, silk slips, and nightshirts. Apart from the fabric that José Antonio had brought us, we had my mother's elegant dresses, which hadn't been worn in twenty years, and which we unstitched to transform into new, more fashionable styles.

"You better take care of these clothes, Violeta. They're all going into your wedding trousseau," Aunt Pilar warned, scissors in hand, because the time had come to cut my braid.

Everyone, even my mother, who rarely stood up from the bed or the wicker chair, came to send me off at the station. I traveled with a hatbox and three heavy suitcases, the same ones we'd used years before when we'd escaped into Exile, and an enormous picnic basket that Facunda had filled with enough to feed all the other passengers. At the last minute, so that I couldn't reject it, Fabian reached through the train window to hand me an envelope full of money along with a love letter written with such passion that I wondered if someone had dictated it to him; it was impossible to imagine him expressing himself with such eloquence. He stuttered whenever he had to talk about his feelings, but with a pen and paper his inhibitions were lowered.

Over those last few days the general anxiety in the air spread to me as well; it was the first time I'd be traveling alone. Fabian offered to ride with me as far as the Sacramento station, where José Antonio would be waiting to pick me up, but at the insistence of Lucinda, who had interrupted her summer tour to come back with Abel and say goodbye, I refused.

"Exert some independence; you're not a little girl. You can't let anyone else decide things for you. You have to take care of yourself in this world," she said.

I've never forgotten those words.

. . .

I'D BEEN IN SACRAMENTO a year, working as assistant to José Antonio, when Uncle Bruno called to tell us that our mother wasn't doing well at all. It wasn't the first time we'd received one of these alarming calls. My mother's health had been declining for the past twenty years, and she'd been convinced she was dying so many times that we tended to pay little mind. This time, however, the situation was serious. Uncle Bruno asked us to come home quickly and to contact our other brothers, so that they could say goodbye.

That's how the six Del Valle children were reunited for the first time since our father's funeral. Ten years had passed and I hardly recognized the four of them, who'd now become fathers several times over, respected members of society, and conservative gentlemen of good economic standing. They remembered me as a little girl in pigtails peering out the window of a train, and now standing before them was a woman of twenty-one. Affection must be cultivated, Camilo; it has to be watered and tended like a plant, but we'd let ours dry up.

We found my mother unconscious, shrunken, all skin and bones. I thought we'd gotten there too late, that she'd died before I'd been able to tell her that I loved her, and I began to feel the stomach cramps that always plague me in my worst moments of anguish. My mother's skin was a bluish color, her lips and fingers purple, as the asphyxia she'd been battling for years was finally getting the better of her. Her breathing was labored and irregular; she would go a few minutes without inhaling and just when we thought we'd lost her she'd gasp desperately for air. The aunts had moved her bed into the little sitting room, after removing the table and sofa, so that they could attend to her more easily.

When he heard what was happening, Fabian showed up with one of his sisters' husbands, who was a doctor. It would've been impossible to move my mother; there were a few clinics in the area, but the closest hospital was in Sacramento. The doctor diagnosed her with advanced emphysema; there was nothing more to be done for her, he said, the patient had only a few days left to live. We all agreed that watching my mother suffer like that for days would be too terrible. As a last recourse, when Aunt Pía's magic hands could do nothing to quell her sister's agonizing pain, she called for Yaima to come.

ABEL AND LUCINDA BROUGHT Yaima. She'd descended from a long line of medicine women who had passed down the gift of healing, clairvoyant dreams, and supernatural revelations, which she'd polished through practice and good intention. "Some use their power for bad. Others ask for money to heal, which kills the magic," she said. She was the link between the earth and the spirit world, with great knowledge of plants and shamanic rituals, and she could banish negative energy and restore health. She ordered my brothers out of the house and, surrounded by only my aunts, Lucinda, Facunda, and me, she began the work of helping María Gracia transition to the Other Side, just as a child being born is aided in their passage to This Side.

The Rivas property had finally been connected to the electric grid three years prior, when we illegally ran a cable from the power lines. Now Yaima had us unplug the lamps and the radio; she lit candles, which she placed in a circle around the bed; and she filled the air with sage, to cleanse the energy in the room.

"The earth is our **Mama.** She gives us life, to her we pray," she said.

With a black blindfold over her eyes she slowly ran her fingers over the patient to examine her.

"She can see the invisible with her hands," Facunda said.

Then Yaima took off the blindfold, pulled some powders from her bag, mixed them with a bit of water, and fed the paste to my mother on a spoon. She was unable to swallow much, but some of the concoction made it into her mouth. Yaima picked up her drum, the same one she'd played in her hut the first time I'd met her, and began beating it rhythmically as she chanted in her language. Facunda explained that she was calling on the Celestial Father, Mother Earth, and the spirits of the dying woman's ancestors to come and retrieve her.

The drum ritual lasted for hours, with a single interruption to relight the sage smudge, purify the air with smoke, and give the patient another dose of the medicinal preparation. At first, Aunts Pía and Pilar prayed their Christian prayers; Lucinda observed carefully, trying to remember every detail for her notebook; Facunda echoed Yaima's words in the native language; and I, curled over with stomach cramps, held my mother's hand. After a little while in that closed space filled with smoke, the sound of the drum and the presence of death began to make us feel dizzy and dazed. No one moved. Each drumbeat reverberated through my body, until I finally surrendered to the pain and went into a strange stupor.

I fell into a trance—there's no other explanation for that flight of time and space. It's impossible to describe the experience of dissolving into the black void of the universe, detached from the body, feelings, and memory, unbound by the umbilical cord that tethers us to reality. There was neither present nor past, and at the same time I was part of everything in existence. I can't say it was a spiritual journey, because all notion of the soul also disappeared. I suppose it was something like dying, and that I will feel it again soon when I reach my final hour. I returned to consciousness as the hypnotic sound of the drum finally ceased.

When the ceremony was over, Yaima, as exhausted as the other women, accepted the **mate** that Facunda offered her, and then she sank down into a corner to rest. The smoke started to dissipate, and I saw that my mother was in a deep sleep, free from her torturous asphyxia. For the rest of the night her breathing was imperceptible and effortless; on a few occasions I placed a mirror under her nose to check that she was still alive. At four o'clock in the morning Yaima beat the drum three times and announced that María Gracia had gone to see the Father. I was lying on the bed beside my mother, holding her hand tightly, but her transition had been so gentle that I hadn't even realized she'd passed away.

The six Del Valle children took my mother's coffin by train to the capital, to place her beside her husband in the family crypt. For months, I was unable to mourn her loss. I thought about her often with a hard lump in my chest, going over the years she had been in my life and blaming her for the perpetual despondency, for not having loved me enough and for having done so little to connect with me. I was angry over the opportunities we missed to be mother and daughter.

One afternoon at the office, busy with some orders, I felt the air suddenly chill, and when I looked up to check if the window was open, I saw my mother standing beside the door, wearing her traveling coat and carrying her purse in her hand, as if she were waiting for a train at the station. I didn't move or breathe so as not to scare her away.

"Mom, Mom, don't go," I silently begged, but an instant later she had disappeared.

I began to cry uncontrollably, the torrent of tears purging me from within until there was nothing left of the bitterness and blame and bad memories. Ever since then, the spirit of my mother has trod lightly around me.

9

.....

PROPER MOURNING FOR THE DEATH OF MY mother, along with the outbreak of the Second World War, delayed my marriage.

Fabian's profession was not highly valued since agriculture was stuck in the previous century. On most farms owned by European immigrants they imported machinery from the United States, but small farmers like Bruno Rivas still plowed using mules or borrowed oxen. The cattle they owned were like our Clotilde and Leonor, patient, good-natured cows, but without any delusions of grandeur.

In that province, veterinarians worked like door-to-door salesmen, visiting farms to vaccinate and tend to sick or injured animals; no one got rich doing it. Fabian didn't do the work for the money, animals were his calling. I was used to a simple existence and we had enough for a certain level of comfort, especially with the help of the Schmidt-Engler clan, now resigned to our inevitable marriage. Fabian's father gave him several acres, just as he had done for his other children, and José Antonio offered to build one of our rustic homes, which I designed with future children in mind.

The news of the Second World War in Europe was alarming but distant. Despite U.S. pressure on us to declare war on the Axis powers, our country remained neutral out of self-preservation; we were very vulnerable to invasion by sea and would never be able to defend ourselves in the case of attack by the fearsome German submarines. There were also the many German and Italian communities to consider, and even a vocal Nazi party, whose members marched down the streets waving flags and proudly bearing swastikas on their armbands. There were no Japanese, as far as I remember.

The Schmidt-Englers, like all the Germans in the region, were sympathetic to the Axis powers, but avoided making enemies of Allied supporters. Fabian stayed silent; conflict was not his forte. I didn't understand the details or reasons for the war, and it didn't matter to me who won, despite the fact that my brother and the Rivases had tried to indoctrinate me against Hitler and Fascism. The worst atrocities of the concentration camps and systematic genocide would remain unknown to us until the end of the war, when photos were published and movies about the horrors released.

José Antonio and the Rivases followed the movements of the troops, which they marked with pins on a map of Europe, and it was obvious that the Germans were devouring the continent one bite at a time. In 1941 Japan bombed an American base at Pearl Harbor and President Roosevelt declared war against the Axis powers. U.S. intervention was the only hope of stopping the Germans.

While in Europe men were killing each other, reducing ancient cities to rubble and ashes, leaving millions of widows, orphans, and refugees in their wake, Fabian was occupied with artificial insemination. Of animals, of course, not people. He didn't come up with the idea—it was something that had been done for many years with sheep and pigs—but he had the notion to try it with cattle. Though I'll spare you the details, it's enough to say that the procedure seems terribly disrespectful to the cows. I don't want to even think about how he obtained the bulls' crucial contribution. Before Fabian became successful with his experiments, reproduction occurred according to the laws of nature, a combination of instinct and luck. The bull mounted his girlfriend and, in general, a calf resulted. The best bulls were rented out; the farmer had to transport them, provide a stable, and watch them closely, because they tended to have bad personalities. That explained why the cows often put up a fight.

Fabian researched a way of preserving the semen of pure-bred animals for several days, which allowed him to inseminate hundreds of cows across many miles without having to transport the bull, as long as he hurried. Now the semen is kept for years and travels around the world, so a newborn calf in Paraguay might descend from a long-dead bull in Texas, but back then that would've sounded like science fiction.

Fabian had the support of his father, the only person who immediately understood the advantages of the project, thanks to the army of cows at his dairy farm. They set up a laboratory in an old warehouse, where he developed the technique and the necessary implements. Over the months and years to come he would live his life obsessed with insemination, which to me seemed pornographic, dreaming of its many possibilities: racehorses, pedigreed dogs and cats, exotic beasts at the zoo, or animals in danger of extinction. I admit that I often teased him about his work, though he remained dedicated as ever and unaffected by my sarcasm. The only thing he asked of me was not to ridicule him in front of other people.

I stopped laughing when I saw how his procedure could benefit my father-in-law and other farmers. For many years Fabian was the best-known vet in the country; he was interviewed by the press, gave conferences, wrote books, traveled to tutor farmworkers, and improved the cattle stock of several Latin American countries. His biggest problem, as he often explained, was finding a way to preserve the semen for long periods of time, something he finally achieved in the sixties, I think. Fabian's prestige didn't translate to money; without his father's financial help he wouldn't have even been able to continue his research.

Despite the demands of his work, which left him little time for other things, Fabian continued to ask me, with his German tenacity, to marry him. What were we waiting for? I was twenty-two and had spent two years in Sacramento out of the nest, as he said. But the notion of being out of the nest was a joke; I lived and worked with my brother, who guarded me like a warden, and Sacramento was a sleepy city of prudish, intolerant, gossipy people. I'd had more intellectual stimulation on the Rivas farm than I did in the provincial capital.

MY FORMER GOVERNESS AND Teresa Rivas were lovers at a time when homosexuality was a privilege reserved for aristocrats and artists, the former because they practiced it with discretion, like one of my distant relatives whose name I won't mention, and the latter because they flaunted social norms and religious precepts. There were few openly gay figures: a journalist, a world-famous poetess, a few actors and writers, but there were many more living in secret. Because of machismo, it was more tolerated among women than men.

At first, Miss Taylor and Teresa Rivas lived,

poor as mice, in Teresa's attic apartment, but Miss Taylor soon got work as an English teacher at a girls' school, where she'd work for twenty years without anyone ever questioning her private life. To the eyes of the world she was a spinster, asexual as an amoeba. She didn't earn much, but she also gave private lessons, and that permitted her to rent a little house in a middle-class neighborhood, where they could finally set up the piano. As soon as he was able to, José Antonio began helping them out, since Miss Taylor's salary was barely enough to fund her modest lifestyle.

Teresa Rivas quit her job at the telephone company to devote herself full-time to the feminist cause. She worked with organizations that furthered the rights of women: the vote; custody of children, which before had been exclusive to the father; ability to earn their own wages and labor protection; defense against violence—basically she worked toward many fundamental changes to the law that we take for granted today. She also promoted the right to abortion and divorce, which the Catholic Church condemned in the most incendiary of terms. At that time hell still existed. Teresa said that until men gave birth and put up with husbands, as women do, they should not have an opinion about—let alone decide on—abortion and divorce. She didn't believe that men had the right to an opinion, much less to pass laws on the female body, since they'd never know the exhaustion of gestation, the pain of labor, and the eternal bondage of motherhood.

These ideas were so radical that Teresa would regularly be thrown in jail for publishing her beliefs, creating public disturbances, inciting strikes, trespassing on Congress, and, on one occasion, assaulting the president of the nation during a public appearance. The papers said that a deranged feminist had thrown a ripe tomato at the president at the ribbon-cutting ceremony for a powdered milk factory. Teresa alleged that it was a U.S. conspiracy to replace the miracle of breast milk with prepackaged garbage. She sat in jail for four months, until José Antonio finally managed to get her out.

It was the highlight of our year when these two women came to visit. They brought news of the capital and progressive ideas from the rest of the world, which produced in us a mixture of horror and admiration. I guess at some point José Antonio accepted the fact that Miss Taylor was never going to marry him, but I doubt he ever understood the real reason. At the time, none of us suspected anything more than an extraordinary friendship between the women.

The sustained efforts of Teresa Rivas and other women like her gradually changed our laws and customs. We move at a turtle's pace, but over my long life I can attest to how far we've come. I think that Teresa and Miss Taylor would be proud of what they'd achieved, and they'd continue the fight for what has yet to be done. No one gives you anything in life, Teresa would say, you have to take it by force, and as soon as you get careless they'll take it back.

I never discussed these issues with my mother and my aunts, or with Fabian, much less his family. Behind my boyfriend's back I read the books and magazines that Teresa gave me and talked about them only with Lucinda and Abel, who were almost as radical as their daughter. I felt a mute rebelliousness, a repressed rage, when I thought about marrying, having children, becoming a housewife, and living a banal life in my husband's shadow.

"Don't get married if you're not sure you can spend the rest of your life with Fabian," Miss Taylor said to me.

"He's waited so long for me. If I don't get married soon, I'll have to break off this eternal engagement."

"That's preferable to getting married if you're not sure, Violeta."

"I'm about to turn twenty-five. I'm more than old enough to get married and have kids. Fabian is a nice man and he loves me a lot. He'll make a very good husband."

"And what about you? Will you make a good wife? Think about it, Violeta. I don't believe you're in love. You've always been so headstrong, you should listen to your instincts."

Miss Taylor's doubts echoed my own, but I was engaged to Fabian, we were already a couple in everyone's eyes, and I could see no valid reason for standing up a good man like him. I had the notion that without him I'd be condemned to a life of spinsterhood. I didn't have any talents or abilities that might mark a path different from the one a woman was expected to follow. Instead of motivating me to take my destiny into my own hands, that rebelliousness that Miss Taylor had mentioned felt like a burden. I wanted to be like her and Teresa, but the price was too high. I didn't dare to trade security for freedom.

Fabian and I were married in 1945. It had been an almost-five-year engagement, supposedly platonic, but by then I'd long since lost my virginity, unknowingly, in one of our entanglements. I discovered it later that night when I realized my underwear was stained with blood even though I wasn't menstruating, but I kept quiet, saying nothing to Fabian. Don't ask me why, Camilo. Our skirmishes continued as always: We would get each other all riled up, half-undressed, feeling guilty, uncomfortable, and fearful, only for him to finish in shame and leave me frustrated. Once I moved to Sacramento, he stayed in a hotel when he came to visit and we could've easily met there if he would've allowed it. In the bed of a nice hotel room we could've made love using condoms, which any man could get hold of. They wouldn't sell them to women. We would've had to be very discreet, because if José Antonio had suspected anything he would've killed me, as he threatened more than once. It was my duty to protect his and the family's honor, he would say, but when I asked him what his honor had to do with my virginity he got angry.

"Don't get sassy with me! I bet Teresa's the one putting these ideas in your head!"

In some ways, my brother was a Neanderthal, but I don't think he would've tried to make good on his threat. Deep down he was a nice guy.

Let me go off on a tangent, Camilo, to give you a brief history of birth control, although I know the topic does not pertain to you. My mother was unable to avoid having six children and many miscarriages, until she employed the method recommended to her by the country's first female doctor, who was sharing this information at the risk of arrest and excommunication. Following the instructions in a pamphlet the doctor had given her, which my mother studied behind her husband's back, she douched with glycerin before the act, followed by a solution of warm water and hydrogen peroxide after, using a gadget she kept hidden in a hatbox. She knew that Arsenio Del Valle, who had married solely to carry on his prestigious name by engendering the largest possible number of descendants, would've had a fit if he'd ever discovered the contents of that hatbox. I'd heard him pontificate often about a woman's sacred duty to bring healthy babies into the world, just as his mother had done. When I finally announced that I was getting married, Aunt Pía gave me the elements

I'd need to wash myself, wrapped discreetly in newspaper, explaining their usage in hushed tones, mortified.

In the end I ran out of excuses to put off the wedding any longer, and we announced that we'd be married in October, never suspecting that the world war would end one month before. The typical thing was for the bride to host the wedding reception, but, with great delicacy so as not to offend us, the Schmidt-Englers insisted that the wedding be held at the Hotel Bavaria.

MY AUNTS DUSTED OFF the sewing machine to complete my trousseau, aided by Lucinda, who no longer rode on horseback to teach because she was over seventy years old and her body couldn't handle all that jostling, as she said. They made sheets embroidered with the bride's and groom's initials, and tablecloths of various sizes, but I didn't want them to alter the dress my mother had been married in, which had survived in a box filled with mothballs since the end of the previous century. I wanted my own dress, without any butter-colored lace. Miss Taylor bought a fashionable wedding gown in the capital and sent it to me by train. It was plain white satin, cut on the bias to accentuate my figure, with a veiled hat that made me look like a nurse.

We were married in a lovely chapel built by the first Germans in the region. I was walked down the aisle by José Antonio, the only one of my brothers present, as my aunts cried tears of joy alongside the Rivases, Torito, Facunda, Miss Taylor, Teresa, and many inhabitants of the little town of Nahuel. On one side of the altar sat the family and friends of the groom, tall, luminous, and well dressed; on the other side, my guests looked much more humble.

Marko Kusanovic also turned up, to everyone's surprise because he was close to sixty years old and had become something of a recluse. He had a sparse apartment in Sacramento so that he could supervise the factory. But as soon as he got the chance he would go out to visit the vast pine forests we'd planted to obtain logs without massacring the native woods, or up to the sawmill in the mountains, where he was happiest. The company's administration, accounting, and profits didn't interest him in the slightest; if my brother had not made that vow of honesty, he could've easily taken advantage of the man.

Marko wore a thick beard like a prophet and dressed like a hunter, although he was incapable of killing so much as a hare. As a wedding present he gave me a sculpture he'd carved out of stone, the first we'd heard of his hidden talent. We knew he'd become a father late in life and had a son of about four or five. The mother was a young indigenous woman who worked in a textile factory and was raising the boy until he was old enough to be sent off to a good school. Marko acknowledged the boy, who was named Anton Kusanovic and, according to his father, was extremely intelligent.

"I'm going to give him the best education; he and his mother have a good life," he said to us proudly.

The end of the war, Germany's defeat, and Hitler's death hung in the air like a black cloud over the German colonizers, but of course no one mentioned it at my wedding. Sympathy for either the Axis or the Allied powers was something that defined people at the time and caused unpleasant arguments, which we'd carefully avoided for several years, and no one wanted to ruin the wedding by bringing it up now. The Rivases, my brother, Miss Taylor, and Teresa had celebrated the peace treaty on September 2 with a grilled rack of lamb, mugs of chicha, and Facunda's magnificent baked goods, without including Fabian.

After the wedding, we were finally able to make love naked in a hotel bed, like I'd imagined so many times. My husband turned out to be sweet and considerate, but I wouldn't know the true turmoil of passion until years later, with another man.

The day after the wedding, we took a train to the capital. I hadn't been back since my mother's funeral, when I visited only the cemetery and my brothers' homes, but it was nothing new to Fabian, since he went often for work. The city had changed a lot; I would've liked to stay several days to explore, return to my old neighborhood, and attend the theater, but we were setting off on our honeymoon to Rio de Janeiro, where Fabian was going to teach some courses. Commercial flights had resumed, after being strictly limited during the war years. The experience of flying for the first time meant many hours trapped in my traveling clothes—girdle, stockings, high heels, tight skirt and jacket, hat, gloves, and fur stole—dizzy, frightened, and nauseated, with brief respites when the plane stopped to refuel.

I hardly remember my honeymoon because I got sick with some kind of stomach bug. I spent most of the time staring out the window at the gorgeous Copacabana Beach below, sipping hot tea instead of the famous caipirinhas. When he wasn't working, Fabian tended to me lovingly. He promised that we would return to Brazil another time for a proper honeymoon.

FAITHFUL TO HIS WORD, my brother built our house in one week and crowned it with a double layer of the best local thatch. In the years I had worked for him, José Antonio had prospered more than he'd ever dreamed of and part of his success can be attributed to me, because I thought up many ideas that should've rightly come from the architect. One of the most profitable projects was the community of Rustic Homes on the lakeshore, sold at absurd prices in the capital as vacation homes.

"It's ridiculous, Violeta. We're too far from the capital, no one is going to want to travel so many hours by train or car to come swim in a freezing lake," José Antonio said, but he humored me.

The results were so incredible that he was flooded with investors for similar projects. I took care of finding the appropriate locations and organizing the land purchase and building permits.

"You're going to give me a good commission for every one of these houses we sell," I demanded.

"What are you saying, Violeta! Aren't we family?" he answered.

"That's exactly why."

In those days, while still single, I was very frugal and didn't have many expenses because I lived with José Antonio and there were few temptations for spending in Sacramento. I saved money, got a loan from the Regional Bank where we had the Rustic Homes accounts, bought a plot of land, and financed eight houses, with a community swimming pool and beautiful landscaping to justify the price. I sold them easily, paid back the loan, and repeated the process. I managed to build four communities before getting married and, as I explained to Fabian, I planned to continue investing in that business and any other opportunities that might come up. This was something unprecedented. Women of my social class did not work, and much less out in the provinces, where we were several decades behind the times.

I assured Fabian that work would never interfere with my duties as a good wife, homemaker, and future mother, and he grudgingly agreed. Social disgrace aside, it meant that his wife was going to have one foot in the country and another in the city. I'm stubborn, and when an idea gets into my head I never let it go. So, while he researched, experimented, wrote, and taught, obsessed as a madman, I took care of the domestic expenses and saved. I sent Uncle Bruno a monthly allowance for my aunts; he refused it every time but I deposited the money into an account for emergencies, never in short supply: Clotilde died and had to be replaced, the fence was knocked down in a storm, there was a bad harvest, the well dried up, Facunda's gallbladder burst and she needed an operation.

The fact that I worked, earned money, and maintained the household was offensive to my husband. I felt guilty and tried to downplay my efforts, never making reference to my job in public. If anyone brought it up I said it was a temporary hobby to keep myself occupied and that, of course, I'd give it up when I had kids. Deep down, however, I no longer considered myself impotent and useless, because I realized I had an innate ability to make money. I inherited that from my father, with the difference that I'm prudent while he was reckless. I'm careful and calculated, whereas he cheated and tempted fate.

. . .

WHY DOES LOVE DIE? I've asked myself this question many times. Fabian didn't give me any reason to stop loving him, quite the opposite—he was the ideal husband, never pestering or asking anything of me. He was then, and continued to be until the day he died, a fine man. We lived well on what I earned and the help he received from his family; we had a cozy home, which was photographed for an architectural magazine as an example of prefab construction; the Schmidt-Englers accepted me as another of their daughters-in-law, and I assimilated into the German community, although I was never able to learn a word of their language. My husband had become the country's most recognized expert in his field, and every business idea that popped into my mind was a success. In short, we had a life that looked almost perfect from the outside.

I loved Fabian, but I know now that I was never in love with him, as Miss Taylor had tried to help me see on more than one occasion. Over our five-year engagement I got to know him backward and forward; I married him well aware of who he was and that he'd never change, but he didn't know me well at all and I changed a lot. His friendly and predictable nature bored me, as did his obsession with studs and pregnant cows; his indifference to anything that didn't personally concern him; his rigidity; his immoveable, antiquated principles; his Aryan arrogance, nourished by years of Nazi propaganda, which had made its way here, to the other end of the world. But I can't really criticize him for feeling superior because all of us thought the European immigrants were better than us.

Ours is a very racist society; you've seen, Camilo, how we treated the indigenous peoples. A relative of mine, who was a congressman in the mid-nineteenth century, proposed either making the native population submit by force or exterminating them, as they did in the United States; he called them untamable brutes, enemies of civilization who lived in sin, lazy drunks, liars, and traitors, to use his exact words. This prejudice was so widespread that the government invited Europeans, in particular the Germans, Swiss, and French, to colonize the south in order to improve the race. If we didn't have immigrants from Africa or Asia it was because the consuls had instructions to impede them; Jewish and Arab people were not welcome either, though they came anyway. I imagine that those foreign colonizers, who looked down on the indigenous peoples, didn't have a particularly favorable opinion of mestizos either.

"You're not mestiza, Violeta. All of our ancestors are Spanish or Portuguese; there's not a drop of Indian blood in our family," Aunt Pilar said when the topic came up.

Whereas I harbored the same doubts I'd had before getting married, Fabian never questioned our relationship and did not notice that I was pulling away, because the thought was inconceivable to him; we'd taken vows before God and society to love and respect each other until death. That's a long time. If I'd known how long a life can be, I would've modified that clause in the marriage contract. I once insinuated my frustration to my husband, with the politeness we always used with each other, and he was not the slightest bit perturbed. I should've been firmer and made him pay attention to me. He responded that couples often have difficulties at first, that it was normal, but that over time we'd learn to live with each other, take our place in society and form a family. That's how it had always been; it was a biological mandate. I would feel more satisfied once I had children, since "motherhood is a woman's destiny," he said.

That was our biggest problem: The children did not come. I suppose that for an expert in reproduction like Fabian, his wife's infertility must've been a personal affront, but he never let on, at least not to me. He just asked me hopefully from time to time if we had any news, and on one occasion he commented in passing that artificial insemination in humans had been practiced since the time of the Sumerians, and that, in fact, Queen Juana of Portugal had a daughter by that method in 1462. I told him not to get me confused with one of his cows. Queen Juana was never mentioned again.

I was scared at the prospect of having children, I

knew it would be the end of my relative freedom, but I didn't actively avoid getting pregnant, unless you count my prayers to Father Quiroga, which doesn't technically count as birth control. Every month, as soon as I began menstruating, I heaved a sigh of relief and made my regular offering to the saint at the Sacramento church, where they had a terrifying oil painting of the priest with a shovel in his hand, surrounded by orphans.

My husband wanted a woman as unconditional in her love as he was, someone who would go along with the plans he had for his life, stand behind him, and express the undying admiration he thought he deserved—but he had the misfortune of falling in love with me. I couldn't give him any of that, but I swear that I tried to, tenaciously, because that was the mission that had been assigned to me. I was sure that if I just faked it long enough I would end up becoming the perfect wife he expected me to be, without any aspirations of my own, existing entirely to serve my husband and children. The only person I knew who had defied that social mandate was Teresa Rivas, who openly expressed her horror at marriage because she considered it fatal to women.

I was so good at fooling people with my act as submissive wife that my sisters-in-law, four happy, hardworking Valkyries, joked about my way of spoiling and waiting on my husband hand and foot, like a geisha. That's how it seemed, especially when they were around. I made sure that Fabian felt comfortable and satisfied, just like the women's magazines recommended, because it was easy for me and kept him from prying into my emotions; he was convinced that if he was happy, then I must be too. But the geisha mask hid the face of an angry woman.

The journey of life has long and tedious stretches, step by step, day by day, without anything exciting happening, but memory is made up of the unexpected events that mark your course. These are the things worth passing on. In an existence as long as mine, there have been some unforgettable people and events, and I've experienced the good fortune of not having had my mind fail me; unlike my poor battered body, my brain remains intact. Remembering is my curse, Camilo, but I'm going to skip over the three years I was married to Fabian because they were as uneventful as life in a nunnery, with nothing tragic or splendid to speak of. For him they were highly satisfying years, which is why he could never figure out what the hell happened—why one day I up and left.

10

JULIÁN BRAVO HAD SERVED AS A PILOT IN the United Kingdom's Royal Air Force, making him among the few Latin Americans to fight in the war. He was decorated for acts of bravery and his suicidal midair duels with German planes. According to the rumor, which he had almost certainly started himself, he'd downed more than eighty enemy planes with his Spitfire. One day he fell out of the sky and into my life, his fame preceding him, but even without that romantic past he would've made a powerful impression. He was a storybook hero.

He made a water landing on the lake in his seaplane, carrying two members of the Danish royal family and their entourage; they were making an official visit to the country and wanted to fish in our rivers. They ended up at the Hotel Bavaria, where they were received without any fanfare, like any other guests. The studied simplicity was my mother-in-law's idea and turned out to be the right instinct, because the Danish nobles extended their visit to stay an entire week with us. There, at the Hotel Bavaria, under my mother-in-law's watchful eye and the stifled giggles of my sisters-in-law, I met Julián.

He was sitting on the terrace railing with a foot on the ground, cigarette in one hand and a glass of whiskey in the other, wearing khaki pants and a white short-sleeved shirt that accentuated his athletic torso and biceps. He radiated something sexual and dangerous, like the pent-up energy of a wild animal, which I felt from several yards away. I don't know how else to describe it. Julián's irresistible masculinity remained with him until the day he died, forty-something years later.

I froze, feeling a mixture of terror and urgent anticipation; in an instant my life had taken an irrevocable turn. He must've sensed my impassioned premonition, because he turned toward me with a curious half smile on his lips. He took a few long seconds to put his other foot down, set his glass on the railing, and swagger over to me like a cowboy in some Wild West movie. Later on he told me that he'd felt the same thing: a certainty that we'd lived our lives up to that point searching for each other.

He stopped a few steps in front of me, looking me up and down to appraise me like an auctioneer. I felt naked in my modest white sundress.

"We know each other, don't we?" he asked.

I nodded, mute.

"Come with me," he said, stubbing out his cigarette with one foot and taking me by the hand.

We practically raced down the winding paths of the terraced garden to the beach; I followed him, hypnotized, without letting go of his hand or stopping to consider that I might be seen by my husband and half his family. I couldn't resist him as he fell to his knees in the sand, pulled me down beside him, and kissed me with an unknown and terrifying intensity.

"Our love is unstoppable," he said, and I nodded again.

And so began the passionate affair that would put an end to my marriage and seal my fate. Julián Bravo asked me to meet him in his room and half an hour later we were naked, desperately exploring each other in broad daylight right there inside my mother-in-law's hotel, steps away from my husband, who was drinking beer with the Danes and explaining via interpreter his fascinating technique for artificial insemination. But upstairs on the second floor, between four walls of fragrant boards from the native forests, the sunlight filtering through a curtain of raw sackcloth, on a feather mattress with linen sheets, I learned at age twenty-eight the surprising possibilities of pleasure and the fundamental difference between an uninspired husband and a lover who seemed to have stepped out of an erotic novel.

. . .

UNTIL THAT FIRST AFTERNOON with Julián Bravo, my ignorance of my own body was so monumental that it can only be explained by the time and place I was born into. I was raised by a prudish mother who'd had six children brought down from heaven by Baby Jesus, as she assured me in hushed tones, and two spinster aunts who never mentioned "the nether regions," which was code for the section of the body between the waist and the knees. Aunt Pía died a virgin and the other one, well, who knows; she may have gone to bed with Bruno Rivas in her later years, but she never admitted it to me. As far as Josephine Taylor, she simply showed me illustrations of the human body in a book, because despite her revolutionary ideas she was just as puritanical as my aunts. From her I learned to take off and put on my clothes like a contortionist to avoid vulgar nudity at all costs. I didn't have girlfriends my own age; I never went to school; my severely limited knowledge came from animals mating on the farm. When I got married, I continued getting undressed as I'd seen Miss Taylor do, and Fabian and I made love in pitch-dark silence; I never imagined there were other options, and I think Fabian considered bovine reproduction more interesting than our sexual encounters.

Julián ripped my dress off like a puma with two swipes of his hands, never even giving me a chance to protest. He smothered my first startled exclamation with a kiss, and from that point on I abandoned any hint of resistance, willing my body to come undone and melt in his arms, wishing I could stay right there with the door shut forever and never see another living soul again, only him. He looked me over, assessing my features and making flattering comments about the shape of my breasts and hips, the shine of my hair, the softness of my skin, my smell of soap, and other attributes I'd never paid attention to and that, frankly, were not that exceptional.

He realized that his open admiration embarrassed me so he pulled me almost by force over to the large mirror on the wardrobe, where I saw a naked stranger, trembling, with wild hair, a picture of depravity that would've terrified my aunts but had the effect of relaxing me. By that point there was no turning back. He guided me to the bed and took his time to caress me from head to toe with a slow and delicious boldness, not expecting anything in exchange, murmuring a string of nonsense, compliments, and vulgarities. The contrast between my clumsiness and his skill must've been comical, but that didn't dampen his enthusiasm, only encouraged his efforts to pleasure me.

I hope you're not horrified by this brief reference to sex, Camilo. I feel the need to justify why I submitted to Julián Bravo for all those years. I've had some lovers in my life, but there weren't very many. The ideal is to make love with someone you adore, but that wasn't the case with Julián that first afternoon. There was no love, only desire—simple, brutal, devastating desire, direct and remorseless. Oblivious to anyone or anything else, we were the only man and the only woman in the universe, lost to absolute pleasure. Orgasm was as dramatic a discovery as the revelation of the woman I had hidden inside me: the stranger in the mirror, shameless, defiantly unfaithful, and giddy.

WE SPENT THE ENTIRE afternoon together, and I suppose Fabian must have asked everyone if they had seen me. I heard the bell announcing that the dining room was open for dinner and I understood that I had to shake off my drowsiness. Julián left me curled up in bed, dressed quickly, and left. I don't know how he convinced someone in the kitchen to give him bread, cheese, smoked salmon, grapes, and a bottle of wine, or how he managed to get the meal up to his room without arousing suspicion. We sat on the floor, naked; I drank wine from his mouth and he ate grapes from mine.

I had the chance to observe him, as he had done with me, and appraise him. He was without a doubt the most attractive man I've seen up close: muscular, supple, tanned from head to toe by outdoor sports, as if he sunbathed nude, and he had an irresistible laugh that made his eyes disappear, dark hair, light eyes that shifted between green and blue, and a few deep lines chiseled in his face. I didn't know it that day, but I soon learned that he had a smooth tenor singing voice, and that in one period of dire economic straits he'd earned a living as a cabaret singer in England and the United States.

I didn't go home that night. I awoke at dawn, wrapped in Julián's arms on a nest of wrinkled sheets, damp from sweat and sex, momentarily disoriented, unable to clearly recall where I was. It took me over a minute to fully accept that nothing would ever be the same as before. I'd have to face Fabian and explain what had happened.

"Relax, Violeta. There's a simple solution. Tell your husband that you didn't feel well and so you got a room for yourself to lie down," Julián suggested, but it was an absurd alibi.

"My mother-in-law owns this hotel. If I'd stayed here on my own, she'd know it, because I would have occupied one of her rooms."

"Well, then what are you planning to tell Fabian?"

"The truth. You must understand that I can't go back to him now."

"A lot of husbands will look the other way to avoid trouble. He'll believe anything you tell him," he replied, alarmed.

"Is that how it's worked out for you before?" I asked, with the vague feeling of stepping into quicksand.

"I'm not cynical, Violeta, I'm practical. No one

has seen us; we can avoid causing a stir. I'm not trying to upend your life . . ."

"It's already been upended. What do we do now?"

WE HURRIEDLY DRESSED AND Julián left before I did. I ran his comb through my hair, skipped washing up, and tiptoed down the hallway praying no one would see me. I hid in the garden and a few minutes later Julián picked me up in one of the cars the Danes had at their disposal and drove me to the train station. By ten o'clock I was at the Rustic Homes office in Sacramento with my brother.

"What are you doing here, Violeta? I thought you were supposed to be at the Hotel Bavaria with the Danes."

"I left Fabian."

"Where?"

"I'm leaving him, José Antonio. I'm not going back to him; the marriage is over."

"My God! What happened?"

My brother listened to me with disbelief plastered across his face, horrified as the substitute patriarch responsible for the family's honor. But just as I had expected, instead of judging me or trying to convince me that the mistake could be made right, he simply asked, wiping his forehead with his shirtsleeve, how he could help. Then he picked up the phone and left messages for Fabian at the Schmidt-Engler farm and at the Hotel Bavaria.

Around noon my husband called the office, relieved to know I was with my brother in the city and that everything had been cleared up in the end. He asked when I was coming home so he could meet me at the station.

"I'm afraid you'll have to come here, Fabian. Violeta has something serious to talk to you about," José Antonio told him.

My husband arrived in Sacramento hours later, and we met face-to-face in the office, with my brother standing guard in the next room in case my husband tried to hit me. José Antonio felt it would be completely justified.

"I had a terrible night looking everywhere for you, Violeta. I went all the way to Santa Clara to see if you were with your aunts. Why did you leave without telling me?"

"I just lost my head and had to run away."

"I'll never understand you, Violeta. But it doesn't matter. Let's go home."

"I want us to separate."

"What are you saying?"

"That I'm not going back with you. I'm in love with Julián Bravo."

"The pilot? But you just met him yesterday! Are you crazy?"

He sat down from the shock of the news. In his mind, the chances of me leaving him were as remote as my likelihood of spontaneously combusting.

"People don't just separate, Violeta! Problems

between couples are normal; they are worked out behind closed doors, without causing a scandal."

"We're going to annul the marriage, Fabian."

"You've completely lost your mind. You can't throw a marriage out the window for a little lust."

"I want an annulment," I insisted, so nervous my voice shook.

"Don't talk nonsense, Violeta. You're confused. I'm your husband and it's my duty to protect you. I'll clean up this mess. Don't worry, I'll right this wrong; no one needs to know it ever happened. I'll talk to that scoundrel."

"This has nothing to do with Julián, it's between you and me. We're going to have to annul the marriage, Fabian," I repeated for the third time.

"I'm never going to go along with that sham. We're married in the eyes of the law and before God, society, and, above all, our families!" he stammered.

"Think about it, Fabian: An annulment would set you free too," my brother interrupted, appearing in the doorway as soon as the tone of the conversation began to intensify.

"I don't need to be set free! I need my wife!" he shouted, and all of a sudden his anger vanished and he slumped in his chair with his face in his hands, sobbing.

As you know, Camilo, divorce didn't become legal in this country until the twenty-first century, when I was eighty-four years old and it was useless to me.

Before, the only way out of a marriage was to get it annulled by resorting to chicanery and legalese, arguing the incompetence of the civil registry, typically by claiming an error in the bride and groom's address. It was easy, as long as both parties agreed; all that was needed were two witnesses willing to commit perjury and an amenable judge. Fabian refused to even consider the notion, which he thought was perverse and sordid. He was sure, he said, that he could win me back, that I should give him another chance, that he'd loved me since he first laid eyes on me, that he'd never loved another woman, that without me life had no meaning. He continued baring his soul this way until his voice began to fail and his tears ran out.

JOSÉ ANTONIO SUGGESTED THAT we give each other time to think, and in the meantime I would stay with him in Sacramento, to keep the family from asking too many questions.

In the end, Fabian agreed to call a truce until we'd both cooled off. It coincided with a planned trip to Argentina to inseminate nine hundred cows on a ranch in Patagonia, mixing Holstein, Jersey, and Montbéliarde breeds. He gave me a detailed explanation of the work that was totally inappropriate at that moment. He'd be gone several weeks and I'd have a chance to change my mind. When he said goodbye he gave me a kiss on the forehead and asked my brother to take care of me until he returned, to make sure I didn't do anything crazy.

My brother called Julián at my in-laws' farm, where he'd been invited to help break the horses. As it turned out he was a champion jumper, another of his talents I was oblivious to, and he knew so much about horses that he'd never lost money on a race.

"You'd better come straight to Sacramento, young man. We have to talk," my brother ordered in a threatening tone that did not leave room for delay.

It was impossible to intimidate Julián Bravo. He'd spent several years risking his life during the war, loved extreme sports, had parachuted into the heart of the Amazon jungle, surfed the world's tallest waves in Portugal, and climbed the most inaccessible Andean peaks without guide ropes. He'd danced with death. His unflagging boldness led him naturally into illicit ventures, but that was later, when he was recruited by the mafia. He didn't answer my brother's summons out of fear, but because he couldn't stop thinking about me.

He arrived in Sacramento on the first train the next day, and he stayed with me the rest of the week until he had to return to the Hotel Bavaria and fly the Danes back to civilization in his seaplane.

11

JULIÁN AND I SPENT THOSE DAYS IN clandestine debauchery, with nothing to do except make love and drink white wine. I didn't offer my brother any explanations, but he understood that I could not be dissuaded and that all he could do was wait for the passion to fizzle out so I would come to my senses. I let myself sink into the delicious swamp of a desire that once satisfied was immediately rekindled; nothing could satiate my primordial thirst for that man. I imagined myself lost forever in his arms, denounced the entire world beyond that room—a frozen world, a world without him.

I stayed in his hotel room, naked or wrapped in one of his shirts—because all I had with me was what I'd been wearing when I left the Hotel Bavaria—anxiously awaiting his return, counting the minutes and hours I spent alone. They were many, because Julián couldn't stand being shut inside and went out to go horseback riding at the Equestrian Club or on his friends' ranches. I forgave his absences as soon as I heard his footsteps outside in the hall and saw him in the doorway, virile, smiling, damp with sweat from physical exertion, dominant, and content. The days we were together and the nights I spent pressed against his body banished all doubts and nourished my adolescent obsession with him. I surrendered myself with an absolute submission that now, in hindsight, seems inconceivable. I lost my good judgment and self-possession; nothing mattered, only him.

Afterwards, when he had to leave, I bought enough new clothes to get by and red lipstick to cheer myself up, and I moved into José Antonio's house without any intention of returning to my previous life. I announced this to Fabian when he returned from Argentina and came to get me, carrying a bouquet of flowers. He repeated that I'd get an annulment over his dead body and asked how I was doing all on my own, since it was apparent that the damned pilot had disappeared.

Julián hadn't vanished, as Fabian supposed. He came to see me when his work allowed, and each new encounter added a link to the chain that bound me to him with little effort on his part. After the war he had worked for a time as a commercial pilot, until he was able to buy his own seaplane and make a living transporting passengers and goods to places where there were no runways. He flew his picturesque yellow plane all around South America on private contracts. Back then, the south was known as a paradise for fishing and birdwatching, so he had plenty of clients. I counted the hours and minutes until we could be together, and marked his absences on a calendar each time he bid me farewell.

I think that my blind innocence confused Julián; he couldn't seem to pull away from me as he had undoubtedly planned. He found himself trapped in the spider's web of a love that did not match his adventurous lifestyle. I held on to him with the desperation of an orphan, and I refused to acknowledge the mountain of obstacles that lay ahead, but the thing that ultimately wore down his resistance was the arrival of Juan Martín.

IN ONE OF OUR private conversations, José Antonio asked me if I planned to be Julián Bravo's lover to the end of my days. No, of course that wasn't my plan. I planned to be his wife as soon as I could convince my stubborn legitimate husband to let me. I was so certain I'd be able to marry Julián soon that I wasn't very careful as we frolicked in bed. We took certain measures, but not always; sometimes we used a condom and sometimes we forgot or were in too much of a hurry. I had the idea, without much basis, that I was sterile and that's why I hadn't had children in my marriage. The logical consequence of so much carelessness took me by surprise.

Julián found out I was pregnant during one of his visits, and the first thing he asked was whether it was Fabian's.

"How could it be? I haven't even seen him in five months," I answered, offended.

Red with rage, he paced around the room accusing me of having done it on purpose, saying that if I was trying to use this to trap him I was sadly mistaken, that he would never give up his freedom. He went on and on, until he noticed me curled in a chair, crying, terrified.

He seemed to snap out of a trance; his anger quickly faded and he fell to his knees beside me, murmuring apologies, begging for my forgiveness, saying it was a shock but it was as much his fault as mine and that we could decide together how to solve the problem.

"It's not a problem, Julián, it's our baby," I responded.

That shut him up. A little while later, once we'd both calmed down, Julián poured himself a glass of whiskey and confessed that in his thirty-something years of amorous adventures across four continents he'd never been faced with the prospect of becoming a father.

"So you thought you were sterile too," I said, and

we both started laughing, relieved and excited to welcome the tiny creature bobbing around inside my belly.

I THOUGHT THAT FABIAN would give in when he heard the news. Why would he stay married to a woman who was pregnant with another man's child? I asked him to meet me at a pastry shop in Sacramento so we could come to an agreement. I was nervous, mentally preparing for a fight, but he disarmed me from the outset by taking both my hands and kissing me on the forehead. He was happy to see me, he said, he'd missed me a lot. We made small talk as they served our tea, catching up on family news, and I told him about Aunt Pía, who was having stomach pains and feeling weak. Since Yaima's rituals and remedies had proven useless, Aunt Pilar was going to bring her to the Sacramento hospital for a checkup. An uncomfortable silence followed, and I took the opportunity to tell him about my condition, blurting it out with my face hidden behind the teacup.

He jumped up, surprised, with a hopeful smile dancing in his eyes, but before he was able to get the question out I assured him that he was not the father.

"You're going to have an illegitimate child," he spat, falling back onto his chair.

"That depends on you, Fabian."

"Don't count on the annulment. You know how I feel about it."

"This isn't a matter of principles, it's just cruel. You want to hurt me. It's fine, I won't ask you again. But you have to give me half of our assets, even though I should get everything. I supported you our entire marriage and I earned every penny in that savings account myself so, rightfully, it belongs to me."

"Where did you get the idea that you had a right to take anything when you decided to abandon our home?"

"I'm going to fight you for it, Fabian, even if I have to go to court."

"Ask your brother how that's going to turn out for you. Isn't he a lawyer? The bank accounts are in my name, just like the house and everything else we own. I'm not trying to hurt you, as you claim, but to protect you, Violeta."

"From what?"

"From yourself. You're not in your right mind. I'm your husband and I love you with all my heart and soul. I'll always love you. I can forgive you anything, Violeta. It's not too late to reconcile . . ."

"I'm pregnant!"

"It doesn't matter, I'm willing to raise your child as if it were my own. Let me help you. I'm begging you . . ."

I didn't see Fabian again until a year and a half later. José Antonio confirmed that I couldn't take the money I thought I had the right to; any amount

I'd be able to get would depend entirely on my husband's goodwill. I spent the following months going between my brother's apartment and the office, without seeing anyone except the Rustic Homes clients. I gave my aunts, the Rivases, and Josephine and Teresa the news by phone. Everyone congratulated me, except my aunts, who had suffered greatly when I left Fabian, and for whom the pregnancy out of wedlock was another heavy blow. Their only consolation was that we were far from the family and gossip in the capital.

"Dear God, child, we've never had a bastard among us," Aunt Pía sobbed.

"There are probably dozens of them, Auntie, but they belong to the men of the family, so nobody even keeps count," I explained.

When my belly started to show, I kept out of sight to avoid running into Fabian's family or any friends we still had in common.

MY SON WAS BORN in the Sacramento hospital the same day that Aunt Pía went in for a series of tests; I had my two beloved aunts with me, as well as José Antonio, who had to pretend to be my husband. Miss Taylor and Teresa didn't come because women's right to vote in presidential and parliamentary elections had just been won. Teresa had spent years fighting for this cause, and the victory found her in jail for disturbing the peace and inciting riot.

She was released that very week and got to celebrate the women's vote by dancing down the street.

Julián was in Uruguay and he found out a week later, after the baby had already been baptized and entered into the civil registration under the name Juan Martín Bravo Del Valle. I named him Juan in honor of Father Quiroga, so he'd be protected all his life, and Martín because I'd always liked that name.

That little boy transformed Julián; he hadn't suspected that he'd reached the age where he was ready to raise a child. His son represented continuity, the opportunity to live life all over again through that boy, to give him the opportunities he'd missed, to create a more complete version of himself. Julián wanted to raise Juan Martín to be an extension of himself: bold, brave, adventurous, a lover of life, and a free spirit. But he wanted Juan Martín to have a more serene heart. Julián had spent his entire life chasing happiness, but it always seemed to slip through his fingers at the last minute, when he thought he had it just within his grasp. The same thing happened with his projects, something more interesting always appearing right out of reach. Nothing was ever enough for him, not his decorations as a war hero or his horseback riding trophies, not his flying machine, nor his success in everything he did, not his smooth tenor voice or his talent for being the center of attention wherever he went. That constant search for something better applied to love and affection as well. He didn't have any family, cast off friends once they no longer served his needs, collected women then left them as soon as someone more attractive crossed his path. Julián wished for his son to avoid suffering the same perennial dissatisfaction.

We moved to a small house in an old neighborhood of Sacramento, with century-old trees and wild roses that grew by work of magic from the cracks in the sidewalks even in winter despite the perpetual rain and fog. Julián began to select clients based on geographic location, so that his absences were brief and he could have more time with his son.

We began living together like a normal family and Julián recruited me to help manage his small aerial transport company in a more organized way. As he admitted, laughing, he couldn't add as much as two plus two. We kept two separate books, an official one and another only we knew about. In the first, which the internal revenue service, and sometimes the police, would ask to see, we wrote down the details of every flight: date, destination, distance, passengers or cargo; in the second we kept the true identity of every person. Many were Jewish Holocaust survivors, rejected by almost every Latin American country, who entered clandestinely to start new lives with the help of sympathetic organizations or through bribes. After the war the country had accepted hundreds of German immigrants, taken in by the local Nazi party, which was forced to change its name but not its ideology after Germany's defeat.

From time to time, a criminal accused of wartime atrocities would come over, fleeing justice in Europe, and for the right price Julián would bring them into the country. Jews or Nazis, it was all the same to Julián, as long as they were paying.

AUNT PILAR RETURNED TO Santa Clara, where the summer chores awaited her, but Aunt Pía had to stay on with us to receive cancer treatment at the hospital. As soon as she held Juan Martín in her arms for the first time, she forgot all about his illegitimacy and began gleefully spoiling him. That would be her consolation for the eleven months she had left in this world. She'd sit in bed or on the sofa with the baby on her lap, singing softly to put him to sleep, and it soothed her pain more than the doctor's pills, she claimed.

I had been assured that, as long as I was still nursing Juan Martín, I'd be safeguarded against another pregnancy, but it turned out to be another of the lies peddled to women at that time. Luckily Julián, softened by the influence of his son, reacted without a huge scene, but he made it perfectly clear that this would be the last child. He didn't plan on filling the house with little brats, since just one had him trapped and tied down with responsibilities, and he had already lost enough freedom, he said.

In reality, Julián was just as free as he'd ever been; I never complained about his trips, and as far as being trapped by responsibilities, he was exaggerating, because he contributed very little to the running of the household. He came and went with the friendly ease of a close relative. He wouldn't hesitate to buy the newest model camera or a piece of jewelry for me, but he never paid the power or water bill. I took care of our expenses, just as I'd done in my marriage, without being bothered by it, because I earned enough, but Fabian had taught me a lesson that I'd never forget: It's not enough to simply make money, you have to know how to keep it. This idea, which now seems so obvious, was a novelty in my youth. It was taken as a given that a woman would always be supported by a man, first her father and then her husband, and in a case where she had her own means, whether inherited or acquired, she needed a man to manage her assets. It was unladylike to talk about money, or to earn it, much less invest it. I never told Julián how much I made or spent. I had my own savings and closed business deals without consulting him. The fact that we weren't married afforded me an independence that would've been impossible otherwise. A married woman couldn't open a bank account without the consent and signature of her husband, who in my case was Fabian, but to skirt that obstacle my accounts were registered in José Antonio's name.

12

....

Aunt Pía died at my house, peacefully and with almost no pain thanks to a miraculous plant provided by Yaima, the indigenous healer. Torito had already been growing it on the farm, because it was useful for alleviating all types of pain, and we followed Yaima's instructions, combining the seeds and leaves to make a more potent version. Facunda used it to make cookies, which they sent to me by train. Toward the end, when the poor woman couldn't eat, Torito prepared drops that I placed under her tongue. In her final days, Aunt Pía slept almost all the time, and in her sporadic moments of consciousness she asked to see Juan Martín. She didn't recognize anyone, except the baby.

"You're going to have a little sister," she whispered to him before she died.

That's how I found out that the baby was a girl and began to think up names.

We buried Aunt Pía in the tiny Nahuel cemetery, according to her final wishes, and not in her family's crypt in the capital, where she'd be among dead people she no longer remembered. The entire town turned out that morning to pay their respects, just as they'd all come to my wedding, and an Indian delegation headed by Yaima sang a tribute to her with drums and flutes. It was a brilliant day, the air smelled of acacia flowers, the sky was free of clouds, and a veil of mist hovered above the damp earth, warmed by the sun.

There, beside the freshly dug hole ready to receive my aunt's coffin, I saw Fabian, wearing his formal suit and black tie, blonder and more solemn than ever, as if the time apart had aged him.

"I loved your aunt a lot; she always treated me kindly," he said, handing me one of his handkerchiefs, because mine was soaked.

Aunt Pilar, the Rivases, and even Torito and Facunda hugged him with so much affection that I took it as a reproach: Fabian was part of the family and I had betrayed him. Afterwards they invited him for lunch at Santa Clara, where Facunda prepared one of her specialties: potato pie with meat and cheese.

"I see that man isn't with you," Fabian commented when we were away from the group.

I explained that Julián was flying a passenger to the archipelago, an excuse that was only half-true, because in reality Julián hadn't been readily accepted by my family. Aunt Pilar had planted the idea that he was a womanizer and gambler, who seduced me with lies and destroyed my life, my marriage, and my reputation; that he had gotten me pregnant and practically abandoned me.

Viewed from the outside, it all looked to be true, but nothing is as simple as it seems. No one knows what really goes on within a couple's inner sanctum or why someone might put up with things that others deem inexcusable. Julián was a spellbinding man. I've never met anyone who compared to him, no one with such an ability to captivate others, like a powerful magnet. Men imitated him or tried to challenge him, women fluttered around him like moths to a flame. He was lively, intelligent, a great storyteller and comedian. He exaggerated and lied, but that was all part of his charm and no one called him out on it. He had irresistible means of seduction, like serenading me from the street in his operatic voice to apologize after a fight. I always admired him, in spite of his tremendous defects.

I was proud that Julián had chosen me; it was proof that I was special. Ever since Juan Martín had been born we'd introduced ourselves as man and wife and behaved as a couple in public, even though we were well aware that gossip brewed behind our backs. Just as José Antonio had warned me, I was rejected by certain circles: The wives of his friends wouldn't speak to me, and we lost a couple of clients who didn't want to work with me in the office; I didn't dare go to any of the country clubs because I could be denied entrance. Of course, no one in the German community, much less the Schmidt-Engler family, could stand me. The few times I crossed paths with them they looked me up and down with a disgusted expression, and I could swear that more than one of them called me a slut between gritted teeth.

Julián, on the other hand, went wherever he pleased; he was free of blame, while I was the adulteress, the concubine, the wayward woman who dared to parade around pregnant by her lover. If my aunts, who loved me dearly and had raised me, considered my conduct to be immoral, I could only imagine how harshly others must've judged me. "Don't worry, sooner or later Fabian is going to want to remarry and start his own family, then he'll come to offer you the annulment on a silver platter," Julián said.

His irresistible charm opened doors for us. He would start to recount one of his adventures or sing the romantic songs from his large repertoire and a circle would quickly form around him. I found other women's attraction to him flattering, because I was the one he'd chosen. Julián and I were happy, up until the second pregnancy.

. . .

ALL THROUGH MY PREGNANCY with my daughter, I still thought I was living an extraordinary love story, even though there were clear signs that Julián was already losing interest in me and unsatisfied with his life in general. He was openly disgusted by the havoc pregnancy wreaked on my body, but I imagined it was only temporary. He slept on the living room sofa, avoided touching me, reminded me often that he didn't want another baby, and blamed me for having trapped him again, without acknowledging the fact that he'd played as much of a part as I had.

I think it was only Juan Martín who kept him from leaving. The boy was not yet two years old and his father was already training him to become a man, as he said, which included chasing him around with the garden hose, locking him in dark places, making him do flips in the air until he vomited, or putting drops of hot sauce on his lips. "Men don't cry" was his motto. Juan Martín's toys were all plastic weapons. Torito gave him a bunny, which lasted only until his father returned from one of his trips and got rid of it.

"Men don't play with bunnies. If you want a pet we'll get you a dog."

I refused, because I didn't have the time or energy to take care of a dog.

I imagine that as I gained weight, he became

entangled with another woman, or several. He seemed bored and impatient; lost his temper easily; started fights with other men for the pleasure of hitting and being hit; bet on horses, car races, billiards, roulette, and any other game of chance he came across. But then he'd suddenly transform into the most tender and devoted of partners, he'd shower me with attention and gifts, play with Juan Martín like a doting father, the three of us going on picnics or swimming in the lake. Then my resentment would start to fade and I'd be unconditionally in love once again.

I learned the hard way not to get in the way of Julián's rage, except when I had to defend the boy. If I tried to warn him he was drinking too much or gambling more than he should, I received a battery of insults, or, in private, it might come to blows. He never hit me in the face and was careful not to leave marks. We faced off like gladiators, because my fury was greater than my fear of his fists. But I always ended up on the floor, with him begging for forgiveness and telling me that he didn't know what had happened—that I'd provoked him and made him lose his mind.

After every battle, in which I swore I'd leave him for good, we ended up in each other's arms. These ardent reconciliations lasted a little while, until he'd once again explode for no reason, as if his rage built up so much pressure he had to release it. But we could be happy between those terrible episodes, which didn't always lead to physical violence; in general, it was verbal abuse. Julián had a rare ability to find his opponent's most vulnerable spot. He hit me where it hurt most.

No one knew about our secret warring, not even José Antonio, whom I saw every day in the office. I was ashamed that I put up with Julián's abuse, and more ashamed still that I always forgave him. I was shackled by our sexual passion and the belief that I'd be lost without him. How would I provide for the kids? How would I face society and my family after a second failure? How would I live down a reputation as a woman cast aside? I'd broken my marriage and defied the world to be with Julián; I couldn't accept that the story I'd told was a lie.

TEN DAYS BEFORE MY due date, we learned that the baby was breech. I lamented once again that Aunt Pía was no longer with us, because I'd seen her use her magic hands to turn a baby in its mother's belly, just like she'd do with calves to get them into birthing position. According to her, she could clearly see the child with the eyes of the soul, and could move it with a gentle massage, loving energy, and prayers to the Virgin Mary, universal mother. I went to the farm, and Uncle Bruno took me to see Yaima, but the healing woman had less skill than Pía for a problem like that, and after a chanting and drum ceremony, squeezing my belly, and giving me an herbal tea, nothing had changed. The doctor scheduled me for a Cesarean to avoid unnecessary complications.

Julián and I had just had one of our monumental fights, which often lasted more than a week. While he was off in the capital picking up a group of engineers who were planning to build a dam, a young woman came by the house looking for him, introducing herself as his girlfriend. I can only imagine how that poor girl must've felt when she saw me, bags under my eyes, face smudged with baby food, balancing a belly the size of a watermelon over swollen legs, claiming to be Julián's wife. I felt so sorry for her and for myself that I invited her in, offered her lemonade, and we cried together.

"He said that our love was unstoppable," she blubbered.

"He said the same thing to me when we met," I informed her.

Julián had assured her that he was single, that he'd never been married, that he'd been waiting for her all his life.

I'll never know exactly what happened between the two of them. The days until Julián returned were a roller coaster of opposing emotions. I wanted to go somewhere far away, so I'd never have to see him again—make up a new identity in another country—but I couldn't even dream of it. I was about to give birth and would soon have a two-year-old child clinging to my skirt and a newborn baby in my arms. No. I shouldn't be the one to give up my home. I should kick him out, let him go off with this latest girlfriend, to disappear from my life and from our children's lives.

Three days later, Julián turned up with a tin tank for Juan Martín and a lapis lazuli necklace for me. By that time my tears had dried up and my sorrow had been replaced by a hyena's fury; I started screaming and clawing at his face. Once he was able to calm me down, he unleashed one of his long meandering arguments, bending reality to his cruel logic, clouding my ability to reason.

"What right do you have to be jealous, Violeta? What more do you want from me? I fell in love with you the first moment I saw you. You're the only woman who could've tied me down, the only one I ever wanted as my wife."

"That great love sure didn't last very long!"

"Because you've changed, you're not even a shadow of the girl I met."

"Time has taken its toll on you too."

"I'm the same as I ever was. But the only thing that matters to you is your work, your businesses, and making money, as if I were incapable of supporting my own family."

"You're welcome to start whenever you like."

"Have you ever given me the chance?" he shouted. "You respect your brother more than me! I stay with you because you're the mother of my child, even though you're not the partner or the lover I want anymore. You let yourself get fat, you were deformed by the first pregnancy and I don't even want to think about the disaster of this second one. You've lost your looks, your femininity, and your youth."

"I'm only thirty years old!"

"You look fifty. You're past your prime. With your appearance and your attitude, not even the most desperate man would go to bed with you. I feel sorry for you. I understand this is the price of motherhood. Nature is cruel to women, but it is also ruthless with men, who have to satisfy their needs."

"The kids belong to both of us, Julián. Neither you nor I have the right to be unfaithful."

"I can't live like a monk. The world is full of attractive young women. I know you've seen the way they chase me. I'd have to be impotent to resist."

And he went on like that until I was too exhausted to think straight. Then, when he saw I'd been utterly defeated, he gathered me lovingly in his arms and started rocking me like a baby, consoling me with the promise that we could start over with a clean slate. It wasn't too late to revive our love as long as I did my part and promised him we wouldn't have any more kids and went on a diet to recover my figure. He would help me, we'd do it together, then he'd make Fabian give me an annulment, even if he had to fight him for it, and we'd get married, he said.

And that's how I agreed to be sterilized.

• • •

JULIÁN DECIDED THAT WE should take advantage of the C-section to have my tubes tied. If he'd been my husband, the doctor might have done it without even asking me, but since he wasn't they had to get my consent. I agreed because it was one of Julián's conditions for staying with me, and anyway I thought that two kids was enough, never imagining the immense resentment I'd feel toward him for making me do it.

When Miss Taylor learned what had happened, she asked why he hadn't had a vasectomy if he didn't want to bring any more children into the world. She was ahead of her time. I'd never have dared to propose that solution to Julián; at that time it was considered a punishment reserved for criminals and an affront to masculinity. The threat to my life was of minor importance.

The day my daughter was born the volcano was smoking and covered entirely in snow. Still woozy from the anesthesia, I watched it from the window of my hospital room, majestic with its plume of smoke, blanketed in white under a sapphire sky, and I decided that the girl would be called Nieves. It wasn't one of the names I'd picked out beforehand. Julián agreed to humor me, even though he'd wanted to use his mother's name, Leonora, but that reminded me of one of the Rivases' cows.

The operation didn't go as smoothly as hoped; I got an infection that left me in bed for two weeks, and the wound took a long time to heal, leaving a raised red scar like a carrot on my belly. Julián went out of his way to take care of me; maybe he loved me more than I thought, or maybe he was just terrified at the prospect of being left alone with two kids.

Josephine Taylor got leave from work to come down and take care of me as well for the first month, and we brought each other up to speed on our lives. She told me how Teresa always kept a bag packed with clothes and toiletries in case she was arrested, something that happened often due to her activism and sympathy with the Communist Party, which operated in secret. The police tolerated her as a harmless madwoman, and the other inmates welcomed her like a heroine. The judges, tired of seeing her, would release her after a few days with the useless recommendation that she should learn to behave like a decent woman. Teresa had a surplus of causes to support, after having fought for years with the women's suffrage movement. There was still a lot to be done, Miss Taylor said, listing off a long string of women's rights that I'd never even considered. In a few months women would be able to vote for the first time in the presidential election, and Teresa was going door-to-door explaining the process, because nothing would change if we didn't exercise our hard-won right. I still hadn't even registered to vote.

Miss Taylor was now matronly and overweight, dressed like a missionary, with gray hair and skin covered in fine lines and tiny red veins, but she had the same round blue eyes and retained her youthful vivaciousness. José Antonio stopped by daily, with the pretext of checking up on me, but he was truly there to see the only love he'd known in his life. He'd aged prematurely due to his solitary ways. When I saw him so happy, drinking tea and playing dominoes with Miss Taylor, just like in the old days at Camellia House, I was tempted to make an offering to Father Quiroga so that Miss Taylor would finally accept my brother's marriage proposal. But I could never do that to Teresa Rivas.

BY AGE EIGHT IT was clear that Juan Martín did not physically resemble his father, and had not inherited his temperament either; he was a calm child who could entertain himself for hours on end, while also being a good student, cautious and fearful. He was terrified by the roughhousing his father thought would make a man of him; he had nightmares, asthma, and was allergic to pollen, dust, feathers, and nuts, but he had a precocious intelligence and a charmingly sweet personality.

Julián asked for more than the child could give, and didn't hide his frustration with him. "How long are you going to coddle the boy, Violeta! You're raising him to be a fag," he shouted right in front of Juan Martín. He was obsessively concerned with the topic. He saw troubling signs of possible homosexuality; his son read too much, played with the girls at school, wore his hair long. He forced the boy to drink wine, so he would learn to hold his liquor and never be a drunk; to bet his allowance on games of poker, in order to teach him how to win and lose with dignity; to play soccer, which the child had zero talent for. He took him hunting or to boxing matches, and he became furious if Juan Martín cried over the injured animal or covered his eyes at the brutality of the spectacle. My son grew up with the impossible aspiration of obtaining his father's approval, knowing full well that nothing he did would ever be enough. "You should learn from your sister," Julián would urge him. Nieves had all the qualities he desired for his son.

From the moment she first poked her head into the world, Nieves was beautiful. She was born with her eyes wide open, screaming, complaining, and hungry. By age one she had given up diapers and waddled around the house like a duck, opening drawers, swallowing insects, and charging at the walls. At age six she could gallop a horse and dive headfirst from the highest diving board at the club swimming pool. She had her father's fearlessness and adventurous spirit. She was so pretty that strangers would stop on the street to admire her. She was so persuasive that my brother begged us not to leave her with him because Nieves could convince him to give her anything, like the time she wanted José Antonio's gold tooth and he had the dentist make one to hang on a chain for her. She sang with a deep, sensual voice and Julián taught her his repertoire so that they could perform duets of colorful sailor's songs, inappropriate for her age. She grew up spoiled and selfish. I tried to impose some discipline, but my attempts were undone by Julián; she always got whatever she wanted, and I was the one reprimanded. I didn't have any authority with my kids. Juan Martín didn't need it, but it would've been good for Nieves.

JUST TO SHOW JULIÁN, and not out of love, after Nieves was born I imposed a Spartan discipline on myself to recover something of my previous figure, which according to him had been my only redeeming quality. I wanted to prove that he had been wrong about me, that I had my body and my life under control. I ate only leaves, like a donkey; I hired a soccer coach to submit me to the same rigorous exercise routine as his players; and I updated my wardrobe to be more in line with the latest fashions introduced by Dior, with wide skirts and jackets cinched at the waist. The results, which came in no time, didn't do much to improve things between Julián and me, but did provide the means to make him jealous. This was fun for me, even though I had to put up with his angry outbursts. On one occasion he threw a plate of shrimp in tomato sauce at me because my black silk dress was too low-cut for his liking and I had refused to change. We were at a fundraising gala for a deaf school, where a reporter caught the scene with his camera, and we ended up in the paper, looking like lunatics.

We'd been together several years and people now accepted us as a couple; anyone who questioned our marital status did so out of Julián's earshot. We had prospered, we lived well and were welcomed in society, but we couldn't enroll Juan Martín and Nieves in the best schools, because those schools were Catholic. Despite everything we'd achieved, I lived with a constant knot in my stomach, perpetually frightened without really knowing why. According to Julián, I had nothing to worry about, I was merely spitting at the sky. What more did I want? I was never satisfied, I was a bottomless well.

We were lacking for nothing in material terms, that was certain, but I had the sensation of walking a tightrope, always worried I was about to fall and bring the kids down with me. Julián would disappear for weeks and return without warning, sometimes euphoric and loaded down with gifts, other times exhausted and depressed, never offering explanations for where he'd been or what he'd done. There was no talk of marriage, despite Teresa Rivas's promise that the right to divorce would soon be granted. Fabian still had no girlfriend to speak of, and I had no hopes of him serving an annulment up on a silver platter, as Julián had promised. Nevertheless, legalizing our union, something I'd been obsessed with for years, now mattered much less, because it was increasingly common for couples to separate and become involved with other people. Also, I understood at a visceral level that it was not in my best interest to bind myself legally to Julián. I had more power and freedom as a single woman.

My brother didn't seem to be in any hurry to marry either. "I bet he's a fag," said Julián, who could hardly stand José Antonio, since he was my source of income and my first line of protection against my partner's overbearing authority. His earnings as a pilot were so unpredictable that they seemed more like gambling profits. I, on the other hand, had a steady salary from Rustic Homes, which had grown like an octopus, with tentacles reaching across several provinces. Years prior I'd convinced José Antonio and Marko Kusanovic that, given our country's climate of stormy winters and dry summers, we should invest in insulated panels, like they used in other countries. I went to the United States, studied the prefab construction industry, and we applied the principles to Rustic Homes: a sandwich of fiberglass insulation between two MDF panels. What had started as basic wooden structures used for rural workers, communities of laborers, and beach vacations became the preferred prefabricated homes for young middle-class couples. They all bore our brand: white walls with bright blue doors, window frames, shutters, and a thatched roof.

• • •

IN THE LATE FIFTIES, Julián regularly went to Argentina on mysterious flights that he registered in the alternate account book under a code that only he understood, because they were classified military operations, he explained. This trick of the second set of books, which had been my father's ruin, would cause me great anxiety throughout my relationship with Julián. Juan Perón was moving from one country to another in exile from Argentina, and had been replaced by new rulers dedicated to erasing his legacy and putting an end to any form of opposition. I didn't need to crack the code to know that Julián's trips were related to corrupt money and secret government plots.

He also began piloting flights to Cuba and Miami, as frequent as the ones to Argentina, but these he discussed openly with me. His well-earned reputation as a daring pilot led to his employment by the Mafia. The criminal empire that had been operating in Cuba since the twenties now flourished under the auspices of Fulgencio Batista's dictatorship, controlling casinos, cabarets, brothels, hotels, and drug trafficking, and contributing significantly to government corruption. Julián ran liquor, drugs, and girls, and provided other highly compensated services. From time to time, however, he transported weapons that ended up, by clandestine means, in the hands of the rebels led by Fidel Castro, who were fighting to overthrow Batista.

"So, you're working for both sides. I don't even

want to think what they'll do to you if they find out," I warned him.

But he assured me that he wasn't at risk, that he knew full well what he was doing.

I went with him on one of his trips, where we were received like royalty in the newly inaugurated Hotel Riviera, hosted by a group of arrogant but welcoming men, who gave me piles of chips with which to entertain myself while Julián did his duties. I didn't know they were Mafia until several years later, when I recognized a photo of the famous gangster Lucky Luciano published on the day of his grandiose funeral in New York.

I spent those days in Havana losing at games of roulette, serenaded by the voice of Frank Sinatra in person, sunbathing by the hotel pool where pretty, flirtatious women paraded around in tiny bathing suits. I drank pink cocktails at the famous Tropicana Club and danced at the various nightclubs to the irresistible Afro-Cubano rhythms that had become popular everywhere, and I was regaled with the stories told by my new, short-lived friends. One of our hosts, who must've been high up in the criminal world, invited me to a party at the presidential palace, where Batista greeted me with a kiss on the hand, while military vehicles patrolled the streets outside. No one imagined that the island's perpetual orgy would soon come to an end.

. . .

SEEING THE ROLLS OF bills that Julián placed in the safe, since he couldn't deposit them in the bank without raising a red flag, I suggested that he buy another plane, reserved only for tourists and businessmen, and that he hire trustworthy pilots—a legitimate business, clean and profitable. I offered to finance half of the investment with my savings, as long as we registered the fifty-fifty partnership with a notary. He was furious that I didn't trust his word, but in the end agreed because the idea tempted him. Commercial aviation had to rely on existing airports, which you could count on the fingers of one hand, but seaplanes could land anywhere there was enough water.

That's how Seagull Air was born, and, in time, once we had several planes, the company connected the better part of the country. And I unwittingly fulfilled the dream my father had held since before my birth, of investing in aviation. I traveled often to the capital, where we'd opened an office, because in this country everything is centralized and anything that doesn't happen in the city doesn't exist. But Julián got bored with the company as soon as it was up and running, because it lacked excitement and offered little danger; routine flights were for other pilots, he was chasing more impressive exploits. The company's income went into the official books, and half of it was mine.

Over the years, Julián didn't lose any of his

astonishing energy, which allowed him to drink like a pirate, fly forty hours without sleeping, compete in equestrian competitions, and play several games of squash in a single morning. His bad moods did not improve either, as he exploded like a powder keg at the tiniest spark, but he did stop hitting me. I knew all his secrets and could do a lot of damage to his name.

"You'd better think twice, Violeta. If you leave me, I'll have to kill you," he once shouted at me.

"You'd better think twice too, Julián, because you're going to need more than threats to keep me," I shouted back at him.

We'd reached a vague truce, and I survived on anxiety medication and sleeping pills.

What was I afraid of? I was afraid of Julián's violent outbursts, our battles to the death, which the kids witnessed and caused Juan Martín to have asthma attacks and migraines. I was afraid of the way I fell time and again into his traps, accepting his messy apologies and forgiving him. I was afraid that his "missions" would lead him to prison or death; I was afraid that the authorities would discover our second set of books; I was afraid that his earnings came at the cost of blood; I was afraid of the suspicious men who called him at all hours of the night; and I was afraid that so much fraternizing with criminals had infected him with cruelty. Julián, on the other hand, was not afraid of anyone or anything. He'd been born under a lucky star, and he'd enjoyed impunity through all the many years of living on the edge. He was invincible.

ON NEW YEAR'S EVE 1958, Fulgencio Batista escaped with his closest collaborators on two planes carrying the hundred million dollars that would guarantee his golden exile. In the last days of the dictatorship, when it was clear that nothing would stop the revolutionaries, Julián Bravo made multiple trips to and from Miami transporting fugitives, money, and more than one member of the Mafia with their girlfriends. The revolutionaries quickly occupied the entire island of Cuba and set up a firing squad to execute political enemies as well as those who had gotten rich illegally during the dictatorship, determined to sweep away corruption. Sexual tourism came to an end and the Mafia abandoned their brothels and casinos; Cuba was no longer profitable.

Julián moved his home base to Miami, but I refused to abandon my job with Rustic Homes and Seagull Air, my brother, my friends, my house, and my lifestyle in Sacramento, to go live in a hotel like a tourist in a city where I didn't know anyone. If we'd gone, the kids and I would've been all alone, since Julián spent more time in the air than on land. We visited him regularly, and during those trips he lavished us with attention and gifts, until another mission forced him to once again say goodbye or we had one of our legendary fights, followed by an indecent reconciliation. On one occasion, when I asked Juan Martín what he wanted for his birthday, he whispered in my ear, "For you to leave Dad for good." He'd have to ask me several more times.

13

THE 1960 EARTHQUAKE CAUGHT ME OFF guard. I was with both of my children at Santa Clara—the Rivas farm was still my refuge, my favorite place for summer vacation and relaxation, far from Julián, who never joined us on those trips. Of the old inhabitants the only ones left were Aunt Pilar, Torito, and Facunda. The Rivases had died a few years prior and we missed them terribly. On their own initiative, the inhabitants of Nahuel installed a bronze plaque in their honor at the train station. You should go see it, Camilo, it must still be there, although there are no more trains; everyone travels by bus now.

The farm belonged to Teresa, the only heir because her brother, Roberto, ceded his inheritance, but since she couldn't maintain it, I covered the expenses.

We rented both of the fields to the Moreau family, who had planted vineyards; there was only one cow left, the horses and mules had been replaced by bicycles and a truck, and the pigsty was reduced to a single pig, which Torito cared for like a daughter, since her piglets were his only source of income. We still had chickens, dogs, and cats. Facunda had a modern gas stove and two brick ovens to make her cakes and empanadas, which she sold in Nahuel and other nearby towns.

I never met the husband Facunda claimed to have. In fact, since no one had ever seen him, we thought she'd made him up. Her two daughters lived with their grandparents while she worked until they were old enough to go off on their own. One of them, Narcisa, had three babies in five years, each so different that it was obvious they didn't share the same father. "That girl turned out with loose legs," Facunda sighed as she described the parade of men who filed through the girl's life.

When Uncle Bruno died and the house was left mostly empty, Facunda brought Narcisa and the babies to live there, so she could raise her daughter's kids just as her parents had raised hers. Torito stood in for the fathers that those children didn't have, even though he was old enough to be their grandfather. He must've been around fifty-five, but his age was only noticeable in the teeth he'd lost and his hunched way of walking. He continued taking his long trips to "get acquainted" and by that point I think he must've had a detailed map of the province and beyond etched in his memory.

Facunda mourned the loss of Uncle Bruno as if she were his mother, and I grieved for him like a daughter. The man had adopted me in heart and soul as soon as I arrived at the farm in the time of our Exile, and he showed me unconditional love, just as Torito had. Every Saturday, Facunda took flowers to his grave beside Aunt Pía's, and that's where I'd like you to bury me, Camilo. I don't want to be burned up and have my ashes thrown around everywhere. I'd prefer to let my bones fertilize the soil. Did you know that these days you can bury a body in a biodegradable coffin or wrapped in a blanket? I like that idea; I bet it's cheap.

Aunt Pilar was broken by Uncle Bruno's death. She said they'd become like twin brother and sister, but I prefer to think they were lovers. When I tried to get the full story out of Facunda and Torito, they responded with evasive comments that confirmed my suspicions. Cheers to them. Aunt Pilar seemed older than her seventy-seven years, she walked with a cane because her knees hurt, and she was no longer interested in people, animals, or the land. That woman, who had once been so vivacious and optimistic, turned inward. She spent hours in silence, with her hands idle, staring off into space. More than once I caught her talking to Uncle Bruno. When I suggested that we install a phone at Santa

Clara, she responded, with great conviction, that if the apparatus couldn't communicate with the dead, it was of no damn use to her.

That summer Teresa and Miss Taylor arrived with several trunks and a caged parrot to stay for a while and get some fresh air, they said. The truth was that Teresa had been placed in solitary confinement for her actions in support of the Communist Party, and eighteen months locked in a cell had wrecked her health. She was skinny and gray, with a consumptive cough and dizzy spells that left her disoriented. We went to meet them at the station and Torito had to carry her off the train because the long trip had completely drained her. They'd refused to let me fly them down on one of Seagull Air's seaplanes, as I'd offered.

That night, after the welcome feast Facunda prepared for them, Miss Taylor confessed through tears that Teresa was slowly dying. She had advanced lung cancer.

FOR MY SON, THE weeks we spent each year at Santa Clara were paradise. He seemed miraculously cured of his allergies and asthma and spent his days outside with Torito, who taught him how to drive the truck and take care of the piglets. We'd lose him for hours to his books, lying on the floor of the Birdcage, which was still standing with its sign on the door prohibiting entrance to persons of both sexes. "Leave me here at Santa Clara, Mom," Juan Martín begged me every year, and I silently filled in the rest of the sentence, "far away from my dad." In adolescence Juan Martín gave up trying to please Julián, and the uneasy admiration he'd had for him in childhood transformed into dread. He was scared of his father.

Nieves, on the other hand, hated the farm. On one occasion she complained to Julián that Aunt Pilar was a mean old lady and Torito was a big retard, which elicited a guffaw from her father. I tried to send her to her room for being so disrespectful, but her father stopped me, saying the girl was right: Pilar was a witch and Torito was an idiot. But despite her impertinence and cynicism, my daughter had many admirable qualities. When I think of her now, I see a bird with colorful feathers and a raspy voice, happy, graceful, ready to take flight and leave everything behind, untethered.

Her mettle was proven the day of the earthquake, the strongest that had ever been registered. It lasted ten minutes, destroyed two provinces, caused tsunamis that reached all the way to Hawaii, stranded a fishing boat in the main square of Sacramento, and left thousands of victims. It was a tragedy, even in this country, where we're used to shaking ground and raging seas. The old house at Santa Clara wobbled for a good while before it collapsed, allowing enough time to escape with the parrot's cage through a dense cloud of dust, as beams and chunks of wall thundered down all around us and the guts of the planet let out a tremendous roar.

A huge crack opened up in the ground, swallowing several chickens, as the dogs howled. We couldn't stand, everything was spinning, the world was turned upside down. The quake continued for what seemed like an eternity, and just when we thought it was finally over a strong aftershock followed. And then we heard the boom and saw the flames. The gas stove had exploded and the house was on fire.

In the midst of that chaos, smoke, and terror, Nieves realized that Teresa wasn't with us. We didn't notice the girl running toward the flaming house; if we had seen her we would have stopped her. I don't know exactly how things happened, just that a few minutes later we heard her calling for Torito. We couldn't figure out where her cries were coming from; no one imagined she could've gone into the burning house. Suddenly we saw my daughter emerge from the smoke and dust, struggling to drag Teresa along by her clothes. Torito was the first to reach them. He lifted Teresa's inert body with one arm and Nieves with the other, and he used his gigantic force, multiplied by adrenaline, to move them safely away from the fire. Nieves was ten years old.

That day and night, which we spent outside, shivering with cold and fear, I got the true measure of my daughter's character. She'd inherited it from her father; she had his same heroic nature. She didn't remember exactly how she'd done it and answered our questions with a shrug of her shoulders, not giving it much importance. All we could determine was that she'd crawled through the ruins, dodging flaming obstacles, crossed what remained of the living room to the wicker chair where she'd seen Teresa moments before the earthquake. Teresa had been asphyxiated by smoke, unconscious. Nieves managed to crawl back through that hellscape dragging a weight much greater than her own, on hands and knees because, as she said, she could breathe better along the floor. Teresa's lungs, weakened by the cancer, could not survive the smoke inhalation and she died a few hours later in the arms of her life partner, Miss Taylor.

Nieves had second-degree burns on her back and legs and her hair was singed, but her face was unharmed and she had no emotional trauma. The earthquake that made history was to her just a curious incident she could tell her father about. The highway was blocked and the railroads were twisted, making it impossible to reach the nearest hospital, so we took her to see Yaima that very day.

The thatched huts had been razed to the ground as if a terrible wind had blown through and the air was thick with straw and dust, but no one in the indigenous community had been injured; the people were calmly gathering their scant belongings and herding the terrified sheep and horses. Mother

Earth and the Great Serpent who inhabits the volcanoes had become angry with the men and women, but the Primordial Spirit would restore order. It had to be invoked. Yaima put off her preparations for the ceremony to treat Nieves with a brief ritual and some miraculous unguents.

AFTER TERESA'S DEATH, MISS Taylor bid us farewell and returned to Ireland, where she hadn't set foot in nearly four decades. She hoped to find her brothers and sisters who had been dispersed in childhood, but she gave up after only one week. That country was no longer her home, and we were the only family she had left, as she told José Antonio via telegram. My brother responded with a single sentence: "Wait there, I'm coming to get you."

He brought her back on a transatlantic ship that took twenty-nine days from port to port, enough time to convince her that she'd made a mistake in systematically rejecting him, but that there was still time to remedy the situation, and he presented her with the garnet-and-diamond ring he'd saved since forever. She told him she was too old and sad to marry, but she accepted the ring and put it in her purse.

José Antonio was a very private man and he would never have given me the details of that trip, but I found out from Miss Taylor that they'd agreed to have a "white marriage." When she saw from my expression that I was unfamiliar with the term, she explained that it was a platonic bond, like a good friendship. And yet, their plan to leave the union unconsummated was abandoned by the time they'd reached Panama. José Antonio was fifty-seven and she, sixty-two. They lived together for over twenty years, the happiest time of my brother's life.

Torito and Facunda took care of Aunt Pilar at Santa Clara for the last two years of her life. She slowly shut down one day at a time without any visible ailment, simply losing interest in the human and the divine alike. She'd prayed thousands of rosaries and novenas over her lifetime, but just when she could use the support of her faith the most, she stopped believing in God and heaven. "All I want is to close my eyes and stop existing, to dissolve into the void, like the fog at dawn," she wrote in a farewell letter that she gave to Facunda. It has been many years since then, Camilo, but the memory of my aunts still makes me cry; those women were my fairy godmothers throughout my entire childhood.

Miss Taylor had inherited the Santa Clara farm from Teresa and decided it wasn't worth selling, even though she received a good offer from the Moreaus, who after evicting several indigenous families from their homes had gradually swallowed up the surrounding lands to expand their property. José Antonio replaced the burned-down house with the best Rustic Homes had to offer, and I continued to cover the expenses, which were minimal. Torito had been there the better part of his life, it was his world, and he couldn't live anywhere else. I always made sure to spend a few weeks on the farm each year, no matter what I had going on in my life; and so I was able to remain rooted to that land.

THE PEOPLE IN THE area divided their lives into before and after the quake. They lost almost all their belongings and it took years to replace them, but no one ever considered moving away from the volcano and the geological fault line we sat atop. The fishing boat stayed in the middle of the main square in Sacramento as a reminder of humanity's impermanence and the uncertainty of the world. Thirty years later, covered in a patina of rust and corroded by time, it was photographed for a magazine as a historical monument.

José Antonio coined a phrase that I found too cynical to repeat, "When there's catastrophe, we buy property." But the reality was that we'd never had more demand for our prefabricated homes, since entire towns and cities had to be rebuilt from the ground up, and there was more land than ever available to construct our planned communities.

I began buying gold with my savings, because inflation in our country was soaring; the currency was so greatly devalued that Julián had the idea to buy chips from a local casino and take them to Las Vegas where they had identical ones he could exchange for dollars. He pulled this stunt a couple of times right under the Mafia's nose, but the third time he got scared—the risk of ending up stitched with bullets and tossed into the Mojave Desert was greater than the thrill of danger. In the meantime, the value of my gold increased, legally, in the darkness of the bank vault. The only one who knew I was on the road to becoming rich was my brother, who had the other key to my safe-deposit box.

Fabian Schmidt-Engler showed up one Sunday at José Antonio's house to consult with him as a lawyer on a confidential matter, he said. My brother, who'd always pitied the man for the misfortune of having married me, welcomed him in. A large agricultural community of German immigrants had settled in the area and they needed the services of a discreet lawyer, Fabian explained.

We'd heard disturbing rumors about Colonia Esperanza. People said it was under the command of a fugitive war criminal, that mysterious things happened there, and that it was like a prison, surrounded by barbed wire, no one allowed in or out. Fabian discounted the hearsay. He told my brother that he knew the colony's director and had been to the property several times as a vet. The immigrants lived peacefully, and worked hard, but they sometimes had trouble with the nosy local authorities.

José Antonio thought that the whole thing sounded suspicious and he politely turned the job down with the excuse that he was too busy with the construction company. As they were saying goodbye, my brother casually asked if he'd given any more thought to the subject of annulment.

"There's nothing to think about," Fabian responded.

Nevertheless, a few years later, my husband showed up at the Rustic Homes office to sell me the annulment because he needed money to finance a lab. Someone had discovered a way to freeze semen for an indefinite period of time, and that opened up incalculable possibilities in the world of animal and human genetics. José Antonio negotiated the price, drew up a contract, gave Fabian half the money up front, and deposited the rest after a judge had signed the annulment. A portion of my gold coins went to that cause. Just when I'd least expected it, I was suddenly a single woman.

PART THREE

ABSENCE

(1960–1983)

14

LOOKING BACK, I REALIZE THAT I LOST Nieves well before I thought I did. My daughter was fourteen when Julián decided that instead of our annual trip to Santa Clara she'd spend her vacation time with him, just the two of them, like a father-daughter honeymoon. Julián had lost all hope of turning Juan Martín into "a man," which is to say a man like him. His son was an awkward and idealistic teenager who seemed more interested in reading Albert Camus and Franz Kafka than the **Playboy** magazines his father brought him from Miami. Juan Martín spent his time discussing Marxism and imperialism with a handful of similarly tormented boys instead of making out with one of his sister's friends in a dark corner.

Over the following years, Julián took Nieves on trips and taught her to drive a car and copilot an airplane. When he caught her smoking and drinking the dregs of cocktail glasses, he began to supply her with menthol cigarettes and instructed her in the art of drinking in moderation, something he himself rarely practiced. Very soon Nieves was dressing in provocative clothing and wearing makeup like a model to go out with her father to nightclubs and casinos, where they placed bets at the tables without anyone suspecting her age; their big joke was that people thought she was Julián's latest conquest. The burns she'd suffered at age ten had left only faint scars, thanks, I suppose, to Yaima's treatment. Her beauty, according to Julián, stopped traffic. By eighteen she was singing for tips at hotels and casinos. Julián delighted in showing off his daughter at a prudent distance, but he ran off any young suitor who came near her.

"I'm never going to get a boyfriend if you keep this up, Dad," Nieves would complain.

"At your age, the last thing you need is a boyfriend. That'll happen over my dead body," he responded. He was as jealous as a lover.

In the meantime, I lived here in our country with Juan Martín, who was studying philosophy and history. In his father's eyes this was a waste of time, completely pointless. Since his university was in the capital, I rented an apartment that we shared, but we seldom saw each other; I had one foot in Sacramento and flew regularly to the United States to see Nieves. My son spent long periods of time alone.

By the time the annulment of my first marriage finally came through, I no longer cared about it. I'd become well aware of the advantages my situation offered; I had my freedom for all intents and purposes, and to satisfy the demands of desire I could turn to that impetuous man who after all those years of shared routines, unwilling collusion, and accumulated resentment, could still seduce me with a kiss. Lust can hold us hostage for so long! It was never so humiliating as in my middle age, when the woman in the mirror showed her fifty years of struggle and exhaustion, body and soul. For Julián, on the other hand, age was a choice; he decided he would remain thirty years old forever, and he almost managed it. He was an energetic, unworried, happy womanizer until an age when the rest of us were beginning to contemplate the inevitability of death. "All you regret in the end are the sins you didn't commit," he would say.

The time I spent with Julián was marked by anticipation and anguish. I'd prepare for those visits like a bride, eager for the moment we could finally be alone together, embrace with renewed enthusiasm, and make love with the wisdom of much practice. I'd sleep glued to his back breathing in his virile, healthy, vigorous smell, wake up flustered from the caresses and vivid dreams, then we'd share our first cup of coffee in the morning naked and walk down the street hand in hand, bringing each other up to speed on everything that had happened while we were apart. That's how it would be for a few days. Then the storm of jealousy would begin brewing. I'd take a look in the mirror, comparing myself to the young women my daughter's age, with whom he openly flirted. For his part, Julián criticized my independence, the time I spent away from him, the fortune I had hidden away to avoid sharing it. He accused me of being an ambitious woman; at the time those words were an insult. In truth, he always found a way to get his hands on some of my savings. A constant stream of money ran through his fingers, but he lived on credit and racked up debt.

I must confess, Camilo, that more than once I prayed to heaven that Julián Bravo would crash in one of his airplanes, and I even fantasized about murder in order to free myself of him. I wouldn't have been the first or the last woman to kill her lover because she couldn't stand him anymore.

JULIÁN WAS SO INSISTENT we should live together again that I finally moved to Miami. I didn't do it to please him, but to be closer to Nieves, who'd dropped out of high school, slept all day long, disappeared every night, and never took my calls. She'd lost the little respect she had for me, and had polished to perfection the art of using her father to humiliate me. She adored him; I was the one who rained on her parade: old-fashioned, rigid, greedy, finicky, an old hag, as she called me to my face.

At that time Miami was full of exiled Cubans, some with a lot of money. There were as many yachts in the marinas as Cadillacs on the streets and the restaurants served the best food from the island; the air hummed with Latin music and conversations shouted in that accent of consonants that sound like vowels. The city was no longer the waiting room for death, crowded with old retirees, that it had been before.

Julián rented a remote villa near the sea, surrounded by a curtain of palm trees and a swimming pool with fountains and lights, which required a large staff to maintain. It was faux Mediterranean architecture: vast, sprawling, with terraces of hand-painted tiles, blue awnings, and plants wilting in the heat of their ceramic pots. The interior decorating was as pretentious as its pastel-pink exterior. Julián picked me up and carried me across the threshold like a bride the first time I saw the house, and took me on a tour, proud of the kitchen worthy of any hotel—though I don't cook, and neither did he—the six bathrooms with murals of mermaids and dolphins, the spacious rooms that smelled of mildew and disinfectant, and the turret containing a telescope to spy on the boats that anchored near the beach at night.

The villa became the center of Julián's business activities and his meetings with the people he called his "associates." Some of them looked like government men, in suits and ties despite the heat and humidity; others were Americans in short-sleeved shirts and hats, or Cubans in sandals and guayaberas. There was also a parade of guys with ostentatious rings who smoked cigars, spoke English with Italian accents, and were flanked by terrifying bodyguards—grotesque caricatures of gangsters.

"Be nice to them, they're my clients," Julián warned me when I asked who they were, but the house was large and I was able to avoid crossing paths with them.

After I'd spent only twenty-four hours living in that pink cake of a mansion, Julián set two cardboard boxes full of papers on the dining room table and asked me to help him sort the contents. That's when I realized that his interest in having me at his side was not sentimental but practical; I'd always been his business manager, secretary, and accountant. Everything was in those boxes, from unpaid bills, deeds, instructions, and schedules to handwritten notes not even he could decipher. In my attempt to organize that mess I discovered the true nature of his activities, most of them illegal, as I'd always suspected.

Heavy black suitcases full of cash regularly came and went. There were entire arsenals of weapons in the bedrooms, but Julián, who was never armed, explained that he was just storing it all for his friends. After a week, he abandoned his attempts at deception and told me all about the Cubans plotting against Fidel Castro and the revolutionaries, the

Mafia families who controlled crime in Florida and Nevada, and the CIA, whose goal was to impede the spread of leftist ideas in Latin America by any means necessary.

"There are guerrilla movements in almost all the countries on our continent. You must see that we can't allow another revolution like the one in Cuba," he explained.

"What do you have to do with it? What are you doing for the CIA?"

"I provide transportation sometimes, flights that no one can know about. I gather information from the Cubans and the contacts I have in other places . . . nothing important."

"Do they pay you?"

"Not a lot, but it comes with certain perks. The Americans let me do whatever else I want; they don't bother me."

"Juan Martín says that the CIA is using the Cold War as an excuse to topple democracies and support bloody dictatorships. There's so much injustice, inequality, and poverty, it's not surprising Communism is taking root in our countries."

"It's a shame, but it doesn't concern us. Juan Martín is being brainwashed in that nest of Commies."

"It's the Catholic university, Julián!"

"That may be, but your son is very impressionable."

"He's your son too."

"Are you sure? It doesn't always seem like it . . ."

And that's how our conversations rapidly devolved into fights; any mundane topic could lead to a brutal battle.

I HAVE FOND MEMORIES, for reasons I'll explain later, of Zoraida Abreu. At that time she was a beautiful young Puerto Rican woman, vivacious, who could've been easily mistaken for a pretty airhead. She dressed provocatively, and spoke in a childlike voice, but in reality she was as tough as an Amazon warrior. Julián fell in love with her on one of his trips and, as had happened with me, he couldn't seem to leave her. In my case it was because I got pregnant, in her case I'll never know, but I can imagine that the woman was more of a fighter than he was. Zoraida, who at seventeen had been crowned queen of a Boricua Rum beauty pageant, followed Julián when he moved to Miami. Julián hated all forms of attachment and kept her at arm's length. He lied and said that he was married to me and that divorce was illegal in his country. He also said that he adored his kids and would never abandon them.

She had the gall to invite me for a drink at the Fontainebleau Hotel. I couldn't resist. She was tall, striking, with thick hair that would've been enough to make two wigs, and she showed up dressed in tight capri pants, high-heeled sandals, and a blouse tied at the waist, accentuating her breasts. All the men in the room turned to look when she walked in, and more than one whistled, but despite looking like a streetwalker, she was not vulgar. We ordered a couple of cocktails and she proceeded to tell me straight out that she had been my husband's lover for four years and two months.

"I'm sorry, I just had to tell you because I can't live with lies."

"Do you want my permission? Go ahead, lady, he's all yours," I said. By then I'd finally reached the point at which I no longer cared about Julián's love affairs, and I knew I had no way of stopping him anyway.

"Julián told me you were only still together because you couldn't get a divorce, but that you don't love each other."

"We're not married. If he wants to marry you, he's free to do so."

We spent an hour in strange complicity. Zoraida recovered from her surprise and anger by the second drink, and decided she wasn't going to confront Julián with the truth she'd uncovered. She realized she'd only lose him, and the information could be useful if she waited for the right moment. It was in her interest to let him pretend to be married, which might keep potential rivals away, and it suited me to have him preoccupied by her.

"I'm not a whore—I don't want his money or anything else from him. I don't plan on blackmailing him either. I'm a nice Catholic girl," she explained with impeccable logic.

It was obvious that she didn't consider me a rival; I was harmless, a matronly woman dressed in a two-piece suit like Jacqueline Kennedy, already out of fashion since miniskirts were all the rage. I thought it would be cruel to point out that while we sat drinking martinis, he was probably with another woman. Zoraida believed that Julián would marry her sooner or later. She was twenty-six years old and very patient.

THE CIA CONCERNED ME much less than the gangsters with their black suitcases, the war arsenal we kept in the house, and the unmarked parcels that sometimes appeared at our doorstep. Julián ordered me not to touch them because they might explode. So they sat there, toasting in the sun, until Julián brought in a little man with a face like a rat to take care of the problem. The rat was a war veteran and bomb expert, who examined the package and then proceeded to open it with the delicacy of a surgeon. The first time it was a case of whiskey. The second, several pounds of prime beef—fillets, ribs, steaks—that had been packed in ice, but the long wait in the sun had turned them to a bloody rotting mess. They were gifts from grateful clients.

I once again felt a clenched fist in my stomach, something that always happened when I spent time with Julián. I asked myself what the hell I was doing in Miami.

That summer we were hit by one of those hurricanes that turn the world upside down. The house was on a rise, so we weren't worried about the waves; we simply boarded up the windows and barricaded the doors against the strong winds. It was a memorable experience; the advantage of a hurricane over an earthquake is that you know ahead of time that it's coming. The wind and water battered the house, pulled up several palm trees, and blew away anything that wasn't tied down. When the storm passed, we found a ping-pong table floating in our swimming pool; it belonged to someone who lived half a mile away. There was also a terrified dog on our second-floor terrace; the poor animal had been picked up and deposited there by the wind.

Two days later, as the ground began to dry, Julián realized that the septic tank had overflowed. He panicked and refused to call anyone to repair it, trying to unclog it himself, donning gloves and rubber boots, sinking up to his knees in repugnant muck, cursing at the top of his lungs. I soon understood why he couldn't ask for help. He pulled a filthy bag from the hole, dragged it to the kitchen, and poured the contents out on the floor: rolls of wet bills covered in poop.

Gagging, I saw that Julián planned to clean the money in our washing machine.

"No! Don't even think about it!" I shouted hysterically.

He must've understood that I was willing to draw

blood to stop him, because I'd instinctively grabbed the largest knife in the kitchen.

"Okay, Violeta! Calm down," he begged, frightened for the first time in his life.

He made a call, and a short while later we had two Mafia goons at our disposal. We went to a laundromat and the gangsters paid everyone to leave. Then the men stood guard as Julián washed the poop-covered bills. After that he had to dry them and pack them in a bag. He brought me along because he had no idea how to operate the machines.

"Now I understand what money laundering is," I said.

That incident helped me realize once and for all that it was better to be Julián's lover than his wife. I went back to Sacramento the next day.

I'VE PUT OFF TELLING you more about Nieves because it's a very painful topic, Camilo. Maybe unjustly, I've blamed Julián for my daughter's fate. The reality is that everyone is responsible for their own life. We're dealt certain cards at birth, and we play our hand; some of us lose, but others may play skillfully from the same bad hand and triumph. Our cards determine who we are: age, gender, race, family, nationality, etc., and we can't change them, only play them to the best of our abilities. The game is marked by challenges and chances, strategizing and cheating. Nieves was dealt an extraordinary hand: She was intelligent, brave, bold, generous, and charming, with a haunting voice and striking beauty. I loved her with all my soul, like any normal mother loves her children, but my love couldn't compare to her father's adoration. Nieves was the only person in this world Julián loved more than himself.

They say that all little girls are in love with their fathers; I think it's called the Electra complex, and they eventually outgrow it. Sometimes, however, fathers fall in love with their daughters too, and then feelings can get tangled up like a ball of string in a cat's claws. Something like that happened between Nieves and Julián. He was obsessed with the girl as soon as he saw that she had the qualities his son was lacking; she was like him, of his blood and spirit. Our son could never compete with his sister, and there came a time when he stopped trying and resigned himself to simply hiding in her shadow, invisible. He did this so efficiently that his father practically forgot he existed.

On one occasion, by the pool, I saw Julián rubbing tanning oil on Nieves, as he'd done many times, but something about the scene disturbed me. I called her over so I could rub it on her instead.

"Dad does it better," she teased.

Later on I confronted Julián, and in response he slapped me. It had been a long time since he'd hit me, and he'd never left a mark on my face before. He accused me of being a filthy harpy who tainted everything with my suspicions and jealousy.

THE YEAR I SPENT with Julián in the hideous pink villa in Miami, surrounded by gangsters, schemers, and spies, Nieves lived with us, in theory, but in practice I saw very little of her. The property was far from downtown, and my daughter often stayed the night with her girlfriends, or so she said. I'd find her some afternoons lounging on a chair beside the pool, drinking a piña colada and resting after a night on the town. Sometimes she was in such an altered state from alcohol—and drugs too, I suppose—that she couldn't drive, so she'd call Julián to pick her up. She cured her hangovers with cocaine, which her father always had on hand and considered as harmless as tobacco.

My daughter sang at nightclubs and casinos, which were almost certainly controlled by the Mafia, and Julián sometimes took me to her shows. I can still see her as she was on those nights, painted like a courtesan, wearing a tight sequined dress and dripping with fake diamonds, caressing the microphone and seducing the audience with her husky, sensual voice. Her father applauded ardently and shouted compliments along with the other men in the audience, and my stomach twisted in knots as I prayed to heaven that the show would soon end.

A year later, after I'd moved back home, a man "discovered" Nieves in one of those clubs and took her out to Las Vegas, promising a career onstage as well as his own devotion. I only learned all this after the fact because Julián didn't tell me what had happened until much later. His name was Joe Santoro and he presented himself as a talent agent, but he was really just a two-bit gangster, one of those handsome young American men of little intelligence and fewer scruples who come a dime a dozen. Nieves secretly packed her things and left without telling her father. Two days later, after he'd turned to the police to find her, she called from Las Vegas. Julián immediately flew out to get her, crazed with rage and jealousy. He had connections in Vegas, where he traveled often with his clients to pick up black suitcases. His plan consisted of hiring a hit man to shoot off Santoro's kneecaps, and drag his daughter home.

Julián and the hit man found Nieves in a filthy flophouse that Joe Santoro shared with a group of hippies and drifters. My daughter was lying with her young lover on a sticky mattress, surrounded by beer cans and fossilized pizza leftovers. They were both flying across other universes thanks to a combination of LSD and marijuana, but Nieves was at least lucid enough to understand her father's intentions. Half-naked, with tangled hair and mascara smeared under her eyes, she stood up to the gangster, grabbed his gun with both her hands, and swore to her father on everything holy that if they laid a finger on Joe she'd kill herself.

JULIÁN'S DAUGHTER DEALT HIM the only blow that could undermine his titanic strength. Nieves simply left him, fleeing like someone trying to outrun death. I think that Nieves felt, at a cellular level, something her brain couldn't acknowledge; she had to escape her father's obsession with her and her own dependence on him. She cut all ties in a single snip, refusing to return to Miami or accept any form of help.

The anger that had driven Julián to Las Vegas turned to desperation when he saw Nieves staring him down like an enemy. He offered her whatever she wanted: told her he was willing to put her up in a decent place to live, support her living with Joe Santoro or any other scoundrel she chose. He begged, pleaded, and cried, but nothing could budge his daughter's rock-hard will. He saw that she was just like him, indomitable, bold, and she would do exactly as she pleased with no consideration for anyone else. Like him, Nieves could sow disaster with total indifference. His daughter was a mirror showing him his own reflection.

Nieves stayed in Las Vegas. Julián wanted to be near her, so he could step in if necessary, but she wouldn't see him even from a distance, and he couldn't abandon his business in Miami. I imagine his clients weren't eager to give him up since it wasn't so easy to find a pilot willing to fly at night under the radar or make a water landing in alligator-infested swamps to pick up mysterious packages.

To keep an eye on his daughter, he hired a private detective, Roy Cooper. Roy would eventually play a major role in your life, Camilo. He was an ex-convict who specialized in blackmail, as I later found out, but it wasn't clear whether he earned his living by doing the blackmailing or by helping those to whom it was being done.

Roy's reports were heartbreaking for Julián. His daughter was on a slippery slope that could only lead to death. She stayed with Joe Santoro for a little while, but quickly left him, or he left her, and Nieves ended up on the street. The famous Summer of Love had ended, but the hippie counterculture was still vibrant in many cities throughout the country, Las Vegas among them. Those young, long-haired kids, tattooed, lazy, and content, who wandered all over California and made history at Woodstock, were not as well tolerated in other places.

Nieves joined the many middle-class white kids who chose to live like promiscuous beggars in a haze of psychedelic music and drugs. Roy was right on her heels, sending frequent reports back to Julián. The pictures showed Nieves dressed in rags decorated with little mirrors, flowers in her hair, at an anti-Vietnam protest with a handful of other kids, sitting cross-legged at the feet of a shaggy guru, or singing love songs and panhandling in a public park. She slept in communes, on the street, in a broken-down car—one night here, one night there, a wandering spirit like so many other young people at the time. She was lured by the attraction of aimless freedom, one-night stands, and intoxicating depravity. She embraced the aesthetic inspired by India, but she wasn't interested in Eastern philosophy or the movement's political and social aims. She protested against the war out of defiance of authority, but she had no idea where that country called Vietnam was even located.

JULIÁN'S PLAN WAS TO throw Nieves a rope once she hit rock bottom. Roy had instructions to make sure the girl didn't go hungry, and to protect her the best he could, without revealing his connection to her father. It was easy, because Nieves was lost in a cloud of marijuana smoke and acid-induced hallucinations. Swallowing life in big gulps, she also began to sniff heroin. It was impossible for Roy to keep track of all the men Nieves had casual relations with, since she never stayed with anyone for more than three or four days. In the photos he sent Julián, taken from a distance, they all looked like the same guy: beard, long hair, a necklace of beads or flowers, sandals, and a guitar.

The one person that stuck out as different was Joe Santoro, who still came and went from Nieves's life with a certain regularity. He wasn't just another hippie. He was a small-time dealer of methamphetamines and heroin, so insignificant that the police didn't bother with him. His buyers were office workers, third-rate entertainment industry people, and tourists. The hippies preferred marijuana and hallucinogens, which were passed around freely; the majority looked down on hard drugs and alcohol. We'll never know whether he introduced Nieves to heroin or just supplied her once she was desperate. The path to addiction is straight and well paved; Nieves traveled it quickly.

I didn't know any of this until a year later, because Julián always assured me over the phone and when he visited that Nieves was fine. He told me that she was sharing an apartment with two girlfriends and studying art. He talked to her a couple of times a week, he said, but he didn't see her because she wanted to try her wings on her own for a while. She didn't want me to go see her either, so I shouldn't worry if she didn't answer my letters. On one occasion I even flew to Miami to help get Julián's papers in order, but he found a way to cover up my daughter's absence. I could've tried harder to find out what was going on and I didn't. I'm guilty too.

JULIÁN AND I WERE held together by a perpetual cycle of hate and lust. And Nieves, of course. Juan Martín doesn't count because, if it had been up to my son, Julián and I would've separated fifteen years earlier. It's impossible to explain our obscene pattern of attraction and rejection, passion and rage, fighting and making up; I myself don't understand it. With time we only remember events, emotions fade, and I'm no longer the woman I was back then.

After every trip I made to Miami in those years, I returned to my house in Sacramento or to the apartment I shared with my son in the capital determined to never again heed a summons from Julián Bravo. But inevitably I always gave in, like a trained, beaten dog. He would call me as soon as the chaos threatened to suffocate him so that I could put things back in order, and he came to see me whenever he needed to flee a disaster related to women or money. His presence was a typhoon that completely upset my well-regulated existence and the peace of mind that I felt in his absence. Those were the only times I ever got drunk and smoked marijuana, which according to Julián I needed in order to enjoy life like a normal person. "I like you when you're relaxed. I can't have fun with you when your head is filled with worries and work," he'd say.

This was a recurring source of conflict: my business. I have a nose for making money, as you know, Camilo; I saved, invested wisely, and lived frugally. To Julián my prudence with money was simply greed, another of my defects. He criticized me, then turned around and blew a year's savings in five minutes.

15

MY BROTHER AND JOSEPHINE TAYLOR, the only ones who knew about Julián's abusiveness, criticized me often for putting up with him. At their insistence, I went to see a psychiatrist to help resolve that destructive emotional dependence.

Dr. Levy was a Jewish man who had studied with Carl Jung. He was a university professor and author of several books—an eminent figure. I'd guess he was around eighty, but it's possible he was younger and merely worn down from so much suffering. The doctor knew Julián because he was one of the immigrants Julián had secretly flown into the country after the war. He had lost his entire family to the concentration camps, but that monumental grief didn't leave him bitter; he instead had an infinite compassion for human fragility. I was embarrassed to have a Holocaust survivor waste his time on my miserable emotional problems, but with a glance he put my mind at ease. He closed the door to his office and time stood still in that room crammed with books; nothing else existed: only he and I.

"I've led a banal life, Dr. Levy. I'm mediocre," I said to him in one session.

He responded that all lives are banal and we're all mediocre, depending on who we compare ourselves to.

"Why would you want a tragic life, Violeta?" he asked me, and his voice broke, surely thinking of the suffering he'd witnessed. "There's a Chinese curse that is applicable here: I wish you an interesting life. The corresponding blessing would be: I wish you a boring life," he added.

Thanks to Dr. Levy, who held my hand through the process, I finally managed to leave Julián. He guided me down a long road of introspection, beginning in my childhood at Camellia House, where I discovered my father's body, and traveling the landscapes of my memory: Miss Taylor, my aunts, the Rivas farm, the itinerant school, the assault by Pascual Freire and Torito's rescue, Fabian, Julián and my children, until finally reaching age fifty, weary from conflict and loneliness.

THE FIRST THING I did was inform Julián that he could no longer count on me to clean up his messes, finance his extravagances, pay his debts, work accounting miracles, or pick up the pieces of the disasters he created. I would also never again set foot in the pink cake in Miami; no more poop-covered dollars in the washing machine, gangsters, or spies for me. If he wanted to come see me, he'd have to stay in a hotel and treat Juan Martín with respect. Lastly, he had to know that if he ever laid a hand on me again he'd be truly sorry.

"You're going to need strength and mental clarity to hold him to this, Violeta. I'd advise you to refrain from alcohol when you're with Julián," Dr. Levy said.

Up to that moment I'd never connected drinking with the power Julián held over me.

Julián thought my departure was another of the empty threats I'd been repeating for years, but this time I had Dr. Levy's support. Two months later, tired of begging me to fly to Miami to help him, he found someone else to manage that jigsaw puzzle he called a business but was really a smuggling operation. The new person in charge was Zoraida Abreu, his longtime lover, with whom I drank martinis at the Fontainebleau Hotel. As it turned out, his choice couldn't have been more perfect, because she was an accountant by trade, in addition to being efficient, discreet, and eager to serve him out of love, just as I'd once been. While I'd worked out the crazy numbers of his double books on pure instinct, she was meticulous and had a thorough knowledge of American law. She knew how to manage secret accounts, evade taxes, and launder money. Julián was much better off with her than with me.

I can picture Miss Boricua Rum, all curves and leonine mane, lording her authority over Julián's associates and clients, keeping his short-lived lovers at bay. She'd told me she was methodical, a necessary requirement for her profession, and had little tolerance for squandering money; her parents were very strict and she'd been educated in a school run by nuns. She called from time to time to fill me in on the latest drama or ask for advice. She was imposing, bossy, sure of herself and her opinions, which contrasted comically with her annoying childlike way of speaking. I doubt that Julián was able to intimidate her and I think that in a brawl she'd have crushed him like a cockroach.

Zoraida's presence was a blessing; she helped me cut my last emotional ties to Julián.

AROUND THIS TIME, IRONICALLY, Julián started to visit our country more often. He was there on top-secret missions related to the German commune, Colonia Esperanza, which we'd first heard about from my ex-husband, Fabian. I pointed out that the missions couldn't be all that secretive if he'd told me about them over a lunch of oysters and sea urchin at a restaurant in the port.

"You're my soul, Violeta. You know me better than anyone. I have no secrets from you," he responded.

I refrained from asking him if he had secrets from Zoraida, because it was better that he didn't suspect our unusual comradery.

Julián seldom saw his son. Juan Martín politely declined the few invitations to Miami that his father extended, using school as an excuse, and when Julián came to the capital they interacted as little as possible. They both avoided getting into any deep discussions, especially on politics, which was the spark that could ignite a mutual hostility. For Julián, his son was a permanent disappointment, and to Juan Martín, his father was a crook who'd sold out to Yankee imperialism.

The presidential election had just been won by a Socialist, representing a coalition of leftist parties that Juan Martín had campaigned for tirelessly. His father was convinced the man wouldn't last more than a few months in power because the right wing and the United States wouldn't permit it, but he didn't tell his son that. He preferred to warn him through me.

"Tell your son to be careful. This country isn't going to be another Cuba. It'll be a bloodbath."

I didn't need to ask how he knew.

ROY, THE MAN JULIÁN had hired as a private detective, saved Nieves's life. On one of those hot afternoons in the Nevada desert he realized it had been over a week since he'd sent his client a report.

Spying on the girl was a frustrating job, beneath someone so experienced in criminal enterprise, but it was good money.

He searched in vain for her in the usual places, including the street corners where Nieves might offer herself to passersby on her more desperate days. He didn't tell her father this, but Julián must've suspected, as it was a common recourse for a girl in dire need of another dose. Roy knew that a man like Julián Bravo was familiar with the world of drugs, from production, transportation, down to the ultimate degradation of the addict. It was a painful irony that his own daughter was one of the victims. Concerned, because he'd never lost track of her for so long, Roy asked among the hippies she ran with—groups of young people in vacant lots, far from the champagne and dazzling lights of the Strip—and found out that someone had seen Nieves with Joe Santoro.

It was already dark out when Roy tracked Joe down at a bowling alley—clean, well dressed, and freshly shaved—drinking beer with a couple of friends.

"Nieves? I'm not her babysitter," he rudely responded.

The girl no longer interested him; he merely sold her hard drugs. He didn't use them himself and had warned her that it was usually a one-way trip, he said. Roy grabbed him by the arm and dragged him into the bathroom, where he started with a knee to the groin that knocked the boy flat on the floor, wet with urine. Then he pulled him up by his belt and was about to bust open his nose, when Joe stopped him, covering his face and blubbering that Nieves was "in the bus."

Roy knew what he was referring to. It was a stripped bus with no wheels, entirely covered in graffiti, parked in the courtyard of an abandoned building. Roy had been to that very building, a den of addicts and drifters, hours earlier, but he hadn't thought to check inside the bus. He found Nieves unconscious on the floor, between two young men who were either sleeping or high. He tried to sit her up, but the girl melted in his arms. He slapped her a few times and shook her to wake her up, tried fruitlessly to find her pulse, then finally picked her up and ran with her to his car. Nieves weighed as much as a small child, pure skin and bones.

The detective called Julián from the hospital. It was already close to midnight in Miami.

"The girl's hit rock bottom. Come quick," he told him.

Julián arrived in Las Vegas the next day, piloting a small jet that one of his clients had lent him, and landed at a private airport. Nieves was released two days later, and with Roy's help Julián forced her onto the plane. She'd recovered from the overdose that almost killed her but was suffering terrible withdrawal. Between the two men, they could barely hold her as she fought with a superhuman force, shouting and cursing so loudly that the police would've been called if they hadn't been at a private airport. On the plane, her father injected her with a sedative, which knocked her out for ten hours, enough time to land in Miami and check her in to a rehab clinic.

That's when Julián finally called to tell me what had happened. I had suspected for years that my daughter was on drugs, but I imagined she was using only marijuana and cocaine, which according to her father wouldn't affect Nieves's ability to function normally in the world. I'd managed to ignore the evidence of what was happening to Nieves, just as I hadn't wanted to admit that Julián was an alcoholic. I'd simply parroted his words: that he knew how to hold his liquor, that he could drink twice as much as any other mortal without being affected, that he needed whiskey to help ease his back pain, and other excuses. Nieves had just survived a near-death experience caused by heroin and was in a strict detox program, but I still didn't think she was an addict. I believed Julián: It had been an unfortunate accident, it wouldn't happen again. The girl had learned her lesson.

A WEEK LATER THEY let us visit Nieves in the clinic. She'd gotten over the worst of the withdrawal; she was clean, her hair washed, wearing jeans and a T-shirt, silently staring at the floor. I hugged her, sobbing, calling her name without getting any reaction, but when Julián asked her how she was, she managed to focus her eyes.

"The Beings have chosen me, Dad. I have a message to share with humanity," she said.

The counselor explained that this state of confusion was normal after the kind of trauma she'd suffered and the effects of the sedatives.

I stayed in Miami for the three months that Nieves was in rehab, seeing her as often as they'd let me, at first a few times a week and then almost every day. The visits were very brief and always chaperoned. I learned about the horrors of withdrawal: the terrible distress, insomnia, cramps and stomach pains, cold sweats, vomiting, and fever. For the first few days they eased her pain with sedatives, but after that she had to face the nightmare cold turkey.

During some visits Nieves seemed normal, coming in from the pool or playing volleyball with her cheeks flushed and eyes shining. Other times she begged us to get her out of there, saying they were torturing her, didn't feed her, tied her up, beat her. She didn't mention the Beings again. Her father and I had several sessions with the psychiatrist and counselors, who emphasized the need for tough love, limits, and discipline, but Nieves was about to turn twenty-one and after that we'd have no power to protect her from herself.

The day of her birthday she disappeared from the

rehab clinic. She left with the clothes on her back and the five hundred dollars her father had given her as a birthday gift, despite the psychiatrist's warnings. We guessed she'd gone back to Las Vegas, but Roy couldn't find her. For a while, we had no idea where she was.

JULIÁN WANTED ME TO stay in the horrible mansion while I was in Miami, but I'd vowed to never again spend a night under the same roof as him. If the opportunity presented itself, I knew I'd end up back in his bed and I would regret it. I rented a small studio with a kitchenette, where I had the silence and solitude I desperately needed during that painful period.

Zoraida Abreu didn't live with Julián either; he'd set her up in a luxury apartment in Coconut Grove, where she was close, but he still had his freedom. He never mentioned her to me and he never knew that she and I met regularly at the Fontainebleau, and that I'd grown fond of the woman. She had the balls I didn't.

Zoraida kept Julián on a tight leash, but she didn't feel the need to watch him too closely because she could read his intentions and betrayals with a mere glance. Julián lacked all mystery for her. I asked if she was jealous, and she responded with a loud laugh.

"Of course! I'm not jealous of you, Violeta, because you're part of the past. But if I catch him with another woman, I'll kill him."

She felt perfectly secure in her position as favorite, because she knew every last detail of Julián's illegal activities and he would never be stupid enough to make her mad.

"I have him in the palm of my hand," she told me.

She was waiting, with laudable patience, for the right moment to make him marry her. She did everything possible to get pregnant, without letting him suspect it, because giving him a child would be her trump card. But she hadn't been successful.

"You don't mind, do you? It won't represent competition for your kids, since they're adults now."

During those three months I was focused on Nieves, but I was in close contact with José Antonio. The Socialist president had set up a public housing program to solve the problem of the shantytowns, where entire families were crowded into miserable shacks made of cardboard and plywood, without access to drinkable water, sewers, or electricity. José Antonio applied for a government bid, backed by many years' experience in prefab housing and the prestige of having introduced and perfected the process.

Rustic Homes was the favorite company of young middle-class couples, who worked hard to acquire their first homes. I knew we would lose prestige if poorer people in marginal neighborhoods had similar houses. "Think of the classist prejudice in our country. Let's make the same basic beach houses, but we'll give them a different color and name. Maybe we'll call it My Own Home, what do you think?" I suggested.

We won a substantial portion of the contract because no one could compete with our price. The profit margin was very low, but Anton Kusanovic, Marko's son, who had replaced him the year before, helped us see that we could make it up with the huge volume. The trick was in the speed of producing and installing the homes, and in order to do this we had to offer incentives. We doubled the factory's installations and began to pay the workers a commission, in addition to their salaries, which helped us appease the labor union.

OUR COUNTRY'S POLITICAL SITUATION in the early seventies was disastrous; there was a deep social and economic crisis and the government was paralyzed by constant disagreement among its parties and intransigent opposition from the right, willing to stop at nothing to end the Socialist experiment. The opposition had the support of the CIA, as Juan Martín reminded me regularly and Julián justified, saying that we had to destroy the guerrillas. "There are no guerrillas here, Dad, it's a coalition of centrist and leftist parties elected by the people. The

Americans have no business getting involved," Juan Martín argued.

None of that affected José Antonio and me. We had more work than we needed and our employees were satisfied, which was a miracle amid the conflict and growing violence, strikes and protests, massive demonstrations in support of the government and similar marches in opposition. The country was polarized, divided into two irreconcilable factions; there was no dialogue, no one was willing to compromise. Despite the contract we'd won, José Antonio and Anton Kusanovic were counted among the Socialist government's enemies, as were most owners of large companies, which included many of our friends and acquaintances. I voted conservative, following my brother's lead. The only people I knew who sympathized with the left were my son and Miss Taylor, who at seventy-something years old had not lost the political passion she'd shared with Teresa Rivas. Her role as my brother's wife had not tamed her in that sense.

Juan Martín had transferred schools and now studied journalism at the National University, "a nest of Commies," as his father called it. He was so dedicated to politics that he attended very few of his classes. He was horrified by my neutrality, which he classified as ignorant and complacent. "How can you vote for the right, Mom! Don't you see the inequality and poverty in this country?" he'd say. I did see it, but I thought there was nothing I could do about it. It was a problem best left to the government or the Church, and I did my part by providing jobs for my employees.

So much would have to happen before I was brought down to reality, Camilo. I chose not to see, hear, or speak up during the most critical years. I'd surely have continued on in the same way straight through the dictatorship if the iron fist of oppression hadn't dealt me a direct blow.

16

WHILE OUR COUNTRY TEETERED ON THE brink of tragedy, I spent three years traveling often between Miami, Las Vegas, and Los Angeles. The information about our country that circulated in the United States was biased, parroting the right-wing propaganda and depicting us as just another Cuba. I returned home often for work, each time seeing the chaos and violence escalate as Juan Martín slipped further and further away from me. My son had become a stranger. He talked to me in a condescending tone, the way someone speaks to a pet; he'd given up trying to indoctrinate me, considering it a lost cause, categorizing me as a "mummified relic." He was hostile, with a shaggy beard and dirty hair, skinny and passionate. Little remained of the timid boy he'd once been.

Nieves disappeared for months after leaving rehab. Julián mobilized all his contacts to look for her in Miami, but she hadn't left the faintest trail. He checked with the airlines and bus companies, with no luck. In my search for her, I dove deep into the underworld of panhandlers, addicts, and life on the mean streets. Julián participated in drug trafficking and crime on a larger scale but had never found himself in a squalid alleyway crowded with zombies. He was oblivious to this other realm, though I grew to know it well. What must they have thought of me? A middle-class woman, well dressed and desperate, crying as she asked about a girl named Nieves. Some of the young people I met broke my heart, but I didn't try to save them; my only goal was finding my daughter. I spent a few weeks doing that—the hardest weeks you can imagine, Camilo—and all I found out was that no one in Miami knew Nieves.

That's what we were going through when Roy called to say that he had located her in Las Vegas. He'd given up trying to find her, but happened to cross paths with Joe Santoro, and the boy led him to Nieves. Julián and I flew out immediately.

THE GIRL THAT ROY had seen didn't run with the bands of wandering kids left over from the hippie movement, but instead "worked" the famous Strip with other young people of both sexes. She had very short hair dyed platinum blond, dramatic almost-white makeup, and provocative attire that would've looked gaudy anywhere else, but blended in on the Strip. According to Roy, she slept on the street or in random rented rooms, dealing drugs, stealing, or prostituting herself. Her time in the rehab clinic in Miami had done nothing to help her, and she was right back to her old ways, only more alone and desperate than before.

"I wouldn't be surprised if Santoro was her pimp," the detective told us.

"He's going to regret it!" Julián exclaimed, enraged.

Julián invited Nieves and me to stay at Caesars Palace, where I shared a room with my skittish daughter because she refused to sleep in her father's suite, which had two bedrooms, a living room, a panoramic view of that artificial city, and even a white grand piano, which they told us belonged to Liberace. I felt awkward in her presence, guilty and ashamed. I saw myself through Nieves's eyes, resented and despised; she tolerated her father and me only to get money out of us, but I couldn't hold it against her because my brief stroll through her world was enough to inspire immense compassion. I would've given her everything I possessed in this world, Camilo, if I thought it could've helped her.

The first thing Nieves did was take a long bubble bath. I brought her a cup of tea and found her asleep in the water, almost cold. I helped her out of the tub, and as I was wrapping a towel around her I saw that she had a huge scar across her back.

"What happened, Nieves!" I exclaimed, alarmed.

"Nothing. A scratch," she replied, shrugging her shoulders.

She never told me what had happened, just as she refused to speak of the life she led, or of Joe Santoro.

"I don't know anything about him. I haven't seen him in a year," she lied.

My daughter's worldly possessions fit into a small bag: a pair of pants, sneakers, and makeup; she didn't even own a toothbrush. As I kept her company, or more accurately, kept watch, Julián bought her a suitcase and filled it with designer clothes from the best luxury shops on the Strip. Spending money on her was his way of dealing with the overwhelming panic constricting his chest.

Nieves stayed with us in the hotel for almost a week, long enough to make Julián think he could save her, but I didn't share his optimism. I could clearly see the signs I'd witnessed before: itchiness, insomnia, shivering, cramps, joint pain, nausea, dilated pupils, confusion, and anxiety. Whenever I turned my attention away for a moment, Nieves would leave the room and return calmed; there were always dealers around, and she knew how to find them. I think they even sent drugs up to her, hidden in the room-service tray or the laundry. That brief respite at Caesars Palace ended abruptly, as soon as she'd gotten enough money out of her father. She stole my watch, a gold chain, and my passport, then vanished once again.

This time Julián knew where to find her, and enlisted Roy and another man to kidnap Nieves, just as they'd done before. He refrained from telling me because he knew I would have been opposed. Nieves was walking down the street one evening when a car stopped and she walked over, thinking it was a possible client. Roy and his goon both got out at the same time, threw a jacket over her head and forced her into the car. She fought like a wild animal in a trap, but the jacket muffled her screams. No one stepped in to help her, although I'm sure several people, including some security guards, witnessed the spectacle; it was the busiest time of night for the casinos and restaurants.

Nieves's father checked her in to a psychiatric ward on the outskirts of a city in Utah, where they put her in a straitjacket and locked her in a padded room. She was no longer a minor and her father did not have the authority to take such measures, but nothing was beyond Julián, who always found a way to get what he wanted, sometimes with money, other times through connections.

THE NEXT DAY, JULIÁN explained what he'd done and informed me that we'd be returning to Miami, since Nieves didn't need us; the clinic would let us know when she was ready to be released and we would go get her. By then we'd have a plan to help her, but first she had to be cured of her addiction. Once again, he was cutting me out of my daughter's life.

"No, Julián. I'm going to stay near her," I announced.

We argued, as usual, but he ultimately gave in.

"If you insist on going to Utah, I'll ask Roy to drive you. I don't want you to take a bus."

The trip was two hours across a hot desert landscape; we rode in silence, sweating, with all the windows down because Roy smoked one cigarette after another. The clinic was a two-story concrete building that looked like a convent, with a garden of cacti and rocks enclosed by a line of shrubs and a high fence. There was no civilization for miles, only a vast expanse of desert, sand, stones, and salt mines.

Inside, an Indian woman who introduced herself as the clinic director informed us that she could not speak about the case without the signature of Mr. Bravo, who had not left any instructions with regards to me.

"I'm the patient's mother!" I shouted, ready to attack the harpy like one of the lunatics in her asylum.

"Let's go, Violeta. Come with me; we'll try again tomorrow," Roy urged, holding me back.

I buried my face in his shirt, soaked with sweat and reeking of tobacco, and I started to cry.

Roy booked two rooms at a bed-and-breakfast,

sent me up to shower and change, and then took me out to eat at a truck stop on the side of the highway.

They wouldn't let me see Nieves or speak with the doctors, but I sat in the waiting room every morning until they kicked me out, convinced that my daughter was suffering. I suspected that instead of helping her, their method was closer to punishment. The harpy eventually took pity on me, sitting there day after day. She offered me tea and cookies and assured me that Nieves was fine, resting and recovering, but she wouldn't provide any details as to whether she was in isolation, tied up, or knocked out with drugs.

"How could you think such things, ma'am? This is a modern institution, not the Dark Ages."

During that long and difficult wait I made the most unexpected friend: Roy stayed with me the entire time. I want to tell you about him, Camilo, because he played an important role in your life.

He called himself Roy Cooper, but I suspected it wasn't his real name, because he was a secretive man. I didn't know where he was from or anything about his past, whether he was married or had a real job, even after we'd spent hours together. Julián had told me that he specialized in blackmail, but no one can make a living that way. Roy must have been more or less the same age as me, around fifty years old, and he was in very good shape; he looked like one of those health nuts who lift weights and run like fugitives at dawn. He had coarse features, an unwelcoming expression, and pockmarked skin, but I thought he was handsome; there was a certain beauty in that face of a seasoned gladiator. He dropped me off and picked me up at the clinic, took me out to eat and, sometimes, to the movies, a swimming pool, or bowling.

"You have to distract yourself, Violeta. Walking around crying isn't doing your daughter any good," he said to me.

TELLING YOU ALL THIS, Camilo, it sounds like I cared little for Nieves's fate, but the days were long and hot, and there was a lot of time left over after those eternal hours at the clinic. Roy was my only comfort, and I grew to care for and admire him, even though we had few common interests. I found myself telling my life story to that stranger, who could've been a hit man for a group of narcos, for all I knew.

"You know everything about me, Roy. You have enough dirt to blackmail me, but I don't know a thing about you," I once said to him.

"There's nothing to tell, Violeta. I'm just a lowlife scoundrel."

"Is Julián paying you to watch me?"

"Bravo hired me to trail his daughter in Vegas, that's it. I'm here because I want to be."

"You like my company that much?" I asked him in a flirtatious impulse.

"Yes," he answered, serious.

That night I went to his room. Don't be alarmed, Camilo. I wasn't always the hobbled old lady I am now. At fifty-one years old I was still attractive and my hormones still functioned. I don't feel the need to mention every romantic relationship I've had in my long life—most were brief and unmemorable. I don't regret any of them; quite the opposite—I'm sorry for the opportunities I let pass me by out of prudishness, or because I was too busy or worried about gossip. I spent the better part of my life single and I didn't owe fidelity to anyone, but women of my generation were denied the sexual freedom that men considered their right. A perfect example was Julián, who was chronically unfaithful yet simultaneously jealous. By the time I met Roy Cooper, Julián's jealousy no longer mattered to me; he had become Zoraida Abreu's problem.

I'll spare you the details. It's enough to say that I hadn't had anyone to hold for a few years and Roy Cooper restored joy to my body, the physical pleasure of making love. From that moment on we were together most of the time. I wouldn't have been able to bear those days without him. He was pleasant company, he asked nothing of me, and he helped me get through that challenging time by making me feel young and desirable, an amazing gift under the circumstances.

• • •

NIEVES WAS NOT RELEASED from the clinic. Seventeen days after she'd been checked in, they called to tell us that she had "left," because they didn't want to admit that she had escaped. I think she could've walked calmly out the front door and they wouldn't have been able to stop her, since Julián Bravo lacked any legal authority to keep her locked up, but Nieves didn't know that. I'm sure it was easy for her to slip out between midnight and daybreak, once her dosage of sedatives had been reduced and she recovered her fierce will, but it couldn't have been easy to make her way through that desert landscape or find transportation. She left a note for her father, ordering him not to search for her and saying she didn't want to see him ever again.

I showed up at the clinic as soon as Julián called me from the Miami airport. I'd only seen the waiting room and the strange cactus garden, and I'd pictured the rest of it as a sinister place where sadistic pseudo-doctors drugged and tortured patients with cold water and electric shocks. But the counselor who met with me this time was friendly and willing to answer my questions about the clinic in general, since my daughter was no longer a patient. She told me that we had to wait for Julián to arrive before we could speak to the psychiatrist who'd treated Nieves. In the meantime she walked me through the clinic, which didn't contain the iron-barred cells of my nightmares, but private rooms painted in cheerful pastel colors. There was a game room, gym, spa, heated pool, and even a projection room where they played innocuous documentaries about dolphins and bonobos. They didn't even call their residents patients, but guests.

Nieves's psychiatrist met with us alongside the clinic director. The Indian woman did not shrink at Julián's threats to sue the clinic for negligence.

"This isn't a prison, Mr. Bravo. We don't keep our guests against their will," she announced dryly, and proceeded to explain Nieves's treatment.

During detox, which was the hardest part of the process, they'd kept her sedated so that she could get through it with minimal discomfort. Then she'd had a few days of rest and relaxation, with baths and massages in the spa, until she began to eat normally and was willing to participate in the individual and group therapy sessions. They described her attitude as hostile and mocking at first, but then she began to relax, and her aggression turned to silence. A few days before leaving, she'd begun to talk about her past, and the time before she'd started using hard drugs. Nieves was emotionally immature, they said, stuck at fourteen or fifteen and vacillating between love and hate for her father, an omniscient figure in her psyche. She struggled with a dependence on him and a need to free herself from his control. She'd left the clinic just when they'd started to explore the traumas of her childhood and adolescence. She wasn't able to face her past, they told us. That's when Julián lost his patience.

"I don't see what good any of that did! You did nothing to help my daughter. What a waste of time and money!"

He stood up and left, slamming the door behind him. I watched him through the window, striding quickly down the gravel path of the garden.

I stayed on to listen to the rest of the information about my daughter's health, which I tried to share with him later.

"They're not doctors, they're charlatans!" he shouted at me.

"You should've figured that out before you put Nieves in there against her will," I responded.

Apart from the physical damage from the drugs, my daughter had had a few abortions, and suffered from malnutrition, osteoporosis, and stomach ulcers. They'd also had to give her antibiotics for cystitis and a venereal disease.

Julián wanted to search for his daughter, but this time Roy refused to help him.

"Face it, Bravo, you don't have authority over her anymore; leave her alone. If Nieves wants your help, she knows where to find you."

Crazed with frustration and grief, Julián returned to Miami.

On our last night, I said goodbye to Roy without making love to him, because the ghost of Nieves lingered in the room, watching us. We lay awake for hours, holding each other, and I fell asleep resting against the mermaid tattoo on his rock-hard shoulder. The next day he dropped me off at the airport, kissed me on the lips, and said we'd be in touch.

17

....

As soon as I got home to Sacramento, I broke down in front of José Antonio and Miss Taylor. I'd stopped at the airport in the capital for only an hour layover before flying to the south, because Juan Martín was away in the north with some other journalism students, filming a documentary. I told them about Nieves, cursing Julián Bravo for the damage he'd done to his daughter, for the cruelty he'd inflicted on his son, and for the abuse I'd received from him. They let me unload my resentment and tears. Then they brought me up to date on the situation in our country.

It seems unbelievable that I could've ignored what was happening. My only explanation is that I was too absorbed in my own drama; politics didn't affect my business and I'd had the resources to pay domestic help and buy whatever I wanted on the black market. I'd never had to wait in line to get sugar or oil, the cook did that. My neighborhood, in the capital as well as in Sacramento, was far removed from the chaos on the streets. Very rarely did I have to go to the city center and deal with the traffic and masses of angry people. I found out about the large street demonstrations on television, where the scenes of collective fervor seemed more festive than violent. I didn't give a second glance to the posters of Soviet soldiers dragging children into the Siberian gulags, pasted all over by the right, or the murals of laborers and farmworkers surrounded by doves of peace and flags, commissioned by the left.

My friends, acquaintances, and clients supported the government opposition, and the obligatory topic of conversation was how those leftists in power had violated the constitution, cramming the country with Cubans and arming the people for a revolution that would put an end to private property. If the president appeared on television to defend his agenda, I changed the channel. I didn't like that arrogant man, who was a traitor to his class, a rich kid in Italian suits claiming to be a Socialist. And what was the difference between Socialism and Communism? They were the same thing, José Antonio explained, and no one wanted to see the country become another branch of the Soviet Union. My brother was concerned over the economic crisis, which sooner or later was bound to affect us, and he worried about the negative image we had among our social circle thanks to the government contract for My Own Home. The unwritten rule was that we should be trying to sabotage the government, not collaborating with it, but we weren't the only ones who benefited. Almost all public works were carried out through private contracts.

I met with Juan Martín in the capital when he returned from the north. His documentary was about American companies with a long presence in our country. The government had seized control of the companies because they had been exploiting the region for half a century and owed a fortune in taxes, he explained. This wasn't what I'd heard, but I knew so little about the matter that I couldn't contradict him.

"YOU LIVE IN A bubble, Mom," Juan Martín said, and insisted on taking me to a part of town I'd never visited before.

It was a poor neighborhood where the families like those in the My Own Home program lived, very humble people who needed assistance to obtain a basic dwelling. Until that moment the houses had been nothing more than a blueprint, a point on a map, or a construction model to be photographed. I walked through the shantytown, down narrow alleys of dirt or mud, filled with stray dogs and rats, kids with no education, unemployed young men, and women worn down from overwork. The prefabricated homes became more than just a good business proposal as I understood what they might mean to these families. Everywhere I looked I saw the typical murals of workers and doves in that horrible Soviet realism style, and on the walls of the homes hung photos of the president alongside images of Father Juan Quiroga, both patron saints. I began to see the arrogant man in the Italian suit from a new perspective.

After our walk we stopped at the home of a schoolteacher my son knew. Over a cup of tea, he told me about the hot lunch and fresh milk that the Ministry of Education provided to all students, which for many of them was the only food they'd eat all day. He told me about his wife, who worked in the San Lucas hospital, the oldest clinic in the country, where the doctors were on strike and had been replaced by medical students; about his son, who was completing his military service and wanted to study topography; and about his relatives and neighbors, lower-middle-class people who had been educated in good public schools and free universities, and were knowledgeable about politics and supporters of the left.

"And I could also introduce you to upper-middle-class people who voted for this government, Mom—students, professionals, priests and nuns, people you consider to be **like us**," Juan Martín said afterwards, then proceeded to list the names of several cousins, nieces and nephews, friends and acquaintances with aristocratic surnames. "Oh, and Mom! Just to clarify: That teacher you just met is an atheist and a Communist," he said teasingly.

SEVERAL MONTHS LATER I received a call from Roy Cooper at the office. I hadn't heard from him and assumed he'd forgotten me, although I thought of him often, with nostalgia. He wasn't the kind of man to waste time with small talk, so he gave me the reason for his call in a few words.

"I've found Nieves, and I need help. Can you come to Los Angeles quickly?" he asked.

I said I'd be there as soon as possible.

"Don't mention this to Julián Bravo," he cautioned me.

Roy was waiting for me at the airport in faded jeans, sandals, and a baseball cap. On the long trip down the streets of that city jammed with traffic, I asked him why he'd kept looking for my daughter and how he'd found her.

"I wasn't looking for her; she called me, Violeta. When I helped Bravo kidnap her in Las Vegas, I dropped my card in Nieves's purse. I felt sorry for her, the poor girl . . . In my line of work I have to deal with a lot of despicable people. Your daughter is the exception."

"What is your line of work, Roy?"

"Let's just say I'm a problem solver. Someone has a problem and I solve it, my way."

"Someone? Who, for example?"

"Maybe a celebrity or politician, anyone who doesn't want to get arrested, blackmailed, or appear in the papers. The most recent case was a preacher in Texas who ended up with a dead body in a hotel room."

"He killed someone?"

"No. He took a young man back to his hotel room, where the guy died accidentally from insulin shock, and the preacher didn't call for help because he was terrified of the scandal it would cause. His congregants would not tolerate homosexuality. I had to move the body to another room, bribe the staff and the police—you know, the usual."

"Why did Nieves call you?"

"She has no idea what I do, Violeta. And she didn't know the card she found was that of the man who'd helped kidnap her. She called me in desperation. She doesn't want to turn to her father. She thinks Bravo had Joe Santoro killed."

"My God! That's impossible."

He didn't respond.

Roy Cooper could've called Julián and sold him the information about Nieves at a good price, but he chose to go to Los Angeles and help her. He took me to a part of the city he called the Mexican ghetto, a neighborhood of one-story houses, shops with signs in Spanish, and restaurants selling cheap meals. He explained that he'd set Nieves up in the home of an old friend of his.

Nieves was waiting for us, and when she saw me she came running and hugged me like she hadn't done in an eternity. "Mom, Mom . . ." she said over and over. For a moment I was transported twenty years back in time to the treasured little girl who sat on my lap and let me brush her hair. She looked much better than she had the last time I'd seen her; she'd gained a bit of weight and her face without makeup looked young and vulnerable. She wore her hair short, its natural color, with only the tips still bleached.

"I'm pregnant, Mom," Nieves announced in a shaky voice.

And that's when I looked at her belly, which I hadn't noticed under her loose dress. I couldn't speak so I just kept hugging her, without a thought for the tears streaming down my face.

The owner of the house, a Mexican woman, gave us time to pull ourselves together and then she welcomed me with kisses on both cheeks. She introduced herself as "Rita Linares, seamstress," followed by the traditional greeting, "my home is your home." Her house was similar to the others on the street, a modest cinder-block construction, comfortable, with a narrow yard and tile roof. The furniture, gaudy and unattractive, was covered in plastic; there was an enormous television set and a refrigerator in the living room, and a profusion of fake flowers and painted Day of the Dead skulls.

She showed me to a bedroom with a wide bed,

a crucifix above the headboard, and several framed pictures on the dresser. Nieves explained that Rita had given up her bed and was sleeping instead in her sewing workshop. Rita invited us to the table and, without accepting help, served us a delicious dinner of fish tacos, rice, beans, and avocado. She offered Roy and me a beer, and placed a glass of milk in front of Nieves. I noticed that when she walked by she patted my daughter's head in a gesture so intimate and maternal that I felt a pang of jealousy.

NIEVES EXPLAINED HOW SHE'D left the Utah clinic in the middle of the night aided by the security guard, who told her how to get to the highway, where she hitched a ride on the first truck that passed. Moving from one vehicle to another, she made it to California. I imagined that over the months that followed she'd gotten by in the same way as before.

"The good news is that she's not using now," Roy clarified.

Nieves told me that when the pregnancy was confirmed she decided that this time she wouldn't have an abortion, and she held tightly to the idea of the baby boy or girl growing inside her as she battled her addiction. What the expensive treatment she'd undergone couldn't do, the desire for a healthy baby could. To combat her anxiety she smoked cigarettes and marijuana, drank cup after cup of coffee, and ate too many sweets.

"I'm going to end up obese." She laughed.

"You have to eat double, for you and the baby," Rita responded, serving her another taco.

When Nieves ran out of money because she couldn't get a job and wasn't selling drugs or soliciting clients, she turned to local churches and women's shelters, where she could spend the night. But by seven every morning she was back on the street, which was harder on her as the pregnancy advanced. One day she found Roy Cooper's card in her purse, and on a whim she called him in Las Vegas. As a test, she asked him about Joe Santoro, but he didn't know what had happened to Joe, and that made her trust him.

"He was shot in the back of the head," Nieves told Roy, something she'd found out through the underground network of drug dealers.

Roy assured her that he hadn't had anything to do with it, he wasn't a hired hit man; he'd lost track of the pimp and wasn't in contact with Julián Bravo either. He immediately offered to send her money.

"I don't need money, I need a friend," she answered. "Don't tell my dad where I am," she added.

Roy didn't hesitate. Accustomed to solving problems, he went to Los Angeles to help. It turned out he'd been born in that city, he knew it well and had many friends, acquaintances, and more than one Hollywood client he'd helped out of a difficult situation. Roy had a Mexican stepfather, who moved the family to a neighborhood where he grew up speaking Spanish and fighting hard among Los Angeles's huge population of Mexican immigrants.

"They'll never find me here, Mom," Nieves said.

"Who are you running from, child?"

"From Dad. He killed Joe Santoro."

"You can't accuse your father of a crime like that, Nieves. That's monstrous."

"He didn't pull the trigger, but he's responsible. You know he's capable of anything. I'm scared of him."

"He'd never hurt you, Nieves, he adores you."

"You have a faulty memory, Mom. If he finds me, he'll try, again, to make me do exactly what he wants. He'll never leave me in peace."

Rita and Roy went out onto the patio to smoke and the two of us were left alone.

"Are you going to ask me who the father of this baby is, Mom?"

"It's yours, that's all that matters. I suppose it's Joe Santoro's?"

"No. That's impossible. I don't know who the father is, it could be anyone. I also don't know exactly when it will be born, because my periods were very irregular."

"Because of the drugs?"

"I guess. The midwife calculates that it will be born in October. But you know what, Mom? I don't want it to be born so soon. I want to keep it inside for a long time. I just want to rest in this house with Rita, and sleep and sleep . . ."

. . .

JOSÉ ANTONIO TOOK OVER my work so I was able to stay in Los Angeles. I told only him, Josephine, and Juan Martín about Nieves. When Julián Bravo visited on his missions for Colonia Esperanza, they said I was on a Mediterranean cruise. He might've thought it was strange for a cruise to last so many months, but he didn't ask questions. I found out, through the grapevine, that he was with a woman twenty-something years younger than him, whom he introduced as his girlfriend, and I deduced that it couldn't be Zoraida Abreu. I later found out that it was a woman named Anushka.

To me, the weeks in the little house in the Mexican neighborhood were among the happiest times of my life, a vacation for my spirit a thousand times better than any luxury cruise, where I was finally able to restore a long-lost bond with my daughter. We shared Rita's bed, self-consciously at first—it had been many years since we'd had any physical contact—but we soon grew used to each other. I remember the feeling of sleeping beside her, waking up with her arm thrown over me, a bittersweet memory.

Roy Cooper came and went often from Las Vegas and the other places his curious work took him. He would stay at a nearby motel because there was no other bed at Rita's house, and according to him there was too much estrogen in the air, but in his free time he took the three of us out to eat at Mexican or Chinese restaurants, to the beach, or to the movies. He preferred action movies, with blood and fighting, but he sat through the romantic films we insisted on seeing. He would invite me to spend the night with him at his motel, and I went without offering any explanation to Nieves or Rita, because we imagined they wouldn't want to hear about it.

Rita Linares had come to the United States by foot, through the Sonoran Desert, at twelve years old, in search of her father, and she'd lived undocumented in Los Angeles for over thirty years. She'd been Roy's friend forever.

"He was the only white kid in our whole school. If you could've seen, Violeta, how the other boys picked on him, until he learned how to run fast and hit back," she told me.

She was a widow; her children lived in other states and only got together for Christmas and New Year's; she was lonely—and so she'd readily agreed when Roy called and asked her to temporarily house a pregnant girl with no family. She took Nieves in without hesitation; she needed the company and liked having someone to look after.

Nieves spent the last few weeks of her pregnancy lying in the backyard, tanning in the sun, swollen and exhausted, regularly dozing off. Rita and I sat beside her sewing and talking about our lives, the telenovelas we watched, my country and hers. I asked if she had ever been in love with Roy Cooper and she responded, horrified, that she was a one-man woman, faithful to her husband, "may he rest in peace." We talked about Nieves in the kitchen, where she couldn't hear us. Rita was as excited as I was about the baby's imminent arrival; she'd set up a crib and was making baby clothes.

"I hope to God that Nieves will stay here to live with me. My only granddaughter is with her parents in Portland. It would make me so happy to have a baby in the house," she said. But the idea that Nieves might stay in Los Angeles was crazy; she should return home, where her family could help her.

My daughter had always lived day to day, relying on luck, improvising without plans, goals, or projects. She was like Julián in that way as well. I asked on several occasions what she planned to do once she gave birth, but her responses were vague.

"Why get ahead of ourselves? The future always surprises us," she'd say.

The only thing she'd decided on was the name: The baby would be called Camila if it was a girl, Camilo if it was a boy.

THE THIRD FRIDAY IN October, Nieves woke up in the middle of the night moaning from a headache. Two hours later, on her third cup of black coffee—which according to her was the universal cure for all ailments—she stood up and a large puddle of amniotic fluid splashed at her feet. Rita called Roy, who happened to be in Los Angeles that week, and soon the four of us were in the waiting room of the maternity ward. Nieves wasn't having contractions, she only complained of an unbearable headache.

We waited a long while before they finally examined her and discovered that her blood pressure was through the roof. The hours and days that followed melded into a single night of fragmented images, a kaleidoscope of faces, hallways, elevators, blue scrubs and white lab coats, the smell of disinfectant, doctor's orders, syringes, Roy Cooper's hand on my arm. Eclampsia, they said. I'd never heard that term before.

"I'm fine, Mom," Nieves murmured with her eyes closed and a hand on her forehead to block the blinding glare of the overhead lights.

That was the last I saw of her. They wheeled her away, racing toward the double doors and disappearing behind them, leaving us alone in the freezing corridor.

They told us they'd done everything possible to save her, but they weren't able to stabilize her blood pressure; she had convulsions, lost consciousness, and fell into a coma. They performed a Cesarean section to remove the baby, but Nieves's heart failed and she died minutes later. I am infinitely sorry, Camilo. I would've wanted you to rest for at least a moment on your mother's breast after being born, to breathe in her smell, absorb her warmth, feel her loving hands and hear her voice saying your name.

How long did we wait? An eternity. At some point a nurse placed the baby in my arms, wrapped in a little white blanket, with a blue cap on its head, tiny, wrinkled, light as a puff of cotton, breathing softly.

"Camilo, Camilo . . ." I whispered, crying.

"You're the grandmother, right? Your grandson is fine, but the pediatrician needs to examine him and run some tests," the woman said.

You had to remain under observation in the newborn nursery, where we could visit you; it would only be a matter of days; you were underweight and jaundiced, nothing serious, conditions that normally resolved on their own, they told us, but . . . The nurse allowed me to hold you for a few minutes, then took you away.

They brought us apple juice, and Roy gave me a pill that I swallowed without any questions. I suppose it was a tranquilizer. I couldn't accept what had happened; I didn't understand their explanations; I asked for Nieves as if I hadn't heard them say she was dead. Another person, who introduced himself as the hospital chaplain, guided us to a small nondenominational chapel lined with light-colored wood and lit by the sun shining through the stained-glass windows. There, my daughter was laid out so we could say goodbye to her.

Nieves was sleeping. She looked peaceful and more beautiful than ever, her delicate golden skin and her doll-like eyelashes framed by honey-colored hair with white tips. Roy announced that he would fill out the necessary forms and gestured for Rita and the chaplain to follow, so that I could be alone with my daughter. It was in that hospital chapel, my heart broken from sorrow, where I promised Nieves that I would be mother, father, and grandmother to her son—a much better mother than I'd been to her, the selfless and honorable father she'd never had, and the best grandmother in the world. I vowed to live out the years she didn't get to so that Camilo would never be an orphan, and that I would give him everything and love him so much that he would have enough left over to give to others. All that and much more I told her, sobbing, stumbling over my words, one promise after another, so that she could go in peace.

Telling you all this, Camilo, the stab of pain that sliced through my chest that day comes back in full force; it's a recurring pain that ambushes me out of nowhere. There can't be a pain worse than that one, so great it has no name. I know, I know, who am I to complain? My daughter's death wasn't a punishment. I'm just a statistic, this is the oldest and most common suffering in human history. Before, no one even expected children to survive, so many died in childhood, and it's still that way in a large part of the world, but that does nothing to lessen the horror when you're the mother. I felt like I'd been emptied out from the inside, I was a bloody cavity, I couldn't breathe, my bones were made of wax, my soul had taken flight. And the world still turned as if nothing had happened: I stand up, take one step then another, find my voice and respond, I haven't lost my mind, I drink water, my mouth full of sand, my eyes burning, and my little girl stiff, frozen, sculpted in alabaster—my daughter who will never again call me Mom, who left a tremendous imprint in her passage through my life, the memory of her laughter, her grace, her rebelliousness, her suffering.

They let me remain beside Nieves for hours in that naked chapel. The daylight winked out of the windows, someone turned on lights shaped like candles and tried to put a cup of tea into my hands, but I couldn't hold it. I was with my daughter, the two of us alone, and I was finally able to tell her what I never said when she was alive: how much I loved her, how I'd missed her for years and years. I said goodbye, kissed her, and asked her forgiveness for the sins of withholding and neglect. I thanked her for having existed, promised her that she would live on in my heart and in her son's, begged her not to leave me, to visit me in dreams, to send me signs and clues, to return incarnated in every beautiful young woman I saw on the street, and to appear to me in spirit during the darkest hours of the night and in the rays of the midday sun. Nieves. Nieves.

· · ·

FINALLY RITA AND ROY came to get me. They helped me stand and circled me in an embrace; they held me up until I was able to gather myself, sheltered in the warmth of their friendship. We said goodbye to Nieves with a kiss on the forehead, and they guided me to the exit. It was dark outside.

Two days later, while you were still under observation in the hospital, your mother was cremated. You have to understand, Camilo, that I couldn't leave her body in Los Angeles, so far from her family and her country. I kept her ashes with me until I was able to place the urn in the crypt reserved for our family in the Nahuel cemetery. I go there to visit her.

Once again it was Roy Cooper who came to my aid in the darkest moment of my life. Naturally, in any normal family, I would've been the one to take charge of the baby, but Roy pointed out that, by birth, my grandson was a U.S. citizen and it would be a nightmare to get authorization to take him out of the country. In the absence of a mother or father, a judge would determine his fate, a long process, and in the meantime the baby would have to stay in a foster home assigned by the family court. Roy wasn't even finished explaining the problem before I lost it; the first idea that popped into my head was to steal my grandson from the hospital and disappear with him. Undoubtedly, Julián Bravo could help me smuggle a baby to the southern end of the world, his means of skirting the law were endless.

"That won't be necessary. We'll register Camilo as my son," Roy interrupted.

"What are you saying?"

"Let's pretend I had a brief affair with Nieves. I recognize my paternity and accept the economic responsibility. The boy won't bear my last name, in line with the mother's express wishes. She wanted him to be named Camilo Del Valle, because she didn't want to use the last name Bravo. Do you understand?"

"No."

"I can decide what happens to the baby because I'm supposedly the father. I can grant custody to his grandmother and authorize her to take him back to her country. Forget about Julián Bravo."

"Tell me the truth, Roy: Are you Camilo's father?"

"No, woman, good God! How could you think I'd ever sleep with Nieves?"

"But, Roy, then why . . ."

"Didn't I tell you I earn my living solving other people's problems? This is just one more."

That's how it happened, Camilo. Roy Cooper was listed as your father on your birth certificate, but of course he isn't your dad. He took care of your mother in the last months of her life and lent his name to this ruse out of affection for her and for me. His plan worked and I was able to take you out of the United States without any trouble, and then I registered you here, which is why you have dual citizenship.

. . .

SEVEN DAYS AFTER YOUR birth, they finally released you from the hospital and I walked out of there with you in my arms. You'd recovered from the jaundice that had made you as yellow as an egg yolk, and your weight had improved. They told me that you weren't premature, even though you looked like it. You were very little and ugly—bald, pale, with big ears, and mute—you barely moved and didn't cry.

"This little mouse needs sunshine and Latin music, to make him want to live a little," Roy joked, but it was good advice.

I moved into Rita's house with you, because you weren't ready for travel, and I started the job of fattening you up. At first you wouldn't eat and I got hysterical trying to force the bottle on you, but Rita had the idea to give you milk through a medicine dropper. What a saint. She spent hours at it.

And your grandfather Julián? What role did he have in all this? I called him and explained what had happened; it would've been impossible to hide it from him. For the first time in the many years I'd known him I heard him sob. He cried over his beloved daughter for a long time, unable to speak, and when he did it wasn't to ask for details, but to offer help: His grandson would want for nothing as long as he was alive, he promised. I didn't have the heart to tell him that I would be taking custody of the baby and that I didn't need his help. I simply explained how Nieves had lived after escaping the Utah clinic and the part that Roy Cooper had played.

"Cooper? What does Cooper have to do with my daughter?"

"Nieves called him. He acted like a father to her."

"I'm Nieves's father!"

"I don't know what happened between you and Nieves, but she didn't want you to know where she was or that she was pregnant."

"I would have helped her."

"I can only tell you what happened in the final months of her life. She was at peace, free of drugs, well cared for by our Mexican friend, and the boy is healthy. If you want to see him, you can come to Los Angeles. As soon as I can, I'm taking him home. We'll raise him there among all of us."

Your grandfather couldn't travel to Los Angeles, so he met you a few months later in Sacramento. But he sent Roy Cooper a check and a thank-you note. Roy, livid, tore up the check.

Between the medicine dropper, the sunshine, and the rancheras, joropos, and rumbas on the radio, the little mouse survived, and six weeks later we said goodbye to Roy Cooper and Rita Linares, who had done so much for us, and traveled back home. A baby is a full-time job; it saps your energy, sleep, and mental health. It was a serious inconvenience for a woman of fifty-two, as I was then, but you restored my youth. I fell in love with you, Camilo, which helped me face the challenge of raising a child and transformed my grief over the loss of your mother into a celebration of my grandson's life.

18

Facunda told me about how the agrarian reforms had expropriated several of the farms surrounding Santa Clara, such as the Moreau lands, though they hadn't affected the Schmidt-Englers. My former father-in-law decided that he wasn't going to sell his products at the official price imposed by the government, and he closed down his dairy and cheese factory. The cows vanished overnight; I think they took them across the border, where they could be kept until the country returned to normal.

Ever more concerning rumors were circulating about Colonia Esperanza. A journalist had begun to investigate, calling it an enclave of foreigners who lived beyond the law and were a threat to national security, but no one seemed to pay much attention. The settlers had not committed any proven crime, and they earned the respect of their neighbors by opening a small clinic to treat the locals for free and regularly donating crates of produce to the church to be distributed among the poorest families.

"They're untouchable; they're protected by the military. The special forces are trained there," Julián told me on one of his visits.

I discovered that he was piloting unregistered private flights to Colonia. The army was planning to build a runway there, but in the meantime Julián's seaplane could land on the lake. I asked him what he was transporting for those strange people, but he didn't answer.

Juan Martín was close to graduating from college and had been elected president of the students' association. He walked around wearing a poncho, with long hair and a shaggy beard, as was the style among the progressive youths. He often appeared on television as student representative, and although his ideas were revolutionary, his tone was conciliatory. He warned of the dangers of the opposition's Fascist activities, but he also denounced the tactics employed by far left groups, which did as much damage as the right. That earned him enemies within his own ranks. Everyone lived on the extreme ends of political passion; they didn't want to hear reasonable calls for dialogue or negotiation.

• • •

ELEVEN MONTHS AFTER YOUR birth, a military coup overthrew the government; it was a bloodbath, just as Julián Bravo had predicted. His trips to our country became so frequent it was as if he'd moved here. He was very busy with government business, as he informed me, without clarifying what that business was. We didn't see each other often, because I was settled with you in Sacramento and he spent most of his time in the capital. When he came to the south he rarely even let me know.

The coup was carried out like a meticulous military operation. The armed forces and the police rebelled at dawn one Tuesday in spring, and by noon they'd bombarded the presidential palace, the president was dead, and the country was under military command. Repression began immediately. There was no resistance in Sacramento, quite the opposite: The people I knew applauded from their balconies because they'd spent three years waiting for those heroic soldiers to save the nation from the hypothetical Communist dictatorship. Martial law went into effect anyway. The soldiers were dressed for war in camouflage, their faces painted like Apaches from the movies so they couldn't be identified, and the security forces patrolled the city in black cars. Helicopters buzzed overhead like botflies, heavy tanks and trucks filed past, scarring the asphalt and scattering the stray dogs that roamed the streets. We heard police sirens, gunshots, and explosions. No one was allowed out; all travel by air, train, and bus was suspended; and checkpoints were set up along the highways to catch the fleeing subversives, terrorists, and guerrillas. It wasn't the first time that we'd heard mention of those enemies of the state: The right-wing media had warned they were Soviet agents, preparing for an armed revolution with long lists of people to execute.

Communication was difficult. I couldn't get in touch with Juan Martín, who was in the capital, or even with José Antonio, who lived a few blocks away. Julián, on the other hand, showed up out of nowhere, when I thought he was in Miami, and announced that he had no trouble getting around; he had permission to circulate because he provided essential services to the military junta in power.

"Follow the instructions they give you on television, Violeta. Stay home; don't go to the office until things calm down. If you need me, leave a message at the hotel."

The first three days the country was in total lockdown, no one could leave their home without a special permit or, in the case of a serious emergency, waving a white handkerchief. The soldiers, inflamed, pushed people through the streets and herded them onto military trucks using the butts of their rifles, taking them to some unknown destination. They lit bonfires in the plazas and burned books, documents, and voter registrations, because democracy had been suspended until further notice. All political parties and Congress recessed indefinitely, and the press was censured. Gatherings of more than six people were prohibited, but in many clubs and hotels, even the Hotel Bavaria, people got together to drink champagne and sing the national anthem. I'm referring to the people of means who had been eagerly awaiting the military coup, especially the large landholders in the region, who hoped to recover their property, which was confiscated by the agrarian reform. The supporters of the Socialist government, laborers and farmworkers, students and poor people in general, were holed up in silence, according to Julián Bravo. The television showed the four generals standing between the flag and the national shield, giving orders to the citizens, followed by Disney cartoons. Rumors circulated with a hurricane force, but they were contradictory and impossible to confirm. I locked myself inside my home, as Julián had ordered me to do. I was very busy with you, my grandson, already crawling around every corner of the house, sticking your fingers in the power outlets, eating dirt and worms. I assumed that things would soon be back to normal.

THREE DAYS LATER, WHEN lockdown was lifted for a few hours, Miss Taylor came to see me with the pretext of bringing powdered milk for the baby, which we hadn't been able to get for several months.

Suddenly the store shelves were fully stocked with items that had been scarce before. We sat in the living room to drink my former governess's favorite Darjeeling tea, and she explained the real reason for her visit.

"They raided the university in the capital, Violeta. They arrested professors and students, especially from the journalism and sociology departments. They say the walls of the college are splattered with blood."

"Juan Martín!" I shouted, my teacup crashing to the floor.

"Your son is on the blacklist. He's been ordered to turn himself in at any police station and they're looking for him. As president of the students' association, he's at the top of their list."

"What happened to him?"

"He got to our house last night. I don't know how he managed to cross several provinces in the middle of the lockdown. He didn't come here because this will be the first place they look for him. We have him hidden, but he needs to get out of the country."

"Julián is the only person who can help with that."

"No, Violeta. Your son says that Julián is complicit with the military and works for the CIA, who's behind all this."

"He'd never turn in his own son!"

"We're not sure about that. José Antonio thinks we can hide Juan Martín at Santa Clara, at least for a little while. No one will look for him on the farm.

But how can we get him there? The trains aren't running, there are checkpoints everywhere."

"I'll take care of it, Josephine."

MY ONLY RECOURSE TO save Juan Martín was to turn to his father. I managed to convince him to come to Sacramento to talk to me, even though he was very busy in those turbulent days, as he told me.

"How many times did I warn that boy to be careful? And now you come begging me for help! Isn't it a little too late?"

"That boy is your son, Julián!"

"Look, Violeta, there's nothing I can do. You want me to risk my career? They watch me. If Juan Martín could get to Sacramento in full lockdown, he can find a safe place to hide himself."

"I thought he could go . . ."

"Don't tell me anything! I don't want to know where he is or where he's going. The less I know, the better. I can't be an accomplice to this."

"For once it isn't about you, Julián. Right now Juan Martín is all that matters. Don't you see that they're killing people?"

"We're at war with the Communists. The ends justify the means."

Julián Bravo was a scoundrel who had a terrible relationship with his son. Eventually, though, just as I'd predicted, he grudgingly helped me to get Juan

Martín out of Sacramento. It took him under two hours to get me a travel permit from the regional commander. Those were other times, Camilo. Now you can find out someone's identity in under a minute and even the most intimate details of their life, but in the seventies that wasn't always possible. A second travel permit was issued in the name of Lorena Benítez, nanny.

Thirty-six hours later, as soon as the curfew lifted at 6:00 A.M., I put you into the car, with the clothes we would need and a bit of food, and went to pick up Juan Martín at one of the Rustic Homes warehouses, where my brother had hidden him. The last time I'd seen him he looked like a hairy prophet, but the person waiting for me now was a tall thin woman, her hair tied back with a ribbon and wearing a blue apron: Lorena Benítez. Despite the disguise, you immediately recognized your uncle and threw your arms around his neck. Luckily you were not able to speak yet.

We drove without a word until we left Sacramento, passed the first checkpoint, and got onto the highway headed south. The soldiers on duty were nervous, aggressive boys, armed to the teeth, who read our permits slowly since they were practically illiterate. They examined my ID, made us get out of the car so they could give it a detailed search, even removing the seats, but they threw only a passing glance at the supposed nanny. Our infallibly classist society and the typical **machista** disrespect for women helped get us through that first checkpoint as well as the others along the way.

I asked Juan Martín why he hadn't turned himself in; those who gave themselves up freely had nothing to fear, as they'd said on television.

"What planet do you live on, Mom? If I turn myself in, I could disappear forever."

"What do you mean, 'disappear'? I don't understand."

"Anyone can be arrested—they don't need a reason—and then they deny ever having detained you. No one knows what happened to you—you become a ghost. They've killed several students from my department and taken more than twenty professors."

"Well, they must've done something wrong, Juan Martín," I stammered, repeating the phrase I'd heard so many times among my circle of friends.

"They've done the same thing I've done, Mom: They're defending the democratically elected government."

The train from Sacramento to the farm usually took a little over two hours and it was normally three or four by car. But we were stopped so many times along the way that we spent almost seven hours on the road to Nahuel, exhausted and our nerves frayed. Luckily you slept almost the entire way in the arms of Lorena Benítez, the nanny, who never aroused any suspicions.

. . .

WE ARRIVED A FEW hours before the curfew went into effect, though it wasn't really enforced in that remote region. Torito and Facunda welcomed us without comment, although it must've surprised them to see Juan Martín dressed as a woman. I think they automatically understood that it was a matter of life and death. My son told them in few words what had happened in the capital and the rest of the country. Santa Clara was an oasis of calm.

"I have to get across the border," he told them.

You, Camilo, arrived hungry, dying of thirst, and with your diapers soaked, and went straight into the arms of Etelvina Muñoz, Facunda's eldest granddaughter. Narcisa, her mother, had had her at age fifteen. The girl helped her grandmother raise her siblings and worked on the farm; she had a broad back, strong hands, a round face, and an enormous intelligence. She had never gone to school but could read and write thanks to Lucinda Rivas, who had taught her what she could before she was defeated by old age, and finally death.

That night you slept curled up on a cot between Facunda and Etelvina, and I slept with my son on the wrought-iron bed that had belonged to my mother. I lay for hours in the dark, aware of every sound outside, fearing that a military jeep or police car might pull up at any moment and take

Juan Martín. I went over and over the mistakes I'd made as a mother, how I'd so often failed my son because I was too concerned with work and I let his sister hog all the attention, recalling the little boy with the idealistic spirit who clashed with his father from such a young age. I finally slept for a few hours around dawn and when I woke up, Facunda had already prepared breakfast; Etelvina had taken you with her, perched on a hip, to milk the cow, and Juan Martín was helping Torito with the other animals. The morning was cool and dew sparkled on the leaves as a bluish mist rose up from the earth warmed by the sun. The penetrating aroma of fresh bay leaf brought back vivid memories of my childhood at Santa Clara, a time that would always be sacred to me. We spent the day close to the house so that we wouldn't draw attention, although the property was fairly isolated. We dug some clothes out of an old trunk that José Antonio had left behind years before. The pants, boots, and moth-eaten sweaters would be good enough for the fugitive.

We gathered around the table with cups of tea and Facunda's fresh baked bread, as Juan Martín told us about the cursory trials and arbitrary executions; of detainees tortured to death; thousands and thousands of people arrested and dragged away in broad daylight, in plain sight of anyone who dared to look; of the holding cells, military bases, sports stadiums, and even entire schools filled with prisoners; of the makeshift concentration camps set up to hold the detainees, and other horrors. I thought it couldn't possibly be true, because, until then, our country had been a shining example of peaceful democracy on a continent ravaged by tyrants, dictatorships, and coups. I thought it was merely Communist propaganda. And yet I knew there must've been a very good reason for my son to flee disguised as a woman.

AT DUSK, TORITO BEGAN to pack the necessary items in the bundle he always carried when he went on his trips.

"You're coming with me, Juanito," he said to my son.

"Do you have a weapon, Torito?"

"This," the giant man replied, showing him the butcher knife he used for everything, which he always took with him on his adventures.

"I mean a firearm," Juan Martín said.

"This isn't the Wild West, no one here has guns. I don't suppose you plan to go around shooting things up," I interrupted.

"You can't let them take me alive, Torito. Do you promise me?"

"I promise."

"My God, son! What are you insinuating?" I shouted.

"I promise," Torito repeated.

They left as soon as it got dark. It was a warm

spring night and the full moon gave off enough light for us to watch them walk away in the opposite direction of the road. I had the terrible premonition that this would be a permanent goodbye, but I kept myself from voicing it because we shouldn't call down misfortune, as my aunts always said. Torito was a few years shy of seventy, according to our calculations, but I didn't doubt that he'd be able to climb those mountains and cross the invisible border on foot, with nothing but the clothes on his back, two blankets, and basic equipment for hunting and fishing. He knew the forgotten footpaths and mountain trails that only the old local guides and some indigenous people still used. Juan Martín, on the other hand, who was some forty-five years younger, was unprepared for that adventure, and could be easily done in by fatigue, panic, cold, or a fall off a cliff. He was an intellectual, had never excelled in sports, and had a cautious nature, so different from his sister. Nieves would've been in her element fleeing from an enemy.

19

I SPENT THIRTEEN DAYS AT SANTA CLARA awaiting news of my son and Torito, alongside Facunda, Etelvina, and Etelvina's younger siblings. Narcisa had taken off with her latest boyfriend, leaving her litter of children in the care of her oldest daughter and her mother, and she wasn't able to get back; she was who knows where when lockdown went into effect. Every hour that passed was a torment. I counted the minutes and marked the days on a calendar, wondering why Torito was taking so long to return. It had been more than enough time for him to get to the border and back, unless something terrible had happened. I spent the better part of those days scanning the road and the surrounding fields, so anxious that I didn't have the energy to take care of you, who crawled half naked among the chickens, eating dirt like some feral creature. The other kids were much older and annoyed by the baby following them around everywhere. Trying to keep up with them, you took your first steps, Camilo. I didn't see them, or hear you say your first word: "Tina," since you couldn't pronounce Etelvina. And that's what you've called her ever since.

Facunda kept up her usual routines: She tended the garden and did the chores, she made pies and empanadas to sell, went to the market, chatted with her friends in Nahuel, and returned with the latest news. There was a troop of soldiers quartered two kilometers from Santa Clara, she told me. They had taken a group of tenant farmers away in military trucks and no one knew what had happened to them. The landowners had recovered their confiscated farms by force and were retaliating against the poor farmers who had occupied them through evictions, beatings, and arrests.

There wasn't a single vacationer or tourist to be seen, even though the summer heat had settled in; the plazas and beaches were empty, as were the hotels, with the exception of the Hotel Bavaria, where the military and government officials stayed. In Nahuel the soldiers used the butts of their rifles to herd up a group of young people and make them whitewash the murals painted with political propaganda. They broke a man's jaw in the market for using the word "comrade," which was now outlawed, along with the terms "the people," "democracy," and "military coup." The acceptable term was "military proclamation."

"They're arresting all men with beards or long hair, then beating them and shaving them. Women aren't allowed to wear pants, because the soldiers don't like it, but how are we going to plow the fields and clean out the stables, then?" Facunda asked.

PEOPLE WERE SCARED, AND no one wanted trouble; the most prudent thing to do was to stay inside. That's why it surprised us when a foreigner showed up on the farm, tall as a basketball player, with enormous feet, skin tanned by the sun, white-blond hair, and blue eyes, speaking Spanish like he'd learned it from a dictionary. He introduced himself as Harald Fiske and asked if we had a telephone, because the Nahuel phone center was closed at that time of day. He was one of the bird-watchers who turned up every year, inexplicably, since our variety is pathetic compared to the orgy of multicolored feathers in the Amazon Basin or the Central American jungle.

Harald Fiske was forty years old, with the ungainly body of a boy who'd just gone through a growth spurt, and premature wrinkles from excessive sun exposure. He carried a huge backpack, three pairs of binoculars, several cameras, and a thick notebook full of writing in code, like a spy. He was so oblivious that he was actually chasing after birds during those dark days of the nascent dictatorship, in a nation where the very air we breathed was restricted. He planned to pitch a tent and camp on the beach.

"Listen, don't be stupid. Do you want them to kill you?" I asked.

"I've been coming to this country every summer for years, ma'am. I've never been robbed," the man insisted.

"In place of robbers, we have soldiers now."

"I'm a diplomat," he said.

"Your passport won't do you much good if they shoot before they ask to see it. You'd better stay here."

"I can let him use Torito's bed, but if he comes back tonight you'll have to sleep on the floor," Facunda said.

And that's how the man entered our life, Camilo. He was employed with the Norwegian foreign office, stationed in Holland with his wife and two kids. He said he loved Latin America, that he'd traveled it from north to south, and that he liked our country especially. Facunda took him in like a dopey son, and from then on whenever he came to the south to watch his birds he stayed at Santa Clara.

AFTER THIRTEEN DAYS OF fruitless waiting, Yaima came riding up on the back of a mule. The indigenous healer, who for decades had been unscathed by the passage of time, was at last showing signs of deterioration. I hadn't seen her since Aunt Pilar's funeral, and in truth I imagined she must've died, but despite her appearance of a centuries-old witch she was still as strong and lucid as ever. She'd known me since I was a prepubescent girl, but she'd never shown the slightest interest in me, which is why I was surprised when she arrived with a message for me. Facunda offered to translate, since the woman's Spanish was as limited as my knowledge of her language.

"Fuchan, the big friend, was taken by the soldiers."

Facunda fell to her knees, sobbing, and my thoughts went immediately to my son.

"Fuchan was with another man, a young man. What happened to him, Yaima?" I shook her.

"We saw Fuchan. The other one we didn't see. There will be a ceremony for Fuchan. We will tell you."

That meant that the tribe had given Torito up for dead.

If Torito had been alone, he must've been returning home and that meant that my son might've escaped. I didn't want to imagine even for an instant that the good man had kept his promise to prevent Juan Martín from falling into the hands of the military by any means necessary. We had to save Torito, and the only thing I could think to do was turn to Julián. With his connections, he could surely find out what had happened to Torito and his son.

After all those years, we still didn't have a phone at the farm and we feared that the public phones in Nahuel might be bugged, but I didn't have a choice.

I called Julián's usual hotels in Sacramento and the capital and left him messages saying I'd call back later that night.

"I suppose you're calling me about Camilo's baptism. His uncle will be the godfather, right?" he asked before I could say a word.

"Yes . . ." I answered, confused.

"How is his uncle?"

"I don't know. Can you come?"

"I'm staying at the Hotel Bavaria tomorrow. I have a meeting near there. I'll stop by to see you."

This absurd dialogue in code confirmed the degree of repression we were living with, just as Juan Martín had forewarned. If Julián didn't feel safe, no one was safe. For three years the right-wing propaganda had been sermonizing about the horrors of a Communist dictatorship. Now we were experiencing the real-life terrors of a Fascist one. The military junta claimed that these were only temporary measures, but that they would continue indefinitely, until Christian and Western values were restored to the nation. I held on to the illusion that our country had the most solid tradition of democracy on the continent, that we'd been a model of civic duty in the world, that we'd soon have elections and democracy would be reinstated. Then Juan Martín could come home.

. . .

JULIÁN SWORE THAT HE wasn't able to get any information about Torito, but I didn't believe him. He had contacts in the highest circles of power, and I was sure he could make a simple phone call to find out who had detained him—whether it had been the police, the special forces, or the military—and where he was. It should've been as important to him to save Torito as it was to me, if only to find out what had happened to our son. Imagining the diverse ways Juan Martín—and Torito—could've died was torture for me.

"You always think the worst, Violeta. I bet he's dancing the tango in Buenos Aires," he said.

His mocking confirmed my suspicion that he knew something and was hiding it from me. I hated him for it.

It was useless to stay on the farm waiting for news. I said goodbye to Facunda, who had become the nominal owner of Santa Clara, managing what little remained of the property, and I returned to Sacramento. At the last minute, Facunda asked me to take Etelvina with me, because stuck on the farm, her granddaughter was destined to a life of hard labor, poverty, and suffering.

"She can help raise Camilo. You don't have to pay her much, but teach her everything you can—she's eager to learn," she told me.

That was forty-seven years ago, by my calculations,

Camilo. I never imagined that Etelvina would be more important in my life than the sum of all the men who have loved me.

José Antonio needed me in Sacramento; we had a lot of work ahead of us to save what remained of the company. The military junta was carefully auditing our collaboration with the previous government, and in the meantime the contract for My Own Home was on hold. We were summoned several times to the office of a colonel, who interrogated us like criminals, but in the end they didn't arrest us. We lost a lot, because we'd invested in new machinery and materials to produce homes in record time, but we had other projects in the works. I can't complain: I've never wanted for money, and I was always able to make a good living.

I spent years tormented by uncertainties over the fate of Juan Martín; I mourned both the death of my daughter and the possible death of my son. You were my only consolation. You were a very mischievous child, Camilo, and you never gave me a moment's peace. You were short and skinny until adolescence, when you shot up so fast I had to buy your school uniform three sizes too big so that it would last you the whole year, and new shoes every seven weeks. You had your mother's courage and your uncle Juan Martín's idealism. At seven years old you came home with a bloody nose and a black eye after confronting a much bigger boy who was abusing an animal. You gave everything away, from your toys down to my clothes, which you stole from me secretly. "You demonic little brat! I should throw you in jail! Then maybe you'd learn!" I'd shout. But I was never able to punish you, because deep down I admired your generosity. You were my son/grandson, my partner in crime, my best friend in the world. You still are, I have to say.

I DON'T WANT TO spend too much time dwelling on the long years of the dictatorship, Camilo; it's an old and well-known story. It's been thirty years now since democracy was restored, and the worst of our past has come to light: the concentration camps, torture, murders, and repression that so many people suffered. None of that can be denied, though at the time, there was no concrete information, only rumors. Some people still try to justify it today, saying the measures were necessary to impose order and save the country from Communism. There were dictatorships in many Latin American countries; we weren't the only ones. Those were the times of the Cold War between the United States and the Soviet Union, and we were in the American zone of influence, where there was zero tolerance for leftist ideas, as Julián Bravo had warned. The Russians in turn imposed their ideology in the part of the world they controlled.

On the surface, the country had never been better. Visitors marveled at our skyscrapers, highways, and safe streets; there was no graffiti, no more protests or students barricaded inside their schools on strike, no stray dogs or beggars asking for alms. They all vanished. No one spoke about politics; it was dangerous. People learned to be punctual, to respect hierarchy and authority, to work; anyone who didn't work didn't eat, the slogan went. The regime's iron fist put an end to political games and we stepped into the future, no longer a poor and underdeveloped country but transformed, by force, into a prosperous and disciplined one. That was the official discourse anyway. Inside, however, we were an ailing nation. Inside, Camilo, I was sick with grief over my fugitive son, over Torito's disappearance, and because I would've had to be blind not to see the dire situation faced by my employees, stricken with poverty and fear.

We got used to being careful with our words, avoiding certain topics, never calling attention to ourselves and always obeying the rules. We also got used to the curfew, which lasted fifteen years, forcing womanizing husbands and rebellious teens to get home early. The crime rate decreased dramatically. The government was committing atrocities, but you could walk down the street and sleep soundly at night without worrying about being robbed by common criminals. It was a very hard time for workers, who had no rights and could be fired from one day to the next; unemployment was high, making it a paradise for business owners. This prosperity for some came at an enormous social cost. The economic boom lasted several years, before it came crashing down. For a while we were the envy of our neighbors and the darlings of the United States. We talk about corruption, now called "illicit enrichment," but during the dictatorship it was legal. The military had their hand in everything and always received a cut.

JOSÉ ANTONIO HAD SUFFERED a heart attack and was at home, cared for by Miss Taylor, but he remained the president of our companies. He knew everybody in Sacramento, had hundreds of friends, and was loved and respected. His experience and his contacts were crucial for winning contracts and getting loans, but Anton Kusanovic and I did all the work. We compensated our staff as best we could, but we had to keep costs down to compete in a fierce market.

"At least they have jobs and are treated with dignity, Violeta," Anton reminded me.

Walking the line between justice, compassion, and greed disgusted me so much that I eventually convinced José Antonio to sell our part of the prefabricated home business to Anton, so my brother could spend his final years in peace and I could dedicate myself to other things. It was the ideal moment to invest in property and close business deals. Many people were selling land at bargain prices and leaving the country, some exiled, others because they abhorred the military regime or wanted better economic opportunities. You could buy low and sell high, as had been my father's motto.

I moved with you and Etelvina to the capital, where the residential and commercial market was more varied and interesting than in the provinces. I did well. There was a lot of inventory and I had a good eye as well as strong negotiation skills. I bought properties in excellent locations, even if they were in bad shape; I renovated them and sold them for a substantial profit. In a short time I'd become an expert in construction, remodeling, interior design, and mortgages; that is the basis of what you call my fortune, Camilo, but that term applied to my wealth is ridiculous. My earnings were meager compared to what was earned by those who employed immoral means to get rich at that time. Those people are the billionaires of today.

Etelvina helped take care of you, because you were too young to enter San Ignacio, which was the best school in the country, despite the fact that it was run by priests. That good woman and I spoiled you so rotten that, if you'd been any other boy, you would've been a selfish monster. But you were a delight. The fact that I'd neglected my children when they were young weighed on my conscience, and I made it my mission not to let the same thing happen to my grandson. I arranged my schedule so that I could spend time with you. I helped you with your homework. Etelvina and I went to all your sporting events and horrible school plays, and we spent our vacations at Santa Clara, where Facunda pampered us with her delicious cooking. I only ever left you to go see Roy, that man full of secrets, in the United States.

The apartment we lived in for many years was old, from a time before the winds of modernization reduced spaces and imposed cold glass and hard steel. The building overlooked the Parque Japonés and I got the flat cheap because the neighborhood was out of fashion, even with its mansions and several embassies. I eventually sold it at an exorbitant price to someone who wanted to erect a thirty-story tower in its place. The villas of the nouveau riche rose up like fortresses on the hillsides, surrounded by tall walls and guarded by mastiffs, while the middle class and businesses occupied our neighborhood. The entrance to our building was attended day and night by two friendly doormen, the Sepúlveda twins, so similar that it was impossible to tell which one was on duty. Our apartment took up the entire third floor; the hallways were so wide and long that you learned to ride your bike in them. It had an air of faded splendor, with high ceilings, parquet floors, and beveled-glass windows that reminded me of Camellia House.

At first, the apartment seemed too big for Etelvina, me, and one little boy, but a few months later José Antonio and Miss Taylor came to live with us. My brother's heart was failing and he couldn't receive the same level of care in Sacramento as he would in the capital at the English Clinic, where he often had to be rushed for treatment. He'd arrive half dead, but they always managed to miraculously revive him. They both hated the city's noise, toxic smog, and traffic, so they rarely went out; they became addicted to telenovelas, which they followed religiously along with you and Etelvina. At four years old you knew all about the most violent human passions and could repeat lurid dialogues in a Mexican accent. I couldn't wait for the moment you were old enough to go to school and broaden your horizons a bit.

Those were the hardest years of the dictatorship, when power was consolidated through violence. Still, except for the terrible uncertainty about the fate of Juan Martín and Torito, they were relatively good years for our small family. I was able to help my brother in his old age, I recovered my previous closeness with Miss Taylor, and I made the most of your childhood.

Etelvina ran the house without any interference on my part because I'd never been interested in domesticity; she managed the daily expenses and supervised the two maids, whom she required to dress in uniform. She memorized recipes from cooking shows on television, and learned to execute them as well as any chef. Miss Taylor taught her the old-fashioned, practically obsolete manners that she'd learned at age seventeen from her second boss, that widow in London. To make up for our lack of a liveried butler, like they had in the telenovelas, Etelvina imposed courtly rituals on us. "Why bother having fine china if we never use it?" she'd say, as she positioned a candelabra in the center of the table and lined up three glasses per place setting. You knew when to use the butter knife and the tool to crack crab before you could tie your shoes.

My age didn't slow me down in the slightest. I was nearing sixty but felt as strong and productive as I had at thirty. I earned more than enough to support the family and save without killing myself at work; I played tennis to keep in shape, without much enthusiasm, because the obsession over hitting a ball with a racket seemed absurd to me. I had an active social life, with more than one romantic encounter that interested me for a few days before I moved on without a second thought. My great love at the time was Roy Cooper, but we were thousands of miles apart.

In his way, Julián loved you dearly, Camilo. He was bored by you, and I don't blame him because children are a nuisance, but what he lacked in patience he made up for with enthusiasm. He presented you with gifts fit for a sheik, which riled you up and caused chaos at home. He taught you everything that Juan Martín had refused to learn: shooting, archery, boxing, and horseback riding, but he was irritated that you did not excel in any of these activities. He bought you a horse, which ended up with Facunda on the farm, put out to pasture in the country instead of jumping hurdles and winning competitions at the hippodrome.

You once mentioned that you'd like to have a dog and so your grandfather bought you a puppy. In no time it grew into a huge black beast that sowed terror among the neighbors in our building, even though he was very sweet-natured. I'm talking about Crispín, the Doberman pinscher that was your beloved pet and slept beside you every night until I eventually sent you to boarding school at San Ignacio.

20

I SPENT FOUR YEARS WITH NO NEWS OF JUAN Martín, cautiously asking around here and there, careful not to arouse suspicion. His name was still on the blacklist; the fact that they were looking for him gave me hope that he might still be alive.

Here's what I would finally learn: Just as his father had sarcastically suggested, he spent some time in Argentina, not dancing the tango but working as a journalist. He earned barely enough to get by. With false identification and a pen name, he wrote articles for various news outlets, and sent information about our country's dictatorship and resistance to Europe, especially Germany, where they had compassion for the thousands of refugees who flocked there.

He could've sent me a message, to at least let me know he was alive, but he didn't. His excuse for this terrible silence—which caused me to grieve for him all those years, afraid he'd died in the mountain crossing or later—was to hide his whereabouts from his father.

His friends were journalists, artists, and intellectuals who shared his politics. There was one young woman especially, Vania Halperin, who caught his eye. She was the daughter of Jewish Holocaust survivors, fragile and pale, with black hair, dark eyes, and a face like a Madonna from a Renaissance painting. Seeing that delicate young woman play the violin in the symphony orchestra, no one would've suspected her revolutionary fervor. Her brother was a member of the Montoneros, a guerrilla organization that the military wanted to root out and exterminate. Juan Martín pursued her with the solemn tenacity of a first love, even though she kept him at a distance.

Buenos Aires, sophisticated and fascinating, is the Paris of Latin America; with a vibrant cultural scene, the best theater and live music, it is the birthplace of many world-famous writers. Juan Martín spent his nights in a loft apartment with a group of like-minded young people, discussing philosophy and politics around bottles of cheap wine, dizzy from the cigarette smoke and their revolutionary passion. He didn't regrow his beard to match his bohemian friends, because he had to look like the picture in his fake passport. He relived the euphoric days of his university years: the left-wing government, the awakening of society, the illusion of power in the hands of the people. I say "illusion," because in reality it was never that way, Camilo, not then and not now. Economic and military power, which is the kind of power that counts, has always remained in the same hands. We didn't experience anything like the Cuban or Russian revolutions here, we merely had a few years of a progressive government, like many that exist today in Europe. We were in the wrong hemisphere and ahead of our time, which is why we paid so dearly for it.

Juan Martín was just putting down roots in that magnificent city, when the horror of a military coup played out in Argentina as well. The commander-in-chief declared that as many people as necessary would die to restore order to the country; that meant the death squads could act with absolute impunity. Thousands were kidnapped and forcibly disappeared, just as in our country and others; or they were tortured and murdered, and their bodies never found. We now know, Camilo, about the infamous Operation Condor, established in the United States to put right-wing dictatorships in power across our continent and coordinate the cruelest strategies to stamp out dissidence.

The repression in Argentina didn't happen overnight and it wasn't an all-out war like ours; it was a dirty war that surreptitiously infiltrated all realms of society. A bomb exploded in an avant-garde theater, a congressman was gunned down in the street, the mutilated body of a union leader was discovered. The locations of the torture centers were public knowledge, and artists, journalists, professors, political leaders, and anyone else considered suspicious began to vanish. Women searched in vain for their husbands; later on, a group of mothers dared to march with photographs of their missing sons and daughters hung around their necks. Soon the grandmothers joined them, women whose daughters had been murdered after giving birth in prison, the babies lost in the maze of illegal adoption.

How much did Julián Bravo know about all of this? How far did his participation go? I know he received training in the School of the Americas in Panama, just like the officers responsible for the repression in our countries. The generals trusted him because he was an extraordinary pilot; I imagine that his courage, experience, and lack of scruples opened the doors to power for him. Once, with a bottle of whiskey in hand, he got too talkative and confessed that sometimes the passengers on his plane were political prisoners being transported in handcuffs, gagged, and drugged. He swore to me, though, that he had never thrown one of those unfortunate souls into the sea: That task was left to the military helicopter pilots.

"They call them death flights," he added.

FIRST THEY TOOK VANIA Halperin. They waited for her to finish a Vivaldi concert at the Teatro Colón and then they arrested her in the dressing room right in front of the other members of the orchestra.

"Come with us, miss. Don't worry, it's a routine check. You don't need your violin, we'll bring you right back," they were heard saying to her.

The beating would've begun in the car. It's likely that they arrested her to get information on her Montonero brother, but the family hadn't heard from him in months. The other musicians who had witnessed the arrest notified Vania's parents, then spread the word among their friends and put out a call to try to get her released. She was last reported seen at the Navy School of Mechanics, which functioned as a torture center.

After two more members of the group of young bohemians were kidnapped, the rest quickly scattered. The editor of one of the newspapers Juan Martín worked for met with him secretly in a café and warned him that government agents had been to the office looking for him.

"Get as far away as you can as fast as you can," he advised him, but Juan Martín couldn't leave without knowing what had happened to Vania; he was willing to move heaven and earth to save her.

Nevertheless, that same day, as he was nearing his loft, he glimpsed one of the unmistakably terrifying black cars. He turned around and walked away, slowly, to keep from calling attention to himself. He didn't dare to ask for help from his friends, because he didn't want to implicate them.

That night he slept huddled between the tombs of the Recoleta Cemetery, and the next day, lacking any better idea, he went to a safe house run by Belgian missionaries. The Catholic Church in Argentina was complicit with the brutal repression, even with the infamous death flights, but there were dissident priests and nuns who stood up for the victims, many of them paying for it with their lives. The Belgians hid him for a few nights. They assured him that they'd try to find Vania Halperin—they kept lists with information and photographs of kidnapped persons—and convinced him it wouldn't do any good to expose himself. His relationship to Vania would be discovered, it was just a matter of time. State-sponsored terrorism was coordinated internationally, and if he was on the blacklist in his country he was on it in Argentina too. His only hope, they told him, was to seek asylum at an embassy.

Juan Martín had a contact who turned out to be instrumental in helping him: the cultural attaché of the German embassy, who received the articles he wrote to be published in Germany. Even though the German people had harbored thousands of refugees from our continent, the German government discreetly supported the dictatorships in the Southern Cone of Latin America for trade reasons, and maybe ideological ones as well—it was the fight against Communism after all. The ambassador was a personal friend of a leading general in the military junta, but the cultural attaché took pity on Juan Martín. She couldn't offer him protection within her own embassy, but she drove him to the Norwegian one.

My son was harbored there for five weeks, sleeping on a camping cot in one of the offices, awaiting news of Vania Halperin. He spent every single minute imagining the nightmare that the young woman was surely experiencing, the interrogations, torture, rapes, trained dogs, electric shocks, rats. If they didn't find her fugitive brother, they might even arrest her parents and torture them in front of her.

THIRTY-THREE DAYS LATER ONE of the Belgian missionaries arrived at the embassy with news that the body of the young woman had turned up in a morgue. There was no doubt it was Vania; her parents had identified the body. Destroyed by grief and guilt over having survived without her, Juan Martín left for Europe with the false documentation that the Norwegian embassy provided him.

And then, after he was safe in Norway, I received the most unexpected visit: Harald Fiske, the birdwatcher I'd met at Santa Clara just after the coup in our country. He brought me the news and a brief letter written by my son minutes before leaving for the airport with an embassy employee. It was a cold missive, with no personal details, notifying me that he'd soon be able to give me the information I required about the product. He was writing in code.

"For the moment, he still doesn't want his father to know where he is," Harald told me.

I'd endured the anguish over not knowing the fate of my only living child with relative calm and infinite patience for almost four years, but when it hit me that this Norwegian man had seen my son only a few days prior, my knees buckled and I fell into a chair, sobbing. The feeling of relief was like the rush of adrenaline caused by terror, a void in the center of my body followed by a surge of fire through my veins. My piercing shrieks brought Etelvina running, and soon the rest of the family was gathered around me, crying, as the messenger watched our emotional release, paralyzed with discomfort.

Harald had been at his diplomatic post in Argentina for a year, alone now, since he'd gotten divorced and his children were attending university in Europe. He'd flown from Buenos Aires to give me the news of Juan Martín, how he'd escaped just in time, his life in Buenos Aires up until the Dirty War broke out and he had to go into hiding, his work as a journalist, his discreet existence under a false identity, his friends, and his love for Vania Halperin.

"He didn't want to leave without her," he told us.

We didn't know it then, but the seven years of Argentine genocide would leave more than thirty thousand persons murdered or forcibly disappeared.

• • •

ANOTHER YEAR PASSED BEFORE I was finally able to reunite with Juan Martín. He'd arrived in Norway with his heart in shreds, scared and depressed, but the Norwegian Refugee Council, which had been established after the Second World War, was there to help him. A representative was waiting for him when he got off the plane to show him to the small studio apartment he'd been assigned in downtown Oslo, equipped with the basics for a comfortable stay, including warm clothes in his size, since he'd left the southern hemisphere in summer and it was the dead of winter there. The council, and in particular this nice man, would be his lifeline for the first months, providing money for daily expenses, guiding him through the bureaucracy of getting a resident's visa and identification under his real name. They taught him the societal norms and how to move through the city. Then they put him in contact with other Latin American refugees and enrolled him in language classes. They even offered him therapy sessions, since immigrants were eligible for mental health services to help them adapt to their new circumstances and move on from the past. Juan Martín explained that he'd escaped in time and hadn't experienced great trauma. More than therapy, he wanted to work; he couldn't sit idly by receiving charity forever.

I went to Norway to visit him, accompanied by Etelvina and you, Camilo; you were not even six years old and I doubt you remember. In the long years

I'd spent without seeing my son he had changed so much that if he hadn't come up to us in the airport we would've walked right past him. I remembered him as a skinny, awkward, long-haired boy, but I was met with a solid, balding man wearing glasses. He was twenty-eight, but he looked closer to forty. I felt lost before that stranger, and for a moment that seemed to last a century, I wasn't able to move. Then he finally pulled me to him in a huge hug, burying my face in the rough wool of his sweater, and we went right back to being the same as always, mother and son, friends.

Juan Martín no longer lived in the small studio; he'd moved to an apartment on the outskirts of the city and was employed by the Norwegian Refugee Council as a translator and host. He now helped other refugees like him, especially those from Latin America; he had the advantage of sharing the same language and a common history.

My son took a week off work to show us the country, which I would return to many times over the following years. On each trip I noted the changes in Juan Martín's life: how he learned to speak Norwegian with a terrible accent, how he adapted and made friends, one day introducing me to Ulla, the young woman who became my daughter-in-law and the mother of two of my grandchildren. From his description of Vania Halperin, I think that Juan Martín's second love was the opposite of his first. Ulla was a girl tanned by the summer sun and the winter snow, athletic, strong, happy, and free of the existential and political dilemmas that plagued Vania.

Distance erases the contours and colors of memory. I have letters and photographs of the family that Juan Martín built in Norway; he calls me on the phone and has come to see me in recent years, when I no longer had the strength for such a long trip, but when I think of my son I can't seem to conjure the exact details of his features or voice. His years in the north of the world have alienated him from this land, and he now seems as foreign to me as Ulla and their children. He's much better off in his peaceful adopted country than in this chaotic one. They say that people in Norway are happier than in any other part of the world except Finland. I got used to loving Juan Martín and his family from a distance, without expectations. In theory, I envy large families like the ones my grandparents and parents had—with the requisite Sunday lunches at Camellia House and the security of living in a tight-knit community—but in reality I don't miss it.

DEMENTIA BEGAN TO TAKE hold of José Antonio. He had a series of small strokes, in addition to his weak heart, high blood pressure, hearing loss, and a thousand other ailments that combined to separate him from reality. The symptoms started well before the diagnosis came; first he got lost on the street or forgot what he'd eaten, then he got lost inside the apartment and forgot who he was.

"You're José Antonio, my husband," Miss Taylor said repeatedly, showing him photo albums and telling him about his life, the events enhanced to make his memories happier, but it was a futile effort.

He became afraid of Crispín, thinking the dog would eat him; it was true that the Doberman looked menacing but he was as tame as a bunny and had lived with us for years. The most painful thing about José Antonio's condition was the fear. He wasn't only scared of Crispín but also of being alone, or abandoned in an old folks' home, or that he didn't have enough money, or that there would be a fire or another earthquake, that someone would poison his food, that he'd die. He recognized Miss Taylor but he sometimes asked who I was and why I came to lunch every day without being invited. Once he went out naked, with only his hat and cane; he made it down to the first floor and strolled onto the street. A pair of kind neighbors brought him back before the police had to.

"I was going to the bank to get my money, so they don't steal it from me" was his explanation.

While Miss Taylor and I were greatly distressed to see the illness transform José Antonio into a stranger, Etelvina and you, Camilo, took it in stride. You'd answer the same question a hundred times, console him when he started crying for no reason, distract him when he got scared. He recognized you, but he thought you were his grandson and got mad when Julián Bravo showed up claiming to be your legitimate grandfather.

Several years later, Crispín began to suffer from dementia. You never wanted to admit it, Camilo, but that's what happened. Animals can lose their minds too. Just like José Antonio, the dog got disoriented inside the apartment, he forgot that he'd eaten, barked for no reason with his nose against the wall, was terrified by the vacuum cleaner because he thought it was another earthquake, and didn't recognize me. The friendly dog, who had always welcomed me with a choreographed dance, began to growl every time I entered the house.

My brother died at age eighty, after having spent more than four years in a parallel dimension. He had neither peace nor joy in the final stage of his life, a dark time for him, when we rarely heard his loud laugh. He didn't have love either, because he couldn't accept it; he would get angry with Miss Taylor and rejected her affections, insulting her in terms I'd never heard him use with anyone. He'd always been tall and strapping, but his ill health reduced him to a skinny old man; this enabled us to overpower him when he became aggressive, flailing his cane at anyone who came near. His eyes lost their sparkle and light; he behaved like a spoiled child. His wife endured him with her typical Irish stoicism; she mourned the loss of the man who had pursued her for decades with the perseverance of an invincible lover, and had adored her as faithfully as the best of husbands. That's how she wanted to remember him, not as the furious old man he'd become.

José Antonio's death was painful because he was terrified of dying and fought it off for several long weeks. We all suffered as he struggled to breathe, the air rattling in his chest, writhing, complaining, and shouting for as long as he still had a voice. It was a relief when finally, exhausted, he surrendered. Seeing his corpse, stiff and cold, his skin that yellowish tinge of the dead, the role he'd played in my life, and how much I owed him, hit me like a typhoon. I had very little contact with my other four brothers—who had all died some years ago—but José Antonio had been a sturdy tree that had protected and shaded me ever since the day I was born; he'd assumed responsibility for me that distant morning when I found my father in the library.

A YEAR LATER IT was Josephine Taylor's turn, bowing out with her usual courtesy and discretion. She didn't want to be a bother. She'd been fighting cancer for a while; according to her it was the traces of that tumor the size of an orange from so many years before. It's unlikely, since the orange was removed when she was a young woman and she didn't get cancer until half a century later. She could've tried a round of chemotherapy, but she decided that without José Antonio her life lacked purpose, and at eighty-six she was too tired to fight. I can picture her on those final days, a little old lady like something out of a fairy tale, old-fashioned, lovely, sitting beside the window with a book open in her lap, even though she could no longer read, and Crispín lying at her feet.

You undoubtedly remember that day vividly, Camilo, because you've relived it many times in your nightmares, waking up crying, upset and mumbling, "Miss Taylor." You'd returned home from school rumpled, scruffy, and sweating, as always; you dropped your bag on the floor and whistled for Crispín, calling his name, thinking it strange that he hadn't come to greet you. You passed through the kitchen where Etelvina and I were engrossed by a telenovela, quickly kissing us hello before continuing into the living room. It was winter, so it was already dark outside and we had lit the fire. There, illuminated by the flames and a weak table lamp, you saw Miss Taylor in her chair. Crispín was by her side, his big black head resting on her lap, but she was completely still. You immediately understood what had happened.

PART FOUR

REBIRTH

(1983–2020)

21

Facunda gave me the news by phone before it appeared in the paper, buried in a footnote. She'd found out through her indigenous relatives, who ever since the time of the Spanish conquest, five hundred years ago, had used the same method of passing information by word of mouth. Censorship, so efficient and terrifying, wasn't enough to quell the outcry. It was the first time bodies of disappeared persons had been discovered; these hadn't been tossed into the sea or blown up in the desert, but sealed inside a mountain cave.

A French missionary and activist named Albert Benoit, who lived in a shantytown where the government repression was particularly harsh, found out about the mass grave in the privacy of the confession booth. He was one of those dissident priests who kept count of the victims; he had been arrested and tortured a couple of times and was ordered by the cardinal to keep out of sight and not cause a commotion, but he hadn't listened. Unlike the Catholic Church in Argentina, our priests didn't aid the dictatorship and instead tried to strike the difficult balance between denouncing abuses and protecting those who defied the regime. One of the murderers, a police officer in the rural area near Nahuel who had retired and now lived in Benoit's shantytown, confessed what he'd done and provided the exact location of the cave, on a hillside in a forested area. He gave the priest permission to pass the information on to his superiors.

Benoit wanted to check the authenticity of the claim before he turned to the cardinal, so he traveled to the south. With a pack on his back, a compass in his pocket, and a pick tied to his bicycle, he set off in the direction indicated, skirting police checkpoints. Once he'd left the towns behind, he stopped worrying about the lockdown measures, because there were no guards. He followed a barely visible path, which seemed to have been abandoned for years, and when it was finally swallowed by vegetation, he oriented himself using the compass and prayers.

Soon the terrain forced him to leave his bicycle and continue on foot, thankful that it was summer, since it would've been even harder to advance in the freezing rain. He slept the first night in the open air and walked the better part of the following day until he finally found the entrance to the cave, blocked with boards and rocks, exactly as his parishioner had described.

It was getting dark and he thought it best to wait until the following morning. He'd miscalculated the time it would take him to get there, so his scant provisions had run out and he'd gone several hours without food, but a brief fast would do him good, he thought. The land was uneven, green and more green, all dense vegetation and water everywhere: puddles, lagoons, streams, waterfalls rushing over cliffs, accumulated rainwater, and melted snow. Unlike the tropical rain forest, which he'd known in his youth as a missionary near the border between Venezuela and Brazil, this region was cold even in summer; in winter only the most expert local guides knew how to cross it.

The air smelled of humus, fragrant native trees, and fungus clinging to the trunks. He intermittently glimpsed the red and white flowers of climbing vines hanging high in the branches. All day long he'd heard the tremendous riot of birds, the screech of the eagle, the murmur of animal life hidden by the foliage, but when night fell, the world went silent.

He felt an abyss of loneliness in that uninhabited landscape and he prayed aloud, "Here am I, Jesus, getting myself into trouble again. If I find what I'm looking for I'll have to disobey the cardinal's order to remain quiet. You understand, don't you? Please don't abandon me now, when I need you most." He finally nodded off inside his sleeping bag, shivering, hungry, sore. He wasn't used to physical exertion since the only sport he played was soccer with the kids in town, and every muscle in his body was screaming for rest.

With the first light of dawn he drank water and slowly chewed the last almonds he had left, then he began the task of removing the rocks, pulling the weeds, and using his pick to pry off the boards that blocked the mouth of the cave. When he'd removed the final obstacle, a fetid gust of wind from inside forced him to retreat. He took off his shirt and tied it around the lower part of his face. He once again invoked Jesus, his friend, and entered. He found a narrow tunnel, just tall enough for him to duck into. He carried a flashlight in his hand and a camera hanging around his neck. It was hard to breathe, and with each step the air was thicker and the stench more intense. He was entering a crypt, but he pressed on because the place was exactly as described. Soon the tunnel opened into a wide dome, where he could stand up straight. Then the beam of his flashlight fell on the first bones.

THE DETAILS OF WHAT I'm telling you, Camilo, weren't published until several years later, when Benoit's story finally came to light. No one knew his name or the role he'd played, because if his identity had been made public he'd have paid a very high price for his courage. In his testimony, the cardinal refused to answer any questions that might incriminate the priest, who was protected by the confidentiality of confession. The whole truth finally came out once democracy was restored. Benoit wrote his account of events, there was an exhibition of the photographs he took that day and many more—some shots of the bones in the prosecutor's office and other remains laid out at the police station—and they even made a movie about it.

With the evidence in hand, the cardinal moved so quickly that the government didn't have time to stop him. He was aware that, in addition to his moral authority, he was backed by the Church's two thousand years of earthly power. It was one thing to arrest and sometimes kill priests and nuns, and another much more serious crime for the government to make enemies in the upper echelons of the Catholic Church, including the pope's representative in our country. In those years of government repression, the cardinal had learned how to stealthily help the victims, which tallied several thousand. He had even created a special vicarage with this mission. He gathered a secret delegation to investigate the cave, which included a Vatican ambassador, the director of the Red Cross, a member of the Human Rights Commission, and two journalists.

The cardinal was too old for a mountain expedition, but he traveled with his secretary to Nahuel, where he waited for the others, who had left separately from the capital in order to avoid arousing suspicion. Despite their precautions, the people in the village realized that something serious must have happened for a cardinal to show up in those parts. He was wearing casual clothes, but he was recognized anyway; his foxlike face was easily identifiable.

The cardinal made the first statement to the press from Nahuel after the group returned from the cave. By then the locals were already whispering about the bones that had been discovered. That's when Facunda called me in Sacramento.

"They say it's the disappeared tenant farmers—the ones who were taken right after the coup, do you remember?"

The official explanation was that there had been an accident, that some tourists had suffocated from poisonous gases inside the cave; then they blamed it on a revenge plot by guerrilla fighters, or criminals who killed each other in a shootout. Finally, after pressure from the public and the Catholic Church, as well as the fact that all of the skulls bore a single gunshot hole, the government attributed it to executions committed by uniformed soldiers acting of their own initiative in the heat of battle, eager to save their country from Communism. The men would be duly reprimanded, the officials assured the public, betting on people's short attention span as they bought time to tamper with the evidence.

They erected walls and put barbed wire all around

the cave opening to keep out the people who'd arrived at the scene: journalists, lawyers, international organizations, curious onlookers, and the silent pilgrimage of family members of the disappeared, some coming from far away, with photos of the victims. This time the government couldn't get rid of them using their typical means. The families camped on the mountainside for several days and nights, until all the remains were removed. The authorities went into the cave covered from head to toe, wearing masks and rubber gloves, and they pulled out thirty-two black plastic bags, while the pilgrims outside sang revolutionary songs that hadn't been heard in several years but had not been forgotten. These people had spent years desperately searching for their disappeared loved ones, hoping they might still be alive and that they'd one day return home. Camping right alongside them was Facunda, deformed by arthritis, but as strong as always.

Faced with the fact that the scandal hadn't blown over in a few days, as they'd hoped, the government ordered an investigation and, finally, several weeks later, they allowed the families of the presumed victims to identify the bodies. It was just a way of giving them the closure they demanded, because in reality the forensic experts had already determined who the bones in the cave belonged to, though the report was sealed.

• • •

FACUNDA GAVE ME THE news and I took the train to Nahuel so I could go with her to the precinct. Autumn was showing itself in the color of the landscape and the cold humid air; the rains would soon begin to fall. They'd summoned the families of the farmers who had been detained and forcibly disappeared in the early days of the military dictatorship—among the abducted were four brothers, the youngest fifteen years old, who'd been tenants on the Moreau land. Everyone around there knew each other, Camilo. It's not like now, with industrialized agriculture, land that belongs to large corporations and farmhands replaced by migrant workers, nomadic, rootless. Back then everyone was related; they'd been born and raised there, had gone to elementary school together, played soccer as kids, had fallen in love and married each other. The population was shrinking because many young people had moved to cities in search of better opportunities, so every absence was felt heavily. The men who had disappeared were part of a large family network—they had faces, names, loved ones and friends who missed them.

We waited almost two hours outside in the street; more than twenty women and even a few kids clinging to their mothers' skirts. The majority of them knew each other, were relatives or friends, almost all of them with the indigenous features so common in those parts. Hard work, poverty, and tragedy had marked them with a patina of sadness. They were dressed modestly in the faded secondhand clothing from the United States that was sold at the flea market. The older women and one pregnant woman sat on the ground, but Facunda remained standing, as straight as her arthritis would allow, dressed entirely in black to represent her anticipated grief, with a stony expression that wasn't sorrow but rage. There were two human rights lawyers with us, sent by the cardinal, and a journalist with a television camera.

I was embarrassed by my American blue jeans, suede boots, and Gucci purse, taller and whiter than everyone else, but none of those women seemed bothered by my wealthy bourgeois appearance; they accepted me as one of them, united by the same loss. They asked me who I was looking for, but before I could respond, Facunda interrupted.

"Her brother—she's looking for her brother," she said.

And that's when I realized that Apolonio Toro had in fact been a brother to me. He was more or less the same age as José Antonio and had been part of my life for as long as I could remember. I prayed silently to heaven that we'd find no evidence of his murder, because in this case doubt was preferable to certainty. I often imagined Torito living like a hermit in a mountain cave somewhere, as would be fitting to his character and his extensive knowledge of the land. I didn't want proof that he was dead.

An officer came out and barked instructions at us: We had half an hour, we couldn't take pictures or touch anything, we'd better look carefully because we wouldn't be given another chance. We had to turn over our ID cards, which would be returned when we left. The lawyers and journalists had to wait outside.

We went in.

UNDER A TENT IN the middle of the courtyard, two long tables were flanked by guards. We didn't see bones, as we'd expected to, but pieces of tattered clothes corroded by time, shoes, sandals, a notebook, and wallets, all numbered. We filed slowly past those sad remains. The women, crying, would stop in front of a wool vest, a belt, a cap, and say "This is my brother's," "This belongs to my husband."

At the end of the second long table, when we'd almost given up, Facunda and I saw the proof we didn't want to find.

"This is Torito's," Facunda whispered, her voice broken by a sob.

I'd searched for him and hoped he might return for so many years. But lying on that table was the wooden cross I'd carved as a gift for Apolonio Toro's first birthday celebration, when my mother, my aunts, and the Rivases were all still alive, when Facunda was a young woman and I was a little girl. It hung on a leather string, the wood polished by time and wear, but my name, **Violeta**, could still be clearly made out. I knew that the other side would show Torito's name. A convulsive sob caused me to double over like I'd been kicked in the stomach, and I felt Facunda's arms around me. That's when a whistle blew, ordering us to leave the tent. Without hesitating, blinded by tears, I impulsively picked up the cross and tucked it inside my shirt.

THAT CROSS IS MAGICAL, Camilo. None of my possessions interest you, I know, but when I die, I want you to keep that cross, to hang around your neck and wear always, so that it will protect you like it has protected me. That's why I never take it off. It's charged with the loyalty, innocence, and strength of Apolonio Toro, who wore it over his heart for many years and died to save your uncle, Juan Martín. Torito has been my guardian angel and he will be yours as well. Promise me this, Camilo.

Sometimes our fates take turns that we don't notice in the moment they occur, but if you live as long as I have they become clear in hindsight. At each crossroads or fork we must decide which direction to take. These decisions may determine the course of the rest of our lives. That's what happened to me the day I recovered Torito's cross. I know that now. Until then I'd lived comfortably without questioning the world I'd been born into; my only unflagging objective had been to raise the boy that Nieves had left an orphan.

That night, as I got undressed, I saw the mark

that the crude wooden cross had left on my chest, pressed into my skin by my bra, and I once again had a long cry for Torito, for Facunda, who loved him so much, for the other women who had identified their dead, and for myself. I thought about my house, my bank accounts, the properties I'd invested in and all the antiques and other frivolous items I'd acquired at auctions, of my wealthy friends, my infinite privileges, and I felt overwhelmed by it all. It was as if I was pulling a cart loaded down with all that baggage as well as the weight of wasted time. I never imagined that I'd begin a new life after that night.

22

THE NAMES OF THE VICTIMS FOUND IN THE cave weren't released for several months, and the press didn't dare to defy the censorship laws by publishing them, even though word was out about a group of women who had identified the bodies at the station. The government strategy consisted of keeping the information under wraps for as long as possible, alleging security concerns, as a way of putting off demands to return the bones to the families for dignified burials. The remains had been removed from the cave in bags, all jumbled together, and the work of reconstructing each skeleton was very tedious. It would be much easier to dump them all in a mass grave and forget about them forever, but it was too late for that.

I imagine that Facunda talked to her family and friends about Torito, but I told only Etelvina and Miss Taylor, who was still alive at the time. They were the only two people I had left who still remembered that gentle giant, aside from Juan Martín, who I immediately notified by mail. For years he had been asking what had happened to our dear friend who'd helped him cross the border and was never heard from again. That's why an alarm bell went off when Julián Bravo, of all people, mentioned Torito.

He came through the capital on one of his quick visits for "business," which was how he described his money laundering and smuggling. Out of habit he stopped by to see us and stayed for dinner because Etelvina had made duck with cherries, his favorite dish. He was still as handsome, athletic, happy, self-confident, and seductive as ever.

"Have you missed me?" he asked with a laugh.

"Not one bit. How is Anushka?"

Anushka was an eternally languid model, who never ate—poor woman, she was constantly starving. He had promised to marry her too, just like Zoraida, but managed to keep her at bay for years.

"Bored. And you, Violeta, what have you been up to lately?"

"I was in Nahuel . . ."

"Oh! Because of the thing with the bones in the cave, I suppose."

"How do you know about that? You don't even live in this country. Yes, they found the remains of fifteen disappeared men. The police arrested them in the early days of the military coup, then they murdered them and hid the bodies."

"It's not the first time and it won't be the last," he commented, studying the label on the bottle of wine.

"They laid out pieces of the men's clothes and other belongings from inside the cave. I went with Facunda . . ."

"Did you find anything of Torito's?" he asked distractedly, filling his glass.

It was in that exact moment, sitting at the table before a platter of duck with cherry sauce and a bottle of cabernet sauvignon, that the missing pieces of the jigsaw puzzle that was Julián Bravo finally came together for me. For years I'd had signs, indications, and evidence, but I didn't want to acknowledge the obvious because it would mean admitting my own complicity. I recalled my poor daughter, her tragic life, the drugs, the poverty, the prostitution, Joe Santoro dead from a bullet to the back of the head, Nieves's fear of her father, and Juan Martín's. I also remembered the beatings and humiliations of the past, the Mafia henchmen, the CIA agents, the rolls of bills and the guns, his connection to the dictatorship. How could I have let all that happen?

JULIÁN KNEW WHAT HAD become of Torito—he'd always known—just as he'd known that Juan Martín had taken refuge in Argentina and hid that from me for four torturous years. I can't prove that he was guilty of Torito's death, but it's possible that he turned the man in to get rid of him once he'd saved Juan Martín. It was always preferable to leave no witnesses. In any case, he knew that Torito's remains had been in that cave and that there were other bodies as well.

Around that time Juan Martín sent me the English translation of an in-depth article on Colonia Esperanza, which was published in Germany and circulated throughout Europe.

"Dad does special flights for those people, doesn't he?" he asked.

According to the article, Colonia wasn't the agricultural paradise it claimed to be, but a hermetic compound of immigrants who had come seeking utopia and ended up trapped by a psychopath who imposed brutal discipline on the two hundred persons living under his rule, many of them children and teenagers. No one went in or out without permission; the members received paramilitary training and endured physical and sexual abuse. One person who somehow escaped and managed to get out of the country to testify in Germany said that ever since the military coup, Colonia had functioned as a torture and extermination center for government dissidents. None of that information had been published in our country, thanks to censorship.

Colonia had built a runway for the private planes and military helicopters that transported the dictatorship's prisoners. Julián's relationship to Colonia became abundantly clear, and I understood why he was so well informed and connected: Operation Condor, his cooperation with the CIA and with the dictatorship.

"Dad is capable of anything," my kids had always said.

Julián Bravo's motto was that the ends justified the means. He'd employed the most dubious methods to obtain his ends with total impunity. He declared himself above the limits placed on other mortals. The moment had arrived for me to apply his axiom: His end justified my means.

THE DAY AFTER THAT illuminating dinner I took a plane to Miami to speak with Zoraida Abreu before Julián returned. We'd maintained sporadic contact, so I knew that the love she'd felt for him had begun to wane. As always, I met her at the Fontainebleau Hotel, which had been rejuvenated by a recent remodel. Zoraida was just over forty and still looked the part of the golden Boricua Rum queen, with the same defiant hips, showgirl legs, and fruitlike breasts. She showed up in a yellow sundress more appropriate for the beach. We hugged with an affection born of shared disenchantment. She took off her tinted glasses and I noted the age on her face; plastic surgery had pulled her skin taut but couldn't remove her tired expression.

We brought each other up to date on our lives. Hers was more or less the same as before in her role as secretary, accountant, housekeeper, lover, and confidante to Julián Bravo. She'd given in to his pressure to have her tubes tied, just as I had, because he wanted to make sure that she wouldn't bring any kids of his into the world. Zoraida would forever lament having given up motherhood out of love for that man. When she told me, I wondered how many women Julián had convinced to undergo the same procedure just to avoid the inconvenience of using a condom.

"I'm his jack-of-all-trades," Zoraida told me bitterly.

"He pays you well . . ."

"The money doesn't make up for the mistreatment. I can't have a life outside of him, he's so jealous. He made sure I'll never have kids and now he doesn't even want me; he never sleeps with me anymore."

"You could leave him."

"He'd never allow it, he needs me too much."

"Why are you still with him?" I pressed.

"He'll marry me eventually, even if only to have someone to take care of him in his old age."

"Are you afraid of him?"

"I used to be, but I'm not anymore. Now I just want to punish him. I'm fed up," she said.

"That's why I came, Zoraida." And I proceeded

to tell her about Anushka, who according to Julián was the most expensive woman in his life.

Anushka was smarter than Zoraida and I were. She'd convinced Julián that she was sterile, and in due course she surprised him with a pregnancy; she didn't tell him about it until it was too late for an abortion. It was the end of her career as a model, she said, although in reality she was over thirty-five and hadn't worked in years. Julián refused to get married and never lived with her, but he generously supported her and the daughter they'd had together.

Zoraida had put up with many of Julián's infidelities, fleeting and inconsequential affairs, but she never dreamed that he'd been maintaining a secret lover and daughter for years. She immediately concluded that if he hadn't married the mother of that child, he wouldn't marry her either. She didn't understand how Julián could've hidden it from her for so long or how he provided for that woman without it reflecting in his finances. Those expenses had never showed up anywhere. She kept his official books as well as his unofficial ones, the ones no one else saw, the secret book of illegal transactions. She was smug about the fact that not a dollar passed through Julián's hands without her knowing about it, but she'd just discovered there must be a third book she didn't know anything about. It might not even be the only one—there could be others. She was more hurt by his hidden money than she was heartbroken by his infidelity. She asked me if I had a photo of Anushka and I showed her some pictures I'd ripped from a fashion magazine years prior. Zoraida examined them as carefully as an etymologist.

"This girl has anorexia" was her only comment.

As we said goodbye, she assured me that Julián would curse the day he'd met her.

Zoraida Abreu's revenge was swift and drastic. She'd served Julián Bravo loyally and patiently for nearly two decades, loving him, in spite of everything, with all her passionate heart. The same passion aided her in sinking him, exactly as I'd imagined when I went to Miami to recruit her. The beauty queen was too intelligent to hire a hit man, cause an accident, or poison Julián, like in some detective novel, as I had fantasized doing so many times. The plan she hatched in under two hours, with three martinis in her system, was much more sophisticated.

AS I FLEW HOME, vacillating between guilt over what I'd just set in motion and satisfaction over having served justice, Zoraida Abreu called her first love, a lawyer whom she'd practically abandoned at the altar when she met Julián. The man was married and had three children, but when he got Zoraida's call he rushed to her aid without hesitation. No one could forget a woman like that. Together they worked out the details of the strategy she'd discussed with me.

Zoraida would be protected by anonymity when the lawyer presented her evidence to the criminal investigator for the Internal Revenue Service, turning Julián in for fraud and tax evasion. As proof of his client's claims, and to assure her immunity, the lawyer turned over evidence that would've taken years to gather: the secret books, the names of shell companies in Panama and Bermuda, bank account numbers in Switzerland and other countries, the combinations to the safes where he kept cash, drugs, and documents, his contacts in the world of organized crime. His unpaid taxes for the previous five years alone amounted to several million dollars, as the criminal investigator explained to the prosecutor.

Zoraida also provided information about Julián Bravo's involvement in drug trafficking, which was enough evidence to arrest him and keep him locked up so that he couldn't flee the United States. The investigation, which under normal circumstances would've lasted two or three years, took only eleven months, thanks to all the documentation supplied by Zoraida's lawyer.

I don't know all the legal details, which don't matter much. It has been thirty-five years since then and I think that the only person who still savors that delicious revenge is Zoraida Abreu. I can picture her as a mature woman, pretty, feeling satisfied as she recalls that event, sitting at the bar of some luxury hotel with the olive from her martini between her teeth. I hope she's had a good life.

Julián paid the fine and back taxes with interest, hired a law firm famous for defending gangsters, and managed to get his sentence reduced to four years in a minimum security federal prison for white-collar criminals. He deserved a much harsher punishment, but in the end he wasn't tried for his capital offenses, only for some of his minor sins.

During those years he lost the trust of his former clients, since trouble with the law was the last thing they wanted, and I think even the CIA abandoned him, but he had made a lot of money and a large portion of it was still hidden. When he got out of prison he was thin, strong, and healthy, because he'd spent the whole time in the gym, and he was almost as rich as he'd been before. One day he dropped in to visit, as casually as if we'd just seen each other the week before. By then I'd moved to another neighborhood, but it wasn't hard to find me. He came to tell me that he'd retired from business and had bought a ranch in Argentine Patagonia to spend his old age raising sheep and purebred horses. He said he would like to do it in good company.

"We're both getting old and we're both single. We should get married, Violeta," he proposed.

I gathered that he didn't suspect my involvement in his arrest.

"Let's finally tie the knot. Camilo would love Patagonia," he insisted.

I turned down the offer and asked after Anushka. He told me she'd married a Brazilian industrialist, after confessing that he wasn't the father of the little girl he'd spent years supporting.

23

Allow me to tell you a little more about Roy Cooper, the solver of problems who looked like a boxer from the wrong side of the tracks and who figures as the father on your birth certificate. I loved him so dearly. You met him, but you might not remember because you were very young when the three of us went to Disney World. I think you were seven or eight. It's the only time you ever saw him, but he and I were in regular contact. We would go on vacation together once or twice a year, once you were old enough for me to leave you with Etelvina or on the farm with Facunda.

Roy had moved back to Los Angeles, where he continued practicing his profession. He had plenty of work; it was the ideal city for a man like him, who could slip like an eel among sinners of all varieties:

felons, delinquents, corrupt cops, and nosy journalists. It amazed me how he could be at home in that world, and yet still love me so generously without asking anything in return—not even to be loved to the same degree—and to do what he'd done for Nieves and for you.

It's a bit odd for me to talk about my lover to you, given that you're my grandson and you're a priest, but Roy was special. (I don't put Julián in the category of lover, because he's the father of my children, even though we never married.) Roy was a man of few words, with a bawdy sense of humor and plenty of street smarts; he never read anything besides the sports pages and paperback crime novels. He smelled like cigarette smoke and sickly sweet cologne; he had the rough hands of a carpenter, shocking table manners, and he seemed to dress in secondhand clothes that were all too tight and horribly out of fashion. He looked like some criminal kingpin's bodyguard.

No one would have ever imagined that the man was sensitive and, in his way, quite gallant. He treated me with a combination of respect, tenderness, and desire. Yes, Camilo, he desired me with such constancy that my advanced age and bad memories were wiped clean, and I was once again a sensual young woman. No one made me feel more beautiful and cherished than he did. We loved each other easily, with lots of laughter and not a lot of imagination. It was the opposite of the carnal passion I'd known with Julián Bravo, acrobatic feats in which I often ended up getting crushed. With Roy we repeated the same routine, calm in the certainty that we were equally enjoying ourselves, and then we would fall asleep in each other's arms, comfortable and satisfied. We spoke little, the past didn't matter and the future didn't exist. He knew about Julián Bravo and suspected my reasons for leaving him, but he avoided asking questions; all that mattered was the time we spent together. I didn't dig into his past either. I never knew if he had a family, if he'd ever married, or what he'd done before he became dedicated to his strange profession.

Roy had a modest mobile home, and in it we traveled to different parts of the country for two or three weeks at a time. We especially loved to visit the national parks. It wasn't the most modern or luxurious of vehicles, but it got the job done and never failed us. It consisted of a little room with a table we used for everything, a basic kitchenette, a bathroom so narrow that if I dropped the soap I couldn't bend over to pick it up, and a bed in the back separated from the rest of the space by a sliding door. It had a water tank on the roof, electricity whenever we could plug it in at a campsite, and a chemical toilet. It was large enough for us, unless it rained for several days straight and we had to stay shut inside, but that didn't happen often.

. . .

THE UNITED STATES IS an entire universe; it contains several nations and every landscape imaginable within its territory. Roy and I traveled unhurriedly with no fixed itinerary; we went wherever our momentary whims led us. That's how we ended up driving from California's Death Valley, where the ghosts of those who have perished in the desert wandered under 126-degree heat, to a glacier in Alaska, where we rode a sled pulled by twelve dogs. We would stop wherever we pleased along the way. We took long hikes, swam in rivers and lakes, fished, and cooked in the open air.

I remember like it was yesterday the last night we spent together in the mobile home. I was sixty-five years old but I felt like I was thirty. We'd had an amazing week at Yosemite National Park, in early autumn, when there are fewer tourists and the landscape transforms magically as the leaves take on vibrant red, orange, and yellow hues. We were grilling our dinner over the fire, as we did every evening, fresh-caught fish with vegetables. Suddenly a bear appeared a short distance away, a dark, enormous animal bumbling toward us, so close we could hear him huffing and could swear we even smelled his breath. We'd learned what to do in a situation like this: Remain still, quiet, and avoid making eye contact. But in that moment of panic I jumped with fright and started to shriek.

The bear stood up on his hind legs, raised his arms to the sky, and answered my cries with a tremendous guttural growl that reverberated like a long echo. Roy didn't hesitate. He grabbed me by my jacket and practically dragged me to the RV. We just managed to get inside and shut the door in the bear's face, as he charged at the vehicle and shook it several times, furious, before turning his attention to the food we'd been preparing. Once his hunger had been quelled with our dinner and garbage, he sat to observe the sunset as calmly as a Buddhist monk.

That night we didn't so much as peek our heads outside, eating only canned beans for dinner. At some point the bear left, and in the morning we quickly broke camp and took off. I think I've only been that scared a few times in my life. Since then I've been to the zoo to see the bears several times; they're lovely, from a distance.

On that trip I noticed that Roy's clothes were hanging off him; he'd lost weight, but since he had the same energy as always, I didn't pay it much mind. The following day we said goodbye at the Los Angeles airport. When I hugged him he got emotional and his eyes welled up, something that didn't match the strong macho image he usually projected.

"Send my love to my son, Camilo," he said, quickly wiping away a tear.

He always asked after you and reminded me of the trick we'd pulled by registering you as his son.

I didn't suspect that day that we'd never sleep together again. Roy would die of cancer a year later. He hid his illness from me because he wanted me to remember him healthy, in love, and vital, but Rita Linares gave me the news.

"He's all alone, Violeta. No one has come to see him, he has no family left, and he hasn't allowed me to call any of his friends. When he couldn't take the pain anymore he agreed to come stay with me. We've been friends since school. He's been in my life ever since I first got to this country, when I was a little immigrant girl who barely spoke English. He's always helped me when I needed it, he's like a brother to me," she said, sobbing.

I immediately flew to Los Angeles in hopes that he'd still be at Rita's house, but he'd already been moved to the hospital. It was the same hospital where you were born and where I saw Nieves for the last time, with its wide hallways, fluorescent lights, linoleum floors, disinfectant smell, and stained-glass chapel. Roy was connected to a respirator, still conscious. He couldn't talk, but I could see in his eyes that he recognized me, and I like to think that my presence was a comfort to him.

"I love you, Roy. I love you so, so much," I said a thousand times.

He died the next day, Rita and I both holding his hands.

. . .

YOU GREW UP SO fast, Camilo, that one night you came into my room to say good night and I was startled by the presence of a strange young man. It was Friday, so your school uniform was covered in a week's worth of sweat and grime; you had a messy mop of hair on your head and an exalted expression. You'd lost your bicycle and had to run twenty-something blocks to get home before curfew.

"Where were you? It's almost ten o'clock at night, Camilo."

"Protesting."

"Against what, I'd like to know."

"Against the military, of course, what else?"

"Are you crazy! I forbid it!"

"I don't think you have the moral authority to forbid it," you said, and you winked with that mischievousness that has always managed to disarm me.

It was true that I'd had to get a screw in my collarbone after a scuffle at a protest march, but that was just bad luck. At that time I wasn't yet sticking my neck out; I happened to be walking down the street, got swept up in a crowd, and wasn't able to escape. The police charged at the protestors, beating them, throwing tear gas, and spraying streams of filthy water. One of those powerful streams had crushed me against the wall of a building. I managed the pain using strong painkillers and marijuana for the first three days after the operation, but my arm had been in a sling for a month and I was running out of patience. That night I got my first glimpse of the nightmare that the last four years of the dictatorship would be for me. If you were ready to go to war against the government at age fourteen, you'd never reach adulthood; the military would make sure of it. I went gray with worry over you, you were such a pain in the ass.

We no longer lived in the old apartment across from the Parque Japonés—which is now called Parque de la Patria—because after José Antonio and Miss Taylor died it was too big for us, and also it no longer matched my state of mind. The four of us—Etelvina, Crispín, you, and I—moved to that house that eventually fell down in the earthquake, do you remember? It was far from the center and the military academy, where the majority of the protests occurred. The move was one more step on my road to shedding the frivolities I'd once thought indispensable but that had begun to feel smothering. I got rid of the bulky furniture, the Persian rugs, the profusion of knickknacks, and I kept only the essentials. Once Etelvina had chosen what she wanted to keep for whenever she decided to move into her own apartment, which in the meantime she would rent out, I called my pack of nieces and nephews, with whom I had had very little contact. In under two hours almost everything was gone. We moved with the bare minimum, much to Etelvina's dismay, because she didn't understand my desire to live like the poor when we could enjoy life like the wealthy.

It's hard to make money working; and the harder

the work, the worse the pay. It takes effort not to lose everything and end up on the street. It's easy, on the other hand, to get rich without producing anything, moving money from one place to another, speculating, taking advantage of stock opportunities, investing in the hard work of others. And it's difficult to spend a fortune, because money attracts more money, which multiplies in the mysterious realm of bank accounts and investments. I managed to accumulate a lot before I finally figured out how to spend it.

FIRST IT WAS THE women I'd met the day we went to identify the remains from the cave. Digna, Rosario, Gladys, María, Malva, Dionisia, and several others, especially Sonia, the mother of the four Navarro brothers, short, solid, and sturdy as an oak. She had received the proof that her sons had been murdered, as she'd suspected for many years, but instead of sinking into grief she led the call to have the bones returned to the families and the guilty charged for their crimes. All those women worked the land in the vicinity of Nahuel, and many of them knew Facunda. They were the pillars of their families, because the men who were still alive were either absent or mired in misery. They'd worked from sunup to sundown since they were girls, and they'd continue doing so to the end. They dreamed that their children or grandchildren might finish school, learn a trade, and have an easier life than they'd had.

I started to visit them one by one, almost always accompanied by Facunda. They told me about their disappeared loved ones, what they'd been like when they were alive, how they'd vanished, and the eternal red tape of searching for them by knocking on doors, sending letters, sitting outside police stations demanding information, getting kicked out, silenced, threatened—but they never gave up and always kept asking. They often cried quietly and seldom laughed. They offered me tea, herbal infusions, **mate**. They didn't have coffee. Facunda had advised me against bringing gifts, as it would be humiliating if they couldn't reciprocate. Instead I brought them medicine whenever they needed it, as well as sneakers for the kids, and they accepted that, giving me eggs or a hen in return.

I was integrated into the group little by little, careful to avoid offending anyone. I resigned myself to being different from them without attempting to hide it, because it would've been futile. I learned to listen without trying to solve their problems or give advice. Facunda got the idea to have meetings every other Friday at the farm. She lived with her daughter Narcisa, now a fat, authoritative woman, and a granddaughter named Susana, who I'll tell you about later. It had been over a year since she'd stopped baking because her body couldn't handle all that work, as she said, but with Narcisa's help she could still manage to prepare one of her famous pies for the women on Friday. I attended meetings only once a month, because it was a long trip from the capital.

Around that time I reconnected with Anton Kusanovic and met his daughter, Mailén, a skinny twelve-year-old girl, all elbows, knees, and nose, but as serious as a notary, introducing herself to me as a feminist. I was reminded of Teresa Rivas, the only feminist I'd ever known. I asked Mailén what that meant to her and she informed me that she was fighting against the patriarchy's oppression of women.

"Don't pay any attention to her, Violeta. It's just a phase, it'll pass. Last year she was a vegetarian," her father clarified.

The intensity of that little girl's determination impressed me in that moment, but I soon forgot about her. I never would've guessed she'd one day become so important to me and to you, Camilo.

The rural women taught me that courage is contagious and that there's strength in numbers; what you can't do on your own can be achieved together, the more the better. They belonged to a national organization of hundreds of mothers and wives of disappeared persons, so tenacious that the government had not been able to disband them. The official version denied the rumors about disappeared persons as Communist propaganda and classified these women as subversive unpatriotic extremists. The press adhered to censorship rules and never mentioned them, but they were well known abroad, thanks to human rights activists and people living in exile, who for years had kept up a campaign of denouncing the dictatorship.

In those Friday meetings, over Facunda's pies, I found out that there were many women's organizations that had been active for decades, which not even military machismo had been able to stamp out. Organizing was more difficult under the dictatorship, but not impossible. I got in contact with groups that fought to pass laws legalizing divorce and decriminalizing abortion. The members were working-class women, middle-class professionals, artists, intellectuals. I attended meetings in order to learn, until I finally found a way to help.

24

THE TIME HAS COME IN THIS STORY TO remind you that in 1986, Harald Fiske, the Norwegian bird-watcher, reappeared in my life. I'd seen him before, when he flew from Buenos Aires to tell me that Juan Martín had escaped from the Dirty War and was receiving asylum in Norway. Although I went to visit Juan Martín several times, I didn't overlap with Harald because his work as a diplomat took him from one country to another. He mailed me a Christmas card every year, one of those newsletters that foreigners send to their friends with domestic news and photos of triumphant families. They only tell of their successes in these collective missives: travels, births and marriages. No one ever goes bankrupt, is sent to prison, or has cancer, no one commits suicide or gets divorced. Luckily that stupid tradition doesn't exist in our culture. Harald Fiske's newsletters were even worse than the idyllic families': birds, birds, and more birds, birds from Borneo, birds from Guatemala, birds from the Arctic. Yes, apparently there are even birds in the Arctic.

I think I already told you that the man was in love with our country, which he said was the most beautiful place in the world since we had every type of landscape: a lunar desert, long coastline, tall mountains, pristine lakes, valleys of orchards and vineyards, fjords and glaciers. He thought we were friendly and welcoming people because he judged us with his romantic heart and little real-life experience. However odd his reasons, he decided he was going to live out his final days here. I never understood it, Camilo, because if you can live legally in Norway, you'd have to be demented to move to this catastrophic country. He had a few years left before retirement so he got himself named ambassador to our country, where he wanted to spend his old age. It was the culmination of everything he'd always wished for. He bought a new camera lens powerful enough to photograph a condor on the highest peak of the Andes, decorated his apartment in the sparse Scandinavian Lutheran style that Etelvina made so much fun of, and then he reached out to me.

My last love, Roy Cooper, had died the year before. With his departure I said farewell to all pretenses of romance because I never expected to fall in love again. I was healthy and energetic, the women's group had given my life new meaning, I was learning a lot and contributing where I could. I felt very content and still young when it came to everything besides the wonders of intimacy with a man. Hormones count, Camilo, and by that age mine had already subsided considerably. In another time or another culture—a village in Calabria, let's say—any woman over sixty would be a little old lady dressed in black. That's how I felt where matters of sex were concerned: so much effort for such a brief reward! But my vanity was still firmly intact and, although I'd lost interest in fashion, I still dyed my hair and wore contact lenses. I flattered myself that from time to time people thought I was your mother instead of your grandmother.

Harald began to gradually fit into my routines. First he arranged to go with me, often, to the Santa Clara farm. He would drive me in his Volvo, because the highway was now as quick as the train, and we would stop at little restaurants along the coast where they served the best fish and seafood in the world. "We have the same natural resources, but the food in my country is tasteless," said Harald, who treated our wines with equal reverence. I went to see Facunda and the women in the group, and he went in search of the same birds he'd seen hundreds of times. We stayed at the hotel in Nahuel, which had changed dramatically from the tiny town it had been in the time of our Exile, no longer a single street lined with clapboard houses; now it had a bank, shops, bars, hair salons, and even a massage parlor full of beautiful young Asian women.

Harald quickly became my best friend and constant companion. We went to the symphony in the capital and hiking in the mountains. He even invited me to some of the tedious dinners at the embassy, where he asked me to play the part of hostess, since he didn't have a wife. I got my revenge by dragging him to protest marches, which were ever more massive and daring.

We didn't know it yet, but the dictatorship's days were numbered; the military's monolithic power was crumbling on the inside and fear was beginning to fade. Political parties that had been banned mobilized clandestinely to demand a return to democracy. Harald attended the street demonstrations dressed like an explorer, in shorts, a vest covered with countless pockets, boots, and his camera hanging around his neck. He was a sight to see: very tall and blond, disconnected from reality, excited as a kid at Carnival. "Nothing more entertaining!" he exclaimed, photographing the military men at close range. By some miracle he was never hit in the head or knocked down by a stream of water; he shielded himself from the tear gas using goggles and handkerchiefs soaked in vinegar. He sent the photos he took to the European media.

Meanwhile, you ran away from school to meet Albert Benoit, the man who'd uncovered the cave of dead bodies. That Frenchman was your hero.

He preached the gospel of Jesus the Carpenter and Liberation Theology, condemned as subversive. He stood with outstretched arms before armored tanks and machine guns to keep soldiers from running over his people; he also held back a furious crowd armed with rocks, managing to calm them so they would not be massacred. He once threw himself facedown in front of a military truck to keep it from advancing, always putting himself in the line of fire. And you, Camilo, were right behind him, lost in the jumble of local boys, one more among the poor crowd, facing down institutionalized violence with arms spread wide, just like Benoit. Was it there, with the rocks, bullets, and tear gas in the air, that the seed of your calling was first sown?

Other priests had been arrested or murdered, but Benoit, protected by heaven, was merely expelled from the country. The voices against the military regime rose to a deafening clamor, until the brutal means of quieting them had been exhausted.

ON ONE OF THE trips to the farm, I introduced Harald to the women's group, and they immediately recognized him as the insane foreigner they'd seen examining the sky with binoculars, spying on the angels. Several of those women were embroidering textiles made from fabric scraps sewn over burlap, creating scenes that represented the harshness of life, prison, lines outside police stations, and soup kitchens. Harald thought the cloths were extraordinary and started sending them to Europe, where they sold well and were even exhibited in galleries and museums as works of resistance art. Since the money went entirely to the creators, word got out and soon there were hundreds of women embroidering burlap all up and down the country. No matter how many textiles the authorities confiscated, more always appeared, so the government created a program to commission more idyllic textiles, depicting children playing in circles and rural women with bouquets of flowers in their hands. No one wanted them.

That night, talking to Harald about the group of women, I told him that they had given me a new lease on life, but that I felt my contribution was merely one drop of water in a desert of needs.

"There's so much to do, Harald!"

"You do a lot, Violeta. You can't help every single case that's presented to you."

"How can I protect these women? I met a twelve-year-old girl who told me her ultimate objective was to overthrow the patriarchy."

"Well, for the moment that's a pretty lofty goal. We have to overthrow the dictatorship first."

"What I should do is create a foundation to fund programs, instead of individuals. The laws need to change . . ."

I first made sure that I had enough money to live decently and to support you, and I put the rest into the Nieves Foundation. Even after I leave this world, the foundation will live on, because the endowment, well invested, will gain interest and remain profitable for a long time. Mailén Kusanovic is in charge, even though it should be your responsibility, Camilo. You could do a lot of good with my money, but you lack the talent to run the foundation; you're too distracted. Your theory is that God will provide, but God doesn't provide anything when it comes to money. It is commendable to choose poverty, as you have done, but if you truly want to help others, you're going to need money. I don't want to get ahead of myself, however, I'll get confused. In this part of my story, Mailén was still a teenager, two years younger than you, but much more intelligent and mature. It would be several years before she reentered our lives.

You were at boarding school at San Ignacio, where the priests were supposedly keeping you safe from yourself. How did you escape so often without getting caught? You'd been trying my patience ever since you were a naughty little boy, protected by Etelvina, who always defended you. I sent you to boarding school not to get rid of you, as you accused me, but because I couldn't control you. You seem to have conveniently forgotten all your bad behavior. The final straw was when you and a friend broke into a house you thought was empty, and a woman came out with a shotgun and almost blew your heads off. What did you expect me to do? Ship you off to a boarding school run by priests, of course. Corporal punishment was no longer used—a shame, because some spankings would've done you good.

LET'S RETURN TO HARALD FISKE. Who'd ever have imagined that the Scandinavian would become my husband? I usually say he's my only husband because I always forget I was married to Fabian Schmidt-Engler in my youth. That veterinarian left no traces on my life. I don't even remember having gone to bed with him, but you know I have a selective memory. I used to keep track of my brief and furtive affairs, writing down the names, dates, and circumstances, and even rating them from one to ten for their efforts, but I stopped because it was a pathetic list that took up only two notebook pages.

Harald and I had been seeing each other several times a week as good friends for a while, traveling to the south together and going to marches, when Etelvina planted the notion in my head that he was in love with me.

"What are you talking about, he's much younger than me. He's never insinuated anything of the sort."

"He must be shy, then," she insisted.

"He's not shy, Etelvina, he's Norwegian. In his country they don't have fits of passion like in your telenovelas."

"Why don't you ask him, señora? Then we can clear things up, banish all doubts."

"What does this have to do with you, Etelvina?"

"I live in this house too, don't I? I have a right to know your plans."

"I don't have any plans."

"But Mr. Harald might . . ."

I couldn't get the idea out of my mind, and I started to watch Harald carefully for signs. She who seeks, shall find. He seemed to use any excuse to touch me, and he looked at me with the expression of a lost puppy, I was no longer so sure of myself. A short while later we were in one of those fish shacks on the beach I've told you about, sharing broiled sea bass and a bottle of white wine, when I couldn't take not knowing anymore.

"Tell me, Harald, what are your intentions with respect to me?"

"Why do you ask?" he said, perplexed.

"Because I'm sixty-six and I'm staring down old age. Also, Etelvina wants to know."

"Tell her I'm waiting for you to ask for my hand in marriage," he answered with a wink.

"Harald Fiske, do you take Violeta Del Valle to be your wife?" I proposed.

"It depends. Does the woman promise to respect, honor, obey, and care for me as long as we both shall live?"

"Well, I can at least promise to care for you."

We toasted to ourselves and to Etelvina, happy at the prospect of a future full of possibilities fanning out before us. In the car, he held my hand and hummed the whole way, as I nervously imagined the moment I'd have to take my clothes off in front of him. I've never gone to the gym, I had flaps of flesh on my arms, a roll on my stomach, and breasts that were drooping down to my knees. Nevertheless, the moment of truth didn't come as soon as I'd expected, because there was terrible news waiting for us.

We arrived home to find the dean of the San Ignacio school consoling Etelvina, sobbing because they'd arrested the light of her life. It wasn't the first time the dean had accused you of some evil deed; he'd threatened to expel you after you pooped on top of the school mascot, a turtle, and when you climbed like a spider up the façade of the Central Bank and hung from the flagpole until the firemen pulled you down. But this time it was something more serious.

"Camilo once again escaped from school and he was caught painting anti-government graffiti. There were two other boys with him, but they weren't our students. They ran away, but your grandson was apprehended with a can of spray paint in his hand. We're trying to find out where they've taken him, Señora Del Valle. We should have some information soon," the dean said.

I lost my mind, I admit it. The methods employed by the police were common knowledge, and the fact that my grandson was a minor would not protect him. My thoughts instantly ran through all the terrible stories I'd heard through my foundation and I recalled the victims in the cave outside of Nahuel. In the few hours that had passed they could've already destroyed you.

I'LL NEVER FORGIVE YOU for doing something so stupid, Camilo. You were an idiotic little monster, and you had me scared to death: I still get mad whenever I think of it. You were completely irresponsible; you knew how government repression functioned, but you thought you could once again misbehave without paying the consequences. You and your friends had vandalized the marble base of the Monument to the Saviors of the Nation, a monstrosity built in the purest Third Reich style, crowned by an eternal flame blazing against the capital skyline, marred by your black spray paint. I want to believe that it wasn't your idea, that you were just going along with your friends. You never confessed their names, not to the dean, not to me, not to anyone; you only told me, confidentially, that they were from Albert Benoit's shantytown. The police split your face open. "Who were the other boys?" "Where did you meet them?" "Their names! Speak, you little shit!"

In that situation I'd have given my life to have Julián Bravo there. Your grandfather had always been a man of infinite resources and contacts, and in other times he would've known what to do, whom to bribe. But because of me he'd lost his power and was isolated from the world on his ranch in Patagonia. Even if he answered my call and still had some contacts in the government, he wouldn't have been able to get there in time. I went with the dean to the cathedral to see if we could get help from one of the vicarage's lawyers. I was in such a nervous state that he had to fill out the form for me, while I impatiently counted the minutes we lost to paperwork.

"Have courage, ma'am, this could take a while . . ." he tried to explain, but I couldn't listen; I was too upset.

In the meantime Harald Fiske sprang into action. The Norwegian embassy, like many other diplomatic seats, was disliked by the government because they'd been offering asylum to fugitives of the regime for years. As representative of that country, Harald lacked influence, but he was friends with the United States ambassador, with whom he often went mountain biking. By then, the government no longer had the Americans' unconditional support because the dictatorship was weak and the situation in the world was changing. It wasn't in their interest to support a regime that had fallen out of favor. The United States ambassador had a secret mission to lay the groundwork for the return of democracy in our country. A democracy with conditions, of course.

"The boy is my girlfriend's son. He did something stupid, but he's not a terrorist," Harald told him.

In reality, it was my grandson, I wasn't yet Harald's girlfriend, and you'd been a terrorist from the age of two, but those details were unimportant. The American offered to intervene on your behalf.

I SUPPOSE YOU REMEMBER all too well the time you spent in the hands of the police. I haven't forgotten a single moment of those two horrible days, which would've been an eternity if they'd transferred you to Security Headquarters, where not even the blessed American ambassador would've been able to save you. They beat you until you were unconscious, and would have submitted you to another round if you hadn't been a Del Valle and a student at San Ignacio. Even there, in the dungeons of the police station, the social hierarchy was firmly intact, Camilo. Be thankful that you weren't one of those other two boys who vandalized the monument alongside you. They would've received even more brutal treatment.

They released you in a deplorable state, with your face swollen up like a pumpkin, your eyes blackened, your shirt bloody, and bruises all over your body. While Etelvina iced your wounds, gave you kisses, and simultaneously smacked you for being so stupid, the dean of your school informed me that you had caused too many problems, you got terrible grades because you didn't like doing homework, and your conduct was atrocious.

"Camilo put a mouse inside the music teacher's purse and emptied a bottle of laxatives into the staff lunch. He was caught smoking marijuana in the bathroom and raffling off pictures from dirty magazines to the elementary school boys. In short, your grandson would be better off in military school—"

"That's your fault!" I interrupted, shouting. "How did he get hold of marijuana, laxatives, and pictures of naked women? Who's watching the children at that boarding school of yours?"

"We're a school, ma'am, not a prison. We don't treat our students like juvenile delinquents."

"You can't expel Camilo, Father," I begged, changing tactics.

"I'm afraid, ma'am, that—"

"My grandson is becoming a Marxist and an atheist . . ."

"What are you saying?"

"You heard me, Father. Marxist and atheist. He's at a difficult age, he needs spiritual guidance. A sergeant at some military school isn't going to be able to offer that, is he?"

The dean gave me a murderous look, but after a long pause he began to laugh loudly. He didn't kick you out of school. I've often asked myself if that wasn't one of those crossroads that determine our destinies, which I've talked to you about already. If they had kicked you out of San Ignacio, you might actually be a Marxist and an atheist instead of a priest; maybe you'd be a normal guy, married to some young woman I adored, and you'd even have given me some great-grandchildren. Hey, I'm free to dream.

25

THE WORLD, OUR COUNTRY, AND OUR LIVES changed dramatically at the end of the eighties. We watched as the Berliners, in a single night, used hammers to tear down the wall that had divided Germany for twenty-eight years. A short while later the Cold War between the United States and the Soviet Union ended, and for too brief a time some of us breathed easy with the hope of peace. But there is always a war somewhere. Our wounded continent, with some sad exceptions, began to heal from the plague of caudillos, revolutions, guerrillas, military coups, tyranny, murder, torture, and genocide.

Here the dictatorship collapsed under its own weight, pushed out from below by collective efforts, without violence or too much turmoil, and we awoke one morning to the news that democracy was back. It was something young people had never known and the rest of us had forgotten. We took to the streets to celebrate and you disappeared for a couple of days to the shantytown where you had so many friends. They were preparing a party to welcome Albert Benoit, who had never even unpacked his suitcase in France because he was anxiously awaiting the moment he could return to his adopted land. He received a hero's welcome from the people he'd defended from tanks and bullets with outstretched arms. Some, like you, who had been beardless children when they marched alongside him armed with stones, were now men and women, but Benoit remembered each one by name.

At first we had a transitional government, a conditional and cautious democracy that would last for several years. Democracy didn't bring with it the descent into chaos that the dictatorship's propaganda had forewarned; those who scandalously benefited from the economic system kept their power; no one paid for the crimes committed. The political parties that had survived in the shadows reemerged, along with other new ones; institutions we'd given up for dead were revived, and we tacitly agreed not to make too much commotion so as not to provoke the military. The dictator went calmly home, cheered on by his followers and defended by the right. The press shook off the burden of censorship and little by little the more sinister aspects of those years came to light. Still, the consensus was that we should leave the past behind and focus on building the future.

. . .

AMONG THE SECRETS THAT were aired once freedom of the press was restored were those of Colonia Esperanza, which had been protected by the military for years. Now the new government was finally allowed inside. It had been turned into a clandestine prison camp where medical experiments were performed on the political prisoners, and many were executed. The director escaped unscathed, and I believe he lived peacefully in Switzerland until his death. Do you see what I'm telling you, Camilo? Bad guys have good luck. The whole thing caused a tremendous scandal, confirming the story published in Germany several years prior, which alleged that the members of the colony, even the children, were all victims of a regime of terror.

Some of the people associated with the infamous colony were discussed on television, among them Fabian Schmidt-Engler. He looked very different from the husband of my youth. He was almost seventy, he'd gained weight, and he had very little hair left; if they hadn't said his name, I might not have recognized him. They mentioned the respected and honorable Schmidt-Engler family, which had grown into a dynasty of wealthy farmers and hoteliers in the south. They said that Fabian had served as liaison between the colony and the military security apparatus, but that he hadn't been aware of the atrocities being committed within the compound.

He wasn't accused of any specific crime. I looked everywhere for information on Julián Bravo and his mysterious flights, but I didn't find anything. They mentioned the military helicopters that transported prisoners, but there was nothing about the private planes that he piloted.

That was the last I ever heard of Fabian until he died in 2000, and I saw his obituary in the newspaper. He was survived by a wife, two daughters, and several grandchildren. I heard that the daughters were adopted, as he wasn't able to have kids with his second wife either. I was glad he finally got the family he'd always wanted.

Juan Martín came from Norway with his wife and my grandkids to celebrate the country's political freedom. The infamous blacklist no longer existed. Their plan was to stay a month, travel the country from north to south, and enjoy the best our tourism had to offer. But after only two weeks Juan Martín realized that he no longer fit in here and he made up an excuse to return to Norway. He'd felt like a foreigner there for many years, but those two weeks here were enough to cure him of his nostalgia and the pain of exile, so that he could definitively put down roots in the country that had welcomed him when his own had failed him. Since then he's been back only a handful of times, and he always visits alone. I don't think his wife and kids are as fond of this country as Harald Fiske was.

. . .

MY LIFE CHANGED DURING those years too, as I entered another stretch of my road. According to the poem by Antonio Machado, "there is no road, the road is made by walking," but in my case it felt more like I was stumbling down narrow, winding paths that were often swallowed up by vegetation. Still, I entered my seventh decade with an easy spirit, free of material ties, and with a new love.

Harald Fiske was the ideal companion, and I can tell you from firsthand experience that it is possible to fall in love in old age with the same intensity and passion as in youth. The only difference is that there's a sense of urgency: You can't waste time on unimportant things. I loved Harald without jealousy, and free of the fights, impatience, intolerance, and other things that tend to sully relationships. His love for me was calm, so different from the constant drama I'd had with Julián Bravo. When he retired from the diplomatic service, we chose to live in Sacramento, where we could have a peaceful existence and visit the farm often to spend time in the fresh air. After Facunda died, her daughter Narcisa took care of the property. I rented out the house in the capital and never lived there again, so it wasn't too painful when it was knocked down in the earthquake. Luckily the renters were on vacation and no one was crushed under the rubble.

In Sacramento I bought an old house and Harald busied himself fixing its many imperfections. He'd grown up helping his father and grandfather in the family carpentry business; his first job, when he was a teenager, was as a welder in a shipyard, and his hobby, aside from the birds, was plumbing. He could spend hours happily lying under the kitchen sink. He didn't know much about electricity, but he improvised, and only once did he almost electrocute himself. He was proud of his calloused hands with cracked nails and dry red skin. "Working hands, honest hands," he'd say.

WITH THE RETURN OF democracy, several women's organizations that collaborated with my foundation, free from the oppression of military machismo, blossomed into the groups that are still working to make a difference today. Thanks to them, divorce is now legal and abortion is allowed under certain circumstances. It's true that we've advanced, but at a crab's pace: two steps forward, one step back.

The foundation discovered its mission. Before, it simply handed out money without any strategy, but I was eventually able to give it a more specific focus, which I hope it will continue with even after I die: working against domestic violence. This was inspired by a young woman named Susana, Etelvina's younger sister. You know who I'm talking about, Camilo.

In her youth, Narcisa, Facunda's daughter, had several children by different men, leaving them to be raised by her mother while she enjoyed a string of romantic affairs. She had taken off with her latest lover when the military coup occurred and no one knew where she was for two or three months. She reappeared alone and pregnant, as had happened before, and in due time she had a daughter named Susana. I saw the girl many times at the farm, growing up under the protective mantle of her grandmother, surrounded by older siblings. She'd just turned sixteen when she moved to a town some twenty miles from Nahuel with a police officer she'd met; I got news of her from time to time through Facunda. She told me that her granddaughter led a miserable life because the man drank like a fish and beat her. Susana was only eighteen and already missing several teeth due to the abuse.

One day a woman arrived in Santa Clara with a baby and a little girl barely old enough to walk, both still in diapers, and left them with Facunda and Narcisa. They were Susana's kids. Their mother was in the hospital with a broken arm and several cracked ribs. In a fit of rage, the man had lit into her with his belt and then kicked her until she was unconscious. It wasn't the first time that Susana had ended up in the hospital. I happened to be at the farm for the week when the woman came to tell us what had happened. She said that when she heard the shouting she summoned the neighborhood women, who banded together and armed themselves with frying pans and broomsticks to save the girl.

"We have to defend ourselves as a group. We're always prepared, but sometimes we don't hear in time and it's too late," she added.

I went with Facunda to see Susana, who was in a communal ward, with her arm in a cast, lying on a bed with no pillow, because of the blows she'd received to the head. The doctor told us that the worst part of her job was treating the victims of domestic violence who returned to the emergency room repeatedly.

"One day they just stop showing up. Many women are murdered by their husbands, lovers, sometimes their fathers."

"What about the police?"

"They wash their hands of it."

"In Susana's case, her aggressor is a police officer."

"Nothing is going to happen to him, even if he kills her. He can just claim it was self-defense." The doctor sighed.

By then I'd been collaborating for several years with different women's organizations and I'd learned to work with humility instead of charging in expecting to change reality on my own, as I'd done at first. The organizations had the experience and could come up with their own solutions; my role was to contribute only where I was asked to. But in the case of Susana, because she was Facunda's granddaughter and Etelvina's sister, my blood boiled. I went to

Sacramento to speak with a judge, who had been a colleague of José Antonio but was several years younger.

"The police can't enter a residence without a warrant, Violeta," he responded when I explained what had happened.

"Even if the man is brutally beating someone?"

"Don't exaggerate, honey."

"This is one of the countries with the worst domestic violence in the world, did you know that?"

"It's a private matter better resolved inside the home. It needn't involve the police or the courts."

"It starts with abuse and ends with murder!"

"Well, in that case, the law would get involved."

"I see. So we should sit around and wait for the degenerate to kill Susana so that you can arrest him. Is that what you're telling me?"

"Relax. I will personally make sure that the aggressor receives a strong reprimand; it may even mean his expulsion from the police force."

"If it was your daughter or granddaughter we were talking about, would you be able to relax knowing he was still on the loose and could attack her again?"

SUSANA WAS STILL IN the hospital when the man showed up at the farm on the pretext of seeing his kids—because he missed them, he claimed. He was in uniform and had his gun in its holster. He explained that Susana was very clumsy and had fallen down some stairs. Facunda and Narcisa wouldn't let him see the children, and shouted angrily at him until he left. He vowed he'd be back and then they'd see what he was made of. I realized then that the judge had made me that empty promise just to get me out of his office.

"Susana has to leave that man immediately. The violence will only get worse," I said to Facunda.

"She doesn't dare, Violeta. The man has threatened to kill her, and the kids too."

"Then she'll have to hide."

"Where?"

"At my house, Facunda. I'll go get her when she's released from the hospital. Have the kids ready."

I took Susana—bandaged, skinny, and terrified—along with her two children, to my house, where Etelvina was waiting for them. On the way I had time to reflect on my own past. For years I put up with Julián Bravo's mistreatment without calling it domestic violence, making excuses: It was an accident; he went too far because he'd had too much to drink; I provoked him; he had problems and he took them out on me, it won't happen again, he promised, he apologized. I wasn't legally tied to him and could support myself, yet it still took me years to put an end to the abuse. Fear? Yes, there was fear, but also uncertainty, emotional dependence, force of habit, and the rule of silence that impeded me from talking about what was happening; I isolated myself.

Etelvina helped me see that Susana was lucky because she was protected by us, but there were millions of women who couldn't escape. The Nieves Foundation already funded safe houses scattered here and there for victims of abuse, but much more was needed. Talking to a woman who ran one of those homes and who understood the victims' situations because she'd suffered similar abuse, we came to the conclusion that even if we multiplied the number of safe houses it wouldn't be enough. She told me that violence against women was a dirty secret that had to be aired so that everyone acknowledged it.

"Report, inform, educate, protect, punish the guilty, legislate. That's what we have to do, Violeta," she said.

And that's how, Camilo, I gave the foundation its concrete mission. It has kept me active and involved during what's called the autumn of life, although in my case it has carried on into full-blown winter. Now the foundation is led by Mailén Kusanovic, who at that time was a teenager with a rabid thirst for justice. While that little girl was devoting her free time to feminist activism, you were drooling over a stupid crush. What a headache you've been for me, Camilo.

Susana and her kids, who came to my house planning to hide for a few days, stayed with us for several years. It was dangerous for them to go back to Nahuel, where the man could find them. Harald paid for the girl to get new teeth, and once she'd stopped having to cover her mouth with her hand and finally had a complete smile, we discovered that she looked a lot like her grandmother Facunda when she was young. She'd also inherited Facunda's strength and solemnity. She recovered from the trauma, and as soon as she could send her daughter to preschool she started to work in one of the safe houses that the foundation funded. Etelvina took care of the baby with the same affection she'd shown to you, Camilo. Now that little boy is thirty years old and works as a biology teacher. I have no idea what happened to the police officer; he simply vanished.

26

YOU GRADUATED FROM SAN IGNACIO WITH the worst grades in your class, but with the award for best classmate and as the dean's favorite student, since he loved to debate with you about God and life.

"Sometimes your grandson drives me crazy, Señora Del Valle, but I value him greatly because he challenges me and makes me laugh. You know what he's come up with most recently? That, if God exists—which according to him isn't a fact, but merely an opinion—God would be a Marxist. We'll miss him at school next year," he told me.

At that time you didn't know anything about God or about life, but you did know a lot about women, I believe. From an early age you were always in love, always with a melodramatic intensity. At nine years old you threatened to commit suicide over a sixteen-year-old neighbor who didn't even know you existed until you stole my diamond ring and gave it to her. I suppose you remember. The poor girl, burning with embarrassment, had to bring it back to me.

"Camilo asked me to wait for him to finish high school so we could get married," she explained.

After that grave romantic disappointment you changed girlfriends every few weeks. Etelvina scared all of them away. "Don't you bring any more street-walkers into this house, Camilito," she said of the girls in school uniforms and knee socks.

A little while after you finished high school, when you were already enrolled in the mechanical engineering program at the university, you fell in love with a woman twice your age; you always liked older women. Thankfully I don't even remember her name, and I hope you don't either. You wanted to marry her, but you were barely old enough to blow your own nose, as Etelvina said. Frankly, I don't know what that divorced woman with teenage kids, manager of a supermarket, saw in you; she must've been very desperate to even notice that long-haired and sloppily dressed boy that you were. Well, you still are.

I had to intervene in the matter, because it has always been my duty to protect you, as I promised Nieves I would. First I made a visit to the supermarket with the intention of helping the lady in question see some reason. She met with me in her office, a cubbyhole behind the meat and poultry section. She was fairly plain, in my opinion, but she was respectful toward me as I explained that it was in her best interest to keep away from my grandson, who was a brazen womanizer, alcoholic, and thief—and also had a violent streak.

"I thank you for warning me, Señora Del Valle, I'll keep it in mind," she responded, guiding me politely to the door.

In light of the fact that the supermarket woman hadn't heeded my words, I arranged with Juan Martín for you to take a trip to Norway, in hopes you'd get distracted by some nice Scandinavian maidens. The job offer you received to spend the summer working in the salmon industry hadn't fallen from the heavens because of your merits, as we led you to believe. Harald procured it for you, with some difficulty, because at the time you were good for nothing, and at a mere glance it was obvious you were unruly. The plan was to keep you there as long as possible. It worked, but I never imagined that it would also lead you away from mechanical engineering. You inherited this inclination from your mother's side. Aunt Pilar, as I've told you, was a brilliant mechanic. She could fix any problem and even invented machines, like that apparatus she made to dry bottles, a kind of enormous aerial sculpture that looked like a prehistoric skeleton. She passed her gift down to you through the complex twists and turns of ancestral blood, and you've been able to do more good with that than with your prayers. It's served you well in that dump . . . I mean, your community.

FOR SOME REASON I no longer remember—maybe the case of that little eleven-year-old girl, pregnant by her stepfather, who was denied a medical abortion and died in labor—thousands of women took to the street across several cities. By then we could do so without risk. I ran into Mailén Kusanovic in the crowd, although I didn't recognize her. The skinny, ugly little girl had transformed into an Amazon warrior marching at the head of a group brandishing a banner.

"Violeta! It's me, Anton's daughter!" she shouted in greeting.

She treated me with familiarity, as if we were the same age, and she also congratulated me profusely for participating in the protest, as if I were a decrepit old lady.

Ever since that day I've kept that girl in mind, Camilo. My original plan, before you decided to become a priest, was that you might marry her, but now I have to accept that she's merely your best friend, unless at some point you hang up your robes and throw your vow of chastity out the window. I imagine that vow must be a burden; it might've inspired respect once, but nowadays it only arouses suspicion. No one will leave a child alone with a priest; three hundred clergymen in this country have been convicted as pedophiles.

I invited Mailén for a cup of tea, as was done at the time, to analyze her as a prospect for you. We had privacy because Harald was fishing with a couple of his friends. I don't approve of that cruel sport that involves trapping a poor fish, pulling out the hook, and leaving its mouth bleeding only to throw it back into the sea, where it will suffer a slow death or be devoured by a shark drawn in by the blood. But I'm getting off topic, let's get back to Mailén.

I'd been expecting the screaming and sweaty young woman I'd seen at the demonstration, but she'd clearly wanted to make a good impression because she showed up with clean hair, wearing makeup and pants that were tight around the waist and wide at the bottom, which were in fashion at the time, and white platform boots. Etelvina had made a meringue pie, which our guest accepted a second piece of without concern for the calories; that detail ended up convincing me that she was the ideal girl for my grandson: I like people who can get happily fat.

I knew that she was studying psychology and had three years left until she graduated. She asked me if I'd ever done psychoanalysis, which I didn't take as impertinence, just professional curiosity. It turned out that she knew of Dr. Levy because his books were used in her classes, and she was impressed that I had known him personally. He'd died before she was born. I think she did the math on my age and calculated that I was as old as the pyramids, but she didn't change her friendly tone.

I took the opportunity to tell her about you, a stupendous young man, sensible and of solid principles, handsome, hardworking, and intelligent. Etelvina, who was serving the pie, froze with the knife in the air and asked me who I was talking about. I told Mailén that you had an amazing job contract in Norway—without specifying that you were gutting salmon—and that you'd begun studying engineering before you left and planned to finish your degree when you returned, after coming to visit me in Sacramento.

"I'd love for you to meet him," I added, trying to sound casual.

Etelvina huffed sarcastically and went into the kitchen.

Anton Kusanovic's mother was a pure-blooded native South American, but he took after his Croatian father. He'd married a Canadian woman, who'd been traveling in South America as a tourist but fell in love here and never returned to her country. Mailén told me that it was love at first sight and that her parents remained as committed to each other as on that first day, after having brought seven children into the world. Mailén is the only one who looks anything like that indigenous grandmother: straight raven-colored hair, black eyes, and high cheekbones; the rest of her family could pass for European. The mix of races is very attractive.

I never imagined that while I was trying to get you a girlfriend, you were making plans to enter the seminary.

AT THAT TIME I was deeply in love with Harald, whose enthusiasm kept me young. One of the adventures he pressured me into was a trip to Antarctica. We traveled on a navy ship with a special permit given to Harald because out of courtesy he was still treated as a diplomat, and because he passed himself off as a scientist. That white, silent, and solitary world is transformative, it can change a person forever. It occurred to me that that's how the land of the dead must look, a place I'll soon go in search of my lost loved ones, where I'll be reunited with Nieves and so many others who passed on before me. My husband saw unknown birds and walked with his camera in a huge crowd of penguins. They smell like fish. These days they allow regular tourists; you should go, Camilo, before the continent melts and the seals are all extinct. One of the pastimes aboard the ship was jumping into the sea among chunks of blue ice; they quickly pulled you out before you died of hypothermia. To defend our honor, Harald and I felt obliged to imitate the young sailors diving into the coldest waters on the planet. My feet have been frozen ever since. Harald is the one who came up with those ridiculous ideas, and I followed along uncomplaining because I understood that he had a love of the outdoors in his blood. The truth is I had many frights and sore muscles because of him.

Aside from the vice of bird-watching, so widespread in his country, Harald liked to work with tools, something he shared with you from the start. Do you remember how he taught you the founding principles of carpentry? He said that tools and manual labor were the common language of men and that there were no barriers to communication when two men worked side by side. His ancestors had all been carpenters and woodworkers in the small town of Ulefoss, where he was born and raised in a house his grandfather had built with his own hands in 1880. The last time I was in Ulefoss the population must've been fewer than three thousand, and the principal occupations were still ironworking, carpentry, and sea trade, just like in past centuries. As boys, Harald and his friends would jump across the river on tree trunks floating down it, a suicidal game, because with one slip they could've been flattened or drowned.

Each year during the Norwegian summer, when it never gets fully dark, we went to a cabin hidden in a forest three hours from Ulefoss. Harald had built it, which was noticeable in the details. It must've been about two hundred square feet and instead of a toilet there was simply a hole inside an outhouse. It didn't have electricity or running water, but Harald installed a generator and we had jugs of water. He took cold showers and I gave myself sponge baths, but we shared the sauna, a wooden structure a few yards from the house, where we would sit and steam beside boiling rocks, then take a dip in the freezing stream afterwards. We warmed ourselves with firewood in the cast-iron stove; Harald was good at splitting trunks with a hatchet and lighting a fire with a single match. Birch trees make the best logs and there were many in those woods. He hunted and fished; I knitted and planned new businesses. We ate noodles, potatoes, trout, and any mammal he caught in his traps or with his rifle; and to pass the time we drank aquavit, forty percent pure alcohol, the national drink. Roy Cooper's mobile home was a palace compared to Harald's cabin, but I must admit that I miss those long honeymoons with my husband in that spectacular forest.

At the first sign of autumn, bands of wild geese began to migrate south, a veil of fog would dawn in the air and a mirror of frost on the ground. The nights once again became long and the days short and gray. That's when we'd say goodbye to the cabin. Harald didn't even lock the door, in case someone got lost and needed to stay there for a night or two. He left piles of wood, candles, kerosene, cans of food, and warm clothes for the hypothetical guest.

It was a custom that had been passed down from his father, originally to aid fugitives during the war, when Norway was occupied by the Germans.

I ONCE ASKED HARALD what had been his greatest wish in life; he responded that he'd always wanted to spend his old age in silence and isolation on one of the fifty thousand small islands of Norway's fragmented geography. But ever since he'd fallen in love with me he only wished to die by my side, in the south of my country. It was one of few occasions when he spoke like a troubadour. I'm sure he loved me very much, but it was usually hard for him to express it; he was a man of few words, fiercely independent, as he wanted me to be too, and a little too practical for my taste. No flowers or perfume; a typical gift from him would be a pocket knife, pruning shears, insect repellant, or a compass. He avoided romantic or sentimental displays, which he considered suspicious. If you truly loved someone, what was the need to make a fuss about it? He adored music, but he squirmed with embarrassment at the cheesiness of certain songs, as well as the more melodramatic plots at the opera; he preferred them in Italian, so he could listen to Pavarotti without having to hear the corny things he was saying. He avoided talking about himself, and took to the extreme the Nordic concept of **janteloven,** which meant: Don't think you're so special—remember that the nail that sticks out is the one the hammer hits. He didn't even brag about the bird species he discovered.

On every trip we stopped to visit Juan Martín and his family in Oslo, but only for a few days. I think my son was more comfortable loving me from a distance. He'd lived in Norway for many years, adapting to a culture so different from our own. Nothing remains of that young revolutionary who escaped from the Dirty War; he's now an old man with a large belly who votes conservative. Of course, the conservatives over there are further left than the Socialists here.

27

THE YEAR I SENT YOU TO NORWAY TO RESCUE you from the clutches of that supermarket manager, Harald and I went to see you before going to the cabin in the woods. The Norwegian salmon industry had enjoyed twenty years of prosperity, and the country was the largest exporter of salmon in the world. The Norwegians are admirable, Camilo. They were poor until they found oil in the north and a fortune fell into their laps. Instead of mismanaging it, as happened in so many other places, they used it to extend prosperity to their entire population. And with the same practical inclination, love for science, and government management that had worked so well in the oilfields, they created the salmon fisheries.

Summer took a bit longer to arrive to the fjords where you were working, so you were wearing an orange parka, parrot-green life jacket, wool hat, scarf, rubber boots, and gloves. We saw you from a distance working on the narrow circular walkway around the floating salmon cages; you looked like an astronaut under those skies of pink clouds, surrounded by snowcapped mountains reflected in a calm sea of cold, crystalline waters. The air was so pure that it hurt to breathe. Work in the fisheries was hard, and I liked that there were many women working right alongside the men. If you still had any machismo you'd picked up from Etelvina, never from me, you lost it there.

In theory you should've been able to save your entire salary, but you never were any good at managing money; it slips through your fingers like sand, another way you're like your mother. You blew all your earnings on beer and aquavit for your co-workers, which made you very popular. I was surprised that you didn't have several girlfriends, because the goal of that trip was precisely to keep you distracted so that you'd forget about the older woman. Harald guessed before I did that you were preoccupied with bigger thoughts.

In that fish processing plant the women all looked alike, covered in blue aprons and with their hair tucked inside plastic caps, but on the aquavit breaks you could see that some were pretty girls around your age who were working there at summer jobs or internships while they were at university.

"Have you noticed that Camilo doesn't even look at them?" Harald commented.

"You're right. What is he thinking so hard about?"

"And he's preaching to us about injustice, the infinite needs of humanity, and his anguish over not being able to remedy them. He's anxious and somber, when he should be euphoric in this beautiful place," Harald said.

"He hasn't mentioned the girls at all. Do you think the boy is gay?" I asked.

"No, but I think he might be a Communist or planning to become a priest," he responded, and we both laughed.

On the second day you asked us if we believed in God, and then the joke from the previous day didn't seem as funny. Religion occupied a minimal role in Harald's life. As a boy he'd attended Lutheran services with his parents, but he'd distanced himself from the church many years prior. As for me, I'd been raised with a kind of Catholic paganism, constantly haggling with heaven via offerings, rosaries, candles, and mass, worshipping crosses and statues. Magical thinking. When I left my marriage to Fabian Schmidt-Engler and moved in with Julián Bravo I was expelled from the Church for adultery. It felt like a harsh punishment, because it stigmatized me in my family and my community, but it didn't have a spiritual impact. I didn't need the Church.

That year, 1994, before going to see you in Norway, I paid the annual offering to Father Juan Quiroga that I'd begun making when they arrested you for vandalizing the Monument to the Saviors of the Nation, which is now called the Monument to Liberty. On that occasion I promised the saint, on my knees, that if I got my grandson back alive I'd walk the Camino de Santiago. I had to do it alone, so Harald went to the Amazon while I traveled to Spain. At seventy-three, I was one of the oldest people on the pilgrimage between Oviedo and Santiago, but I advanced at a steady pace for sixteen days, with a walking stick in my hand and a backpack on my back. They were exhausting, exhilarating days crossing an unforgettable landscape, full of emotional encounters with other walkers and spiritual reflection. I relived my entire life, and when I finally arrived at the cathedral of Santiago de Compostela, it was with the certainty that death is merely the threshold to another form of existence. The soul transcends.

That was the first of many reflections I've had on my faith, Camilo.

YOU RETURNED FROM NORWAY sooner than planned, with no intention of continuing university and determined to enter the seminary, against my will. Neither I nor anyone who knew you would ever have guessed that you'd choose that arduous path.

"It's not a calling, it's a whim!" I shouted.

You've reminded me of this outburst at least a hundred times since then. I was about to march straight to whoever was in charge of the Jesuits, to tell them what I thought of the matter, but Harald and Etelvina stopped me. You were almost twenty-two years old and it wasn't your grandmother's place to intervene.

"Don't worry about Camilito, señora, he'll never last with the monks. I'm sure they'll kick him out for being so spoiled," Etelvina tried to console me.

But that's not what happened, as we all know. You had fourteen years of studies and preparation ahead of you, followed by a life of priesthood.

The only way I can make sense of your spiritual transformation, Camilo, is rereading something you wrote to me several years later, from the Congo, after you were ordained. You might not remember that letter. Some men in the community you worked with, that you served, attacked the mission, set it on fire, and murdered two of the kind nuns with machetes. You were saved by some miracle—I think you'd gone out to get provisions for the school kids. It made the world news and I almost lost my mind with worry, because I'd had no word from you.

Your letter took a month to get to me. You wrote: "For me faith is a total commitment. My commitment is to everything Jesus represented. What the Gospels say is true, Grandma. I've never seen gravity, but I have evidence that it exists at every moment. That's how I feel about the truth of Christ; it's a monumental force that manifests itself in everything and gives meaning to my life. I can tell you that, despite the doubts I have about the Church, with all my faults and limitations, I'm profoundly happy. Don't worry about me, Grandma, because I'm not worried about myself."

You went into the seminary and left a huge void. Etelvina and I cried as if you'd gone off to war; it was hard for us to carry on without you in our lives.

IN 1997 FACUNDA DIED at age eighty-seven. Until then, she'd been as strong and healthy as ever, but she fell off the horse that your grandpa Julián had given you, a beautiful animal that had a happy life on the Santa Clara farm and was Facunda's preferred mode of transport. They determined that she hadn't died from the fall, but that her heart had stopped while she was in the saddle. In any case, my good friend had a sudden, painless end, as she deserved. We held a wake for her on the property where she'd spent the better part of her life, and for two days there was a steady stream of friends, neighbors from Nahuel and other nearby towns, and the indigenous population of the region, many of whom were her relatives. There were so many people that we had to have the wake outside, where we placed her coffin under a fragrant awning of flowers and laurel branches. I'm sorry you weren't able to attend, Camilo, because you were completing your novitiate; Harald took hundreds of photos and videos—you can ask Etelvina to see them.

The Nahuel parish priest gave the service and then

there was an indigenous ritual to bid Facunda goodbye. The participants arrived in their ceremonial dress and carrying musical instruments, because the farewell is sung. We couldn't let people go hungry, so we grilled several lambs on the spit, served with ears of corn, tomato and onion salad, fresh-baked bread, sweets, and a lot of aguardiente and wine, because grief is easier to bear with alcohol. The rule for a wake is that the animals killed must be entirely consumed; no food can be wasted. An old man from the indigenous community who had replaced Yaima as healer led the ritual in his language, which I couldn't understand, but they explained that he told Facunda she'd ceased to exist and that she shouldn't return in search of her children and grandchildren. She should surrender now to the sleep of Mother Earth, where those who had left before her resided.

The old man sent final instructions for Facunda's spirit to help her in her passage to the plane of her ancestors by blowing cigar smoke onto a live chicken and sprinkling it with drops of liquor before he twisted its neck and threw it onto the fire, where it was reduced to ashes. The men who were still sober carried the coffin to the Nahuel cemetery, because Facunda had always said that she wanted to be buried beside the Rivases and not in the native burial ground. Those who could followed the procession on foot, the others rode in the two vans I'd hired for the occasion. It was a short distance, but we'd had a lot to drink. The ceremony concluded at the gravesite, where we said our final farewell to Facunda's body and wished her spirit safe passage to the Other Side.

In addition to Facunda, to whom I was tied by so many bonds, we also lost Crispín that year. The dog was ancient, deaf, half-blind, and crazy, things that often come with old age. The veterinarian wasn't convinced animals could have dementia, but I'd seen my brother José Antonio move deeper and deeper into the labyrinth of memory loss and I'm telling you, Camilo, that Crispín's symptoms were identical. He died in Etelvina's arms, his belly full of a beef fillet that she had ground up for him, because he had few teeth left. He was given a merciful injection by the same vet who hadn't believed the dog was senile. I stayed as far away as possible because I couldn't bear to witness the end of that loyal animal. It would've saddened you greatly not to be with him in his final moments, so we told you that he died peacefully lying on my bed, where he'd slept ever since you went off to boarding school.

WHEN YOU ENTERED THE seminary I had to learn to love you from a distance. I can't tell you how difficult it was, Camilo, until I got used to writing letters. One day you'll read the ones you wrote to me and relive the effervescence of your youth with Jesus as your companion, and those intense years studying philosophy, history, and theology, throwing open the windows to human knowledge. You got lucky with your professors; they taught you how to learn, to acknowledge what you don't know, and to ask questions. Some of them were truly erudite. Do you remember the old man who taught you canonical law? In the first class he told you that you were going to learn the law backward and forward . . . so that you could find the loopholes to free the human being. I think you took the lesson to heart because that's what you've always done.

You also found loopholes for yourself. The bishop recently called to scold you for marrying a lesbian couple, both dressed in white, beaming. He waved their wedding picture, which had been published on Facebook, in front of your face.

"That looks more like a first communion," you joked.

"You have to annul this marriage and issue an apology!" the bishop ordered.

You found a loophole in the vow of obedience. "I'll decide later whether to communicate your demands to the press, Your Eminence. But I can't annul the marriage, as that would go against my conscience, because I believe that every human being has the right to love. I'll face the consequences."

You told me this by phone, and I wrote it down so I wouldn't forget, because that was exactly your response when you were little and I caught you doing something bad. You'd tell me "I can't say I'm sorry because it would go against my conscience, Grandma. Every human being has the right to throw eggs with a slingshot. But you can punish me if you want to." By age ten, you could already argue like a Jesuit.

YOU NEVER WANTED TO tell me why they sent you to Africa, but I suspect you went as a punishment or so they could silence you when you tried to report pedophilia among some of your colleagues. Or maybe you asked to go as a missionary because of your passion for danger, which is to say, for the same reason you convinced your grandpa Julián to take you swimming with sharks when you were eleven years old. I almost died when I found out that they'd lowered you down in a cage with a camera in an ocean infested with those carnivorous beasts, as your grandfather drank beer with the ship's captain.

At first that Christian mission to the Congo seemed like a romantic adventure, fit for a nineteenth-century novel: young idealists spreading their faith and improving the living conditions of "barbaric" people. I was impressed to hear that you were studying Swahili, since you'd barely learned English and butchered it with your terrible accent. You were excited by the prospect of putting your hands to good use doing something besides reciting mass, but the overly optimistic tone of your letters put me on red alert. You were hiding something from me.

You sent pictures of the broken-down vehicle

you fixed up using parts you'd made yourself in a forge, of the kids in the school cafeteria you'd built with your own hands, the well you were digging in the village, the brave Basque nun, the African nun who made you laugh, and the puppy you thought was male but turned out to be female. All the time, you carefully avoided mention of the community you lived in. I didn't know anything about Africa, its diversity, its history, or its misfortunes. I was incapable of distinguishing one country from another and supposed that there were elephants and lions all over the continent. I decided to do some research and discovered that the Congo is an enormous country rich in natural resources, but it's also one of the most violent places in the world, more dangerous than any war zone.

I wheedled the truth out of you letter by letter and gathered that you were emulating Albert Benoit, that missionary who had died a few years prior in the shantytown he'd dedicated his life to. I attended the funeral in your place; the capital was paralyzed by the heartbroken crowd that marched behind his coffin to the cemetery. You hoped, just like that French priest, to suffer alongside the most vulnerable and share their fate, whatever that may be. I learned about the local tribal conflicts, war, poverty, armed bands, refugee camps, the brutal mistreatment of women, who were worth less than livestock, and the fact that life could be lost at any moment for no reason other than bad luck. You told me about the boys who'd been child soldiers, recruited at age eight by force and required to commit atrocious acts such as killing their mother, father, or brother, so that the blood on their hands would bind them to the militia and forever isolate them from their family and tribe; of the women who were raped when they went to the well to gather water, and how the men couldn't go in their place because they'd be killed; the corruption, greed, and abuse of power, the brutal heritage of colonization.

Here, you'd always been rebellious. You were infuriated by injustice, the class system, poverty; you railed against the hierarchy of the Church, against superstitious religion, against the stupidity and close-mindedness of certain politicians, businesspeople, and so many priests. In the Congo, where there were much more serious problems, you were happy; you were a carpenter and a mechanic, you gave classes to the kids, planted vegetables, and raised pigs. It wasn't your country, you didn't expect to change it, just to help wherever you could. "I'm better suited to working with my hands and resolving practical problems, Grandma, I'm no good at preaching. I'm a failure as a missionary," you wrote me. You returned humbled, Camilo. That was your greatest lesson from the Congo.

You now live in a community that was no more than a trash heap before you got there. I was moved when you took me to see it, so clean and orderly, with modest but decent homes, a school, workshops for different trades, and even a library. I was moved most of all by the shack with a pressed dirt floor where you live with the dog and cat who've adopted you. You know what, Camilo? I felt a pang of envy, a desire to be young again and start over, to throw all the superfluous things I have out the window and keep only the essential, to share and to serve. I know that you are completely happy among those people. You've accepted that you can't change the country much less the world, but you can help some individuals. You've been guided by the spirit of Albert Benoit. You don't know how many times I've thanked heaven that you were young during the dictatorship and that, despite so much reckless behavior, you were able to escape the claws of repression. The bishop may pull on your ears, and there are people who accuse you of being a Communist because of your work with the poor; but during the dictatorship you'd have been exterminated like a cockroach.

I PROMISE THAT I'VE long abandoned the plan of setting you up with Mailén Kusanovic. Of course I'm joking when I tell you to hang up your robes and marry her. I have only a breath of life left in me and I don't want to waste it on impossible dreams; I know that you'll be a priest until death. Yours, not mine. It was a coincidence that she reappeared on the horizon when you were in Africa, I didn't go out looking for her.

Mailén had heard about the Nieves Foundation, since it had been in existence for many years and had a good reputation, and she reached out with a proposal. She was no longer a girl, she must've been over thirty, but it didn't take me long to find out that she was single. At that time everything at the foundation passed through my hands; I had only a secretary, because I was trying to spend as little as possible on administration. Mailén was surprised to see me behind my desk because she didn't associate me with philanthropy, and I was surprised that she had never wavered from the feminist objectives she'd held since she was twelve years old. She needed the support of my foundation for a project that would provide birth control and sex education.

We'd just elected the first female president of the republic, a woman who prioritized women's issues, and was especially focused on combatting the epidemic of domestic violence, which she called a national disgrace. I had several meetings with her when she assumed the presidency, because my experience was useful to her. The mission of the foundation coincided exactly with her aims. That meant that the Nieves Foundation began to receive government support, acquired greater visibility, and attracted donors that still today, so many years later, help fund it.

"I thought that the new Ministry for Women already had a project like the one you are proposing in the schools," I said to Mailén.

She helped me see that, as always happens, the funds weren't enough to reach the isolated rural areas and indigenous communities. She explained that she had several volunteers and the material that the government had provided, but they needed vans for transportation and a budget for gasoline and accommodations while they were on the road. What she was asking for was reasonable; we ran the numbers and came to an agreement in under fifteen minutes.

We went from the office straight to dinner at a restaurant where the food was a blow to the liver, but delicious. Before dessert came I'd suggested she come work with me at the foundation.

"I'll be ninety in a few years. I don't plan to retire, but I need help," I told her.

And that's how Mailén reentered my life, this time for good.

Since then she's been like a daughter to me, and has become part of our tiny family. Naturally, in under six months she was managing the Nieves Foundation. Hiring her wasn't a matchmaking strategy, Camilo. It's enough to know that she's your best friend and she treats you like a brother; when I'm gone, she'll take care of you, since she has a lot more common sense than you do. Her job is to keep you from doing too many stupid things.

. . .

I ENTERED THE LAST decade of my life still healthy and accompanied by Harald, so I didn't feel that I was nearing the land of death. Most of us spend our lives denying the irrefutable fact that we're going to die, and that doesn't change even at age ninety. I continued to believe that I had a lot of time ahead of me, until Harald died. We were a romantic elderly couple; we went to bed at night holding hands and woke up with our bodies entwined. Since I'm an early riser, I would wake up before him and spend a beautiful half hour dozing in the darkness and silence of our bedroom, giving thanks for so much shared happiness. That's my way of praying.

My vanity lasted for as long as he was with me, because he found me pretty. Do you remember what I looked like before, Camilo? You came into my life when I was more or less the age that you are now, but I looked a lot better than you do. Too much kindness will wear you down, I've warned you. The bad guys have more fun and reach old age in better condition than saints like you. If hell no longer exists and heaven is in question, it doesn't make sense to put so much effort into being a good person.

I miss Harald a lot. He should be here with me now, holding my hand in my final days. He'd be eighty-seven years old. Compared to the century I've been alive, that's nothing. At eighty-seven I was still a young woman learning to dance the rumba for exercise, since I found the gym too boring, and taking a canoe trip over the turquoise waters of the Futaleufú River in Patagonia, with some of the roughest rapids in the world. Just picture it, Camilo, eight insane people in a yellow rubber raft, wearing life jackets so that our cadavers would float, and helmets, to keep our brains from spilling out if our heads were cracked open against a rock.

I loved that man so much! I can't forgive him for abandoning me. He was so healthy that I was totally unprepared for his heart to suddenly burst. He had the lack of courtesy to die before me, even though he was thirteen years younger. It happened on my ninety-fifth birthday; he died in the middle of the party, with a glass of champagne in his hand. Harald had a nice life and a nice death. He went out singing, drinking, and in love, but for me it was a heavy blow; my heart broke.

28

AT AGE SIXTY-FOUR I FELT DEFEATED AND ready to surrender to old age, but then Torito's cross guided me onto a different path and gave me purpose, a new life, a chance to be useful, and a marvelous freedom of the soul. I shed a large part of my material burdens and fears, except the fear of something bad happening to you, Camilo. I lived the next thirty-five years with the same energy I'd had in my youth. The mirror reflected the inevitable passage of time, but inside I didn't feel it at all. Since my aging process was gradual, elderliness snuck up on me. There's a big difference between being old and being ancient.

My survival instincts keep me alive well beyond what dignity should allow. In the last three years Mother Nature, ever implacable, has stripped me of my energy, my good health, my independence, leaving me the ancient woman that I am today. I didn't feel old when I turned ninety-seven, because I was actively involved with my projects, I had curiosity about the world, and I still got angry over a battered woman. I didn't dwell on death because I was excited by life. I had carried on for two years without Harald, the man I'd been happiest with in all my long existence, but I wasn't alone because I had you, Etelvina, Mailén, and the many other women I worked with at the Nieves Foundation.

And then, as you know, I fell on the stairs. Nothing serious. It was followed by a routine operation to replace my hip and several months of physical therapy until I learned to walk again, but I could no longer do it without the help of a cane, then Etelvina's firm arm, a walker, and finally, the wheelchair. The worst thing about the wheelchair is that my face is at the height of people's belly buttons and the first thing I see are their nose hairs. Goodbye to driving, my second-floor office, the theater, and the foundation, which is now run completely by Mailén, although in reality it had been for years. I had to accept that I needed help. The daily humiliations of dependency are less painful if you accept them with humility. Nevertheless, my body's disability brought me an unexpected gift: It freed up an immense amount of space in my mind. I no longer had responsibilities and could spend my time writing this story for you, little by little, and preparing my soul for its departure.

I decided to come to Santa Clara after the hip operation, because I assumed these would be my final days and it seemed a shame to spend them in the city. Etelvina was born in this place and we're both happiest here. To think that when we came to this idyllic farm with my mother and aunts we dubbed it Exile, with a capital "E." It wasn't our exile, it was our salvation. This is the same prefabricated house that my brother built to replace the Rivas home when it was knocked down and burned in the 1960 earthquake. It's held up well since then. I've simply had to change the thatch on the roof every four years, and I installed heating, because the cold and damp seep in during winter. It's surrounded by jasmines and hydrangeas, and there's a purple bougainvillea framing the entrance. I brought my bed and a few pieces of furniture; it's very cozy and I feel that the walls are imbued with the presence of those who lived here before: my mother and my aunts, the Rivases, Facunda, and Torito.

Here, I'm near the Nahuel cemetery, where my loved ones lie—even Harald, because his children agreed to let his body remain here, in accordance with his wishes. They came to the funeral with their families, as tall and blond as Harald, and they got sick to their stomachs as soon as they got here, which always happens to civilized people. Your mother's ashes reside there in a ceramic urn and there is a grave for Torito, even though we will never know if the bones they gave us belonged to him or to another man. And there in that same cemetery is where you'll bury me, in the biodegradable coffin we have waiting in the Birdcage.

I KNOW YOU'VE BEEN digging through my drawers in search of the savings that Etelvina and I have hidden out of precaution. It's prudent to keep cash on hand, in case we're robbed, because if we don't give them anything they might cut our throats. Remember that it happened once before and we were scared to death by those bumbling idiots who crawled through a window and took off running when I started screaming at the top of my lungs, but next time our luck or my lungs might fail us. I think that was in Sacramento, though; it would be very odd for something like that to happen here.

Those bills tied up with Christmas ribbon won't do any good tucked away. Soon, in a matter of days, Etelvina is going to give them to you to put toward your magic ration cards. You didn't tell me about them, but there was an article in the paper and they talked about it on television, saying that even billionaires, who don't normally give to the poor because it's sexier to give to the symphony, are donating to your cause. According to Etelvina, they do it more out of guilt than kindness. She explained that you give out cards to families going through a rough time, so that they can buy on credit at their small neighborhood grocery stores and at the end of the month you pick up the tab. This guarantees food on the table, saves the family the humiliation of receiving charity, and keeps small shops in danger of closing in business. It's a good idea, you do have good ideas from time to time.

Remember that everything in storage in Sacramento will go to Etelvina for her apartment, where she plans to move as soon as she's free of me. She'll finally be able to sleep late, have breakfast in bed, and take vacations to the farm, which already belongs to her. She'll live in the peace and quiet she deserves. I assume everything you inherit will go directly to the poor, which is why I'm leaving you only money, minus a sum for Etelvina and the portions that correspond to Juan Martín and the foundation, as stipulated in my will. You're going to be surprised, Camilo. You'll have enough to open hundreds of magic accounts.

It would be pointless to ask you to spend a little on yourself, even though you need new clothes and you should really replace those boots with the holes in the soles. I guess priests' robes have gone out of fashion, just like nuns' habits; you always wear the same faded jeans and the vest that Etelvina knitted you a thousand years ago. Maybe Mailén will do something about it. You are truly poor. Of the three vows you took to become a priest, the vow of poverty is the easiest for you to comply with.

I might have failed Juan Martín and Nieves as a mother because I was too caught up in my passions and my work, but I've been a good mother to you, Camilo. You're the greatest love of my life, and it started when you were swimming around in the amniotic fluid of Nieves's belly. She loved you from your first spark of existence, and in order to protect you, to make sure you'd be born healthy, she gave up the drugs that had been the center of her life during all those tumultuous years. She's never left you, she's been with you always; I imagine you feel her presence, just as I do. My love for you was solidified the first time I held you in my arms, and from that instant it has only grown and grown, you can be sure of that. It couldn't have been any other way. You are an exceptional man, and it's not just my senility speaking, half the country would agree with me, and the other half doesn't count.

My emotional lineage ends with you, although there are others who will carry on my bloodline. In the photographs Juan Martín sends me, his family appears before landscapes of pristine snow and ice, smiling with too many teeth and a suspicious excess of optimism. That's not the case with you. Your teeth leave a lot to be desired and you've had a pretty hard life. That's why I admire you and love you so much. You're my friend and confidant, my spiritual partner, the greatest love of my long life. I only regret that you didn't have children, but we can't always get what we wish for in this world.

There's a time to live and a time to die. In between there's time to remember. That is all I've done for these past days, silently filling in the missing details to complete this testament—a sentimental legacy, more than a material one. I haven't been able to write by hand for several years now, my handwriting has lost the elegance it once had, which I learned from Miss Taylor in childhood, and is now almost illegible, but my arthritis doesn't keep me from using the computer, a useful extension of my crippled body. You laugh at me, Camilo, and say I'm the only hundred-year-old woman with one foot in the grave who's more interested in her computer than in praying.

I WAS BORN IN 1920, during the influenza pandemic, and I'm going to die in 2020, during the outbreak of coronavirus. What an elegant name for such a terrible scourge. I've lived a century and I have a good memory, in addition to seventy-something diaries and thousands of letters as evidence of my passage through this world. I've witnessed many events, I've amassed a lot of experience, but either because I was too distracted or too busy, I haven't acquired much wisdom. If reincarnation is real, I'll have to return to Earth to make up for what I'm lacking. It's a terrifying prospect.

The world is paralyzed, and humanity is in quarantine. It is a strange symmetry that I was born in one pandemic and will die during another. I saw on television that the streets of the cities are empty, voices echo off the New York skyscrapers and butterflies congregate on the monuments in Paris. I can't have visitors, and that allows me to say goodbye slowly and peacefully. Activity has stopped everywhere and anxiety reigns, but here at Santa Clara nothing has changed: The animals and plants don't know about the virus, the air is pure, and the calm is so profound that from my bed I can hear the crickets beside the lake in the distance.

You and Etelvina are the only living souls who can visit me, the rest are spirits. I'd like to say goodbye to Juan Martín, tell him how much I love him and that I'm sorry I didn't get to know his children better, but he isn't able to come; it's too dangerous to travel right now and many flights are canceled.

Luckily I have you here with me, Camilo. Thank you for coming, and for staying. You won't have to wait long, I promise. I worry about you distributing aid in places where the illness is causing tremendous mortality. Take care of yourself. There are a lot of people who need you.

GOODBYE, CAMILO.

This is the end. I'm waiting, accompanied by Etelvina, my cat Frida, the stray dogs that roam the farm who come to lie at my feet from time to time, and the ghosts that surround me. Torito is the most present, because this is his house and I'm his guest. He hasn't changed, he's the same big, sweet man that I saw walk away for the last time with Juan Martín. He sits on the bench in the corner carving little animals out of wood, silent. I've asked him what happened on the mountain, but he just shrugs his shoulders in response. I also asked him what it's like on the Other Side of life and he told me that I'll soon find out.

I've been lying here for several days, remembering, dying, maybe a week now. The hemorrhage occurred all of a sudden, without warning, as I was watching the news of the virus on television; I didn't get to prepare myself as well as I would've liked, and now there's a lady, who must be death, sitting at the foot of my bed, motioning for me to follow her. I can't distinguish clearly between night and day, and it doesn't matter, because pain and memory aren't measured with clocks. The morphine puts me to sleep and transports me to the dimension of dreams and visions. Etelvina had to remove the painting of the Chinese farmers that always hung across from the bed because that usually immobile couple, with their picnic basket and cone-shaped straw hats stepped right out of their frame and started walking around the room, dragging their slippered feet. Effects of the morphine, I suppose, because I'm lucid, I always have been; my body can't take any more, but my mind is intact. The itinerant farmers walked to Camellia House, where my father was smoking in the library, waiting for them. They brought him rice of hope on a platter.

If the doctor was wrong and I'm not dying, it will be a major letdown. But that's not going to happen. From time to time I rise up like a column of smoke and I see myself from above as I lie in this bed struggling for breath, so shrunken that my shape under the covers is barely visible. Oh! That magnificent experience of leaving the body to float in the air! Free. Dying is a tremendous effort, Camilo. I suppose that there's no rush because I'm going to be dead for a long time, but the wait is exasperating. The only thing that makes me sad is that we won't be together, but as long as you still remember me I'll be with you in a way. When I asked you if you're going to miss me, you responded that I'll always be sitting in a rocking chair inside your heart. You can be so cheesy sometimes, Camilo. I don't think you'll miss me, because you're very busy combatting poverty and you won't have time to think about me, but I hope that you'll miss my letters. If my absence makes you sad, Mailén will console you; I think she might be in love with you. I'm sure your agreement to remain just friends won't last; I've lived too long to believe in something as ridiculous as a vow of chastity. Also, I've heard you say that chastity isn't the same as celibacy. Leave it to a Jesuit.

Etelvina cries when she thinks I can't hear her. She's been my best friend and main support through my clumsy old age when I've needed help just to go to the bathroom. Soon I'll abandon this helpless body that served me so well for an entire century but has finally given up.

"Am I dying, Etelvina?"

"Yes, señora. Are you afraid?"

"No. I feel content, and curious. What will be on the Other Side?"

"I don't know."

"Ask Camilo."

"I did, señora. He says he doesn't know either."

"If Camilo doesn't know, it must be because there's nothing there."

"Come back to haunt us, señora, and tell us what it's like to die," she said with that sarcasm of hers.

It's true that I feel content and curious, but sometimes I'm also frightened. Waiting on the Other Side may be total desolation, eternal wandering of the sidereal plane calling out for help over and over. No. It won't be like that. There will be light, a lot of light. My moments of uncertainty are very brief. Life pulls me back in and it's hard for me to leave it behind.

Etelvina wants me to confess and take communion, since you're already here; she's afraid that my many sins might condemn me. I agree with you that confession shouldn't be a habit, it is enough to confess a few times in your life, when there's a pressing need to free the soul of guilt. Also, I haven't had much occasion to sin in the last twenty years, and I've already paid for my previous mistakes. I've been guided by a simple rule of conduct: Treat others as I want them to treat me. Still, I've hurt people. I did it without cruel intentions, unless you count Fabian, whom I betrayed and abandoned because I couldn't control myself, and Julián, because he deserved it. I don't regret what I did, because it was the only punishment I could think of.

My feet feel colder than ever before. I don't know if it's day or night, sometimes the dark stretches on for so long that it mingles with the previous nights and the following ones. If I ask Etelvina what day it is, she always gives the same answer: "Whatever day you want it to be, señora, every day is the same here." She's wise, she's already figured out that only the present exists. And you, Camilo? What do you think of death? The question elicits a smile; you still have your dimples and your eyes disappear when you laugh, another way you resemble your mother. You'll soon turn fifty years old and you've witnessed more cruelty and suffering than most mortals, but you've kept your childlike innocence.

AFTER A CENTURY, TIME is now slipping through my fingers. Where did those hundred years go?

I can't confess to you, Camilo, you're my grandson, but if you like, you can absolve me of my sins to put Etelvina at ease. Guiltless bodies float lighter on the sidereal plane and turn to stardust.

Godspeed, Camilo. Nieves has come to get me. The sky is beautiful . . .

Acknowledgments

Many people contributed to the writing of this story. Some helped me in my research or inspired me, others served as models for certain characters, and my editors and translator made the existence of this book possible.

I am especially grateful to:

Juan Allende, my brother, who always helps me with research and reads the first draft.

Johanna V. Castillo, my agent at Writer's House in New York, who edited the manuscript.

Luís Miguel Palomares and Maribel Luque, from Balcells Agency, who have represented me for forty years.

Lori Barra, who directs my foundation, where I've learned about the strength of women in the most traumatic circumstances.

Felipe Barras del Solar, who inspired the character of Camilo Del Valle.

Berta Beltrán, who served as model for the loyal Etelvina.

Beatriz Manz for sharing with me her childhood in the countryside.

Roger Cukras for his stories about the Mafia and for his unconditional love.

Scott Michael for instructing me on the tax evasion penalties imposed by the United States.

Elizabeth Subercaseaux for her novelist's eye and her support as a great friend.

Mikkel Aaland for the information about Norway and its people.

Jennifer and Harleigh Gordon, whose tragic lives inspired the character of Nieves.

To Google and Wikipedia, indispensable for historical documentation.

ABOUT THE AUTHOR

Born in Peru and raised in Chile, Isabel Allende is the author of a number of bestselling and critically acclaimed books, including **A Long Petal of the Sea**, **The House of the Spirits**, **Of Love and Shadows**, **Eva Luna**, **The Stories of Eva Luna**, and **Paula**. Her books have been translated into more than forty-two languages and have sold more than seventy-four million copies worldwide. She lives in California.

IsabelAllende.com
Facebook.com/IsabelAllende
Twitter: @isabelallende
Instagram: @allendeisabel

LIKE WHAT YOU'VE READ?

Try these titles by Isabel Allende,
also available in large print:

The Soul of a Woman
ISBN 978-0-593-40143-9

A Long Petal of the Sea
ISBN 978-0-593-17205-6

For more information on large print titles, visit
www.penguinrandomhouse.com/large-print-format-books